Praise for *The Good Teacher*

'The tale of a good teacher who follows her moral compass and risks damnation. A decade long journey that culminates in a gripping John Grisham-like-climax. A book club favourite. It's not surprising that movie producers are circling around *The Good Teacher*.'
– Mark Naglazas, *The Sunday Times Magazine*

'Just finished reading PJ Kelly's book *The Good Teacher* and I really enjoyed it. It is written in a similar vein to classic Jodie Picoult books where a social issue is questioned and challenged and those who work with vulnerable children in our communities will find it engaging. Great first novel for PJ Kelly.'
– Maggie Dent,
author of *Saving Our Children from Our Chaotic World*

'I just finished reading PJ's book – what a cracking story, I couldn't put it down. I hope someone out there is optioning it for a movie or TV series – it's got everything – interesting plot, great characters, tension, drama, pathos, black comedy and even a courtroom drama. At its centre is one of the most important moral and philosophical issues of our times and a dilemma to solve. Wonderful – many, many congratulations.'
– Jenny Davis, author of *Dear Heart*

'What an incredible debut. So well written and I loved that this was so relatable as a teacher and, I would imagine, eye opening for people not in education. Brilliant story and hard to put down.'
– Jessica Sanders, Deputy Principal and teacher

'It will have you questioning what is right and wrong in this thrilling moral dilemma. A great contribution to the literary world from a local author which I enjoyed immensely.'
– Jennifer Merigan, *Have A Go News*

'Date night – cheese, wine, the couch and *The Good Teacher*. Two nights in a row, this one's a keeper. I can't put it down.'
– Beck Strong, Education Assistant

THE GOOD TEACHER

P J KELLY

ETEXT PRESS

Published by eText Press Publishing 2017

This is a work of fiction. Names, characters, places and incidents are products of the author's imagination or are used fictitiously. Any resemblance to actual events, locales, or persons, living or dead, is entirely coincidental.

ISBN: 978-0-6480692-4-9
Language: British English

Typeset in Adobe Caslon Pro and Tw Century MT Condensed by eText Press Publishing, Joondalup, Australia.

Cover design by P J Kelly, typset by eText Press Publishing
Images: Kho via 123RF.com (olive tree), Natstco via istockphoto.com (hands), Iakov Kalinin via 123RF.com (wheat field) and royalty free via Acclaim Images and used by permission of US Department of Defense (passenger plane and clouds).

To all the teachers of the world.

Where would we be without you?

"It is not living that matters, but living rightly."

Socrates

Children and Community Services Act 2004

Part 2 — Objects and principles

Division 1 — Objects

6. (d) to provide for the protection and care of children in circumstances where their parents have not given, or are unlikely or unable to give, that protection and care

9. *Principles to be observed*

In the administration of this Act the following principles must be observed —

(a) the principle that the parents, family and community of a child have the primary role in safeguarding and promoting the child's wellbeing;

(b) the principle that the preferred way of safeguarding and promoting a child's wellbeing is to support the child's parents, family and community in the care of the child;

(c) the principle that every child should be cared for and protected from harm;

(d) the principle that every child should live in an environment free from violence;

(e) the principle that every child should have stable, secure and safe relationships and living arrangements;

(f) the principle that intervention action (as defined in section 32(2)) should be taken only in circumstances where there is no other reasonable way to safeguard and promote the child's wellbeing;

(g) the principle that if a child is removed from the child's family then, so far as is consistent with the child's best interests, the child should be given encouragement and support in maintaining contact with the child's parents, siblings and other relatives and with any other people who are significant in the child's life;

(ha) the principle that if a child is removed from the child's family then, so far as is consistent with the child's best interests, planning for the child's care should occur as soon as possible in order to ensure long-term stability for the child;

(h) the principle that decisions about a child should be made promptly having regard to the age, characteristics, circumstances and needs of the child;

(ia) the principle that decisions about a child with disability should be made giving special consideration to any difficulties or discrimination that may be encountered by the child because of the child's disability and should support the child's full and effective participation in society;

(i) the principle that decisions about a child should be consistent with cultural, ethnic and religious values and traditions relevant to the child;

(j) the principle that a child's parents and any other people who are significant in the child's life should be given an opportunity and assistance to participate in decision-making processes under this Act that are likely to have a significant impact on the child's life;

(k) the principle that a child's parents and any other people who are significant in the child's life should be given adequate information, in a manner and language that they can understand.

PART ONE

1

FRIDAY 12th MAY 2005
12:20PM AUSTRALIAN WESTERN STANDARD TIME
MARVALE PRIMARY SCHOOL

The shrill ring of the lunchtime siren pierced the calm of the classroom. Voices rose as young minds anticipated the sun-drenched playground awaiting them.

Miss Bell reclined in her high-backed chair and sighed. Respite really hadn't come quick enough.

The small group of children surrounding her scooped up the collections of coloured counters and blocks scattered in front of them. Their teacher waited only for the high-pitched wail to end. Talking over the top of it was pointless and, as surely as it had invaded the confines of her classroom so, too, would it gradually fade to nothing.

'Stop, look and listen,' she sang.

'Stop, look and listen,' echoed the children, all twenty-eight eager faces turning her way.

'We need to pack everything up before we can go to lunch,' announced Miss Bell. 'And please, no running,' she added, chaos having already spilled across the room, an explosion of busy bodies darting around pale blue desks, excited eight-year-olds crisscrossing from one side of the classroom to the other.

Miss Bell had been looking forward to this day for months and she watched with extra detail as her students tidied their desks with zeal, zipping bulging pencil cases shut and standing quietly to attention. She marveled at how regimented they could be, their resemblance to a small battalion of soldiers a welcome reprieve from the bedlam of the morning. Peace had been restored.

They stood proudly, their arms folded tightly across crisp yellow polo shirts, their backs straight and chins up. How easily they fell into line when they wanted to go and play. Everything else was such a struggle and holding their attention was always an effort.

Miss Bell got to her feet and strolled toward the front of the room, her knee-length blue skirt and white blouse a crumpled mass of creases and crinkles. She took a long last look at each student, savouring the cheeky grins and innocence-filled eyes that greeted her sentimental gaze.

'She's really taking her time,' thought Lisa Johnstone from her desk at the front of the class. She was a particular favourite of Miss Bell's and the exuberant smile that she projected today was cause for celebration alone. She'd had an excellent morning. Her math was improving and she adored the class book her teacher was reading about a young girl called Alice.

'I wish I could live in Wonderland too,' commented Lisa earlier that morning, during a guided reading session. The whole group found that funny. Lisa, though, was serious.

Miss Bell selected James Hartley to open the door to freedom. He was the closest and as he heaved the door inward and wedged the doorstop in place, the sweet smell of hot sausage rolls wafted past. Heads turned and noses wriggled. A gaggle of hungry tummies groaned in unison.

It was a Friday and the school canteen always put on a good spread but Miss Bell wasn't even mildly tempted. She had eaten nothing all morning, yet the aroma of hot food didn't even register with her overworked mind. Her senses were on high alert for factors out of her control. Eating wasn't a concern.

'Good afternoon class.'

'Good afternoon Miss Bell,' came the rushed reply, her students already pouring out through the open door.

Miss Bell removed the blue hair elastic from around her ponytail and shook her blonde hair free. She was a pretty woman with fine-boned features and smooth skin, her relaxed nature concealing the softer lines of her thirty-seven years. She was feeling her age today, though, and took a deep breath as the last child disappeared out the door.

Fridays were usually the easiest day of the week with a timetable that started with an English block in the morning and finished with a Math session straight after recess. Today's lunch break would be followed by an hour of Art and then Indonesian, both of which were taken by specially trained teachers in other locations of the school. Miss Bell liked to spend the last two hours of the working week marking student work, as well as tidying her classroom in preparation for a fresh start on Monday.

Not today though. She wouldn't be doing anything to do with teaching for a long time and as she ruffled her fingers through her hair, she acknowledged that today was the beginning of a new life. Today was the first step in her own flight to freedom.

12:23PM

Miss Bell considered her well-organised classroom and allowed a flood of more recent memories to wash over her. Swathes of colour-filled paintings hung in linear arcs across the ceiling, strung like vines, from wall to wall. The display to her left was filled with acrostic poems, each piece handwritten in marker pen and mounted on black card. She loved exhibiting her students' work. It was a reminder to parents of the hard graft that went on inside these walls each and every day. She never slackened the pace and loved every minute of her day, but as her mind surveyed the fresh set of paintings still hanging from the wooden racks at the rear of the class, it was the fire that destroyed this block three years ago, that flickered its way into her thoughts. Long black streaks of smoke-stained bricks ran like scars across the upper sections of the back wall.

Miss Bell lived locally even back then and was woken by the piercing wail of the fire-truck sirens as they tore past her house toward the school. She hadn't even bothered to get dressed, dashing down the road in her dressing gown only to watch in horror as a team of firefighters fought valiantly against the huge inferno already licking the walls of her classroom. A decade of resources and memories disintegrated before her tear-soaked eyes, the whole roof quickly crumbling under the intense heat of the blaze.

Worse was to come the next day as she watched the children arrive, devastation and confusion wrought heavily across their stricken faces. Their silence alone was painful enough to witness and the tears that fell from those young eyes would never be forgotten.

The rebuilding process had taken longer than expected but it was the little jokes she shared with her class during these down times that helped her breathe life into the idea of renewal as a concept that could succeed. The affected classes were moved into hastily erected demountables.

The younger children were the first to shows signs of recovery and Miss Bell began to realise, that whilst painful at first, rebirth brought with it new opportunities and a renewed hope.

'I miss all my old stuff,' cried Annie Smith, a few weeks after the fire. She'd held everything in and was finally allowing herself to grieve for the possessions she had lost.

'I know Annie,' said Miss Bell. 'So do I.'

'Why did the fire take them away?'

'Because that's what fire does, but like a forest we will grow back bigger and stronger,' explained her teacher, putting to good use the lessons she had been given by the school psychologist in how to counsel her students.

'Will it happen again?' asked Annie.

'No, it won't happen again,' said Miss Bell. 'We'll make sure of that.'

Providing certainty to the children was of paramount importance and Miss Bell had taken great care to ensure their emotional and physical well-being. She felt their welfare was strongly linked to her own.

Today was a salute to that process of regeneration and as she wandered into the broad corridor that ran like a backbone between the classrooms of Red Block, she allowed her fingers to slide across the engraved letters of the bronze plaque that commemorated this building's restoration. The Lord Mayor had been invited to cut the silk ribbon that symbolically reopened these rebuilt classrooms. There had been much fanfare and celebration, with the whole community invited and involved. Miss Bell had used that day to quietly celebrate the start of her own restoration project, redeploying the same steely determination that had been so instrumental in surviving the fire, to reconstruct her own damaged life.

'You coming for a cuppa?'

Miss Bell withdrew her hand from the plaque and spun nervously around to see a smiling Nancy Robinson staring at her. Her whole body tightened as a cast of words jostled for position. Talking with colleagues wasn't part of her plan.

'Hi Nancy. Umm, yes. Be down in five,' she mumbled unconvincingly.

'You okay?'

'Yeah, I'm fine. It's been a long week.'

'It's been a long year.'

Nancy had been a good friend since she'd arrived at the start of last year. They'd shared many serious conversations after school, unloading the emotional baggage of the day upon each other and, as Nancy departed, Miss Bell watched her exit the building with a heavy heart.

She would miss the bricks and mortar that built this place, but it was the wonderful people that kept her here. They were the reason she'd stayed so long.

She crossed her fingers and prayed they wouldn't be drowned in suspicion, innocent casualties weighed down by the aftermath of her actions. They knew nothing of her plans yet every member of staff would be in for a fight all the same and, as her heart began to quicken, she strode purposefully from the building before she could change her mind.

2

12:31PM

Miss Bell found Jacob and Lisa Johnstone huddled together in a corner of the undercover area. Jacob was in Year Five but he was always quietly slipping his way into the Junior Primary area, the need to sit with his sister always greater than any desire to obey the rules. He was fiercely protective of her and no one had sought to deny him that role.

Several other individuals were spread out across the carpet, some still finishing their fruit and biscuits, others unsure of just who to play with. Most of the children had already taken flight, out across the paved area or down the bottom of the hill, scattering themselves across the oval.

Lisa and Jacob looked up at Miss Bell as she approached, the smiles of the last lesson already doused by the rumblings of two empty bellies. Miss Bell lowered herself to their eye level and knelt softly on the floor beside them.

'Hi Lisa, hi Jacob,' she said gently. 'How's everything going?'

They shrugged their shoulders in unison. Economy of movement is what the experts called it. 'Why speak when you have nothing to say?' is how the school speech therapist had explained it away. It just made Miss Bell sad. Children should be the spark that makes everyone else light up. They are the future. Not these two though. Their flame had almost been extinguished. They saw their own future through a dark and uninspiring lens.

Miss Bell considered the contents of the torn brown paper bags on the carpeted floor in front of them and frowned. A small bag of potato crisps and three boiled lollies lay untouched and unwanted. Anger simmered in her own belly at the neglect this lunch bag exemplified. It might have looked enticing if accompanied by a healthy sandwich and a piece of fruit, but she knew this was all they had and it made both them and her miserable. It was another reminder of the love and care that was absent from their lives, their hollow eyes and skinny bodies proof that what they were eating was neither going to fill them up nor make them grow stronger. Weakness was all it would produce and they hated the way it made them feel.

Miss Bell thought of the children as autumn leaves, starved of sustenance, preparing to detach from life and fall forgotten to the ground. These two siblings were a pale imitation of what they should have been. Frail ghosts that inhabited this world but rarely enjoyed it.

The Community and Services Act 2004 - Principle a) the parents, family and community of a child have the primary role in safeguarding and promoting the child's wellbeing.

Miss Bell's first contact with the Johnstone family came early last year. Jacob was assigned to her class and it was during those first few tortuous months that she began to suspect he was a child born into a house of neglect and shame. It broke her heart, those first few weeks of February, seeing him shuffle up to school each day in the same unwashed uniform and barely-there shoes. Jacob knew he looked a mess and often tried to convince those around him that the battered old trainers struggling to hold onto his feet were just sentimental favourites. That a clean pair of Nikes lay unused under his bed. These were the sorts of lies and distractions that littered his life and Miss Bell realised immediately that he was trying to hide an uncomfortable truth. He was too young to realise that you can't erase a history of poverty with words alone.

She took Jacob under her wing. He was a clever boy and old enough to know that a better world existed. It was this gulf between he and the other children that made him hate who he was and Miss Bell was quick to identify with these feelings.

Her own childhood had been one of luxury and pampering. She was cared for by two adoring parents and whilst there were no brothers or sisters to play with, she wanted for nothing, and they loved her with everything they had. Then just when she was old enough to realise how good life was, it was ripped away from her. She empathised with Jacob and Lisa. Felt a strong connection to them and their plight. She knew how it felt to hate who she was.

'You want to go on a trip?' asked Miss Bell.

Jacob's eyes flickered with interest. 'Where to?'

'To a magical place where the ocean is warm and all of the buildings are white.'

'Who'll be there?' piped up Lisa.

'People. Us,' Miss Bell explained. 'It's a popular place and they make the best burgers ever.'

'Really?' inquired Jacob, hunger ripping through him.

'Really,' smiled Miss Bell. 'Fresh bread and the largest meat patties the world has ever seen.'

'When do we go?' asked Jake, mouthwatering images flooding his mind.

'Now if you like? We can just drop everything and go if that's what you want?' Miss Bell had rehearsed this sentence many times over. She knew that Jacob missed being in her class, so spending the afternoon with her would sound like fun and anyway this was a decision the children could make for themselves. School was their refuge. Their mum and dad hated it here and had long since given up exerting any control over Miss Bell's jurisdiction.

The siblings communicated quickly with their eyes. 'Let's go,' they chimed, a shared happiness cemented with high fives.

Miss Bell marveled at the way these two communicated so seamlessly. It was more a survival instinct born from desperation, than a secret language sparked by imagination but having no family of her own, Miss Bell had always been in awe of the bond they shared.

Growing up, she'd always fantasised about having a sister or a brother to play with and just when her parents had announced her dreams were only six months from delivery, fate stepped in and tore those dreams to shreds. It was a memory she'd long tried to forget.

A wet morning during the winter of nineteen eighty-two heralded the beginning of the end and as thick sheets of rain blanketed the southern suburbs of Perth, two disconsolate policemen climbed wearily from their patrol car and made a harried approach toward the red-bricked portico of a modest two-storey house. It was far from the future failings of Marvale but as a light fog hovered over the wet grass of the front lawn, the chill of bad news settled upon this doorstep and never left.

These unlucky men in blue had earlier borne witness to the horrific aftermath of an alcohol-fuelled car crash and as the knock of knuckles on wood resonated across this cold façade of suburbia, the front door swung open to reveal a fourteen-year old girl in pink pyjamas.

'Hello,' she'd croaked, a young voice filled with uncertainty, fear having already wriggled its way into her words.

'Good morning,' replied Officer Ackford. 'Is your name Jessica Bell?'

A nod. 'Yes,' whispered the teenager, her insecurity only just audible above the torrent of rain upon the red tin roof.

'Can we come in?'

'I'm not meant to allow strangers in to the house. Mum and Dad's rules.'

'We understand,' replied the officer, his face bristling with the mention of the girl's parents, the bloodied mess of their bodies, still an all-too-vivid memory.

'Is there anybody else staying in the house with you? A babysitter perhaps?'

'No. I'm old enough to look after myself,' she explained.

And it was true. She was already a very capable young lady even back then, but taking care of yourself for one evening is completely different to suffering a whole lifetime as the sole surviving member of your family.

'Mum and Dad should have been home by now,' she added. 'They probably got held up somewhere.'

The officers struggled to make a clear distinction between the unavoidable horrors of this world and the injustices that are forced upon the innocent.

'Your parents won't be coming home,' said Officer Ackford, and as the fatal words continued to fall from his mouth, the body of the little girl inside the pink pyjamas crumpled to the floor and her young heart broke into a thousand pieces.

Miss Bell had spent the rest of her life repairing the damage as best she could, and having collected every fragment that fell that day, the last piece of the jigsaw was finally being returned to its rightful position. Today's events would make her whole again. Could make her whole again.

3

12:40PM

Jacob and Lisa stayed close as Miss Bell walked quickly across the tarmacked surface of the school car park. She swore under her breath in memory of an earlier reluctance to park closer to the school's buildings. A departure from her habitual routine might have drawn unwanted attention. Trouble was it meant walking the entire length of the car park and it seemed to be taking forever.

The sounds of young children playing spilled out from the Marvale Kindergarten, which backed onto this section of the school grounds. Duty teachers in bright orange vests watched every leap and swing as children as young as four got to grips with the ropes, bars and slides of the colourful playground.

'There's Mrs Hammond,' noticed Lisa, waving in the direction of her old Kindergarten teacher.

'Not now Lisa,' hushed Miss Bell, 'She's concentrating on the little kids. Keeping them safe.'

'She's a nice lady,' said Lisa.

'Yes, she is,' smiled Miss Bell.

What Lisa didn't know was that the dedication she saw as kindness had led to the downfall of Mrs Hammond's marriage and subsequent ugly divorce. As Jess knew all too well, this job often came at a cost and with the highest rate of divorce in the government sector, it wasn't a reality the local politicians liked to talk about. For Jess, her work meant there wasn't room in her life for anything remotely romantic.

'Which one's your car?' asked Jacob a little too loudly.

'The blue one. Just over there.'

'Looks shiny,' said Lisa.

'I clean it a lot,' explained Jess, that same fastidious attention to detail currently drilling holes in her watertight getaway plan.

The Community and Services Act 2004 – Principle (b)
the preferred way of safeguarding and promoting a child's wellbeing is to support the child's parents, family and community in the care of the child.

She had met Mr and Mrs Johnstone repeatedly over the past year and a half. At first casually, with an invitation to the parents for a low-key meeting in the classroom after school. It was an attempt at building a mutually beneficial relationship. Jess always saw this as her first port of call. A chance to inquire about any short-term problems, such as the children's consistently late arrival at school. Any deeper-set issues could be introduced and worked on as the year progressed. She had found this approach had produced great results kick-starting other parents into positive action. For Gary and Tracey Johnstone, though, it was an opportunity to display surprise and ignorance, followed quickly by a raft of empty promises to 'look into it'.

'So, you weren't aware of the need to sign his diary each night?' she asked them at the first session.

'No,' answered Gary, his chin covered in dark stubble, the stench of alcohol coating every word. 'Little bugger's been hidin' it, hasn't he!'

'And the bags under his eyes?

'Nightmares,' explained Tracey, her short black skirt and red singlet revealing more skin than was recommended for the grounds of an educational institution. 'He suffers sweats and tremors. I nurse him back to sleep most nights.'

When the situation deteriorated further, Jess set up a case conference in the hope that the added pressure of the Deputy Principal's presence would force Gary and Tracey to accept the gravity of the situation.

It was pressure they were all too keen to avoid and by simply not showing up they succeeded.

On numerous occasions the scheduled meetings would come and go, with no reason for their absence offered. Jess began to despise them for the apparent enjoyment they derived from wasting the time of anyone concerned for the welfare of two precious lives they, themselves, had brought into this world.

It went even less productively when they did show up. They weren't what you would call good listeners and the meetings usually ended with Gary Johnstone shouting abuse and being escorted off the premises.

'They're my bloody kids you know!' he'd hollered in Jess's face one afternoon. 'I'll do what I want with them!'

'That's not how the law works,' explained Jess, her voice struggling to stay calm in the face of such aggression.

'I make the fuckin' rules, not you,' yelled Gary.

'Well that's not actually true,' interrupted the Deputy Principal, Rupert Small, rising from his chair, intent on making the most of his size. He was very tall and seriously overweight, an imposing combination and a useful tool in situations like this.

'Well that's not actually true,' mimicked Tracey, as she stared defiantly up at him.

'That's it. I'm putting in a report to DCP, outlining my continued concerns in regard to the parenting of Jacob and Lisa Johnstone,' announced the deputy through gritted teeth. 'Expect a visit in the next couple of days.'

'Bastards!' roared Gary.

'Get out of my office,' said Rupert.

'Make me!' Gary's invitation was instinctive, but as Rupert stepped forward to remove him, Tracey grabbed her vile husband and hauled him out into the reception area.

'Pricks,' she'd shrieked as they slipped out through the main entrance, Gary's upturned finger almost getting jammed in the hastily slammed door.

Jess's frustration during these altercations was palpable and it was during the ensuing bouts of darkness which inevitably followed that she first cultivated the astonishing plan she was about to enact.

The lack of meaningful progress at a school level meant that whilst the paper trail was growing, any real change was non-existent. Jess knew that documented plans only worked when all parties were on board. Words are only effective when met with action and Jess's own colleagues had grown numb to the gravity of this growing problem. They had become frustrated to the point where the only process they could control was the documentation of these failures. With the right words entered on the right pages and the school now legally protected from future attack, the real goal of the children's welfare could be placed out of sight and out of mind. It was a well-drilled approach that kept the lawyers at bay and the parents in denial but it was one Jess vowed to change.

'Quickly now, into the car,' she said , turning the last few metres of carpark into a restrained sprint. She opened the left rear door of the Prius, allowing Jacob and Lisa to slide in along the back seat. 'Buckle up, okay?'

She closed the door and glared across the roof of the car. The Principal's office had a clear view of her parking spot and the blinds were currently open. Jess knew her actions couldn't be excused.

She looked in through the side window of the car and watched as the flashy interior of her Prius caught the children's attention. They were smiling as they played with the lights in the roof and the muffled sound of their merriment was music to her ears. The scream of guilt wasn't powerful enough to drown out what was important. The two children, now in her care, were happy and, in that moment, she knew what she had to do.

12:52PM

The shiny blue Prius glided out through the gates of the school and onto the road. The silence of the electric motor added to the serenity inside the vehicle with Jacob and Lisa watching the houses and trees on their familiar streets drift by. An old lady walking her dog barely noticed the car and Jess prayed she'd been successful in adding anonymity to their exit.

The digital clock on the dashboard clicked over to 12:54pm. Jess swung left off Ridge Drive and onto the freeway on- ramp. She was conscious that every second was being counted. Even the smallest detail of this fateful day would eventually be documented frame by frame. Her every move would be dissected and analyzed. Whatever had brought her to this point was now just a recorded element of the past. A new, brighter future was ahead and there would be no turning back.

Jess had always been a nice girl but the saying 'Nice guys finish last' had been trumpeted all too often throughout her life. Nice had finally lost its appeal.

4

1:30PM
MARVALE TAVERN

'Kids alright?' asked George from behind the bar.

'When they keep their mouths shut, they're great,' slurred Gary Johnstone, a combination of beer and spirits already working their undiluted magic on his inhibitions. He was such a regular here, the bar stool he sat on bore his name, engraved down one leg in a drunken scrawl with a switchblade.

The bar was empty except for these two and the stink of smoke and sweat hung in the air like incense. A drab mixture of old paintings and mirrors grazed the cream rendered walls, the uneven texture collecting dust in every hollow. It wasn't the healthiest of hangouts but then neither were the people who frequented it.

'You on pick-up today?' asked George, as he restocked the fridges behind the bar.

'If they're lucky. Depends how I feel. Anyway, they're big enough and ugly enough to walk home by themselves.'

'You're being too harsh,' replied George, a sly smile betraying a ruddy face scarred with pockmarks. 'That Lisa's a bit of alright.'

Gary screwed up his face. 'My Lisa?'

'Yeah, nice hair. And she's got great, long legs,' drooled George.

'She's eight years old, you pervert.'

'I know that, you tosser, but you can see she's got the makings of a stunner.'

'When you seen her? I ain't ever bought her in here.'

'Down the shops, and at the park. I bump into other people's kids all the time. I can usually spot the family resemblance.'

'Fuck off. Cannot.'

'Can too. It's part of being a good barman. I've a strong memory for faces.'

It was true, George never forgot who his customers were, friend or foe alike. 'He keeps 'em close,' thought Gary and much as he hated someone ogling his own daughter, he knew he'd do well to keep George happy.

'Well, you're gonna have to wait a few years before you can have a taste of that one,' said Gary.

'She for sale then?'

'Everything's for sale mate. Give her a few years and she'll be a working girl just like her mum.'

'I'm a patient man. I can wait.'

They toasted the moment, the clink of glasses echoing off the grimy walls.

'You wanna do a job for me?' asked George.

'Whereabouts?'

'Yanchep. You might not get back in time for the kids though.'

'I'll take the risk.'

'You got your car here?'

'Sure have. Trusty rust bucket goes everywhere with me.'

'But will she make it back?'

'Oath she will. Doesn't look like much but she's got a hell of an engine.'

'Alright then. Give me a sec.'

George disappeared through a door at the back of the bar. Gary skulled his drink, a minor spill down one side of his mouth. He was wiping his chin with his forearm when George reappeared, a small brown package in his right hand. He placed it on top of the bar.

'The address is written on the bag,' explained George. 'Don't knock. Just leave it inside the old tyre leaning against the house. Go down the right side. You'll see it.'

Gary nodded. 'Right side of the house?' he whispered.

'Yep. You got it covered?'

'Got it!'

'Don't fuck it up this time.'

Gary blinked several times, swallowed hard. 'Yeah, sorry.'

'And remember,' grinned George as he pushed the paper bag across the bar top into Gary's hands. 'You never got it from me!'

5

1:43PM
PERTH INTERNATIONAL AIRPORT

Jess parked her car in long-term parking and slotted enough money into the machine for a full week. The longer they could avoid discovery the better. Seven days and it wouldn't matter what the police found. They'd be long gone.

She placed the ticket on the dashboard, while the children waited on the curb in front of the car. She glanced up at them through the windscreen, side by side, holding hands, both wearing big smiles. They'd got through life together and Jess knew how deeply their bond ran.

Lisa and Jacob's suffering was well known to everyone on staff at Marvale Primary. The litany of problems they'd faced had been well documented since they first dragged their feet into pre-primary and anyone who came into contact with them struggled with the pain and injustice of watching two kids get dealt bad card after bad card.

'God knows why they ever had children,' vented Jess after she'd first met both parents back in 2003. Obviously never wanted them. Always handed them back after the school holidays like they were someone else's pets. They acted as if having the children home for two weeks was them doing the school a favour.

When Jess discovered a university research article that proposed a link between the creation of the taxpayer-funded Baby Bonus in the late nineteen nineties and a rise in neglected children born since then, she wasn't at all surprised. Having a child so that you can get your hands on a cool eight thousand dollars in benefits would appeal to many of the senseless parents she had dealt with. If it wasn't for the money, she doubted whether Gary or Tracey would have ever created anything of real worth. But they did. Twice. And, so, the suffering and the payments began.

Jess still bristled at the memory of Lisa standing in the doorway of her classroom, wearing the same unwashed uniform she'd departed in when the holidays had begun two weeks beforehand. She'd grown close to Lisa during first term and a special protective bond was already taking shape. It was the continuation of a relationship initiated with Jacob the year before, but that day, when Lisa appeared at her door, tears dripping down her cheeks, she knew her crying had a more desperate edge to it than was normal, even for her.

'What's the matter Lisa?' Jess knelt beside her, equal doses of concern and anger moulding her words.

A shrug of her shoulders was all she could manage.

'Where's Jacob?'

Another shrug. She couldn't even make eye contact.

'Do you want to come in?'

A nod.

Lisa smelled so bad that Jess had to call the front office for help. She knew this needed the corroboration of an eye witness, someone who could help document its horror.

Evelyn Noakes arrived a few minutes later with a change of clothes for Lisa. Evelyn was the school registrar and had worked at Marvale for twenty years. She was nearing retirement and had seen a lot in her time but this scene brought her to tears too. Unable to speak, she handed the clothes to Jess in silence.

'Here you go Lisa. It's a change of clothes,' Jess explained. 'I'll walk you to the showers so you can have a good wash before you put them on.'

Jess understood that Lisa had come early to avoid any uncomfortable stares from the other kids. She was a clever girl in that regard and trusted that her teacher would know what to do. Life was forcing independence upon her. She would be a survivor just like Jess. She had to be.

Jacob turned up an hour later in the same condition. The school day had already started. Apparently, he'd tried to hide in the back yard. Gary found him and gave him a whack across the head before pushing him up and out the side gate.

Jess conducted a thorough review of these events over the following days. It turned out that Gary and Tracey hadn't paid their water bill so it had been switched off. They said they'd forgotten. Confirmation of a long day at the pub told Jess that Gary had spent all the money on alcohol. Either way, no water meant no showers and no washing machine. The children hadn't washed for two weeks.

Jess lifted two small blue suitcases from the boot of the Prius. She had purchased them especially for this trip. Shopping for the children had been a wonderful experience. It had made her feel better than she had in years.

Jess, like her mum and dad, was a born giver, but when everything was taken from her, she failed to see the point anymore. It had become an unbalanced equation in her mind and the losses she had been forced to endure drove any feelings of generosity hard against the headstones of her parent's grave.

Birthdays were no longer a celebration but a reminder of what she'd lost. Christmas was absolute torture, so she locked herself away during these periods of darkness, sometimes for days on end.

'Here you go kids, your very own suitcases.'

Lisa and Jacob looked down at the luggage then back up at her.

'What are they for?' asked Jacob.

'To carry our clothes,' said Jess.

'Must be a long trip?' said Jacob.

'Where are we?' asked Lisa.

'Perth Airport,' replied Jess. 'You've been here before, haven't you?'

'Nah. Never.' explained Jacob.

The roar of engines thundered across the car park. The children looked skyward.

'Wow,' said Jacob.

The children watched in awe as a huge plane climbed steeply into the endless blue.

'We'll be on one of those soon,' said Jess.

Lisa and Jacob stared, their mouths and eyes wide open.

'I've never been on a plane,' breathed Lisa.

'Same,' leapt Jacob.

'First time for everything,' said Jess, already sweating over the fact that not all first times go well. It brought to memory Mrs Hammond's recount of the school's first contact with the Johnstone family. It was a day that will be etched into the memories of those who were there. The first day of kindergarten usually throws up a few surprises but the Johnstones had it in spades. The lurid stench of alcohol on the breath of both parents was an ugly sign. The dark shadows under the eyes of the children were a warning. Their lack of speech was a bright red flag.

Scariest of all though was their lack of excitement. The room was filled with toys and games yet Jacob and Lisa just stood there, sullen and still, like statues of despair. The Education Assistants were deeply suspicious.

None of the other children appeared to know who Jacob and Lisa were. Their parents had kept them hidden, but going to school was the law and they'd fronted up after a few discreet, yet pointed phone calls from the school Principal. Yasmin Neates never shied away from confrontation and she had politely informed Mr and Mrs Johnstone of the need for Lisa and Jacob to attend classes.

It was a decision their parents had been putting off. They knew they weren't good at this job and they didn't care, but the searing weight of insinuation and blame was currently boring into them like a blowtorch. Gary and Tracey didn't stick around long, drifting off before any tricky questions were asked. They scarpered like rats from a trap, their children as indifferent to their departure as they were to the world around them. There were no tears or cries for mum, just a blank stare and a collective silence.

And now, as Jessica Bell guided the children across a zebra crossing just outside the airport building, she considered the treadmill of social workers, therapists and police they had endured, forced to run from department to department by the same unhealthy and abusive parents who had given birth to them. They had come a long way since that first day, but after four years in the school system, all anyone had really discovered was that staying in the cycle and surviving it was a hell of a lot easier than changing it or getting out. Red tape and the stone-cold face of law made that almost impossible.

The yellow and blue school uniforms stood out more than Jess would have liked and she made a mental note to dispatch them quickly. The school crest could be easily tracked. Deep down she hoped the staff at Marvale might understand and even approve of what she was doing; happy that someone was finally helping Lisa and Jacob escape the vicious cycle they had been born into. The school had done what it could within the parameters of the law. Many teachers had tried and failed before Jess. The Johnstone family file was as thick as a phone book, filled with transcripts, examinations, reports and assessments. It was all good evidence, but it had proved ineffective in bringing about justice. It was only proof that the system was powerless to protect Lisa and Jacob Johnstone. Two of the innocent one-percenters, who the system failed to accommodate, their lives falling through the cracks.

When Jess first received the children's files from administration, she was advised to sit down and take a deep breath. The office knew what she was taking on, but they couldn't have predicted the impact it would have on her life.

The desperation and relief on the face of last year's teacher would have given Jess a clue.

Ashen faced and resigned, Mrs Harvey had spent the Christmas holidays trying to shake off a nagging sense of failure. February came around and the chance to pass on this heavy weight of responsibility was too great to pass up. Quit or die trying. It was an act of self-preservation.

This year would be different. Jess would not take the easy way out. She would do whatever was necessary to avert disaster. It was a decision that would set Jess apart from the rest.

The Community and Services Act 2004 – Principle (c) every child should be cared for and protected from harm.

The sliding glass doors of the Departure Terminal parted in silence. Jess knew that these automatic sensors weren't the only electronic eyes watching them; the CCTV camera perched high above the doorway a mere introduction to the extreme levels of security required by an international airport.

Her reconnaissance mission here last month had detailed a multitude of devices. She realised she couldn't avoid their detection and set about asserting some control over what they would see. She also knew she couldn't control the viewers on the other side, the security officers watching her every move; men and women, trained in the art of suspicion and deceit. Would they see two children being coerced into an airport or a happy family going on holiday? She glanced down at the children and saw smiles on their faces. Mission accomplished.

It had been twelve weeks since the idea to flee first surfaced in Jess's mind. A notion that could have been lying dormant and repressed for months, set free one cold foggy morning during a routine jog around the local park. It scared her at first, that such a thought could be her own. She ran past several people walking their dogs and feared they knew what she was thinking. Did the guilt show on her face? She erased the idea quickly from her mind, gone before it could be assessed for plausibility.

But it wasn't going to go away.

This strong craving for justice was not to be denied and she winced in discomfort as it continued to catch her off guard, knocking at the door of her thoughts during those quiet moments. And slowly but surely it nudged its way into her heart and as her resolve weakened, so, too, her courage grew. She was short on solutions to a problem that wouldn't go away and here in front of her was an answer. It no longer mattered how brazen and immoral it appeared to be. It just might work.

The early morning runs became spirited and rich as she threw around various scenarios, dissecting them with a passion she hadn't felt for a long time. Jess did her best thinking before the rest of the world woke up. The crisp clean air providing her ideas with a precision and clarity that the white noise of the day drowned out and swallowed.

She would have preferred to talk with someone; throw around ideas and maybe hear a contrasting opinion, but ideas like these cannot be discussed. Jess realised early on that to allow another person into her plan would have rendered the whole idea unworkable. Like a serial killer in the making, she had to go through it alone. No one could know what she was planning.

'I'm hungry,' said Jacob, his disgruntled taste buds succumbing to the sweet aromas flowing from the Dome coffee shop.

'Let's check-in first and then we'll get something to eat.'

'It's like a shopping centre,' said Lisa, taking in the enormity of her surroundings. The children appeared overawed by the massive panels of steel and glass that encased them, the cavernous roof reaching high above the concourse, a spider web of painted metal beams arching from one side to the other.

'Where are all the planes?' asked Lisa, this flicker of curiosity something the teachers of Marvale had tried to nurture and protect.

'Outside on the runway,' said Jess, kneeling down to share Lisa's view of the world. 'See that big television screen over there,' she pointed, her educator's hat still on, 'That has all the numbers of all the planes that are either taking off from here or landing. It tells us what country they have come from and where they are flying to next.'

'Are we going on one of them?' asked Lisa trying to contain her excitement.

'Yes, we are,' said Jess. 'See the one halfway down the list. It reads EK125 flying to Dubai and leaving at 1500 hours.'

'Fifteen hundred hours,' exclaimed Jacob. 'But there's only

twenty-four hours in a day. We'll be waiting forever.' A twinkle in his eye hinted at mischief.

That was one thing Jacob had going for him; a great math brain. He could soak up numbers until the cows came home. Just lapped them up. Would quickly make sense of a problem and then spew out an answer like it was obvious all along. He often used this ability as a source for humour but he really was something of a prodigy given his background.

It's another reason Jess bonded with him so quickly. She was a math head too. Loved the exactness of it. Loved the fact that emotions couldn't get in the way. A calculation was a cold hard fact. Two plus two equals four. It was this same deliberate approach to life that helped her decide to run. Abuse plus Neglect equals Freedom. They were the sum of all parts and she was the solution.

'Are mummy and daddy coming?' asked Lisa. It came out of the blue, but it was both the question Jess had been dreading and the one she had prepared best for. She knew it would come and understood how to handle it.

'No, not this time, but they told me to look after you and to have a good time.'

'Will we be gone long?' asked Jacob.

'Just long enough to see everything we want to see and eat a lot of really good food.'

This made Jacob and Lisa smile. Miss Bell often spoilt them with special lunches.

'Will they have movies on the plane?' asked Lisa.

'And video games?' added Jacob.

'Of course they will. You can do both,' explained Jess.

Jacob and Lisa cheered and laughed. It was a sound Jess had become addicted too. So pure and untainted, it was solid proof of the real promise that lay within. Residing deep inside these two young lives, it had found a secluded spot, a place that could not be reached by the horrors they'd had to endure. A spark that was endangered, yet alive, awaiting the day when it would re-ignite the fires of their potential.

The Community and Services Act 2004 – Principle (d) every child should live in an environment free from violence.

Jess unzipped her larger suitcase and lifted out two K-Mart bags. 'Surprise! I brought a change of clothes for you both to wear on the plane. You don't want to stay in these old uniforms all day.'

Lisa and Jacob peered inside the bags. 'Cool,' said Jacob, lifting out a pair of blue denim jeans.

'The change rooms are just over there,' directed Jess.

Lisa held up a beautiful pink and white dress and her smile said it all.

'You like it?'

'Thank you, Miss Bell,' she giggled, wrapping her arms around her teacher's waist. Lisa didn't get enough affection at home and her self-esteem had taken a battering. Jess wasn't much of a hugger herself but Lisa's embraces always softened her and she looked forward to breaking down some of the emotional barriers they had both erected.

The siblings carried their clothes, walking hand in hand toward the change rooms. Jess watched them and wondered if they would ever look at her like a son or a daughter would.

'Don't get ahead of yourself,' prompted the quiet voice of reason. 'First we need to get on that plane and fast.'

6

1:52PM
SUZIE'S SALON

'I know. Can you believe it?' whispered a young Chinese woman as she rested her elbows on the glossy white surface of her desk. 'She still not know,' she continued, dipping her brush into a small bottle of nail polish and applying a fresh coat of blood red paint to the fingernails splayed in front of her.

'If she was my best friend I'd tell her,' said Tracey Johnstone from the other side of the counter. 'She needs to know.'

Tracey was in her Friday night best; a bright red top covered in sequins, a blaze of sparkles amid the fluorescent tubes of the small nail salon. Her blonde hair matched the razzle-dazzle of her clothing with its teased-out frizz and light sprinkle of glitter. A short black skirt rode up her thighs like an elastic band, two red high heels dangling loosely off her feet.

'Is this the first time,' said Suzy, her own light pink uniform no match for the glitz of Tracey's get-up.

Tracey leant in closer. 'Nah, I slept with Steve too,' she whispered, her manicured eyebrows arching their backs.

Suzy's hands slipped, making a mess of the nail she was working on. She grabbed some tissues. 'You too?' she said. 'But you her friend?' She dabbed at the skin around the nail.

'This was a couple of years ago. I hadn't met Anna yet.'

'How you meet Steve then?'

'At a footy party. Grand Final day I think. It was a corker.'

'Oh. So just the once?'

Tracey held up several fingers on both hands. 'We did it eight times. He was pretty good in bed.'

Suzy lifted the brush and carefully slotted it back inside the small bottle it came with. She screwed the lid on tightly.

'What are you doing that for?' said Tracey. 'You haven't finished.'

'You not… do good thing,' stammered Suzy. 'He married man. You as well.'

'He came on to me. I wasn't chasing him.'

'But you not say no.'

'I'd had a few drinks and one thing led to another and before I knew it he was inside me.'

'Sssssss,' hissed Suzy, her hands up over her ears.

'Don't be such a priss. It's the bloody truth that's all.'

'You speak too ugly. Please stop.'

'Who you calling ugly? Bloody slope head!'

'You not nice. Please go!'

'Hey, I'm the customer here. I'll do what I fuckin' want.'

Tracey wrenched the bottle of polish out of Suzy's hand and unscrewed the lid. She slid the brush out of the bottle and draped it carefully across the surface of one of the three, as yet unpainted nails. 'You chinks are all the same. Think you're so high and mighty with your shitty little beauty shops. Only reason I come here is cause you're so bloody cheap.'

Suzy trembled. There was no escape. Behind her was a wall. She had to go past her customer if she was going to get away.

Tracey turned her attention to the next nail. 'You need to be nicer to people like me, or we won't put up with the stink you give off.' She looked up and stared Suzy straight in the face. 'I like sweet and sour on my chicken not up my nostrils.'

Suzie's face turned quickly to anger. 'You go now!' she demanded, launching herself to her feet.

'You kickin' me out?'

'You can keep bottle, just leave!'

Tracey placed her hands on the counter and leant forward, looming over Suzy like a giant. 'What if I decide to stay and tell you a few secrets about your own husband.'

There was movement from a doorway at the rear of the salon. An older Chinese man stepped forward. 'Is there a problem Suzy?'

'Yeah,' answered Tracey, turning to give him her full attention. 'You chinks are in my country and I want you to fuck off back home. That doable you reckon?'

'No, it is not,' glowered the man, who was now striding toward them. 'But you going back to the dump you came from is.' He yelled out something in Chinese, which made Tracey even more furious.

'What'd you say?' she sneered, the wet brush still in her hand, small red droplets falling to the floor. Tracey spun and glared at Suzy, her voice louder. 'What'd he say?'

A younger man stepped through the same doorway at the rear of the salon. 'He say that trash needs to be taken out and that it looks really heavy so he need some help.'

'I'm a paying customer,' harked Tracey. 'I have rights.'

'Not anymore,' said Suzy. 'I ban you from coming back. We not want to see your ugly mug again.'

'How dare you!' Tracey sank back into her chair and tried to coat her last unpainted nail. The men took positions either side of her.

'Out,' directed the younger man, pointing the way to the front door.

'I have one more nail to do,' said Tracey.

'Out!' he repeated.

'Don't you fuckin' touch me!' said Tracey.

The men exchanged some final words in Chinese before they grabbed an arm each and lifted her off the chair. Tracey flicked the nailbrush at the older man splashing his right cheek with polish. She knocked the small bottle off the table, spilling its contents like blood across a hospital floor.

Tracey struggled to free herself from their grip as she went kicking and screaming toward the front door.

'You're hurting me,' she yelled as they dragged her down the aisle, red high heels scraping along the white floor tiles. 'This is racism,' she hollered as the door was opened and she was thrown out onto the sidewalk. 'Slit-eyed bastards,' she hissed just before the straps of her oversised leather handbag got caught in her shoes, trapping her legs and tripping her heavily upon the cement pathway. The salon door banged shut behind her, the older man locking it and flipping the 'Open' sign hanging on the door so that it read 'Closed'.

Tracey lay strewn across the concrete, her skirt halfway up her bum and a scatter of red sequins littering the ground beneath her. She untangled her legs and struggled to her feet. 'Little fuckers,' she shouted at them through the glass. Her dress was torn, revealing one leg of badly laddered pantyhose and the hint of a bright red G-string.

She thrust the clasp on her handbag open, reaching inside and pulling out a tube of lipstick. She uncapped it and stepped menacingly toward the salon window. Her smile was coated with sarcasm as she used the lipstick to scrawl the words 'Ching Chong Chinamen' upon the glass in poppy red. The older Chinese man appeared at the window, his face inches away from the glass and just above the last word. This made Tracey smile even more. He lifted a phone to his ear but she was in no hurry and having taken the time to apply an exclamation mark to her thoughts on multiculturalism, she carefully wound down the shaft on her lipstick and dropped it nonchalantly into her bag.

She pulled her skirt down, straightened out her top and gave the old guy a one-fingered salute, her only unpainted nail raised in anger and revenge. She blew him a kiss before turning and sauntering off up the pathway, seemingly without a care in the world.

7

2:00PM
MARVALE PRIMARY SCHOOL

Amy Tanner glanced at her leather-strapped wristwatch and thanked the Lord for small mercies. She called all the noisy bodies of RED4 to attention and told them to hand in their artwork and line up at the door. 'One more hour to go,' she thought to herself. Another chaotic school week was almost over.

The students hustled and bustled their way around the grid-like maze of large brown worktables. They carried their colour-filled crayon creations toward the shelves at the rear of the class, before continuing their journey toward the exit. They were also looking forward to the end of the school week.

Amy watched the Year Four's assemble themselves into a loose line and considered how the lesson had gone. Forgetting to do a 'Circle' and talk through any issues from lunch was an oversight, which had led to a classroom disagreement between Dave and Neil.

Amy realised that she had also neglected to call the roll, which she quickly grabbed and completed while the children waited to go. She looked over their heads and identified them all, one by one. Well nearly all. Everyone was there except for Lisa Johnstone. Not unusual she thought to herself. Probably completing an extra session of remedial reading with one of the education assistants.

Amy had always considered Lisa to be a promising artist. Her work was often different to everybody else's and special in its own unique way. She always took direction well, yet still allowed her mind to run free with the possibilities the task offered. Lisa would have to catch up on today's lesson and Amy pledged to check in with one of her favourite Year Four artists early next week.

The sounds of a fresh batch of rowdy children started spilling in through the doorway. Amy couldn't hear herself think, her desire for a calm and peaceful art room no match for the chaos of the transition period between lessons. This time of the day and week often resembled a battleground, as one class left and another arrived.

'If only it was good energy,' thought Amy, then she might have enjoyed these handovers between Art and Indonesian. Encouraging the students to throw these sparks upon a canvas, rather than into the mischief and mayhem they always brought, was a challenge she often failed. Today was almost over she thought, and this 'load of hullabaloo' would be gone in sixty minutes.

Amy drew on her reserves of strength and stood tall, shouting above the din, instructing her old class to march forward. As soon as the last set of feet stepped out, her new class stepped in, threading themselves in through the green door and past the stainless-steel sinks that lined the entrance to her room. They poured themselves into the vacant spaces of her classroom like hot water upon a cracked riverbed.

'Circles please,' yelled Amy over the top of the clamour, children fighting over stools, battling for places beside friends as if their lives depended on it.

2:03PM

Sujitha Tran cajoled RED4 down the footpath toward her classroom. The last hour had not gone well and she was exhausted. She'd complained to the Principal about the crazy scheduling of Art and Indonesian together at the end of the week.

'These silly kids just don't know how to do anything but fight,' she'd explained passionately to Yasmin Neates.

Sujitha had come from the sheltered territory of the private school system and wondered how the teachers put up with this kind of misbehaviour all day, every day. Her principal just smiled. 'You'll get used to it,' she'd suggested.

The class looked pretty complete today, observed Sujitha as they filtered in through the doorway. 'Lots of bodies,' she thought. 'Must do the class roll.' But a disagreement over seats sucked away her attention and the day rolled on like it always did.

Except something was different. The class was not complete. There was one person missing and her continued absence was going unchecked.

8

2:05PM
PERTH INTERNATIONAL AIRPORT

'Check in time is closed I'm afraid.' The tired lady behind the Qantas counter was nearing the end of her shift. A gold embossed nametag labelled her as Bonnie Shelford, Ground Staff.

'I am so sorry but we left our passports at the house and had to return all the way home to get them,' said Jess, her quiet distress seemingly believable. Lisa and Jacob were still too enamoured with their new threads to take any notice of the adult conversation happening above their heads.

'I appreciate your situation Miss Bell,' explained Bonnie, 'but it is company policy and I must follow protocol. Security is our highest priority.'

Jess should have been frantic but her preparation for this moment had been meticulous. Arriving late wasn't a mistake. It was in fact an important part of her plan.

Her Level Three security clearance had provided her with relatively good access to the Education Department database, helping her to investigate legal precedents where desperate parents had sought to flee a country with children in tow. When some files proved to be above her security level, she had simply 'borrowed' the deputy principal's password and downloaded them anyway. She liked to think she was accessing them under Freedom of Information laws but she knew that was a lie and as she got deeper into the program, she realised that nothing would stop her fulfilling her plan. Legal or illegal, it didn't matter anymore.

These national databases were filled with folder after folder, cataloguing case after case where a custody dispute had led to a family member snatching a child during school hours. Some sort refuge within state boundaries, others wanted the speed of a plane and the safety of an international border. What caused their efforts to fail? What brought their run for freedom to a sudden halt? Each case ensured she learnt one more detail about what not to do.

In several cases the escapees were stopped at the departure gates, interrogated and later arrested. The cause? A red flag, raised as soon as the passenger list for the flight had been automatically scanned by immigration for arrest warrants and flight risks. When check-in closed the manifest of travellers booked on that flight was instantly shared across several government departments and agencies. Information retrieval was paramount post 9/11 and this data was used to prevent any wanted criminals from leaving the country. Shared custody cases and the like, anything which involved the courts, was also flagged, often preventing frustrated parents from absconding to some far off Middle Eastern desert, where the reciprocal rights of law were as worthless as a grain of sand. Jess wasn't sure if the three of them would have flicked any switches but circumventing this potential difficulty was important to her. She decided they would have to take a chance and check-in after closing.

'I understand how important protocol and security are but please don't punish the children for my mistake,' said Jess. 'They are so excited about our holiday. This would devastate them.'

Jacob and Lisa looked up and smiled on cue. Jess knew from experience that when required they could project a happiness and contentment that belied the truth. It was how their parents had tricked social worker after social worker.

Well trained in the art of deception, it was the only thing that

Jess could thank their parents for.

Bonnie gazed at the children. She'd had a tough upbringing herself and now her adult life was slowly careering out of control. 'Two is a great number,' she thought to herself. 'One of each.' That was what she'd envisaged her own family being made up of, but at thirty-five her window of opportunity was quickly passing. Here in front of her was a woman who had everything she'd ever wanted. Beauty, great clothes, and two children. 'Should have been me,' cursed Bonnie before the click-clack of the keyboard suggested she'd made up her mind.

'I've allocated you a window seat Miss Bell.' A simple smile told Jess not to be too effusive; nothing on record, business as usual.

'Thank you.'

'Passports?'

Jess slid three dark blue booklets across the counter.

Accessing the children's passports had proved surprisingly easy once the decision to break the law had been made and she acted out her plan one cold April morning.

The heavy autumn rain that had been forecast was already falling when she slid the rusty key out from under the clay flowerpot. It was exactly where Lisa said it would be. Information Jess had extracted during a lesson in creative writing.

The back door to the house opened with a nudge and Jess stepped forward nervously. She took a deep breath to calm her nerves but instead of feeling better, a foul stench assaulted her nostrils and she winced with distaste. She swallowed hard and bit her bottom lip.

She gazed up the hallway, her eyes taking time to adjust to the darkness. There were piles of stuff on both sides of the corridor: boxes, old clothes, miniature televisions, travel magazines. She stepped forward and wove her way past the eclectic mix of household rubbish.

The internal layout of the house was a mystery and trawling through each room could have proven tedious. She needed to be quick. Tracey and Gary's whereabouts were unknown.

She stepped through a doorway to her left and scanned the room. Two large windows were heavily curtained, small patches of light seeping in around the edges where the drapes were faded and torn. A mixture of junk was stacked waist high against the walls of the room, a two-seater couch and television taking center stage. The aroma here was a mixture of sweat, smoke and alcohol, a still life of overflowing ashtrays and empty bottles littering every surface.

Jess retreated into the main corridor and took a few steps to her right. Another doorway, this time leading to a dirty bathroom, its tiled walls spared the collections of junk. The grime covered tiles though were more visible than Jess would have liked; the grout, an unforgiving black; loose strands of hair, scattered everywhere. Mould sprouted from every corner, the blackened hem of the oversized shower curtain, draping through the muck of a damp floor.

A rusted showerhead hung loosely down the wall, holding on to the chromed flexi arm by a frayed length of brown string, a failed attempt at repair. A thick trail of green lime scale ran down the wall and into a drain, itself choking on clumps of hair. A flash of Lisa standing in the doorway of Jess's classroom, as filthy as a stray dog. It made her wonder if she'd ever felt the clean embrace of a warm bath.

Up the hall further was the kitchen, a similar state of disrepair, grime coating every surface, mould splattered dishes piled high across the counter. Jess had found the last few minutes sad and disheartening but it was the state of the children's room that really ripped her heart out.

The stench coming from the end of the passage was almost unbearable and having adapted to the reek that had almost smothered her at the start of this quest, Jess continued cautiously toward the source. By the time she peered around the doorway, she was already choking back tears. Two cot-sized mattresses blurred her vision, arranged side by side on the floor just inside the room. Each bed was besieged by piles and piles of junk, lining the walls and floor of the room. Two torn couch cushions served as pillows, with a stained brown blanket draped carefully across both mattresses. The image of Lisa and Jacob sleeping amongst such filth broke Jess in two and she fell to her knees sobbing. A wave of despair crashed over her, bile rising in the pit of her stomach, her body wrestling for control.

The last room she had visited that day had proved to be her salvation, discovering the children's passports, buried under a pile of unpaid bills in the closet of Gary and Tracey's bedroom. Their double bed wasn't any better than the rest of the house, the same piles of rubbish filling the outer edges of another unloved and chaotic space. It was all so symbolic of their own head space and Jess felt a deep sadness for the whole family.

She flicked through the passports quickly. It had been Tracey's parents who had applied for them. They were the only people in Lisa and Jacob's life capable of filling out such complicated documentation. John and Eileen Johnstone were the glue that held their daughter's life together, loaning her money when finances were stretched and taking the kids off her hands when she struggled to cope. They loved their daughter but she was hard work.

But it was love that wasn't reciprocated. The ugly heads of jealousy and favouritism reared early last year when John and Eileen organised a trip to Bali for the kids.

Tracey had argued that it was she who needed 'a bloody good break' and when her parents refused to change their plans and include her in the holiday abroad, accusations of kidnapping and abuse were thrown around like cheap red wine. The flights were cancelled and John and Eileen were instantly frozen from their grandchildren's lives.

Jess had heard a lot about the grandparents but had only ever seen them once. The local rumour mill had gone into overdrive, the unsubstantiated accusations flying mercilessly across town. Everyone knows anyone in Marvale and with a high proportion of fractured families, many reconstructed from the unkind rubble of divorce, Jess knew better than to listen to the school gate mafia. She had been the butt of their banter on many occasions and knew all too well that trying to communicate with these mean-spirited mothers was as useless as the bendy rulers their children brought to school.

Jess tracked John and Eileen down herself and discovered two, kind and loving individuals. People who would have made a hell of a lot of difference to the lives of their grandchildren. They were as stable as you could get. Their daughter and her choice of a partner were not. Their exclusion from the children's upbringing made Jess's decision that much easier.

The Community and Services Act 2004 – Principle (e) every child should have stable, secure and safe relationships and living arrangements.

The fact that the passports were produced in 2002 was a lucky break for Jess. In 2004, the Department of Foreign Affairs started producing passports with chips in them that linked a family together. Children younger than sixteen couldn't leave the country unless two things accompanied them; either a parental passport with the same chip on the same flight or a letter of permission signed by their legal guardians. Jess had been relieved to discover that this technology was not retrospective and that older passports would not support this new feature.

Having found what she wanted, Jess stepped out onto the steps at the rear of number 23 Dalton Crescent, closed the door behind her and vowed never to return to this soul-destroying dump. She returned the key to its hiding spot and retreated down the steps with both passports tucked safely inside her jacket. She didn't look back.

Bonnie looked the three of them over then glanced quickly at their passport photos, completing the three-part visual check. The questions she had in her head went unasked because her last-minute decision to slip them into the flight meant that she had a time limit hanging over her head. Just thirty seconds to fill in the blanks on screen then press enter. The security clearances would not be completed. She knew that but to hell with it. She could see that this woman was a good person. She'd been well trained to spot a security risk and Jessica Bell did not fit any of the flight risk profiles.

This decision marked the end of Bonnie's days as a Qantas employee.

SEND. She hit return. 'Have a nice flight Miss Bell,' smiled Bonnie.

Jess slid the passports back in her handbag. 'Thank you, Bonnie, we will.'

2:53PM
GATE 12, PERTH INTERNATIONAL AIRPORT

The sign at Gate 12 was already illuminated, signaling the open nature of the flight. Jess and the kids entered the roped off section which was heaving with passengers, some seated while others hovered around the ticket desk hoping for an early invitation to board. Jess observed a handful of security officers dotted around the edges.

'Stay calm and keep to your plan,' she reminded herself. One more hurdle to climb over and the most dangerous section of their escape would be complete. Once out of the country she knew they would be harder to stop.

'Ladies and gentlemen,' sang a pretty voice. 'Flight EK125 is now open for boarding.'

Jess observed her fellow passengers as they jostled for position, a queue quickly forming from the chaotic jumble of impatient bodies. A lack of certainty tugged at the hem of Jess's dress, playing havoc with her poise. Her plan was going perfectly but an old friend named doubt rose to the surface once again, plaguing her with questions.

She'd experienced a massive lack of confidence some sixteen years ago, here at this very same airport. Her twenty-first birthday celebration had been spent alone and adrift. With very little in the way of family and friends, she had come impulsively to the airport, a hastily filled suitcase and unused passport all that she carried. She was trying to escape the darker memories that were strangling her and hoped that a new country would provide a fresh start. It proved to be a successful decision and one she was hoping to repeat.

'This is us guys,' she said softly. 'You ready to get on the plane?'

'Ready,' they replied in unison, their patience both admirable and concerning. It was a slightly robotic trait and something they often displayed in class. The school psychologist, Maria Barnaby, said it was a result of either a home life that was not stimulating them or an environment within which they were too frightened to act or think of their own accord.

Maria and Jess had chatted many times after school, usually about these two precious pupils. Maria was an intelligent woman with an adult family of her own. She had the academic knowledge of an expert in her field and the maternal nous of a mother, so when it came to understanding children, she was always right on the money. Jess had mined her colleague's reserves for advice and information.

It was Maria who'd first reminded Jess of the Code of Ethics for teachers that stated a clear expectation to '*make decisions that put the welfare of the child above all else*'. This same Code also demanded that teachers be '*accountable for their students' welfare*' and '*place the student's best interests above the teacher's personal interest or benefit*'. Jess was going one better, deciding to put her whole life on the line for sake of these children.

The Community and Services Act 2004 – Principle (f)
intervention action should be taken only in circumstances where there is no other reasonable way to safeguard and promote the child's wellbeing.

Jess pulled the boarding passes from her coat pocket. She checked the details, growing comfortable with the anonymity offered by the crowds. Suddenly a beeping sound leapt from her watch, unwanted attention raining down on her. She'd set the alarm last night so she would know when the tick-tock of the schoolyard clock would no longer be on her side. She'd assumed awareness of this moment to be advantageous but the many eyes that bored her way were far from beneficial and panic once again shook her like a rag doll. She wrestled with her wristwatch and fumbled the boarding passes in the process, the thick white cards somersaulting their way toward the carpet. A security guard stared at her like she was a ticking time bomb, the intermittent beeping of the timepiece growing in volume. Jess slid it from her wrist and pushed every button she could find.

'You dropped these,' said a deep voice.

Jess looked up and gazed into the green eyes of an older man. He was wearing a dark blue suit and tie. Jess's mind was on full throttle the alarm almost boring a hole in her brain.

She absent-mindedly accepted the boarding cards without a reply.

'May I?' he offered, taking possession of the problem watch. He held down both side buttons until the beeping stopped.

'Old trick,' he smiled, returning the timepiece to Jess. 'Are these your children?'

'Yes.'

The man knelt down to meet Jacob and Lisa at eye level. A flash of light from the badge on his left breast caught their attention. Lisa thought the engraved font was very pretty, although the words escaped her decoding skills. 'Captain Brian McLay' read Jacob.

'Hi kids.'

Lisa and Jacob didn't reply, they just stared.

'It's okay, I just wanted to give you these.' Captain McLay opened the plastic bag he was carrying and passed both of them a small pencil case shaped like a plane, the word Emirates embroidered across one side. 'There's a full set of coloured pencils and Textas inside.' He reached inside again and pulled out two huge colouring-in books. 'I'll give these to your mum to carry onto the plane for you.'

Jacob's eyes opened like saucers and Lisa let out an infectious giggle. The Captain rose to meet Jess's eye level.

'Here you go Miss Bell,' he said, handing her the books.

'Thanks.' Her hands were trembling beyond control.

'My pleasure. Could I escort you through the gate? It'll be a lot quicker.'

'That's okay, we're fine.'

'C'mon. The kids can start work on their colouring books and you can finally relax. I think you deserve it.'

Jess was breathing hard, her brow lined with crease marks. 'Alright, that would be nice.'

'Good. Please follow me.' The Captain guided them down one side of the queue. Jess looked down at her watch as it clicked over to 2:59. School was almost out but they weren't on the plane yet. That was a problem and Jess knew it.

9

3:00PM
MARVALE PRIMARY SCHOOL

The home time siren spilled out across the playground, flooding the cream-coloured paving of the deserted quadrangle and sweeping down toward the classrooms.

Young faces transformed into brightly lit beams of freedom, their teachers breathing a collective sigh of relief. Final directives were given out as chairs were quickly stacked, bags were rashly packed and floors were poorly cleaned. The end of the school week had finally arrived.

Sujitha Tran waited for her class to settle. She was a patient woman but even she had a limit. Her classroom was darker than most, even with the lights on. She liked it that way though; felt it calmed the students and made the teaching space more peaceful. The smells of jasmine rice and coconut wafted playfully around the class, escaped grains of rice dotting the desks like snowfall, the children dropping their empty paper patty pans into the rubbish bin.

'Selamat siang,' said Sujitha, her smile a little forced.

'Selamat siang Ibu Tran,' replied the packed class with an impressive harmony that was often missing from the rest of their day. The paper roll sat unchecked on the teacher's desk. There was only one empty seat in the far-right corner of the room. Specialist teachers saw the whole school pass through their doorway, some three hundred and sixty-two children in total, so it was understandable that Sujitha did not remember exactly who should have been in that chair.

The flu was sweeping through the school so an absent child wasn't that big a deal at the moment. Anyway, an absence doesn't need to be investigated until a student has been away three consecutive days. She could always check with the class teacher later if she needed to find out who was missing.

Sujitha opened the door to the outside world, stepping aside just in time to allow the children to spill out in threes and fours, their juvenile impatience forcing a squish of bodies through a gap only wide enough for two at a time.

They ran up the slope toward their classroom, the whole school on high alert as parents weaved young children carefully past the rush of bigger bodies. Excited students zigzagged haphazardly through any gap they could find, chrome plated scooters complicating this flow of madness as wheels spun without warning, bags swinging dangerously though the air.

The upper primary students of Blue Block stepped free of the four walls that enclosed them, making hushed arrangements to meet up at the park. Jacob wasn't part of anyone's plans. He was now just a missing piece of data like his sister. No one even spoke his name. Some kids are good at being invisible. Others just fade away.

The school perimeter resembled a hive, a swarming mass of bees suffocating every exit. Cars pulled in and out of the pick-up zones, spiriting uniformed passengers far from the confines of the black garrison fence that surrounded Marvale Primary. It was Friday afternoon and everyone's minds had already left the buildings of this educational institution. Now they were just waiting for their bodies to catch up.

Up the hill in Red Block, Jess's class had been empty for over two and a half hours. She'd taken nothing with her. Her laptop computer lay open and unwanted on her desk, its metallic body dormant beside the same stack of exercise books she collected and marked each week.

'Beer o'clock,' said a middle-aged man as he strode into her empty classroom, his cropped hair a scrunched mass of browns and greys, his tie askew, the knot loose and low beneath the shirt collar.

'Jess?' A glimmer of confusion crossed his face, the answer to his own question an unexpected one. Jeff Simpson had worked with Jess every day for the past three years and it was unusual for him not to know where she was at any given time. They taught all their subjects together, combining both of their classes into one big happy family. Today had been slightly different due to his attendance at a Curriculum Development course in Joondalup. He had missed his good friend and teaching partner and had left the lecture early, looking forward to catching up over a cold beer. But she wasn't here. He left the classroom slightly perplexed and continued his search for her warm smile and easy company.

10

3:02PM
GATE 12, PERTH INTERNATIONAL AIRPORT

'Good afternoon Captain,' smiled the well-groomed stewardess from behind the ticketing desk at Gate 12.

'Afternoon Hayley. This is Miss Bell, and these two little people are Lisa and Jacob. Could you please check them in as Express guests? They have a very long flight ahead of them.'

'Of course, sir.'

Jess watched this exchange with detachment. They were conversing about her, yet she'd planned to remain invisible. Captain McLay didn't know it but he was both helping and hindering her in equal doses. Jess hadn't broken any major laws yet but every step forward made it more difficult to see the events of the day clearly. Adapting her plan to these sorts of changes was not easy and navigating her way through the difficulties that arose felt like she was fumbling for guidance through a maze without walls.

'I'll leave you in Hayley's capable hands,' said the Captain.

Jess tried to shake off the doubt that cloaked her. 'Thank you,' she smiled.

'Bye,' said Lisa with a little wave of her little hand.

'See ya, Lisa,' replied the Captain. He gave her a soft-handed high five then turned to Jacob. 'Nice meeting you son.' Captain McLay shook the boy's hand before turning and walking briskly down the tunnel toward the plane. Jess watched him go, unsure whether his attention was a flirt with danger or just a crazy dream.

'Afternoon Miss Bell,' said Hayley.

'Hi,' croaked Jess. It was all she could get out of her dry, tacky mouth.

Guilt was a heavy burden and not something Jess carried easily. She had always tended toward the safest route and today was proving a massive departure from that lifelong strategy.

'Can I have your boarding passes please?'

Jess took the passes from her pocket and passed all three to the stewardess.

'Thank you.'

Lisa and Jacob watched as Hayley guided each card into a slot and waited for the machine to beep. Her long brown ponytail swayed from side to side with each check of the monitor. If they'd watched her any longer she could have inadvertently hypnotised them.

The Captain's aftershave lingered in the still air of the terminal, his perfumed scent reminding Jess of her teaching partner, Jeff Simpson, and the hell she was about to put him through. What she was experiencing now was nothing compared to the microscopic scrutiny his actions would be put under. It was a teacher's worst nightmare and the suspicion he'd have to endure would become a stain that could never be completely removed.

Her eyelids eased closed and she imagined Jeff back in his classroom, thumping his desk with frustration, tears sliding down his cheeks, anger and concern wearing him out like a seesaw. His clouting of the desk morphed into the clip clop sound of footsteps as Lisa walked passed him, her arm in a sling, her head and eyes cast down toward the floor. A white cast of plaster enveloping her forearm.

'Miss Bell,' said a voice, its familiarity running in contrast to the images. 'Are you okay?'

'I must be strong,' thought Jess, as she ushered the many painful memories from her mind. She dragged her eye lids open. Hayley was closer now, having stepped around the counter, her face filled with concern.

'I'm okay,' replied Jess. 'Just tired. It's been a long day.'

Hayley returned the boarding passes. 'Look after yourself and have a nice flight.'

'Thank you.' Jess turned and treaded off down the airbridge toward the plane.

'Excuse me, Miss Bell.' It was Hayley's voice again. Jess stopped, took a deep breath and turned slowly.

'Don't forget your children.' Lisa and Jacob were still standing at the desk staring up at the beautiful lady, mesmerized by her smile and her smooth skin and her foreign fragrance. They had never met anyone as glamorous or beautiful as her before. 'She must be a princess,' thought Lisa, her narratives often revealing a penchant for the comforts of an imaginary castle.

Hayley lowered herself to the children's eye level. 'Your mummy's waiting guys. I'll see you on the plane.'

'Really,' said Jacob.

'I promise.'

Jess waved them on. 'C'mon kids, I know she's beautiful but she's also a very busy woman.'

Jess was a beautiful woman as well, but it was the damage that lay within which she couldn't conceal; the pain she had to endure each day. Experience had taught her that love and truth were deeply connected. When one is broken the other is also damaged. Love had been torn from Jess at an early age and a darker truth had stepped in to stem the pain. Love and loss were now inseparable, making Jess a complex individual.

'See ya, Hayley,' smiled Jacob as he walked through the doors. Lisa was quicker to cut the cord, running up to Jess and grabbing her hand.

'You must stay with me at all times, okay?' insisted their teacher. 'We need to look after each other.'

Jacob nodded. The extra responsibility of looking after his little sister always scared him. It was an expectation his parents had forced upon him from the time she was born. Sometimes they would disappear for days and taking care of her exhausted him. Lisa was oblivious to the extra burden Jacob carried. He wasn't even allowed to go over other people's houses after school because he had to stay and look after her. That's why he liked being at school. His load was lighter there. The teachers took great care of Lisa and they were always in control; always knew what was happening and where everyone was. 'It's like they have eyes in the back of their heads,' he sometimes observed.

Jess's own eyes were a cause of concern, the lights around her appearing to flicker, reality continuing its battle against the intermittent flashes from the past. The same visions of Lisa's fractured arm continued to badger her brain. She remembered the complaint Tracey had filed against Gary for child abuse. It was quickly withdrawn when DCP got wind of it but it became widely known that Gary had accidentally snapped both the Radius and Ulna bones of Lisa's forearm during an argument over the dishes. Their little bodies were so frail that such indiscriminate force just snapped them like a piece of chalk.

Jess struggled down the tunnel, the walls beginning to drift from side to side, her failing eyes starting to lose focus. She knew she'd made a huge error in not eating any lunch. Exhaustion and stress weren't the only battles she was waging. Hunger was now rendering her body useless and as the light of the afternoon slowly faded, so too did the hope that she carried in her heart. She'd considered all the dangers except for this. Controlled all the external factors only to be unraveled by internal ones.

The deceit of darkness gradually overcame her, tempting her with the peace and serenity that she had been searching for all her life. Her eyes were failing and her legs were next to go, her body simply crumbling to the floor.

'So close, so close,' she stammered before the thud of the carpeted floor greeted her head, a final act of fatigue that forced her into a deeper sleep than she could ever have imagined.

11

3:30PM
MARVALE PRIMARY SCHOOL

Jeff Simpson collapsed into a staffroom chair and lifted a cold stubbie of beer to his mouth.

'Long day Jeff?' inquired Tim from the other side of the table.

'Too fucking long,' he replied. 'Thank god it's Friday.'

Jeff took a swig from the bottle, the instant relief in his body palpable. He dragged it from his lips and swallowed. 'Aaaaahhhh. That's better.'

Several teachers had gathered around one of the square wooden tables that furnished the well-lit staffroom.

'Where's Jess?' asked Yasmin Neates. 'You two are normally inseparable.'

'Don't know. She wasn't in her room when I got back from my course.'

'I haven't seen her all day,' chimed in Rupert Small, the Deputy.

'She was definitely here this morning,' said Nora Sloane, the school librarian. 'She came in and got some books with her class just before recess.'

Evie Harmon poked her head in through the door that led to the atrium. 'Hey everyone.'

'Coming for a drink?' asked Tim.

'Nah, still got a heap of work to finish. Had a few playground issues with the wee ones. Need to write it all up in the SAER file.'

'Was Robert Costa involved by any chance?' asked Yasmin.

'Does a bear shit in the woods?' Evie's comment drew a laugh from those present. 'Anyone spoken to Jacob Johnstone today?' added Evie.

'No,' answered Rupert. 'Probably off sick with the flu like the rest of them. Twenty-five kids away today. That's two-point-five per classroom.'

Rupert loved his stats. He could objectify any situation and turn it into a group of numbers, collate the info into a graph, print it off in colour and then dissect it for everyone to see. The desk jockeys at Silver City devoured his sheets of data like chocolates.

'Jacob was definitely here this morning,' explained Tim. 'I had his class for sport first up. I remember because he arrived late as usual.'

'Was he hungry?' asked Yasmin.

'I didn't ask. He sat out most of the first game.'

'I saw his little sister Lisa in the library, too,' answered Nora.

'That's who he was protecting at recess,' explained Evie. 'Someone's been teasing her.'

The use of Lisa and Jacob's names was poignant. The invisibility cloak that Jess had draped over their departure was rapidly dissolving.

'Whose Lisa's teacher?' asked Evie.

'Jess is,' answered Jeff.

'She's usually always here with you alcoholics?' said Evie.

'We were just thinking the same thing,' agreed Yasmin.

Jess had started off quietly at the school, leaving the social occasions to those who enjoyed them most. Jeff's arrival had changed all that and they'd both become permanent features here over the past few years.

Some of her closer acquaintances knew that alcohol had been a coping mechanism during her teenage years. What they didn't realise was that it had come to fulfil the same purpose recently, the stresses and strains inherent with this job growing in size. It was an uncomfortable paradox. Most of the problems she experienced as a teacher could be linked directly back to the parents who treated liquor like a fix-all solution. Now she was back on that loaded wagon.

Before she came to Marvale she'd been a clean skin. Ten years without a drop and she was proud of it. Now, though, two beers at Friday drinks would set her up for another two when she got home and by eight o'clock she'd be fast asleep on the couch, her problems all gone. She'd wake up some time during the late-night home shopping infomercials and stumble robot-like to her bed. This was her end of the week routine and it rarely got broken.

These last few years had been especially tough. A new teaching partner in Jeff had gone some way to sharing the workload but she had her own private demons to fight and they were not open for discussion. Jeff was a great friend and they had a lot of fun together. He had made her life at Marvale happier, filling it with laughter and smiles. But he also voiced a real concern for some of the children in their care and it was these discussions that formed the catalyst for Jess to formulate and enact her plan.

Jeff spoke about the issues Jess saw but never mentioned. His strong ideals made her decide to be a different kind of teacher. One who never shied away from the tough stuff. Lisa and Jacob were a case in point. She would not stand back and watch as they passed on through. She was going to be the difference in their lives, not just the documenter.

'If she's not here soon, I'll have to file a missing person's report,' joked Tim.

'I certainly missed her today,' said Jeff. 'First course I've been on without her. It really sucked!'

'You two should get married,' grinned Yasmin.

'That's the worst idea I've heard in ages,' said Tim. 'You seen them argue?'

'We don't argue,' said Jeff, 'We discuss.'

'Gets pretty heated,' replied Tim.

'We're both passionate people.'

'Exactly! So, like I said, get married already.' Yasmin finished her plea to much applause. The strong friendship they had built had kept them both in this profession past their use-by dates. Jeff always felt that ten years was a good grab of time to be a teacher. After that, burnout was a common affliction and he wanted to avoid it. But they both enjoyed the camaraderie and support their relationship provided and found it hard to give it up. They depended on each other. They both loved working together, but that's as far as it went. They were as inseparable as brother and sister: a grown-up version of Jacob and Lisa.

The truth was they hadn't missed a Friday drinking session in over three years. Until today. He wasn't showing it but Jeff had started to worry. 'If she wasn't here, then where could she be?'

12

3:45PM
11 ANGLE WAY, MARVALE

Tracey sucked on a cigarette from the comfort of a torn and tattered couch. She flicked the embers into a small glass ashtray balanced precariously on the armrest beside her.

'Don't see these much anymore,' said Tracey, indicating the ashtray.

'People won't let you smoke inside is why,' explained a woman in the armchair opposite. 'Secondhand smoke is bad for the children,' she mimicked. 'It's all bullshit is what I reckon.'

'I prefer the smell of nicotine to the stink of kids,' said Tracey, taking a sip from the wine glass in her hand. 'Someone should make an air freshener called Smoke.'

'Makes my house smell like a pub. Like I'm out havin' a good time.'

The sound of bodies racing in through the front door drew a sigh from both women. 'There goes that feeling,' said Tracey, her shimmery outfit at sharp odds with the dull shades of the living room.

Two young children burst into the lounge room, chests puffing under stained yellow shirts, bright red school bags secured to their backs.

'Hi mum,' said the older boy. 'Hi Mrs Johnstone.'

'Hi Teo. Hi Lizzy,' replied Tracey.

The little girl just smiled.

'Drop your bags in your rooms and you can go off and play,' ordered their mother. 'Leave us adults alone with our vices.'

'Did Jacob go to school today?' asked Teo.

'Yeah, of course he did. Was a bit late, but yeah he went,' said Tracey.

'Never saw him at recess or lunch,' said Teo.

'Must have got a detention,' said Tracey. 'He's always getting himself into trouble.'

'I saw him talking to Miss Bell at lunchtime,' said Lizzy. 'She took both your kids for a walk to the office I think.'

'Probably for food,' said Tracey. 'I give what I have but those meddling teachers always try to give more. Making bloody softies out of my kids.'

'Should stick to education,' said the other woman. 'Leave us to sort out their diets.'

'If only they could do that right,' said Tracey. 'My Lisa's way behind the other kids. Thick as two bricks because of those lazy arse teachers.'

The other woman looked at her children. 'All right you two, piss off. And don't forget your chores.'

Teo and Lizzy nodded as they disappeared up the hallway in a rush of footsteps.

'Your two critters will be home by now, won't they?' said the woman.

'Yeah. Gary's on pick-up today,' said Tracey. 'My afternoon off.'

'He much of a cook?'

'Hah. That'll be the day. They'd have to break their teeth on a frozen sausage roll before he'd even try to turn on the oven. Useless in that department.'

'What is he good at?'

'Being a dickhead. He's got expert qualifications when it comes to fucking up. Just like your ex.'

'Yeah, good riddance to that tosser.' The woman drained her glass.

'Gary will be gone soon too if he doesn't buck up his ideas. He isn't bringing in any dough and he's getting fat and lazy.'

'They always do. You want another drink?'

'Fuck yeah.'

13

4:00PM
FLIGHT EK125

Jess tried squeezing her eyes open, the bright lights of the cabin an intense reminder of her place in the waking world. A throbbing headache provided added discomfort, a small bout of turbulence emulating the unease that troubled her from within. She tried to swallow but her mouth was too dry, the aftertaste of vomit an unwelcome remnant of the last few hours.

She tensed her stomach muscles to sit up, a deep ache from her abdomen adding to the casualty list. She looked left and right. The seats beside her were empty. Across the aisle a man in a suit stared at the screen in front of him, headphones locking him into a fictional world of his choice. Jess tried to haul herself up off the chair but a seat belt was still secured around her waist, its unforgiving tension dragging her down, draining her of the limited energy she had. A surge of vomit made her hesitate and as the cabin once again began to drain of light, she took heed of the warning signals and slumped back into her pod-like chair and slept.

'Hi kids, how are you?' Hayley knelt down beside the children.

'We're okay,' replied Jacob. 'Is Miss Bell going to be okay?'

'Of course, she is,' smiled Hayley. 'Your mum just needs to rest.'

'She's not our mum.'

'She's not?' said Hayley, 'I just assumed she was.'

'That makes an ass of you and me,' remembered Lisa.

'Indeed, it does. Who taught you that?'

'My pop,' smiled Lisa. 'He likes all that funny stuff.'

'Obviously,' said Hayley. 'Anyway, Miss Bell is having a little sleep in First Class where she's being taken care of by a nurse.'

'Can we see her?' asked Jacob.

'Of course, you can but we want her to get as much sleep as possible first so Captain McLay has a little surprise for you.'

Jess awoke with a fright, her eyes flickering with uncertainty. She fumbled for the buckle across her lap and unclasped it. She grabbed the arm rest to her left and lifted her body across and into the empty seat beside her. Hauling her weary body to its feet, she stepped into the aisle. The passageway toward the next cabin was clear, her legs unsteady.

A set of red drapes separated the two cabins and she drew them to one side. A sea of people greeted her, the overpowering smell of food adding to her sense of nausea, mouths chewing, faces laughing. She fumbled in her pockets for the boarding passes. Empty. She scanned the seats ahead of her.

An empty block of seats down the left-hand side of the cabin caught her attention. 'We booked a window,' she remembered. Her legs pushed on without question, hustling her down the aisle, careful short steps, her balance slowly improving.

The vacant seats were filled with pillows and blankets. Colouring-in books and a pencil case wedged into the seat pocket in front. She glanced up at the seat numbers. K7, 8, and 9. A smile. A memory. The lady at check-in. Her voice announcing their seat selection.

Jess gazed hurriedly up and down the plane. Her view was obscured, the long distances to the galley testing her recovery, reality slightly blurred and unbalanced. Hayley was up the far end, talking to another stewardess. Jess strode up the aisle, the twinkle of lights and the hum of twin engines magnifying the confusion.

'Excuse me, Hayley.'

Hayley turned around. 'Miss Bell, are you okay?'

'Yes. I mean no.' She paused for breath. 'Where are my children?'

'They're safe. Everything's okay. Sorry, I didn't realise you were awake.'

'Where are they?'

'They're with the captain.'

'Why. What's happened?'

'Nothing. He just wanted to show them the view from the cockpit.'

'They're upfront?'

'Yes. Captain McLay is showing them how he flies the plane. Come. I'll take you there too.'

Jess took a deep breath.

'Can you make it?' asked Hayley.

A nod. 'I'll feel much better once I've seen them.'

They left the confines of Economy, the wider spaces of First Class much easier to navigate. They eased down a narrow corridor, towards the nose of the plane, a thin grey door down one end. Hayley knocked twice and the door swung inward.

The darkness on the other side was eerie, a bank of coloured lights on either side. The sound of muffled voices and a large window filled with puffy white clouds.

'This is amazing,' exclaimed Jacob.

'It's like magic,' said Lisa.

She couldn't see them. 'Hi guys,' called Jess, a strong desire to make contact with the voices.

'Hi Miss Bell,' they tuned back, 'They turned the lights off for us. How cool is this.'

'It's cool but I really wish I could see you.'

'Sorry Miss Bell, I'll put the lights back on.' It was the familiar voice of Captain McLay, the instant buzz of electricity, filling the smaller than expected cockpit with a yellow light.

'Are you okay?' asked Lisa as she stepped forward and hugged her teacher's legs. The comfort of her embrace was welcome relief and Jess rested her own arms across the child's shoulders.

'I'm fine now. Sorry for scaring you,' she said.

'I thought you'd died,' said Lisa. 'I cried.'

Tears welled up in Jess's eyes. 'I just fainted, that's all. I haven't eaten all day. I was a very silly girl.'

'How's your head?' asked Jacob. 'You really hit the floor hard.'

'Did I? Yeah, it's pretty sore.'

'Don't worry kids,' said Hayley. 'She'll make a full recovery in a few hours. Did you enjoy it up here?'

'Of course,' said Jacob. 'I want to be a pilot one day. This is the coolest job on earth.'

'Which you can clearly see below us,' said the Captain. 'Would you like a peek, Miss Bell?'

Jess took a step forward and looked out through the tinted windows of the cockpit. The geography below resembled a patchwork quilt of green and yellow squares.

'Is that Australia?' she asked.

'No, we left Australian airspace one hour ago. Below us is India, then soon the Middle East.'

Jess shrugged off her anxiety and swelled with pride. 'We've made it,' she thought. They were now in international airspace.

14

5:30PM
MARVALE PRIMARY SCHOOL

The staffroom groaned with inebriated laughter.

'Why don't you call her?' suggested Tim.

'And say what?

'That she's a loser with a capital L,' joked one of the assistants, a thumb and pointy finger spelling it out against her forehead.

'Just to check that she's okay,' corrected Tim. 'It's not like her to be absent without a reason. I'd be worried if I was you.'

'No wonder you're both bloody single,' said Yasmin. 'Leave the poor woman alone. She can do what she wants.'

'I'll text her,' said Jeff.

6:00PM
FLIGHT EK125

Jess unfolded the concertina door to one side and slid the small silver knob to the right. The internal light of the toilet cubicle flickered to life. She lowered the toilet seat and rested her weary legs. The sight of her reflection in the side mirror drew a grimace, her skin all blotchy and red like a Margherita pizza. Her hair was pulled of her face in a tight ponytail, the harsh lights exposing every pore. She pressed the home button on her iPhone and waited as the screen lit up. She opened the Messages App. A green light told her there was a new message from Jeff Simpson.

Where are you???

It was so simple. Three words. But they meant so much. 'They're looking for me,' thought Jess and she knew what she needed to do.

She lifted the phone to her lips and kissed the screen. Her eyes were closed and she took a long, moment to reflect. Told herself to be stronger, faster, better.

She lowered the phone, pressed the off switch and swiped the red slider, watching intently as the apple icon powered down and disappeared.

'Goodbye.'

She lifted the phone above the sink, the screen facing downward and drove the glass face hard against the butt of the stainless-steel tap. A muffled thud as a splinter of small cracks burst across the unprotected display. Jess smashed it callously against the faucet three more times, turning it into a busted mass of twisted metal and broken glass. She shook the damaged segments free, watching as they tumbled into the blue water of the chemical toilet. Jess ripped out the electrical board and snapped it in half. The shattered hardware somersaulted into the water like a chunk of plane wreckage. Her phone was no more. Jess pressed the black button above the toilet, the hissing sound of air sucking both the waterlogged debris and her old life down the chute and out into the chilly atmosphere of high altitude. The communication lines between her old life and her future were gone.

15

8:00PM
MARVALE TAVERN

'Where's Trace?' asked George.

'Workin'. Friday nights her busy night.' Gary was still seated on his favourite stool. Smoke wafted through the air, the popular drinking hole now packed with George's favourite crowd of tradies and checkout chicks.

'She should pull in a bit of dosh, I reckon,' continued Gary. 'Maybe pay off some of me debts.'

'She still does alright then?' asked George, as he wiped the dust from a clean glass.

'Yeah. She's got her regulars. It's either that or hairdressing and she's shit at that.'

'That's pretty damn obvious. Your mop looks like it was cut by a three-year old.'

Gary ran his fingers through his hair. 'Shut up, baldy. At least I still have some.'

George grinned. 'What streets is your wife workin'?'

'Baker Street. Been there a few years now. They all know her.'

'That's in Leederville? Long way from home.'

'Yeah. Its where the posh people live. Lots of money. Handy to the train too. I don't have to pick her up.'

'Great. It's on my way home too. I might do a drive by.'

'Really. Didn't know you fancied her.'

'She's alright. Wouldn't mind some action.'

'You can take it off the money I owe you if you want?'

'Thought I might get a freebie for allowing you past my usual limit.'

Gary's smile faded. He'd gone four digits into the red earlier that week after stuffing up a job.

'Yeah alright.' He didn't want to offend his bank manager. He knew George could bring him to his knees in a flash. Owed him everything. He'd been drinking on that same Tab for the last few months and was fully aware that he couldn't afford what he was having. Debt was something he lived with. Expected he'd die with it as well.

8:15PM
LEEDERVILLE

Tracey waited in the bitter cold of Baker Street, every heaving breath driving a funnel of mist between her lips. The warmth of the day had long disappeared but Tracey was a hard woman, used to a hard life. She would have preferred to be home in front of the television but Friday's were her busiest night and, hell, she enjoyed the sex it brought her.

A blue Camry pulled up to the curb.

'Evening Tracey,' said a man through the wound down passenger window of his well-polished car.

'Hello, hello. Fancy seeing you around here.'

'Thought I'd drop by and chance my luck.'

'Had a chat with someone about you today,' smiled Tracey.

'Hope it was good?'

'Not for me. Got me ass kicked.'

'Funny that. It's your arse I'm interested in.'

'Half price for you, Stevie.'

'Then jump in.' He leant across and heaved the passenger door open.

Tracey discarded her half-finished cigarette upon the footpath and ground it into the concrete with the tip of her shoe. She sashayed over to the car and got in.

'Your place or mine?' she asked, dropping into the comfort of the heated vehicle.

'Mine,' grinned Steve. 'I've got a little surprise for you.'

16

9:30PM AWST
FLIGHT EK125

Hayley strode up the aisle, a silver tray of drinks balanced expertly on her palm.

'Here you go guys.' She passed a wine and two lemonades to Jess, Lisa and Jacob.

'Thank you,' said Jess. 'Are you sure it's okay?'

'I checked with our doctor and he said that a small dose of alcohol would do you the world of good. Apparently, it'll encourage your body to circulate the blood faster, thus returning much needed nutrients to your system.'

Jess smiled. 'I definitely feel like I need it. Thought I was a goner back there. How close were we to missing the plane?'

'We had you on a stretcher and were about to take you to hospital,' explained Hayley. 'It was the children who changed our minds.'

Jess looked across at the children. Lisa and Jacob were both seated to her right, a glass of lemonade in their hand, a set of headphones glued to their ears as they gazed hypnotically at the small television screens in front of them.

'They told me that you hadn't eaten all day,' continued Hayley. 'They were also really worried about being separated. It was risky but I took a punt that you'd just fainted. I could so easily have been wrong.'

'They can be very persuasive when they want to,' said Jess.

'Lucky for you.'

'I know. I can't tell you what it means to me. To us.'

'I'm just glad you're feeling better. Buzz me if you need anything else.' Hayley swung her ponytail and disappeared up the aisle.

Jess lifted the cold glass of wine to her nose and breathed in its sweet aroma. She took a sip and scanned the details of their flight on her private screen. Flight EK125 was now flying at an altitude of twenty thousand feet above the Arabian Sea. The distance between her and the storm that was brewing back at Marvale was increasing by a rate of six hundred and fifty kilometres per hour.

Jess wanted to enjoy this milestone, a glass of Sauvignon Blanc her chosen reward. She took another quiet sip, allowing the chilled wine to run across her tongue and down her throat. The tension in her shoulders eased as she relaxed into phase two of her plan.

'Is that nice?'

Jess swallowed, Jacob's question catching her off-guard. 'Yes, it is.'

'Can I have a taste?'

'No. It's not for kids.'

'Mum and Dad let me.'

'Well I'm not sure that's a good thing Jacob.'

'But I like it. Makes me feel all wobbly.'

'That's exactly why you shouldn't be drinking it.'

'Dad says it's good for us. Shuts us up.' Jacob laughed. Jess was tongue-tied. 'One time, Lisa couldn't stand up straight she'd had so much. Kept falling over. We were all laughing at her.' Jacob's smile slowly disappeared. 'Dad wasn't happy when she spewed all over the couch.' Jacob looked up at Jess. 'Does drinking make you mad?'

'No. It either makes me happy or sleepy.'

Jacob smiled. 'That's good.'

Jess hadn't planned to drink around the kids. She knew this liquid was the source of many of their parents' problems. It was also the indelible stain that had destroyed her own family. But she wasn't about to spirit the kids off into a monastery and live a life without temptation. No, she had to keep a balance. That was what the good life was about and that was where she was taking them, to a place where life was lived to the full. Where love and kindness abounded because the people were truly happy. Happy with the beauty that surrounded them. A place untouched by the myriad problems that beset the bigger cities.

It was a little place Jess had stumbled upon after she'd escaped the loneliness of her twenty-first birthday. Having cycled alone through Europe, she'd rolled into a busy seaport, the loud horn of an incoming ferry blasting her future wide open. That afternoon she gave her bike away to a homeless man and booked a ticket on the next boat out.

It was during this ride that she stumbled across the most beautiful seaside town. The people looked so happy and the smell of warm pastries filled the air. The warmth of the summer sun on her skin eased her mind and the gorgeous sandy beaches beckoned her with open arms. She got swept up in its cheeky embrace and after the madness of Europe she decided to stop and rest.

She rented a small apartment and got a job waiting tables at a seafood restaurant along the boardwalk. She spent her days at the beach reading books and meeting people. A nap each afternoon re-energised her for the buzz of the night, the whole village coming out to party. Jess discovered a lot of positives about herself during this time, rediscovering both life and love.

She'd never wanted to leave. The European Union however had other ideas and after six months of heaven, her visa expired and life once again got complicated. Having rented a car for a day trip to the mountain village, a simple parking ticket drew the unwanted attention of local police and having checked her records, they informed her politely but firmly that she had stayed one month too long and must leave as soon as was practical.

Moving on was something she had done extremely well in the past, but she wasn't ready to go this time. This place had captured her heart and mellowed her mind and as the boat left the harbour, she refused to wave goodbye to the friends she had made and to the town she had loved. Instead she made a promise to come back one day. It was a pledge she was going to keep. Sharing this special place with Lisa and Jacob made her return even more enticing.

17

SATURDAY 13TH MAY
2:00AM
23 DALTON CRESCENT, MARVALE

Tracey fumbled with her key ring. It was adorned with a silver anchor, the chain ensnared around the house key. She untangled the mess and slid the key inside the brass lock. The front door eased open.

'Wait for me,' slurred Gary as he navigated the pathway behind her. Walking in a straight line was proving difficult.

The whole house was dark, a reflection of Tracey's own state of mind. Steve's visit hadn't gone well. His surprise was news that his wife had found out about their affair and he blamed Tracey for being a big mouth. Having interrogated her for an hour or two he dropped her back in Leederville with a warning to 'Stay outta his god damn life'. Tracey felt battered and bruised. Business had been slow after that and George turned up just as she was about to clock off. She'd tried to talk her way out of it but he wasn't in the mood for a chat. He wanted action, his put downs and party tricks throwing her emotions further into shadow. He could be a real bastard when he wanted to. Worse, it was a give-a-way shag.

She switched on the lounge room light.

'We'll do it in here,' she said.

Gary eased through the doorway, both hands out in front of him like a blood thirsty zombie.

'Hurry up shithead,' she yelled.

'Sssssshhhhhh, you'll wake up the kids.'

'Who cares! Just give me the fuckin' gear would ya!'

Gary felt really bad. Tracey often spoke poorly about both him and the kids, calling him a lazy no-good husband and a lay-about but tonight he'd done those labels proud. The drink had got to him again. He wanted to get off the grog but George was a hard man to say no to. He'd managed to save the night by calling Trace with word he'd scored some cocaine from a dude at the pub. Gary knew he couldn't afford it, even at the cut price of fifty dollars a hit but he was too drunk to worry about money. George paid for it. He was clever like that. Knew that when people owed you enough, they were yours to do with what you liked. He enjoyed owning people. It was part of his business model.

'Where is it?' asked Tracey.

'In my pocket.' He fumbled in his jeans but kept missing the pocket.

'You're fuckin useless. Come here.'

Tracey was impatient. Wanted to feel that floating sensation again and the rush of happiness that came with it. It'd been two months since they'd last scored and she'd been craving it.

She slid her right hand into his pocket and pulled out the dirty white cloth like it was a rabbit's ear. 'Nothing there.'

'Must be in the other one.'

Tracey shoved her fingers into his other pocket and smiled. 'Thank fuck.'

'I like having your hands in my pants,' grinned Gary, as Tracey pulled a small plastic bag of white powder up and out of his jeans.

'Don't get too excited. I'd prefer George's cock to yours.'

'What?'

'At least he can get hard.'

'That's not my fault. It's the booze.'

'That's not my fault,' she mimicked back. 'You're such a fuckin' loser.'

'But I got the drugs for you.'

'So, let's bloody use them alright.' Tracey poured the contents of the bag onto the table top. A noise up the hallway startled them.

'Told you we'd wake up the kids,' said Gary.

'Well just fuckin' tell them to go back to sleep.'

'You do it. I'm too pissed.' Gary slumped back in his chair.

Tracey just stared at him her jaw clenched. She got to her feet and stepped out into the hallway. All was quiet. She waited. A grey cat stepped out from the kitchen.

'It's only the mangy cat.'

He scampered past her and out the front door.

'You left the door open, you grommet,' said Tracey.

Gary didn't move. 'Ooops.'

Tracey closed the door and sat down. She just wanted to forget the world even existed.

18

4:00AM AWST
DUBAI INTERNATIONAL AIRPORT

Jess and the kids had slept well on the plane and were now enjoying the sights and sounds of Dubai International Airport. They strolled amiably past the busy restaurants and shops that lined the concourse, navigating the flow of international travellers who whizzed past them. Jacob was mesmerised by all the activity and glossy surfaces, every scene repeated on the high shine of the polished marble floors. Patterned walls of cream and brown swirls were duplicated around every corner, each new turn identical to the one before, like a giant maze where shopping was your only goal. Well-labelled corridors fell away to the left and right of the main strip, each one leading to a departure gate, refuelled planes waiting to take you anywhere and everywhere.

Jess stopped and stared out through the tinted glass panels which shielded them from the outside. The moon was low, the brisk desert winds blowing hard across raised dunes, tiny grains of sand peppering the buildings transparent outer skin.

'Does mum know we're with you?' queried Lisa.

'Of course she does,' answered Jess. 'Do you want to send her a postcard? And one to your grandparents as well?'

'Okay?'

'Can I draw them a picture,' asked Jacob.

'Sure.'

The Community and Services Act 2004 – Principle (g) if a child is removed from the child's family then, so far as is consistent with the child's best interests, the child should be given encouragement and support in maintaining contact with the child's parents, siblings and other relatives and with any other people who are significant in the child's life.

'Thank you, mam,' said a young lady, her head covered with a Burqa. She accepted the American Dollars in Jess's hand and provided some change. Jess figured it was harder to trace cash and had purchased a range of foreign currencies back in Perth.

'Thank you.' Jess took ownership of a small plastic bag with the shop's logo on the side.

She slid across the bench seat beside Lisa and Jacob.

'Here you go.' She lifted the purchases out of the bag one by one. 'A postcard each to write on, a pen each to write with and a plane each for inspiration.'

'Cool plane,' remarked Jacob as he taxied the replica 747 across the table and whizzed it through the air. 'Vrooooommmm!'

Jess smiled; making them happy was getting easier by the minute. 'I was born for this job,' she thought to herself.

Lisa held her new pen between her fingers, poised for action, waiting for that first idea. 'What should I write about?'

'Whatever you want to, Lisa.'

She had lots of questions swimming around in her brain. The last fifteen hours had been very eventful.

Jess turned her attention to Jacob who was still playing pilots. 'I'll scribe for you,' she suggested, sliding his postcard across the table. He wasn't very good at spelling and writing only made that obvious. 'What would you like to say?'

Jacob guided his plane into landing. 'Hi mum, hi dad. Having a great time. Much better than being at school. Miss Bell's here with us too, so it's a little bit the same, just better. That's all. Bye.'

Jess wrote down every word, her teacher's print very clear and legible. She knew that there was no need to disguise her handwriting. They'd know who took the children.

Jess added two kisses at the end through force of habit. 'You can draw a small picture just here if you want?' she suggested, a small space below the address still empty.

'Okay. I'll draw a plane.'

'Good idea.' Jess passed him the pen then turned back to Lisa. 'How's the writing going?'

'How do you spell because?' asked Lisa.

'B-e-c-a-u-s-e,' spelt Jess, watching as Lisa copied down each letter, then smiled proudly. 'What have you written about?'

Lisa covered the postcard with her non-writing hand. 'Not much. Just stuff.'

Jess knew Lisa liked to keep things close to her chest; was never one to share work with the class. It wasn't a confidence problem; she just liked her privacy. Jess had shared this observation with the school psychologist.

'When you consider the openly hostile environment that she has been forced to grow up in,' mused the psych, 'A little bit of secrecy might to be a good thing'.

Jess had agreed with her. 'It's a coping strategy that will benefit her in the long term.'

4:30AM AWST

Jess stopped beside the bright red walls of a traditional British post box. She looked down at the postcards in her hand. Lisa's was on top and though she had promised not to read it, the scrawled handwriting and poor spelling drew her in.

> *Dear nan and pop i am in airput now. I mis you Wen i see you nekt. Can you tak me to park and swings. mum and dad shout wen i aks to see you because i sad you not come. Luv Lisa. XX*

Jess allowed a sigh to ease from between her lips as she slid the postcards in through the slot. She hoped this offering of words would quell some of the fear being experienced by the wider Johnstone family. She didn't care about how Tracey and Gary were feeling. They were beyond help.

19

11:00AM AWST
23 DALTON CRESCENT

'Fuck! Where are the kids?' It was almost lunchtime and Gary needed a piss. All that beer had to come out somewhere. The pores on his face could only handle so much. He'd stumbled up the hallway, passed the kids' room and saw a problem. Their beds were empty and then he remembered.

'Fuck! Fuck! Fuck!' He certainly had a way with words. His vocabulary was unusually small for a man of his age but he made up for it by repeating the same word, over and over again. Like it had a different definition if you said it more than once; one fuck equals surprised; two means worried and three means angry. 'Those little bastards are going to be in big fuckin' trouble when I find 'em,' he roared.

'Shut the fuck up, Gary,' screamed Tracey, 'I'm trying to sleep.'

Gary stormed into the bedroom. 'The kids are gone you silly bitch. If we don't find them, the cops will come sniffing around.'

'Check next door or the park,' said Tracey, unfazed by Gary's aggression. 'They probably woke up early and went out to play like they usually do.' She was always so casual, even in a real emergency. This time it exhibited as a loathing, bordering on hate.

Three years ago, this animosity almost brought about Lisa's

demise. The whole family were at a New Year's Eve party in Marvale. Supervision for the kids was non-existent and Lisa had discovered the swimming pool out the back of the house. A broken gate helped her navigate a direct route to the moonlit water and never having been taught to swim, she was battling to stay afloat as soon as she jumped in.

Luckily Tracey had also stepped out the back, the temptation of a cigarette a blessing in disguise. She saw the splashes and walked toward the fence. No one else was there and adding to the confusion on Tracey's face was the lack of noise coming from the thrashing, the base and treble of the stereo inside the house all but drowning out her younger child's wrestle with death. Tracey's confusion quickly turned to anger when she realised who it was. She never screamed for anyone's help or ran over to save her child. She just waited, her daughter's silent screams continuing to fall on deaf ears.

It wasn't until Lisa was almost done fighting, her body spent and exhausted, that Tracey strolled casually up beside the pool fence, her mind consumed with thoughts of reprisal rather than survival.

'I bloody well told you to steer clear of this pool, you stupid child,' she'd seethed as her six-year-old daughter continued to cough and splutter her way to a watery end. Her Year One teacher's premonition of 'dead before age ten' would have come true if it wasn't for Tracey's belated intervention, stepping past the rusted gate just in time to see her daughter take a last desperate gasp of air before she sank below the surface. Tracey grinned when she saw her daughter's body disappearing toward the bottom of the pool. She knew her daughter would be beholden to her forever.

Tracey grabbed the long steel handle of the leaf net which was leaning up against the fence. She lifted it above the edge of the pool and shoved it hard, in through the water and toward Lisa's limp frame.

The reinforced plastic frame of the net wedged hard against Lisa's ribcage, causing a jolt of pain to awaken her primal instincts, surging for one last act of survival. Her tired arms grabbed hold of the net and a second chance at life. Tracey hauled her catch toward the side of the pool and the safety of the limestone pavers that lapped over the edge.

Lisa's head emerged from the water and into open air, a fit of coughing and spluttering heralding a sudden intake of life-affirming oxygen. Her shoulder collided painfully with the edge of the pool, instinct driving through any distress, grabbing the ledge and hanging on. Tracey did not lend a hand or rush to her daughter's side. She stood her ground, triumphant and unrepentant.

Lisa dragged herself gasping from the pool and slumped upon the paving at her mother's feet. There was no audience present to recount Tracey's act of heroism. The party music continued to rage on without them, a contradictory chorus of drunken voices, belting out the lyrics to the old Guns and Roses track *Sweet Child of Mine*.

Tracey stared down at her daughter, gave her a nudge with her foot.

'You owe me,' she said, before discarding the net angrily toward the ground. Tracey was a woman of few words and as she stormed out through the gate and back toward the house, she prayed she could make up for the drinking time she'd lost.

Since that day, her hate for Lisa had only grown stronger. She'd had a rough night after the false tranquility of an impure hit and sleep was now her number one priority. She didn't care that Gary was worried about the kids. She cared only for the soft call of her pillow.

'Their beds are still made,' yelled Gary from the doorway, his voice shaking. 'I don't think they slept here.'

Tracey kept her eyes closed. 'They must have. What time did you give them dinner?'

The stuttering silence seeping out of Gary's mouth was a sign of the bursting panic building within his fragile body. Gary knew the answer to the question, but he was scared to hear it. More so, he hated the fact that it would only add to the incompetence of the previous day. He'd been caught red-handed a few times in his life with nowhere to run and no one to hide behind. He'd have to add today to that growing list.

'I wasn't here. I was at the bloody pub.'

Tracey opened her eyes like a snake waking to the sound of a mouse. 'Did you see them when they came home from school?'

'I told you already. I was down the pub.'

The bed creaked as Tracey shifted her weight. 'Have you got shit for brains? You're fuckin' kiddin' me, aren't you?'

Gary shuffled his feet. He hated being talked to like this but he knew he'd messed up. Big time.

The awkward silence that followed forced Tracey to lift herself up into a seating position. 'You know the DCP are watching us. You know we'll lose them next time we fuck up. And the money too.'

Gary stepped back into the room. 'I'll find 'em. You stay here in case they come home. I'll go look around the suburb. Stay here, alright?'

'I'm not going any fuckin' where. This is your mess. You tidy up your own shit.'

Gary hustled himself out the front door like a battered puppy. His bare feet navigated the broken pathway, before hopping across the weed covered verge and out onto the cracked concrete footpath. He had never been an athlete and looked like he was always a hair's breadth from a heart attack. A fast walk was the best he could manage.

A desperate wheeze accompanied Gary's every step, the cowardice and fear coursing through him was a default mechanism to a challenging situation. He couldn't fathom what it would mean if he couldn't find the kids. Not because he was worried about them. No way. It was all about his own survival.

He stopped walking. 'Fuck! Fuck! Fuck!' he screamed, as the empty streets swallowed up his cries. He sat down, a growing anxiety keeping him seated and desperate on the edge of the gutter.

20

2:00PM AWST
CHARLES DE GAULLE AIRPORT, PARIS

'Okay kids, no more plane flights,' promised Jess.

'Yippee,' exclaimed Lisa and Jacob as they glided down the escalator toward a vast room filled with weary travellers. Jacob watched as hundreds of suitcases cruised in circles on shiny metal turnstiles. Lisa concentrated on the metal grill beneath her feet, scared of the sharp teeth on the edge of every step.

Jess smiled as a large sign above welcomed them to Charles De Gaulle Airport.

'There are a lot of people here,' she said, 'So let's hold hands until we are clear of the chaos.'

The children held tight as they walked toward turnstile three. Jess observed the controlled mayhem surrounding them. Small groups of security personnel prowled the edges of the hall, their dark suits a reminder of the serious nature of their jobs. The relative anonymity of the plane had been enjoyable.

'There's one of our suitcases,' she said, releasing the children's hands. 'Stay here.' She dashed forward through the deep crowds that surrounded the luggage carousel. She leant in between two people and grabbed a large blue suitcase.

'Non!' insisted a French accented voice to her right. Jess looked across and saw an elderly man staring accusingly at her. 'Is my suitcase,' he said, almost annoyed.

'Sorry, but my one looks just like this,' said Jess, fumbling with the tag hanging from the handle. 'Olivier Gustaph, Paris France' read the blue and white card and Jess felt a flush of embarrassment. 'My apologies.'

The old man took ownership of his suitcase and wheeled it gruffly away. 'Sacre bleu,' he muttered under his breath, a few bystanders eyeing Jess with suspicion.

She backtracked through the growing hordes of people, all jostling for prime position. 'Be patient,' she thought. 'Wait your turn. Take your time.'

She expected to see the children at any moment, but as she moved further away from the carousel an uneasy fear rose unabated. They had been on the run for almost twenty-four hours and whether the alarm had been sounded yet or not was simply out of her control. Keeping the children safe, however, was but having returned to the exact spot where she'd left them, she burned with the guilt and horror of a bad parent.

A massive contradiction now stared her squarely in the face. Two missing Perth children were now also missing in Paris and there wasn't a soul she could trust to help her find them.

She took a few deep breaths and tried to clear her mind, a growing mountain of debris cloaking her good sense. The spot where she left the children was now swarming with people, her vision limited to just a few feet. Her taller than average height provided an advantageous view across the swaying sea of heads but Lisa and Jacob were small. Too small to spot above the mobs of passengers continuing to pour down the escalators. The arrivals hall was quickly becoming a complex war zone.

'Jacob, Lisa,' called Jess, all emotion removed.

'Jacob, Lisa,' she repeated over the din, a hint of desperation creeping into her words. Jess forced her way through the impatient packs as politely as she could. Hope was the only thing driving her forward, the expectation that Jacob and Lisa could appear at any moment her only wish.

'Attention please,' burst a woman's voice over the public announcement system. 'Would Madame Jessica Bell please approach a member of the airport staff.'

Jess almost missed the broadcast. Her name pulling at her attention.

'I repeat, would Madame Jessica Bell please approach a member of the airport staff.'

This time she heard every word. A growing anxiety magnified her insecurity and she drifted off to one side of the vast hall, seeking refuge upon a low bench seat. A massive concrete pillar towered over her, dwarfing Jess and her ambitions. The desire to vomit was surprisingly powerful and she struggled to quell it. Spewing all over the floor was hardly going to bring her the privacy she currently craved.

Her embattled brain sifted through a raft of possibilities. The best-case scenario was that they had found the children and wanted to reunite them all. Worst case was that the Marvale Police had already sent out an alert. One would bring a happy end to her current problem. The other would ensure that the drama and pain had only just begun.

Jess had spent many nights agonizing over her decision to take Jacob and Lisa. It was an act of desperation and the illegalities were undeniable. If caught she would do time in prison. The length of the sentence would rest with a judge. Could Jess survive being locked up again.

An overnight stint in a police cell when she was nineteen had given her a brief and bitter taste of life behind bars. It had also cemented her view of the legal system as both a cruel and ignorant beast. A machine which placed too much emphasis on punishment and not enough on motive.

Jess had knocked a man unconscious during a fight in a bar. That part was true. She'd gone there for a few quiet drinks, holidaying alone in the Margaret River region, taking some well-earned time away from the overbearing nature of city life. It had been five painful years since her parents departed and she still hadn't found happiness. Her victim would certainly know this.

He had been harassing his girlfriend all afternoon and it was a situation Jess wouldn't tolerate any longer. She hated bullies which made her view from the bar very unfortunate, forcing her to suffer through several repeated acts of degradation and violence toward the young woman. A lack of action by the male bar staff forced her to step in.

Jess approached her target and communicated her displeasure with his behaviour. He laughed in her face, a barrage of words only escalating the situation.

The man then reached across and grabbed Jess's hair. 'Get the fuck away from me or I'll rip your hair out,' he'd hissed. 'You bitches are all the same.'

He released Jess from his grip and shoved her away with his other arm. But he was wrong. Jess wasn't like all the other girls and it was this piece of misinformation that brought him to his knees.

Jess had performed excellently during the self-defence courses set up by her free-thinking therapist. He'd introduced them as a way of channeling her anger into something positive. He may not have approved of their use here but twenty seconds later and she had her assailant pinned down in a position of great pain and what she hoped was judicious surrender. But he wasn't giving up, mouthing off at her like he was in a winning position. A final strike to the head and he was out for the count.

The security staff were slow at stepping in, finally dragging her away and holding her in custody until the police entered the premises half an hour later. She expected them to see it her way but this small town was also small-minded and it closed in on her like a venus fly trap.

The police spoke to a few witnesses, got some background on everyone involved. Turned out that this poor excuse for a man was the son of a well-respected family in the area and all fingers were now being pointed at the outsider as the source of trouble. Even the young girl she'd tried to protect refused to speak out against her malicious boyfriend and with the evidence stacked against her, Jess was jailed on a charge of Grievous Bodily Harm.

Jess spent a lonely night in a cramped concrete cell. She received a police escort out of town early the next day. Her trial would come later.

The man's girlfriend spoke up a few weeks later, her conscience getting the better of her once the not-so-super summer holiday was over. Jess received a simple letter in the mail advising her that her prior conviction had been overturned and no record of this event would be recorded against her name. This had been fortuitous later, when a criminal record could have thwarted any hope of entering the teaching profession. Jess shivered at the memory of her time behind bars. The experience and loss of her most basic rights had scarred her, but she had buried it deeply, like she always did with any dark periods. Like she always would.

But that was in the past. The polished surfaces and high watt glimmer of Charles De Gaulle airport were a million miles away from the rustic buildings of the wine regions of Western Australia. Jess felt like she was being forced into another corner and like a boxer hanging on through the dying seconds of the final round, she told herself she would not allow these old fears to hem her in. She stood calmly, located a staff member and began the long walk toward fate.

'Excuse me. I just heard my name over the speakers.'

'Ahhh. You are Miss Jessica Bell?' the lady clarified.

'Yes.'

'You have lost something?'

'My children?'

She smiled. 'Follow me please.' The woman strode off across the polished concrete floor. Jess stared down at the woman's brisk steps, keeping just a few metres behind her. She felt the eyes of the world upon her but, in reality, she was still just another tourist in one of the most visited cities in the world. No one gave her a second thought.

'This way Madame,' directed the lady, her outstretched right arm dragging open an oversized steel door. Jess stepped through and allowed the chaotic sounds of the last few minutes to fall away, the heavy door easing itself closed behind them.

The vast open spaces of the baggage hall were replaced by a long corridor of glossy white walls. Jess followed the official up the hallway. It appeared to go on forever, the whiteness of the space embodying a lightness of being that belied the pressure that weighed heavily on her. She felt trapped but knew only that she had to keep moving forward, accepting the finality of the destiny that lay in wait. She prayed the children were down here somewhere. That, in itself, would bring some relief.

'Next door on your left please.'

Jess did as she was told, stepping in through a smaller door way and into a box like space. It had white walls and no windows, the floor occupied by two black chairs and a simple wooden desk.

'Please take a seat Miss Bell. Someone will be along to see you shortly.' The woman closed the door behind her, the twisting lock a source of concern, leaving Jess trapped and alone with her thoughts.

The dimensions of the room were strangely reminiscent of her cell in Margaret River. 'What have I done?' she asked herself. 'I'm no better than Gary and Tracey. I've only had them for a day and already I've lost them.' She berated herself, forcing her confidence to its lowest ebb, allowing despondency to reach for a foothold in the gloom.

Just then the door clicked open and in ran Jacob and Lisa, the sound of their voices lifting Jess' mood. She opened her arms just in time to receive their desperate embrace. Lisa's sobs tore her in two, her skinny frame draped across her teacher's shoulder, arms flung around her neck. Jacob kept his composure, a picture of concentrated quiet, embracing the two of them, his feet still firmly on the floor. This was how they both handled trauma. One lived inside of it, without any emotional control whatsoever. The other one, outside of it, always watching, reacting with detachment and sometimes derision.

The official watched on happily. Family reunions were her chance to feel good about this job. She had sensed Jess's desperation and having children of her own, knew that reuniting them would be both rewarding and pleasurable. It was a shining light in her day, otherwise overshadowed by drug busts and drunk passengers.

'I found them beside the money exchange window. They told me they'd been yelled at by an angry old man. They couldn't understand a word he was saying and he harassed them until they had no choice but to move on.'

Lisa eased herself off Jess's shoulder. 'It was so scary. I couldn't see you,' she stuttered. 'I wanted…'

Jess rested a finger against Lisa's lips. 'Sssshhhhhhh. It's okay now. I've got you back.' Lisa collapsed back upon her teacher's shoulder, a small whimper escaping from her mouth. She wiped her eyes with Jess's shirt and rested her head.

'Thank you for looking after them,' said Jess.

'It was our pleasure,' replied the official. 'You have two beautiful children.'

'Thank you.'

Jacob looked up at the lady. 'Will our luggage still be sliding around on those spinning things?' he asked.

'No. I have organised for them to be collected. This way please.' The lady led them back into the corridor and up towards the double doors that led to the arrivals hall. Jess carried Lisa in both arms as the doors were opened and the organised chaos of Charles De Gaulle airport burst upon them once again.

'Passports please,' said a female customs officer from behind a panel of glass.

Jess passed three blue booklets over the top of the counter, the drain of the last half hour all too evident on her face. Lisa and Jacob stood patiently on either side.

'Did you enjoy your flight?' asked the customs officer.

Jess tried to concentrate. 'Yes, thank you, it was very pleasant.'

'You packed all your own luggage.'

'Yes, I did.'

'And the children?'

'I packed for them as well.'

The officer smiled, looking over the passports and then at each of them. She lifted her stamp. Bang, bang, bang!

'Welcome to France.'
'Merci,' said Jess, pulling out the only bit of French she knew.

21

2:50PM AWST
MARVALE

Desperation had taken a hold of Gary. He'd been searching for close on four hours, trapped by the fear of going home empty handed. Facing Tracey wasn't worth his trouble. He was better off sticking his head in the sand.

'Where the fuck are you?' he mumbled under his smelly breath, stumbling barefoot and clueless up the street. He looked like he felt, ripped jeans creeping down his backside, a torn surfie t-shirt under a faded black Adidas sports jacket. It was what he'd slept in and having looked everywhere he could think of, he was lost, both mentally and physically.

The park had been empty. The shops were the exact opposite, so crowded and noisy it gave him the shakes. He even checked with the neighbours and some of his kids' friends. These were people he never socialised with. It was hard enough trying to force a friendly chat, let alone plying them for information about his missing kids. They didn't like him and he felt the same. Thought he was bad news. Gary was actually proud of his reputation. 'Rather be bad news than no news,' he'd chided. 'Rather be something than nothing.' They were zeros as far as he was concerned. Lived by the rules, played by the rules and sometimes even made the rules. He was proud to be the rebel who just broke them all.

He wasn't feeling so heroic now though. One more house and he'd have to think of another plan. His feet were getting sore. He'd realised quickly that forgetting his shoes had been a mistake, his badly cracked heels weeping sweat and blood.

At first, being shoeless had made him feel like a kid again. Life was simpler back then. Not a worry in the world. Gary had grown up in a small country town where everyone knew each other. Had a real sense of community. He laughed at the contradiction he now lived.

Most people in this suburb knew him too, but not for any of the right reasons. He was an outcast; as unwanted as the fungal infection that split the skin of his heels in the first place. Tinea had ravaged his feet since childhood. It was somewhat symptomatic of the diseased family relations that led to his eventual departure from that small town. He thought about the river he used to swim in and the trees he used to climb.

'Ow!' Gary stubbed his big toe against a raised slab of concrete. 'Fuck!' he yelled, bending down to check out the damage. His nails were long and dirty but they were still in one piece. There were no signs of fresh blood, which was a blessing because he wasn't good with too much of that yucky red liquid. His own father used to tease him about it, labelling him 'a bit of a wuss,' especially after he fainted aged ten having sliced deep into his thumb with a saw. He'd hated being put down by a man he looked up to. Their relationship deteriorated during his teenage years, most of the attention directed toward his younger brother, a karate champion and doctor in the making. Gary felt like a cupboard without handles. No one complained because they never really cared what was inside.

He stood up and stared at the house opposite. He'd seen his kids playing there before and willed this to be the home that gave him the answers he so desperately needed. The well-dressed parents of number sixteen had also waved to him at school a couple of times and he'd swallowed hard at the perverted idea of having to talk to them. 'Fuckin' show offs' he thought to himself. Expensive clothes weren't welcome in his neighbourhood. He could feel the distaste and anger already rising from his gut as he walked up the front path toward the bright red door. He noted the colour choice was probably based on that 'stupid Feng Shui crap'. Tracey used it on her nails. Gary had enough brains to know that a red door was a display of power and control so he prepared himself for a demonstration of his own strength. He knocked hard on the front door, his closed fist a veiled threat, his spread legs an indicator of action. The door swung open a few seconds later to reveal a portly man in black chinos and a crisp white polo.

'You seen my kids?' Gary wasn't one for niceties.

'Good morning,' replied the man.

'Not really. So you seen them or not?'

'You're Lisa and Jacob's dad, yeah?'

'And you're Humpty Dumpty. Yeah, of course I'm their father. Can't see anybody else here can you?'

'No, I can't.' He extended a hand. 'I'm Craig by the way.'

'Are you gonna answer my bloody question or not?' Gary's patience was shot.

'Umm, no I haven't seen them.'

'Shit.' Gary punched a clenched fist into an open palm.

'Everything alright?'

'Do I look alright?'

'No. You look a bit stressed. Is there anything I…'

'And you look fat. Thanks for nothing arsehole.' Gary turned his back and started to walk away.

Craig looked down at his potbelly and thought about calling after Gary. Common sense told him that sometimes these kinds of people are better left alone. You never know how they'll react. 'Good luck.' It was an inside thought that came out a bit louder than planned.

Gary was already halfway down the path but he wasn't out of earshot. He stopped, turned around and glared up at his neighbour. 'What'd you say?'

'Good luck.' The sarcasm of his earlier delivery was gone. 'Hope you find them.'

Gary made his way back towards the front door. 'You'd be praying for that wouldn't you?' Gary reached the front steps.

'Of course I would.'

Gary took the steps one at a time and stopped just in front of his adversary. 'Or else I'll be back,' he said, his middle finger thrust hard into the man's chest. 'You understand?'

A step back. 'Yeah. I didn't mean…'

'You didn't mean what? To annoy me?' Another decisive prod and Craig was forced to retreat further into his own house. 'So, when I turn and leave, just keep your big mouth shut.' Prod. 'And get back inside your happy little house.' Prod. 'Then close the fuckin' door and start praying.' Prod. 'Not for my kids, but for yourself! You don't want to see me again. Not today. Maybe not ever.' Prod.

Craig nodded his head in submission.

'That's it, good boy. Now close the door and don't even think of opening your smart arse mouth again.'

Craig closed the door slowly. Didn't want it to slam. It eased closed and clicked shut. He breathed a sigh of relief.

Knock. Knock. Knock. Craig thought about opening the door. Knock, knock, knock. A bit louder this time. He turned the knob and opened the door, the gap just wide enough to see Gary's grinning face.

'I said keep it closed.' A nod and the door was quickly closed once again. Silence.

Gary smirked at his handy work. It was easy to scare people. Intimidation was something he'd learned at school. School! The kids! Shit! Where are they? Anger returned, followed quickly by guilt. 'Why did I have to go and forget to feed the kids? Fuuuuuuuuccccccckkkkkkkkk!'

He actually felt really bad about it. Was excellent at feeling guilty after the fact. It was a trait he displayed with most of the shoddy things he did. Just always seemed to get waylaid with offers and enticements. This time it had been the promise of a job from George, which Gary knew had turned into a right bloody run around. Spent more on petrol than he'd received in payment.

There was a soft spot for the kids buried way down deep inside this cracked shell of a man and it was times like this that he realised his errors and knew he'd let them down. These moments of vulnerability were the difference between the good and the bad in Gary, but now, as he felt remorse crawling through him, he acted as only he knew how and flew into a rage, denying himself any real culpability. He was so full of lies that if you removed them all, he would have imploded within his own incompetence. Gary was much better off projecting blame onto others and continuing to crash through life. His second chances were long gone. Gary was on borrowed time.

He pounded along the footpath in the general direction of home when a police car cruised around the corner up ahead. Gary visibly flinched at the sight of the blue and white checked vehicle. They were never welcome in his life but recently they'd become more of a feature. He suddenly realised that his present dilemma was altogether different to his usual life. Someone had to tell the police his kids were missing. Going home and telling Tracey that it was all his fault was going to be hell. 'The pigs in their pretty blue uniforms could do it for him,' he thought. 'I could get a lift back to the house as well.' His feet were really sore.

You see Gary was always thinking of how life could benefit him. That's what made him tick and, as the cops cruised closer, Gary was in two minds. To tell or not to tell? That was the question.

22

2:55PM AWST
CDG AIRPORT, PARIS

Two uniformed gendarmes watched on as Jess and the kids hurried across the carpeted foyer of the airport. The sleek silver trolley in front of them held three suitcases and a small piece of hand luggage. Jess was trying to stay incognito but paranoia told her that everything she did was noteworthy. Her whole body screamed with exhaustion but stopping to rest was clearly out of the question.

She was keen to get out of the airport and into fresh air. The air-conditioned warmth was annoying her, making her feel dirty and stale. Her clothes felt clammy against her sweat-laden skin and her hair needed a wash.

She checked her watch. It read seven fifty-five am. She'd adjusted it to local time on the plane when the pilot advised them over the intercom that they were preparing for landing. He'd given the temperature and the time of day and wished all the passengers a safe and happy trip.

Perth was seven hours ahead of mainland Europe, which meant it had been exactly twenty-four hours since they'd left Australian soil. Had the alarm been raised? Were their names and descriptions being circulated by Interpol yet? It had been plain sailing so far. Almost too easy. The sign she was looking for caught her eye and she quickly followed the arrow. The children followed the trolley down a tiled corridor off the main hall. They stopped outside the door to the women's toilets. Jess checked that no one was watching before she ushered Lisa and Jacob in through the entrance. She pulled the trolley in after them.

'Quickly. Over there,' whispered Jess, her arm guiding them toward a row of open cubicles. The restroom was spacious and clean, large white tiles covering both floor and walls. One side was all sinks, taps and mirrors and Jess caught sight of their reflection. The light here was softer, kinder than the harsh glare of the airplane toilet and she smiled. They looked like a family. Felt like a family already.

'What are we doing in here?' asked Jacob.

Jess ignored his question, grabbing her suitcase off the trolley. 'Follow me,' she said and the children trailed her into the cubicle on the far left. They all squeezed in before she closed and locked the door behind them.

It was a tight fit. Jess leant in between the kids, lowering the toilet seat lid so that Lisa could sit on it like a chair. Jacob stood to her left, his arms by his sides making the best of a cramped situation. The height differential between the three of them was exacerbated by the close confines of this white walled box, so Jess knelt down onto the cold hard tiles and looked them both in the eye.

'Okay. This is where our excursion gets really interesting.' The deeper she got into this whole scenario the more anxious she became. 'We're going to play dress-up now okay?'

Lisa screwed her face up in confusion.

Jacobs eyes showed a flicker of enthusiasm. 'Like superheroes?' he asked.

'And princesses?' said Lisa, cottoning on to the idea.

'Sort of. Imagine you're a secret agent and you have to disguise yourself so that no one will recognise you.' Jess grimaced at how close to the truth this really was.

'Sounds cool,' said Jacob. Lisa soaked up her brother's

excitement and sat wide-eyed, listening to every word.

'I'm going to make myself look very different as well,' said Jess. 'I'm going to cut my hair really short and dye my hair brown.'

Lisa and Jacobs faces were almost comical, their eyes wide and mouths open.

'Does that sound a bit strange?' she asked.

They both nodded. 'I won't recognise you,' said Jacob.

'That's the whole idea,' smiled Jess. 'What would you like to change?'

'Can I go spiky and blonde?' asked Jacob.

'Sure, if that's what you want.'

'Cool! I'll look like a punk rocker.'

Jess smiled. 'This could be fun,' she thought. Lisa though was quiet, very quiet.

'How about you Lisa? What colour would you like your hair to be?'

A light shrug from two weary shoulders. Lisa liked her hair. People told her she had beautiful golden curls. It was a compliment she depended on. Not much else came her way in the form of positive reinforcement. Her locks were a big part of her and she really didn't want to change them.

'Maybe a new style as well?' suggested Jess, her hands trembling. She loved Lisa's curls too but they made her stand out too much. They had to go.

Jess checked her watch again, an irrational fear of time gaining traction. They had entered a new phase of her plan and she knew it didn't include gentle persuasion. The tick tock of the clock was everything now and tough decisions needed to be made.

'You need to think of a new style otherwise I'll have to choose.' Her smile was gone.

Lisa's eyes started to well up with tears as the confusion of the last twenty-four hours finally caught up with her. Jess brushed the first tear drops away with tenderness but she knew she could not allow her own emotions or the wishes of others to slow them down. She had to be strong, so she ignored the second batch of silky tears and just got down to business.

France has seen many atrocities during its time. Two world wars were waged upon these shores and what Jess was planning paled into insignificance when compared to the horrendous acts carried out on the battlefields of the Western Front. But Lisa's little world was all she knew and in her eyes what her wonderful teacher did next was unthinkable.

23

2:59PM AWST
MARVALE

The police knew exactly who he was. Officers Gates and Harris had dealt with him too many times to either forget or forgive. Their dislike for the vagrant up ahead was palpable.

'What's that piece of shit doing up and out at this time of day?' asked Officer Harris as he steered the car along the road.

'Looking for a score probably,' replied Gates, who often knew his targets' habits better than they themselves did. 'Let's trail him. Give him the shits for a while.'

The police car cruised past Gary before completing a U-turn and coming slowly back around. It was enough to drive Gary mad, the hum of the car engine audible behind him, the threat of the siren annoyingly close.

His uptight body language made the officers smile. They thought following him was funny. Gary wasn't seeing the funny side at all.

They trailed him for a few hundred metres as he shuffled unhappily along the footpath. He didn't know what the hell to do. His house was normally the safest place to go, but the 'bloody cops' were pestering him and the situation with the kids meant that home was the last place he was welcome. He was going to tell them everything until he saw the faces of Gates and Harris. They'd enjoy his pain too much. Couldn't allow them the satisfaction.

Hunger too was gnawing at his belly but he hadn't brought any money with him; wasn't even sure if he had any coin left anywhere.

'These cops are seriously fucking up a really fucked-up day,' thought Gary.

Officer Gates had radioed headquarters for an update on Gary's profile and they'd reported back with no current arrest warrants or unpaid fines.

'He's doing okay for a low life,' said Gates. 'About time he cleaned up his act.' Gates knew his kind though and it wouldn't be long before he reverted to type.

'Where are his shoes?' said Officer Harris.

'Let's ask him?' Gates was keen to address him face to face.

Gary heard the fresh rev of the engine and felt the car edge closer. They trawled past him before pulling over into the curb.

Officer Gates wound down his window as Gary tried to hustle past. 'Morning Gary.'

He tried ignoring them and kept on walking. He hated doing what the police wanted. Officer Harris pressed lightly on the accelerator and trailed alongside the target.

'Don't ignore me,' said Gates. 'I might get suspicious. Think you've got something to hide.'

'Sorry.' Gary kept his gaze on the footpath.

'Going for a stroll, are we?'

'Yeah.'

'Nice day for it.' The cold wind and grey sky made this observation a large exercise in sarcasm. It made Gary's blood boil. 'Take a load off,' smiled Gates. 'I want a chat.'

'I'm busy.'

'It wasn't a suggestion.'

Gary stopped and turned to face them. Knew that when they gave a direct instruction it was better to give in than to fight.

'Jump in back,' said Gates.

'I'm alright out here. Like you said, it's a beautiful day.'

Officer Gates smiled. 'Everything alright?'

Gary tried to put on a brave face but he was no hero, the traits of a coward running a thicker line through his blood than that of a hero. He stared at the two thorns sticking in his side and considered blurting out all his demons. He was neither strong nor daring and like a freshly hatched bird about to tumble to its death, his bottom lip started to quiver, the nest of twigs he was resting on beginning to snap under the weight of circumstance. The turmoil he was feeling inside wanted out and as his heartbeat thundered inside his head he struggled for composure, too scared to answer even the simplest of questions, lest his emotions boil over altogether.

'Where are your shoes Gary?' asked Harris, leaning across the gear stick so that Gary could see his grinning face.

Gary shrugged his shoulders. He wanted to turn and run but he had nowhere to go. It was a quandary he wasn't smart enough to solve and the cops soaked up the uncomfortable silence, staring at him with satisfaction. Gary steeled himself for one more sentence. Tried to let his pride do the talking. He looked down at his boney feet and thought about his past.

'I like the feeling of being barefoot,' he joked. 'Makes me feel like a kid.' Just mentioning the word kid gave him goosebumps and he rushed to part ways. 'I gotta go boys. See ya round.' Gary forced his legs into a jog and headed up the alleyway to his right.

The officers looked at each other.

'What do you reckon?' said Harris.

'Let him go,' said Gates. 'He's not worth it.'

'He's up to something though.'

'Idiots like him are always in some sort of trouble,' said Gates. 'Follows them like the plague. We'll just wait for the call and then he can tell us where his shoes really are.'

Officer Harris laughed as Gary disappeared into the next street.

The police car pulled away from the curb and accelerated quickly away.

24

4:00PM AWST
CDG AIRPORT, PARIS

'Just a small car please,' said Jess, 'We're not going far.'

'Of course, Madame.' The young lady behind the Avis desk was all smiles.

Lisa and Jacob stood silently behind Jess. One harrowing hour had passed since they'd first entered the toilets and they were now virtually unrecognisable from the children who'd departed Marvale so unexpectedly. Jacob's wavy brown hair was gone, replaced by a blonde buzz cut that would almost have looked natural if his complexion wasn't so pasty and white. He wasn't smiling but he still felt super cool.

Lisa's sad red eyes, spoke of the pain and discomfort she had suffered. All of her long blonde curls were gone and her head was now covered with a brown pixie cut which made her look like a cross between an indie rocker and a fairy. She was still cute. She could pull off any style but she wanted to feel like a princess and Miss Bell had taken that from her.

Chopping off Lisa's golden locks had been a harrowing experience for all of them. There was nowhere to hide in that tiny white cubicle, so they had endured each other's pain in a stifled and unhappy silence. Lisa's muffled tears had distressed

Jacob so much that he had turned his back on her and closed his eyes, choosing to ignore what was going on. It was a skill he'd developed back in Marvale. The sound of his sister's suppressed sobs always tore at his heartstrings, becoming tough and sinewy in the process. He knew how to bury his feelings and in times of trouble that's exactly what he did.

Miss Bell's actions had conjured up the echo of one of his father's fiery outbursts, his gravelly voice driving tears from their bodies with a force that was both emotional and physical. Jacob often felt like his whole body was going to implode with emptiness but his own whimpering worked to find a rhythm that would provide him with the comfort of sleep. He would awaken much later to an eerie silence.

But that was in the past and now it was his favourite teacher, Miss Bell, who was the one perpetuating these same emotions. Of all the things that had happened today, it was this strange turn of events that concerned him most.

Lisa had been too emotional to speak, each swish of the scissor blades slicing through her misery, her sadness compounded by the clumps of hair sliding down her back. The short bursts of breath she took between cuts, were just enough to stay alive.

Haircuts had been a nuisance in her home. Tracey often bemoaned that 'they cost good money they didn't have'. It was a luxury they'd done without, especially once Nan and Pop had disappeared from their lives. Lisa remembered how a trim from her Nan was something she used to look forward to. Those soft gentle hands gliding through her hair and the love that oozed from every touch. Lisa's first feelings of being a princess were when she was with her Nan and she often looked like one when she returned home.

Tracey hated it when her daughter looked better than she did and she said as much without any fear that Lisa would hear her stripped-back hatred. Lisa thought that her teacher was different but it seemed not. She didn't want what was happening to her but Miss Bell ploughed on through her tears without emotion or care. There were no gentle hands here. There was no love on display.

The only thing missing were the 'bad words' thought Lisa and it broke her little heart.

Jess felt like vomiting with every cut. She had actually dry-wretched twice, managing to halt the churning in her stomach only by summoning all her loathing for an uncaring world. She allowed these emotions to fester, the poison they produced driving her forward with determination and desire. These abhorrent feelings weren't something she had calculated on but she needed them as much as she despised them and part of her started breaking inside, as agony ripped at her heart.

She had put a lot of research into this section of the journey. Spent time back in Perth learning how to mix dyes and cut hair. She'd even set aside an hour for the job knowing the dye had to be given time to take effect. The proliferation of CCTV cameras around every corner meant becoming invisible would be a huge advantage and the changes she could grind out now would be well worth the pain in the long run.

The Avis lady checked the screen for any available cars.

Lisa tugged at Jess's jeans. 'Can we go home?' she asked. 'I don't want donuts anymore.'

Jess knew the kids were getting tired and even a little suspicious. She had a plan to combat that but needed them in the hire car first. 'Soon Lisa, soon.'

Jess's long blond hair had been cut short making her appear years younger. She had never been a great sun worshipper and her face was relatively free of the lines and creases associated with squinting. The rimless glasses on her face added an air of intelligence and the jeans and t-shirt presumed she was on holiday. For the police in Perth she was becoming more important every hour, yet they would have struggled to recognise her here today.

The change of wardrobe had also been a good idea. Jess had searched EBay for some French kids clothes. Jacob wore a small replica team shirt from French football's number one team, Paris Saint Germain, and a pair of black Adidas tracksuit pants. Covering his feet were black Adidas trainers and he really looked like a young soccer fan.

The truth was he didn't even know the rules of the game.

Lisa on the other hand looked like a Eurovision contestant with a bright pink t-shirt with the word 'Beautiful' written across the front and a little white skirt that was a mix between a mini and a tutu. On her feet were a pair of pink converse shoes. Both collections were noteworthy and full of description, which in Australia would have made them stand out, but here in Europe, where children dressed older than they were, they were just one of the crowd.

The young woman behind the counter waved to the children while she waited for Jess to fill in some forms. She had two kids of similar ages and understood how they felt. Travelling was always tough on the little ones.

Jacob prodded Jess's thigh. 'Why do we need another car?' he asked. 'Where's your blue Prius?'

Jess was caught off guard by Jacob's utterances. Mixing old information with new was dangerous and needed to be avoided.

'It's at home,' whispered Jess. 'We'll use this hire car for the rest of the journey.' Her nostrils flared slightly, an animalistic reaction to fear.

'But I don't want a pastry anymore,' said Lisa. 'I want my home and my…' Jess cut Lisa off like she'd never done before and the anger that leapt from her mouth surprised everyone.

'Shut up and stop whining,' she shouted. 'I know it's been a long trip but we'll be there soon.'

Lisa and Jacob cowered back in fright. This woman no longer looked nor acted like their teacher. They were instantly reminded of their parents. This was not what they had signed up for. The pastries and the warm swim were miles away from this cold glass building and the emptiness they felt inside was growing with every passing hour. Their lips started trembling as tears once again began welling up. But Jess could not deal with their sadness, her own despair threatening to consume her. She had to keep moving. She turned her back on the children and gave it one last go.

'Sorry about that,' she said to the Avis woman, the forced smile a contradiction to the feelings she felt inside. 'Long flight.'

'I understand.' Dealing with weary travellers was part of her job and she had been trained neither to combat nor oppose their strong emotions. Her boss always said 'Empathy is your greatest tool. They are not angry with you. They are just tired. Do not fight it. Just go with it.'

She clicked the mouse. 'Here are your keys madam.' The jingle-jangle of the key ring a welcome sound amid the tension of the moment.

'Thank you,' said Jess, the keys falling softly into her hand.

'Your car is waiting just outside these doors and to your left. Drive safely Mrs Anderson.'

Jess grabbed the trolley and pushed it toward the glass doors. Jacob stared up at the Avis woman, a burning question on the tip of his tongue. Lisa stayed with him as Miss Bell moved toward the exit. Jacob was reluctant to cause any more trouble but he was really confused. 'Who was Mrs Anderson?' He prayed Miss Bell hadn't been given the wrong car. He stepped forward wanting to query the mistake. Miss Bell was already angry with them, and he didn't want her getting angry with the nice lady behind the counter as well. He looked at the lady and went to speak.

'Jacob!' came a thundering declaration from across the floor. He turned and stared at his teacher, her eyes piercing straight through him. 'Hurry up or I will leave you both here.'

Jacob grabbed Lisa's hand and walked a quick line toward Miss Bell. They had never seen her shout like this. No one had.

25

4:40PM AWST
PARIS

The red Citroen crawled along the busy freeway, a bout of early morning traffic threatening to choke every escape route. Cars sat bumper-to-bumper, blinkers everywhere, drivers changing lanes, horns blaring as impatience became frustration and French tempers flared.

The atmosphere inside the Citroen was in stark contrast to the mayhem outside of it. An eerie quietness had descended on its fatigued inhabitants. Jess tried hard to concentrate on the road ahead, a lack of sleep proving detrimental to the art of driving. Lisa and Jacob sat without emotion on the backseat, the large steel framework of Charles De Gaulle airport disappearing through the rear window behind them.

French road signs hung from every bridge and off ramp. Translating them was a welcome diversion from the emotional outpouring she was about to generate.

'Get it done now,' she thought to herself, 'Then you can stop worrying about it and concentrate on getting safely to your destination. The kids can cry themselves to sleep if necessary,' she reasoned. 'And when they wake up you'll be half way there. Halfway to heaven.' It was both a harsh truth and a cruel reality.

Jess pressed the lock button on her armrest. All four doors were now secured, the quiet click of the electronic locks of little concern to the innocent minds of her fragile guests. She was about to break their hearts but love was her guide and so do it she must.

The traffic thinned out and soon she was gazing out across the large paddocks of freshly rolled hay that bordered both sides of the road. The centre of Paris had been easily avoided, her easterly route a quick exit from the capital. She had experienced the beauty of the French countryside on her previous visit to this part of the world and pondered its ability to evoke strong images of great contrast. Her father had been a dedicated historian of the theatres of World War One and often recycled some of its more romantic events into quiet bedtime stories. It was a memory she remained fond of, his wistful voice a sound that refused to be dimmed by the passage of time. Jess had become well versed in the many famous battles fought here, her father's versions a starry-eyed partner to the modern-day images of dead bodies and severed limbs that lay strewn across these farms. No one tries to glorify war anymore. It is a senseless act where the only sure things are that rain will fall and blood will flow, both eventually becoming one with the soil.

Her father's death was also a senseless act and he had joined his storied subjects far too soon. Jess realised first hand that, as it is with war, it is the living who are left to contemplate the horrors of life after their loved ones have passed.

The beauty of peacetime had proved a much kinder place for the French, allowing survivors to rebuild battered lives, attempting to rediscover their belief in a better world. Jess knew it was just as important to remember, as it was to forget, which is why her next act was a stain she knew could never be removed: a mark as powerful as a bullet, leaving a wound that would scar the children for years to come.

The painted white lines of the road kept order upon the freeway. For Jess, they also represented a guide toward the future she had so lovingly planned and it was crucial she keep her new family moving in a forward direction, while she went about the ugly job of extinguishing the past.

Being successful wasn't all glory though and a sense of pain was an unavoidable reality. The private therapist who was brought in after the fire at school had taught her how to deal with grief and the expected feelings of negativity but there were some emotions you couldn't control. Jess's worse nightmare was that the papers would slander and attack her motives with lies and innuendo. Getting away with something like this was one thing, controlling all that comes after it was another issue altogether. The papers would jump and run with whatever was presented to them, plain gossip becoming half-truths before blatant lies morphed into cold hard fact.

Jess knew Tracey and Gary had a long and detailed history of abuse. Their brushes with the law were well documented and could not be ignored. Jess was quite the opposite: a teacher of children, a trusted professional who had taken every possible step to secure their safety. Surely all of this would come to the surface once she and the children were gone. Everyone would come to understand why she had taken such drastic action, even if she couldn't present the truth herself. Those who knew her would defend her character and stand up for her beliefs.

That was all she could hope for.

Europe was full of stories of dramatic abductions and mysterious disappearances and the three of them would be added to Interpol's missing persons list, the trail ending here in Paris, their new lives buried beneath many layers of secrets. A new life and a new start, for her as well as the children.

Jess was trying to ensure the long-term stability of this new life by first erasing a few details of their past. She had a great future mapped out for them but first a horrible task. It was the most diabolical part of her whole plan.

The Community and Services Act 2004 – Principle (ha) if a child is removed from the child's family then, so far as is consistent with the child's best interests, planning for the child's care should occur as soon as possible in order to ensure long-term stability for the child.

She had realised a few weeks ago it would come to this. These last few alterations could make the future more complete and the forthcoming days easier for both her and the children. It would be very painful and no doubt involve a flood of tears but it had to be done and not for the last time did she steel herself to do that which she did not want to. Enough with the talk. Action was now required.

'Lisa and Jacob,' she said calmly, checking their reflection in the rear-view mirror. 'I have something to tell you.'

The children appeared detached from their own reality. They were no longer sure what was happening to them but they were too tired to speak. Information overload had already numbed this new world. What more could there possibly be?

'It's about your parents.'

They both looked up. Jess had their attention.

'They're dead.'

26

5:00PM AWST
MARVALE TAVERN

Gary looked like death warmed up. Large sections of his brain had gone to sleep, the cerebral cortex only just functioning enough to get him onto his favourite stool. Any intellectual promise of his youth had been squandered years ago, which is why he found this current and very complex situation so hard to deal with. It was easier to avoid a problem than face it, so Gary had a general rule of thumb. When in crisis, head to the pub.

It was late afternoon by the time he stumbled in through the front door of the Marvale Tavern and took up residence on the same stool in the same corner of the same bar as he had for most of yesterday. This whole mess had started here and, now that it was unraveling, he found a comforting bedfellow in the repetition and ignorance of the previous day. Most people hate to repeat the same mistakes but Gary was a rare beast who often struggled to identify where life's mistakes actually began.

He stamped a closed fist on the bar. The tavern was starting to fill with the Saturday afternoon footy crowd and he hated waiting for a drink. The clamour of skin on wood got the attention he was seeking.

'You all right?' asked the pretty blonde behind the bar. She was pouring a pint for another customer and had a generous smile.

'Nah,' said Gary.

'You look terrible.'

'Thanks for the pick-me-up Sandy.' Gary knew he hadn't washed before he left the house but wasn't aware of how bad he actually looked and smelt.

'Sorry Gary. Truth hurts. You after a drink?'

'Yeah.'

'Usual.'

'Yeah.'

Sandy finished what she was doing before turning to get a clean pint glass from the cooler. Gary watched her as she cruised up the bar. He'd wanted a piece of Sandy ever since she appeared behind the bar a few months back. She worked the weekend shift and George had already told him how *talented* she was. Now he wanted his own sample.

Gary grabbed his crotch and shifted on his seat. He wasn't thinking about making babies. Gary had never wanted kids but neglected to put two and two together. He just wanted sex. Separating these two acts was unfortunately beyond him.

Sandy had her own issues.

She was only twenty-two. Had her whole life before her. Wanted kids. Wanted fame. Wanted money. Those three don't easily go together and truth be told her acting talent was only as long as her legs. She'd make a good mother though. Had a good heart. Came from a big family. Was good to her younger brother and sisters. She just needed some protection from the seedier side of life. Her natural talents were going to get her in trouble and before she knew it she'd be in too deep to get out. She often crossed her fingers and hoped for some good luck, but she should have crossed her legs instead.

'Here you go.' Sandy's perfume wafted across Gary's nostrils as she placed the cold beer in front of him. Her tight white t-shirt made him smile. Lust was surging through him.

'Add a shot of whisky on the side will ya honey?' Gary was feeling lucky.

5:05PM
23 DALTON CRESCENT

Tracey's luck had just about run out. She was still sleeping and would have preferred to stay that way. It took her a long time to recover from a night on the drugs and as she got older, she slept more and more. Oblivion was a holiday as far as she was concerned: the ugly truth of life too boring and broken to repair.

Gary liked to put his head in the sand but Tracey still had half a brain and knew better. She could be clever, conniving and downright devious but she wasn't at her best today. Her best was long gone. All she could do was snore and wheeze, enjoying the last few hours of an ignorant slumber.

27

9:00PM AWST
FRENCH-ITALIAN BORDER

The children slept peacefully on the faux leather seats of the Citroen. Jacob's head was nestled comfortably between the cushioned softness of the backrest and the smooth upholstery of the side door. Lisa had draped herself across the back seat, her head resting on her brother's legs. They looked at ease now but a set of blotchy red circles around their eyes was clear evidence of the tears they'd shed. More proof lay beside Lisa's head, Jacob's fist still clenched tightly, the anger he'd displayed yet to disperse from his body. They looked like angels now, but twenty minutes ago, all hell was breaking loose.

'Dead. What do you mean?' seethed Jacob.

'They passed away this morning,' said Jess. 'Nothing could be done to save them.'

'What happened?'

'A car accident. Late last night. They were killed instantly.'

It was all propaganda yet the falsehoods were rolling off Jess's well-rehearsed tongue like a runaway train. Real emotions were being discarded like debris as the fabrications and fibs forced their way through in a blur of disgust. Jess was channelling her own experiences, an echo of that knock on the door which brought her own world crashing down around her. Revisiting the past was uncomfortable but her journey was at a very uncomfortable stage and it couldn't be side stepped.

Lisa was a blubbering mess. 'Can we see them?'

'No. It's better this way.' Jess clenched her teeth and concentrated hard on the straight lines that split the road. The images she was conjuring up forced a fever of hate to brew inside her. She'd lived through such traumatic news herself and knew how damaging it was. 'How can you be so mean,' she scolded herself, experiencing every word like a bludgeon to the head.

Jacob acted out his pain, punching the headrest on the seat in front of him.

'Fuck,' he yelled.

Jess spun instinctively, holding Jacob's gaze momentarily before turning her attention back to the road. She'd heard Jacob swear before, but not with such fury. He had his father's disease. It would be another issue to resolve, but now wasn't the time.

'Take us home!' said Jacob, his words weighted with emotion, every letter carved from stone.

Tears welled up in Jess's eyes as she allowed the final words to ooze out like a poison, killing off all hope of a return to anything which resembled their life before.

'I won't,' she said. 'You're staying with me now. I'll be looking after you from here on in.' Pain ripped through the children like scissors through paper. Jess was in control and she wanted to sever every connection she could find to the suburb of Marvale.

Jacob's resolve was stronger than she'd expected but eventually he snapped in two, his sobs ripping hard upon Jess's ears. There is no greater pain than a child's and after everything that Jacob had been through, it was this moment that she felt most keenly. Jess could never have known what her young charge was thinking, the fatal news informing Jacob that his old life had died with his parents.

He felt love for them, of course, because that was what life expected of him but he hated them too. They'd fallen so short of his demands and as the news of their demise sank in, he felt his body relax more than it had done for many years. The pain of living a lie came pouring out.

Jess endured their tears. She questioned everything she had done and the decisions that lay ahead. She would always regret having spoken the words that broke Lisa and Jacob's hearts. Words that would one day come back to haunt her.

But the car was quiet now and she steered the red Citroen across the border between France and Italy, mentally ticking off another important checkpoint on their journey.

Thirty hours had passed since they left Australian soil and they were further into this new life than she had ever thought possible. The reality of a life on the run was a concept she was adjusting to. Summoning the courage to live a life of vigilance would test her further and Jess felt the paranoia normally associated with life on the wrong side of the law. That constant threat of discovery forcing you to always look over your shoulder and the need to always be aware of what was behind you as well as in front. In the absence of friends, her only constant companion would be fear.

The flashing lights up ahead made the hairs on her skin stand on end. The midday sun illuminated the metal body of the police patrol bike, a lone policeman, his arm out, directing her toward the side of the road. Jess glanced over her shoulder at the children. They were still sleeping.

She prayed for them to stay that way.

She slowed the car and pulled over toward the edge of the mountain road, stopping just behind the motorcycle. The officer approached the car, his smart green leather jacket and black trousers, a stylish nod to the nearby city of fashionable Milan.

The hum of the French engine died with the twist of the key, the absence of noise waking Lisa and Jacob from their slumber. Jess didn't know that sleeping children loved the gentle rumble of the working chassis. It would have been valuable information. What she did know was that their waking was a factor which could only complicate the situation she was about to face.

The officer strolled toward Jess's side of the car and she wound down her window.

'Buongiorno signorina. ID please.' His accent was thick and coarse.

Jess passed her Greek driver's licence through the window. The officer accepted it with gloved hands.

'Miss Apostolides. Welcome to Italia. You travel through my beautiful country for what reason?'

'Holiday. We are returning from a camping trip to Spain.'

'Lots of sun. You enjoy?'

'Yes. Thank you.'

He turned his attention to the children who were watching this exchange quietly from the back seat.

'Hello children. You must be tired after your big holiday?'

Jess waited nervously for their answer. Lisa and Jacob nodded their sleepy heads, a blur of planes, cars and deaths muddying the finer details of their lives.

'Sorry, but they are very tired,' said Jess.

'I understand. Are they your children?'

'Yes, of course.'

'My apologies signora. I mean you no offence but in this job nothing is ever as it seems.'

The officer continued his observations in silence. Jess didn't know whether to hold the man's gaze or to look away. The officer walked up one side of the car and around the back. The children craned their necks to watch him through the rear window. Jess followed his progress in the side and rear vision mirrors. The clip clop of his boots only increased the tension as he strolled down the opposite side and back around the front. It was twelve seconds of hell.

'The car appears to be in working order signora.'

Jess nodded. 'Thanks for checking.' The officer returned her Greek driver's licence.

'Thank you for your patience Ms. Apostolides. Have a nice holiday.'

'Thank you, officer.'

He stepped away from the car, his outstretched arm indicating for Jess to rejoin the highway. She took his cue, switching the car on before accelerating slowly away from another crime scene. Forgery, fraud, impersonation and kidnapping made a long list of misdemeanours, her every move a felony that would later be entered, addressed and filed.

'Was he a policeman?' asked Jacob.

'Yes, he was.'

'He sounded funny,' said Lisa.

'He's Italian,' said Jess. 'We're in Italy, just north of a city called Milan.'

'Why did you tell him we'd been on holiday?' asked Jacob.

'I didn't want to talk about your mum and dad in front of you,' said Jess, twisting the rear-vision mirror to make face-to-face contact with the children. 'I thought it might make you sad.'

'Oh. Okay. I understand.' Jacob looked down at his hands. 'I had a dream about them,' he said calmly.

Lisa looked across at her brother. 'Was it a good dream?' she asked.

'Not really. We were in a car, driving somewhere and another car crashed into us. Lisa and I were thrown out and we landed beside the road on our feet like we were gymnasts. I could see mum and dad stuck in the front seat. The car was all smashed up and they had blood all over their faces.'

'Were they dead?' asked Lisa.

'No.'

'Did they say anything?'

'Yes, they did. They said goodbye. I could feel their breath against my skin. Like a whisper.'

'Were they in pain?'

'No, they looked kind of happy. Like they knew where they were going.'

'Did you say goodbye?'

Jacob looked down at his sister. 'Yes Lisa, we both did.'

Her brother placed an arm around her shoulders which made her smile. He meant the world to this little girl lost. Jacob looked across at Jess who was feeling a mixture of pride and relief. This boy was amazing and the dream was a present from heaven.

'It's all up to you now,' whispered Jacob.

'Thanks,' she whispered back. The hardest part was over.

28

11:00PM AWST
23 DALTON CRESCENT, MARVALE

Tracey crawled from her catnap exactly thirty-one hours after her children had left the country. Having looked at her watch and after calling out repeatedly for someone to get her a glass of bloody wine, the lack of response spiked a bout of worry, which quickly turned to panic.

She hauled her naked body from underneath the doona and stumbled awkwardly from room to room, the rising dread rendering her speechless, a nagging sense of déjà vu hitting home. These debilitating rushes of anxiety had become a common thread lately. Trouble found her more often than she liked and she'd grown tired of its presence. Fear was telling her she'd lost control of her own destiny for the umpteenth time. 'Here we fuckin' go again.'

She'd created this crazy life for herself. Fallen pregnant with Jacob a few months after meeting Gary. They were hastily married, the pressure from her church-going folks too much to resist. Not in the local parish mind you. No, they decided to escape to some country town where a brief ceremony ensued. Only immediate family were invited. Tracey was just eighteen years old and it was the beginning of a run of big mistakes.

Ten years on and 'those bloody kids were still causing her grief'. She'd not seen their sallow faces since Friday morning and that was usually a reason to celebrate but the dislike she felt for them was magnified tenfold by tonight's uncomfortable absence. She usually liked it when the kids weren't around but this was different. This affected her financial future!

They'd be together, of course, wallowed Tracey. Her children were virtually inseparable and the loneliness that gnawed at her own heart often cauterised any effort she made to reach out to them. Tracey had a brother too, but they'd been estranged for a few years now. She found trouble so easy to find, yet love, he was always running the other way.

Tracey wasn't an island and she badly needed someone to talk to. She made some quick calculations in her head. Tried to read the different futures that each action would invoke. Ignorance encouraged her to open a cask of wine and sloth told her to go back to bed. Tracey hadn't always been useless and her conscience was telling her to call the cops. She was out of wine anyway and having slept all day she was no longer tired. Calling the cops was the only option left so that's what she did.

The police received Tracey's panicked phone call just after midnight. 'My kids are gone!'

'Do you have any idea where they might be?' asked the clerk.

'No. I've spent the whole day looking for them.'

'Is there an ex-husband in the picture?'

'He's out searching the streets for them. And he's not my ex, although he might be if we end up losin' them.'

'Is he the father of the missing children?'

'Of course he bloody is.' Tracey's whole body was shaking. 'What do you think I am?'

'I didn't mean to offend you, mam. These are just routine questions.'

'Fuck routines. Just find my bloody kids, alright!'

An All-Points Bulletin went out to every officer on duty. Phone calls were made to the region's hospitals and cinemas and all the local parks in a five mile radius were combed. They also visited every pub in the immediate vicinity, just in case someone knew or had seen something of interest.

11:55 PM
MARVALE TAVERN

'Everything all right, officers?' is how George greeted them, his tavern heaving with customers, most of them watching the Saturday night footy on the big screen.

'Evening George,' said Officers Gates and Harris. 'Just on the lookout for a couple of kids.'

Gary Johnstone's ears pricked up from his stool at the far end of the bar. Hearing the word 'kids' had made him go all wobbly so he gripped the counter and took another gulp of his White Russian. He was well hidden, a wall of sweaty bodies between them and him. The television commentary was loud but he could still hear little snippets of the conversation. He'd consumed six pints and had only recently moved onto the spirits. The stress of the afternoon needed a clean wipe and it was working.

'Just wondering if you'd seen them in here,' said Gates. 'A boy and a girl, aged eight and ten, missing since yesterday.'

'No, I haven't,' said George. 'I'm not a big fan of kids drinking alcohol. Don't usually get many coming in here.' His sarcasm came as naturally to him as breathing and George scanned the smoke-filled room for further inspiration. His flock were all in various states of alcoholic poisoning, their blotchy, animated faces dissecting the game's big moments. He looked back at the officers. 'There are heaps of big kids in here, but no one that young.'

Gary was sweating. The alcohol that had subdued his mind was now prying open a chasm of guilt and shame, the cowardly events of the last two days flooding back like a tsunami.

'Shouldn't you be closed anyway?' asked Officer Harris. 'It's gone eleven thirty.'

'Closed-door policy,' said George. 'These are my after-hours drinkers. Practically members.'

'Yeah, well we walked in pretty easily.'

'You guys are VIPs. Do you fancy a drink?'

'Thanks, but no thanks,' said Gates.

'How about you turn down the music for us, though,' said Harris, 'And ask your members if they've seen the missing kids. Then you can usher them out and shut up shop for the night.'

'But the footy's not over yet.'

'It's not a live game,' smiled Harris. 'Collingwood's my team. The games been over for an hour and they lost by five.'

'But this lot don't know that,' said George, indicating the drunken crowd. 'They came in especially to see it. Look at the score. It's a nail-biter.'

'Like I said, my team lost. Leave it on and you'll end up on the losing end too.'

'They all look like they've had enough anyway,' said Gates. 'Wouldn't want them to drive home drunk, now, would we?'

'Of course not,' said George, resigning himself to the ultimate power of the law.

George stepped between the crowds and up toward the big screen. He pulled the remote from his pocket and hit the power button, turning the big screen off and sending the whole place into an uproar.

'What the fuck you doin' George,' asked a punter amid the chorus of disapproval.

'Its closing time,' he shouted. A chorus of abuse rained down on his bald head. He waited for the disgust to die down before directing their gaze toward the two well-dressed men in blue uniforms standing tall and mighty near the bar.

'Two of our finest would like to say a few words before you go,' said George.

The whole mob went quiet, placing their drinks on the tables surrounding them.

Officer Harris spoke first. 'Evening ladies and gents. We are on the lookout for two children. Their names are Lisa and Jacob Johnstone. They are eight and ten years old and live locally.'

Gary could feel everyone's eyes boring into the back of his head which was totally imaginary. His back was turned to everyone, lest the officers or anyone else identify him. He'd kept to himself all evening. He wasn't that popular anyway and watched the coppers speech via the reflection in the mirror behind the bar. He felt as small as the little cocktail umbrella that graced the fancy drink he cradled so preciously.

'They live in Dalton Crescent so you might have seen them around town,' explained Officer Gates. 'About this height,' his right hand out flat at his waist. 'They go to the local school and are the children of Tracey and Gary Johnstone.'

A sideways glance from his bald mate behind the bar froze Gary like a mannequin.

'George has kindly agreed to close-up shop,' said Officer Harris, 'So please finish your drinks and come and see us if you have any information whatsoever. It's very cold outside and we need to find these kids before it's too late.' The rumble of voices rolled across the tabletops, the wiser patrons leaving straight away, while others returned to the comfort of their beverages.

George started cashing up the till. He was always eager to count his money, hoped the coppers hadn't prevented him from taking his usual Saturday night windfall. Owning a pub in this suburb was like winning Lotto every weekend. His customers were some of the poorest in the state but they sure spent up large on alcohol. It was this contradiction that had originally brought him across the Nullarbor and it was a truth he was keen to suck dry.

Another of life's contradictions sat sheepishly down the far end of the bar and George couldn't, for the life of him, fathom why he was still here. He'd already willed him to get out, staring across at him when the coppers finished their spiel and the first rush of drinkers piled out the door. He should've leapt of the stool and quietly disappeared into the night. George didn't want to get embroiled in whatever was going on with the Johnstone children.

Gary felt too paranoid to make any moves. Sipping his drink kept the hiss of panic at bay. He hadn't wanted to be the first to leave. Was sure the coppers or one of the patrons would have recognised him.

He watched in the mirror as a couple of drinkers started a conversation with the coppers and decided that now was his chance. He had to go while they were distracted. He slipped off the stool and headed straight for the door.

It should have been easy, but two hours spent teetering on that ungainly wooden stool had sent Gary's legs to sleep. Add that to the alcohol washing through him and he'd already been stripped of any sense of balance. His first step onto the hard wooden floor was shaky at best, his second step lacked confidence and grip, a dangerous mixture of beer and perspiration coating the floor with a slippery film. He lost traction with planet earth, his feet flying out from underneath him like a carpet of marbles, sending his upper body clattering into two bikies. Their drinks fell with them, off the table and shattered on the sweat-stained floor.

'What the fuck,' is how the first bikie made sense of what was happening.

'Fuck me,' is what the second one said, having quickly identified the red-faced offender.

All hopes of a quiet exit were gone. Gary had successfully done the exact opposite. His arms and legs were splayed out upon the floor, his right hand bleeding from cut glass, his vision a blur of colour. Luck had deserted him a long time ago.

'Where are the pigs,' he asked, his bleary-eyed bearings all confusion and no control.

Two sets of hands reached underneath his armpits and hauled him off the floor. 'We're right here?' said a voice he recognised.

Gary could hear George in the background trying to calm the two bikies down, promising them a fresh beer. But it was the righteous tone of the men who'd grabbed him that sent shivers down his cowardly spine. His vision cleared and he looked left then right and found himself caught deep in the blue eyes of Officers Gates and Harris. He was dead in the water.

'Shit!'

'Mr Johnstone,' said Officer Harris. 'What a nice surprise finding you here.'

Gary acted dumb. He was good at that. 'What's so surprising

about it? I always spend Saturday night here.'

'So do I,' mimicked Officer Harris. 'Looking for ratbags like you.' Harris found it quite distasteful that this little crook was here getting pissed while his children were lost and possibly terrified. He would have expected nothing less.

'Did you hear our little speech?' asked Gates.

'Nah, I was in the toilet.'

'Well it might just interest you.'

'Really,' slurred Gary. 'Why's that?'

'We've been to see your lovely wife and she told us you were out searching the streets for your little darlings,' said Harris. 'Excuse me if I'm wrong, but whilst it might be dirty and grimy in here, it's not exactly the streets.'

'I was out lookin'. You saw me.'

'Looking for your shoes,' said Gates. 'You never mentioned any kids.'

'I was scared. You guys pissed me off with your smart-arse smiles.'

'Sorry about that.'

'Anyway, I was really sad cause I couldn't find 'em. I love my kids.'

'Sure you do,' said Harris. 'That's why you're in here and they're out there, somewhere. Could be dead for all you know.'

'Shut up. They're not dead.'

'Do you know something we don't?'

'No. I bet they're just hiding that's all. Little bastards do that sometimes.'

'Who are they hiding from?' asked Gates.

'You checked with the grandparents. They're always nicking them.'

'Been there, done that. They're actually a really nice couple.'

'Weak as piss is what they are.'

'So, you like them then,' said Gates.

Gary scratched his head and looked away.

'Your children have been missing for almost forty hours now,' said Harris. 'That's a pretty serious amount of time to be hiding.'

'They'll turn up.'

'Just like that,' said Gates. 'Might even pop in here and have a drink with Daddy will they?'

'Not now they won't.' Gary watched another patron slip out the front door. 'Look, if you haven't got anything decent to ask me then I'm bloody going home.'

'Too right you are,' said Harris. 'Your wife is waiting for you and she isn't going to be very happy when she finds out where you've been.'

'She won't find out.'

'Oh yes she will,' smiled Gates.

It took Gary an hour to complete the twenty-minute stumble home, his drunken stupor forcing him to sway from footpath to road and back again. This crazy zigzag pattern meant he'd covered about three times as much ground as was necessary. He'd also bumped into more lampposts and rubbish bins than a blind cat, with the bumps and bruises to prove it.

When he finally staggered up the steps to his house, he was so exhausted that the day's events paled in comparison to his desire for sleep. He stumbled in through the front door, tip-toed up the corridor and collapsed upon his bed.

He never noticed Tracey asleep in the lounge, curled up like a dog on the couch, the house phone still in her grasp.

Gary was asleep soon after his head landed face down on the edge of the stained brown pillow, a gravelly snore quickly escaping his squashed nose. His breath stank, his bedroom stank and his life stank. Even his dreams had the reek of failure. He'd made it home. His kids hadn't.

29

SUNDAY 14th MAY
1:00AM AWST
CROATIA

Jacob and Lisa stared wide-eyed out the backseat window as the world continued to rush past at ever increasing speeds. They'd never seen so much of their planet in such a short space of time and their brains were at sixes and sevens, trying to make sense of this wild stream of information.

The grieving process had proved a massive drain on their psyche and Jess was loath to interrupt the tranquility of the road. She drove without conversation knowing full well they had to process it by themselves and in their own good time. It couldn't be rushed. She knew that from personal experience.

Jess hadn't coped well with the death of her own parents. Their demise catapulted her off the rails and down the slippery slopes of adolescence. Fourteen was a terrible age to experience such loss and whilst still not of legal drinking age, it didn't stop her mixing with the wrong groups and swallowing her way to oblivion. She was a tall girl and an early bout of maturity meant she had little trouble fooling the bottle shop boys down at the corner store. It helped that they fancied her too.

Tricking her well-meaning carers was also easy. Moving in

with the goodhearted neighbours across the road had been her only choice. Mum and Dad had both been raised in single-child families and having moved half way around the world, grandparents were a feature of family life she had never known. She didn't want to relocate to dreary old England anyway and Mr and Mrs Swanson were good family friends and members of the same church. They had no children of their own, so it was easy to adapt at first and Jess did not want for attention.

It was a move her parents had suggested in their Wills and the Swansons were very happy at first; Jess was the child they'd always prayed for. But Jess wasn't a child anymore; she was what the hushed tones of the parish pews referred to as damaged goods. The Will had been agreed to many years earlier, when her family unit was securely intact and happy. Now she was bristling with anger and always on the lookout for trouble.

Mr and Mrs Swanson were at a loss as to how to handle her aggression and their efforts towards restraint and regulation drove Jess further and further away.

The disillusionment and angst she harboured during those teenage years meant she was subsequently interrogated and harassed by wave after wave of mental health experts. Do this and take that was all they ever offered her. Repeat prescription after repeat prescription. Drugs to stop nature taking its natural course; her body forced to accept a fact it just wanted to repel. The doctors didn't have the patience to wait for her to be ready in her own time.

She ran away fifteen times in total. There were no easy solutions to her ills, so when she turned eighteen the Swansons gave up trying and said she could look after herself. They signed over the Trust account her parents had created and helped her buy a house. They washed their hands of responsibility, announcing during one particularly heated evening that she could buy as many bottles of whiskey as she wanted. And she did, filling the empty rooms of her new pad with the despair and hopelessness of liquid laughter.

This newfound independence didn't quite work for her either. Neither the alcohol nor the irregular counselling sessions could help her forget who she was and the trial medications she was forced to take made her feel woozy and depressed. She was a ragbag collection of emotions, often flat-lining when words were too hard to come by.

That was almost twenty years ago but the memories of those bad old days still remained with her and, like a line drawn in the sand, she viewed them with detachment and isolation. She vowed never to cross to that side again, employing those old feelings of hate and fear to safeguard against any repetition of those errors from her past. It was an emotional guarantee she made to herself every morning in the mirror.

That is why Lisa and Jacob represented a second chance. Another chance at a life she had searched long and hard for. It was the final solution to all her woes. Teaching had given her the tools to take the leap and now she had her new family and all the possibilities of the world ahead. There was no need to force a new understanding upon the children. Give them time to heal and a new future could be enjoyed and not endured.

She glanced into the rearview mirror, happy that Lisa and Jacob could only see the beauty of the land that drifted past them, the late afternoon sun falling in a soft arch across the forests, penetrating the wild pines that grew on both sides of the road. The children knew nothing of the bloodshed and horror that had so recently visited the people of Croatia, a war of hatred that had burst upon the news at the same time as Jess's own life had exploded into tiny pieces. The sheer number of atrocities carried out here had helped Jess appreciate that she was just a tiny cog in a much larger machine of human malice. A vicious construct that snapped people's hearts like matchsticks.

The only good reason for looking back now, was to make sure they weren't being followed.

The English-speaking radio station she'd stumbled onto had not mentioned anything about a trio of Australian fugitives. She wondered how quickly news travelled. What was happening back in Marvale? Had they even noticed that the kids were gone?

That old world and her part in it, already seemed so far away.

30

7:00AM AWST
23 DALTON CRESCENT, MARVALE

'Rap, rap, rap.' The rattling sound of knuckles on glass thrust Tracey from her dreams. The living room couch groaned as she sat up quickly and collected what was left of her mind.

'Mr and Mrs Johnstone,' called an authoritative voice through the frosted glass panels of the front door. 'It's the police. Please open the door.'

'Shit,' thought Tracey. 'The kids. They must have found them.' She grabbed a half empty bottle of vodka off the table and rolled it under the couch. The sound of glass on glass told Tracey there was another bottle of something under there. She smiled.

'Is anyone home,' called the officer.

Tracey hauled her body to its feet and dragged it into the hallway. 'Coming,' she croaked, her throat dry with a mixture of worry and excitement.

The morning sun was already pouring in through the glass, lighting up the rubbish-strewn hallway. Tracey navigated her way past a pile of plastic shopping bags and pizza boxes, already anticipating the threat of the two alien-like silhouettes visible through the door ahead of her.

'They've probably still got the kids in the car,' she thought, before twisting the lock and drawing the door inward. A hateful burst of morning light revealed its true strength, scorching her eyes and momentarily blinding her. She lifted a hand to shield her face as the finer details of two blue uniforms came into focus.

'Morning Mrs Johnstone,' greeted Officer Harris. 'May we come in?'

'Where are my kids?'

'We haven't found them yet, but we'll explain more inside,' he continued, his arm directing her back inside.

'What do you mean you haven't found them?' Tracey turned down her hallway and into the lounge. 'Where the hell are they then?'

'We have some news as to that question,' said Officer Gates as they stepped into the lounge.

Tracey stopped them in their tracks. 'Good news?'

'Good and bad,' said Harris. He and Gates stepped past her and took a seat on the old couch. Tracey sat down opposite them on the edge of a tattered and torn armchair.

'What the fuck does that mean? Let's not play any bloody games all right?'

Officer Gates scanned the room.

'Is Mr Johnstone available?' asked Harris.

'I'm here,' came a gruff reply as Gary shuffled out from the light filled hallway and into the semi-darkness of the lounge. He was still struggling to stay upright.

Tracey got to her feet. 'You okay honey,' she asked. She was on her best behaviour.

'I just need a coffee.'

'There'll be time for that later,' said Officer Harris. 'Please. Take a seat.'

Gary let out a groan before he navigated his way across the room, toward another armchair in the far corner. He sat down heavily.

'We can confirm that Lisa and Jacob have left the country,' said Officer Harris.

'What?' Tracey's face was all screwed up.

'How?' asked Gary. 'They're our kids.'

'Passport records show they left Australia at three pm on Friday. They flew to Dubai where they caught a connecting flight to Paris.'

'That's fucking crazy,' said Tracey. 'They've never even been on a plane before. How the fuck would they know how to do all that?'

'They had help,' said Gates. 'Their teacher, Miss Jessica Bell, is our prime suspect at this stage. Her passport matches their own movements and they left on the same plane.'

Tracey closed her eyes and clenched her teeth. 'Fuckin' bitch?'

'Did the frogs catch them?' asked Gary.

'The frogs?' said Gates.

'Yeah, the fuckin' Frenchies.'

'Oh. No, not yet,' replied Officer Gates. 'The trail ends in Paris.'

'What the fuck does that mean?' asked Tracey. 'The trail ends in Paris,' she mimicked.

'Please stay calm Mrs Johnstone.' Harris held up his palm. 'It's better if we all keep a clear head.'

'That's easy for you to say. I've been drinking myself silly with worry. Just explain yourself will ya.'

'They've simply disappeared,' said Harris. 'No one has seen or heard from them for nineteen hours.'

Tears started sliding down Tracey's reddened cheeks.

Gary leaned despondently back in his chair. He wasn't thinking about the kids and he wasn't interested in comforting his wife. He knew trouble was coming his way and he fought hard against the tide of emotion that was about to engulf him.

Harris and Gates went on to explain that the missing person's files on Lisa and Jacob Johnstone had been upscaled to a full-blown federal investigation. The local police had been instructed to pass on all their information to the Australian law enforcement agency. Their first act was to feed all that information onto the French police, who had tried, without much success, to trace the three Australians.

Two French officers were deployed to comb every inch of

Charles De Gaulle airport. Questions were asked of some of the employees who worked there. Some people had seen the family; others had not. No one spoke to the lady at the Avis Rent-a-Car because she was off duty. The new guy on the desk was oblivious to the identification crimes of the previous shift. Australia was on the opposite side of the world anyway. What effect could these three possibly have on the people of Paris? As long as the tourists kept pouring into the most visited city in the world, then everything was fine.

The gendarmes dug no deeper than necessary and having finished their inquiry, left the crime scene no wiser than when they arrived. Forty hours had passed since they'd left the country and not an ounce of progress had been made. Our fugitives were getting away and all hell was about to break loose.

31

MONDAY 15TH MAY
7:30AM AWST
MARVALE PRIMARY SCHOOL

A small herd of reporters jostled for prime position around the gated entrance to Marvale Primary School. Like ants to a lollipop they could taste the sugar in the developing international saga that had begun to swirl around this educational institution.

'Oi mate,' yelled the school gardener. 'Watch the plants please. Your killing them.'

Evan Nash was the mild-mannered gardener of Marvale Primary but he'd been unexpectedly placed on gate duty today and already these media types were proving to be more nuisance than a field of weeds. He'd been charged with the responsibility of ensuring only teachers and staff came through the gate. Keeping the journalists at bay meant that the small gardens he'd so lovingly established either side of the car park entrance were taking an absolute hammering.

'Oi you lot! Stick to the footpaths and get out of my gardens. You're a bunch of bright sparks. It shouldn't be that hard.'

Yasmin Neates was the school principal and she watched on calmly from behind the net curtains of her office window. She had caught whiff of the foul wind blowing her way when the

Education Minister's media liaison had called yesterday afternoon to warn her of the growing disquiet surrounding the unexpected developments regarding two of her students and a teacher on her staff. Prior to that phone call she had been oblivious to the events of the previous two days, happily enjoying a couple of quiet wines at a friend's house. She sensed the enormity of the situation and that 'shit was about to start hitting the fan'. Her school was slap bang in the middle of it all.

Yasmin had a secret though. Far from the terror and dread that would course through most Principals during a crisis of this size, she lived for these moments. Being forced into a corner brought out the best in Yasmin. She loved a challenge and after forty years at the coalface of the education business, she knew this problem was as big as they came. She rubbed her palms briskly together. Retirement was still a couple of years away and this might just be her crowning glory.

Jeff Simpson strolled down his street toward the alley which would deposit him directly across the road from the main entrance to the school. He walked to work almost every day, his house just a few blocks away. Arriving on foot kept him in good health.

A keen journalist spotted him as soon as he emerged onto the road and sensing an opportunity the young man made a beeline for him. The rest of the pack quickly turned and followed, a swarm of cameras and microphones jogging Jeff's way. Miss Bell's teaching partner was out of the information loop, the wild advance of the media horde throwing him into total confusion and mild fear. 'What the hell is going on,' he thought as their gamut of devices and cables protruded inside his personal space.

'Mr Simpson, you taught with Miss Bell,' said a young man. 'What do you think made her kidnap two students?'

'What?' laughed Jeff, managing to prevent several expletives from escaping his mouth. 'What are you talking about? How do you even know my name?'

'Jessica Bell has kidnapped Lisa and Jacob Johnstone,' said another voice, this time a woman. 'She's on the run. How does that make you feel?'

'Sorry, but I don't know what the hell you're talking about. Jess wouldn't do that. She's not that sort of person.'

'When was the last time you saw her?'

'Friday. She…' Jeff paused as memory of her absence from drinks drove a spike of apprehension through his spleen.

'Let him through. Let him through,' yelled Yasmin as she drove herself through the pack of reporters and grabbed Jeff's hand. 'Come with me,' she said, the drive of her words both demanding and protective. They walked quickly toward the school gate, the media pack hustling after them, tripping over each other in a race for the best coverage.

'Have the parents been notified?' called out a man in a suit.

'Open the gate,' instructed Yasmin.

Jeff kept his head down as a barrage of questions were thrown at him. He had absolutely no intention of saying anything, his mind a mass of conflicting emotions, a wretched reservoir of tears welling up inside of him.

The gate slid open and Jeff and Yasmin slipped inside. His boss let go of his hand and glared back at the journalists.

'Don't even think about following us!' she hollered. 'You'll only pass through here when we invite you to. Not before, not after and maybe not ever.' She was immediately hit with a salvo of questions but she was unmoved by their pushy questions and protestations. 'Close the gate,' she commanded, and Evan the gardener took great delight in hitting the button once more.

The black metal gate eased closed and the sudden feeling of breathing space was a welcome respite from the bustle of bodies on the other side. A wall of microphones and voice recorders were thrust between the square black bars of the gate but they had protection from their advances, for now.

Yasmin threw her right arm around Jeff's shoulders and guided him away from the throng. They walked slowly across the car park toward the administration block, Jeff trying valiantly to regroup his swirling emotions.

'Sorry about that,' said Yasmin. 'Probably should have sent an email out to all the staff.'

'Is it true?'

'It looks like it might be,' said Yasmin. 'The police have been in contact with me and it's their opinion that the case against Jess is firming up.'

'I can't believe it. Why would she do it?'

'It's too early to tell Jeff. Making assumptions at this stage will only get us into even more trouble. We must stick to the facts and speak as a group. They'll want some individual quotes so that they can try and tear us apart. If they can smell a rat, then we'll all be in the poo.'

'This is an absolute nightmare.'

'It sure is,' said Yasmin.

7:45AM AWST

A shiny white Mazda groaned to a halt in front of the overcrowded gate to the school. The driver's window descended, revealing a smiling Rupert Small, sharply dressed and totally composed. A gabble of microphones stabbed his way.

'Do you work here?' asked a male reporter.

'Of course I do. I'm the Deputy Principal.' Rupert couldn't hide how much he hated it when people didn't instantly know who he was. 'Read the badge!' He hit the car horn which blared across the car park and the gate started opening.

'Do you have any comment to make?'

'Yes.' Rupert cleared his throat. 'I have known Miss Bell for four years. She was a quiet lady who has always kept to herself. I do not in any way support her actions and I am working in tandem with the Education Department and both the local and federal police to apprehend her as soon as possible.' He revved his engine.

'What made her so quiet?' inquired a man wielding a Channel Nine microphone.

'A lot of things. She saw the world differently to most.'

'Can you give us an example.'

'Sorry, must fly.' Rupert put his car into first gear. He still drove a manual. Liked the racing car feel.

A female journalist thrust the passenger door open and jumped in. Rupert was startled but focused.

'Do you believe she's innocent?' she asked.

He smiled. 'I believe what the facts will tell us.'

'What is your gut instinct?'

'You tell me. You're the one with the microphone.'

'You think she did it don't you.'

'No comment,' grinned Rupert. 'Now please get out of my car.' She did what he asked before he accelerated through the gate. The spoiler on the rear of the car clipped her hand-held microphone, sending it spilling across the concrete driveway.

Evan watched the deputy's car screech past him. 'Morning Rupert.'

There would be no reply. It was a routine Evan liked to play out each day. Rupert Small wasn't one to acknowledge the existence of the little people around him. Evan knew where he stood in the hierarchy of the school. He was a good reader of people and he could smell imminent danger.

8:15AM AWST

'You said what?' screamed Yasmin Neates. She was shrill and to the point.

'You heard me,' said Rupert.

The staffroom was a hive of activity, a stunned audience of teachers watching their bosses argue, hot cups of tea and coffee on the tables in front of them.

'But we need to be impartial,' said Yasmin. 'We must not make any assumptions.'

'I'm not going to let her take us down as well.'

'She hasn't been convicted of anything yet.'

'Yet,' said Rupert. 'She will be though. I'll make sure of that.'

'You bloody fool. I expected more from you.'

'Wrong again!' Rupert turned on his well-heeled shoes and strode down the hallway to his office.

He disappeared inside his doorway and slammed the door shut.

Rupert never had anyone's back but his own. And now in the school's time of need all he would be was a liability. Yasmin was gutted. She took a second to compose herself before lifting a small silver bell off the table beside her and giving it a couple of shakes. 'Ting-a-ling-ling-ling'. The bell had special significance, a present from Miss Bell last Christmas. Using the bell today would, she hoped, signal her intentions.

'Sorry to interrupt you all, but I wanted to bring everyone up to date with the disruption currently swirling around one of our teachers and two of our students. I have closed Marvale Primary for the day to attend to this issue, so please, under no circumstances are any children to be allowed access into your classrooms. I am sure we will get a few turning up due to the late notice, but they must be either sent home or directed to our front office so their parents can be contacted. I have locked all of the gates into the school, so they shouldn't even make it that far.'

A light murmur filled the room as the assembled staff soaked up the news. Yasmin waited patiently for it to settle.

'This doesn't mean however that you can return home. I require all staff to remain onsite so that we can manage the fallout from this news and whatever else becomes necessary as the case unfolds. No one is to talk to the media and please refrain from calling your family and friends for the next few hours. I want to keep this in-house. I am the spokesperson and I will be addressing the media shortly. I accept that you will need to discuss this amongst yourselves, but please hold off from making any judgments. Prejudice, whether for or against Jess, will only hinder our search for the truth. I have been in contact with the police and I know some of the facts as they stand this minute, so I will try to answer any questions you have?'

A flurry of arms was raised.

'Are we, as a school, in trouble?' asked Tim.

'No. As long as we, as a school, or as individuals, have not assisted Jess in taking these children, then we have nothing to fear.'

Many eyes looked over in Jeff's direction and he felt the heat of their stares.

'I knew absolutely nothing about this crazy idea,' said Jeff.

'It is exactly this sort of prejudice that I was alluding too,' said Yasmin. 'No one should be placed under any more scrutiny than the next person. We can only deal in facts. If you think you have information that might be of interest, then please come and see me.'

'Do the police know where she has taken them?' asked Nancy.

'No. They have flight information that she left Australia with both children and flew as far as Paris, but it is not clear if they flew on from there or what form of transport they used after that. I will keep you up to date with developments as they happen. I'd rather you stay informed through me, rather than relying on rumours generated by the media.'

'Who has she taken?' asked Nora Sloane.

'Lisa and Jacob Johnstone,' said Yasmin. 'Year four and five. I'm sure you all know them.'

'Why now?'

'She taught them both. Jacob last year and Lisa this year. She's had a lot to do with both children and their parents. Tried many times to have them removed from their family, as have many of us. Looks like she may have allowed it to get personal.'

'Damn right it got personal,' said Rupert, having returned to the staff room. 'Both children come from a troubled family. The worst kind if you ask me. Took up a hell of a lot of my time. I told Jess on countless occasions that they weren't worth the effort.'

'Rupert, please,' said Yasmin.

'I hate these kind of shitty little families, you all know that. But this is just giving them what they want. What Jess has done will throw everything I have worked for, back fifty years. The government will have a field day with us.'

'What if the police never find her?' asked Jeff.

'Fat chance of that,' laughed Rupert. 'It's not if but when. She's a teacher for god's sake. What does she know about the art of kidnapping? Word has already gone out to the Federal Police,

Interpol and the EU. She can run but she can't hide.'

Yasmin rang her bell in an effort to return the focus back to her.

'As a school we must stick together,' said Yasmin. 'Managing the fallout from this will take strength and perseverance. The regional director has already given me a grilling. Mark my words, the department is looking for a scapegoat. Let's make sure it's not one of us.'

'How are the parents doing?' asked Evie.

'Terribly. They are understandably worried sick. We might not think much of their parenting skills but they love their children and want them back as quickly as possible.'

8:30AM AWST
DALTON CRESCENT

Tracey dialed a number on the house telephone then waited.

'Centrelink, how can I help you.' The voice on the other end was human.

Tracey tried to control her breathing. 'Hi. Can I speak with someone about the Family Carers Allowance?'

'Sure. Putting you through.'

Seconds passed. Tracey shuffled nervously in her chair. Officers Gates and Harris were long gone and she had moved to the upright comfort of the kitchen table. Cups and plates lay unwashed around her but she wasn't interested in doing any cleaning. She only had money on her mind.

The purring tones of a ringing phone put her on alert. 'Family Benefits,' said a short, sharp, female voice.

'Hi. I have a question about the Family Carers Allowance?'

'Fire away,' replied the woman.

Tracey didn't mince her words. 'If someone's children were kidnapped and disappeared on the other side of the world, would they still receive their allowances?'

'That's a big if. Haven't been asked this one before,' said the clerk.

'I was just wondering.' Tracey steered clear of accepting too much responsibility for the question. 'It's for a story I'm writing.'

'You're an author?'

'Yes.'

'How exciting. Well then, let's see. Are the police going to be aware of the disappearance?'

'Yes. I mean they would be told straight away and a search would begin.'

'And this is for both benefits A and B we're talking about?'

'Yes, both of them.' Gary and Tracey had been on the receiving end of tens of thousands of dollars, all of it deposited into their accounts, courtesy of the Australian Government. The payments started when the kids were born and Tracey loved lining up at the bank every Tuesday to withdraw the cash. They weren't what you would call financially astute and had grown to depend on this cash injection as much as the ants crawling across her counter depended on her penchant for filthy dishes.

The news from the police had concerned her. Would the events of the last few days affect the flow of money now that the kids were overseas and officially missing? The nice lady at Centrelink was being very helpful.

'If the police have launched an investigation,' said the clerk, 'and if that investigation was ongoing and not solved or closed at any time in the first three years then the payments would continue to flow for all of that time.'

'For three years? said Tracey, searching for clarification. She had been burned by the white-collar workers of Centrelink before and knew that sometimes what they said on the phone was different to what they told you in person.

'Yes,' replied the clerk. 'And then at the end of three years, if the case is still unsolved, then a lump sum equal to six months of the A and B payment would be released to the parents before the allowance was cancelled.'

'A lump sum?' Tracey could not hide the smile in her voice. 'About how much is that?' Tracey wasn't one to budget. Grand totals were what she liked.

'That depends on the benefit being received. But an average individual could be looking at around fifteen thousand dollars.'

'Wow?'

'That's each parent.'

'Bloody hell!'

'Is that good news for your story?'

'It's better than I'd hoped,' smiled Tracey as she did a little jiggle on her chair, her mind dizzy with delight.

'Was that all miss?' asked the clerk.

'Yes, thank you very, very much.' Tracey put down the receiver and burst with joy. 'Fuck yeah, fuck yeah,' she sang, getting to her feet and completing a little dance upon the patterned linoleum. She skipped out of the kitchen and up the hallway.

'Gary,' she yelled. 'Wake up you little mad man. It's time to celebrate.' She turned into the lounge room and knelt down beside the couch. She reached underneath the frame and dragged out the bottle of vodka. She reached under again, remembering the earlier clink of glass and pulled out a half bottle of Jim Beam. Tracey smiled like she hadn't done for a long time. Life, she felt, had just turned a bloody big corner and all the dark clouds that had been hovering were clearing away to reveal a ray of light.

'Gary,' she yelled impatiently, climbing to her feet and falling back upon the worn cushions of the three-seater. 'Get in here. We've got some drinking to do.'

Tracey unscrewed the lid on the vodka and took a swig straight from the bottle. Her mouth was a patchwork quilt of stained teeth, a spill of vodka dripping from between her lips.

'What are you yelling about?' grumbled Gary as he stepped in through the lounge door, wearing nothing but a stained pair of jocks.

'Get dressed you fat fucker,' laughed Tracey. 'We just won lotto!'

'We don't even play it.'

'We do now. And the gods are smiling on us.'

Gary scratched his balls. 'I don't know what the hell you're going on about. I'm going back to bed.' Gary shuffled back up the hallway and closed the bedroom door.

'Party pooper.' She gave the hallway the finger. 'Means there's more for little old me,' sang Tracey as she closed her eyes and took another swig from the bottle.

32

2:00PM AWST
ATHENS

The first rays of the morning sun crept over the peak of Mt Lycabettus and cascaded down upon the six-lane avenue of Dimitry. The Gates of Apollo loomed large as the red Citroen glided by, ancient history watching over present-day Athens. The streets were already busy as yellow taxis veered from lane to lane, their drivers with a morning coffee in one hand and the steering wheel in the other.

Jess kept her tired eyes peeled for the large green road signs she had been tracking since she crossed over into the birthplace of truth and democracy some two hours ago. It was here that civilisations first started philosophising about the morality of right and wrong. Jess would have welcomed their advice, the conflictions of her own morality continuing to drive her to distraction.

The children were looking good, both wide eyed and engrossed in this strange new world. A mysterious place far from the suburban streets of home.

Sleep had come easily amid the space and comfort of the back seats and now that they were well rested, the events of last two days had eased to the backs of their minds.

'This place is awesome,' said Jacob. 'Can we get out and explore?'

'Not today,' said Jess. 'Maybe another time. It sure is a beautiful city.'

'Why all the columns?'

'They were part of the temples, built to honour the gods that lived here.'

'Like Jesus?' asked Jacob.

'No, these gods were Greek. They lived on Mt Olympus with names like Zeus and Apollo. They fought many wars. It was the original battleground between good and evil.'

Jess felt a strong connection with Greece's tumultuous past and having carried her guilt here, she hoped to discard it once and for all on the ancient ruins scattered throughout this amazing country. Greece had been subjected throughout history to conquest and occupation. Ripped apart by the outside forces of hate, jealousy and greed, the weakness of its geographic make-up meant that the islands were almost indefensible. For how do you protect a country so fragmented and disparate?

It was this very characteristic that had drawn Jess here. Disappearing within such a puzzling jigsaw of disjointed islands appeared as simple as attacking it.

She steered the hire car toward the intersection ahead, a maze of overhead wires allowing the traffic lights to float above the traffic. She took a right turn past a derelict building, its cracked and decaying concrete façade making it a modern-day ruin. The road ahead was gridlocked and noisy, horns blaring, drivers yelling. Four-storey buildings bordered both sides of the road, her eyes directed toward a skyline dominated by two huge ocean ferries, their sterns rising high above the street, dwarfing everyone and everything around them.

Jess allowed the Citroen to crawl forward, the symphony of engines echoing off the concrete buildings. More boats appeared as the horizon widened, the sheer width of their girths throwing the streets below into shadow.

A procession of ticket booths were already abuzz with people, this human flood of travellers a daily occurrence. Foreigners hauled huge suitcases, while locals on mopeds zig-zagged their way through the traffic. The only slice of sanity appeared to rest upon the decks of the white and blue hulled ferries, small pockets of onlookers smiling down from above at the turmoil of this crazy world below them.

Vehicles poured into the hulls of the boats, queues having formed in every direction. This was the organised chaos the Greeks were famous for and Jess tried to relax, recalling her first visit to these shores almost twenty years prior. Back then it was just as vibrant and colourful and her time here had taught her to let such events take their natural course.

'Are we travelling on one of those?' asked Jacob, pointing at the huge ferries.

'Yes, we are,' said Jess. 'Pretty cool, hey.'

'Sure is big.'

'Bigger than me,' said Lisa, and they laughed.

Jess hustled the Citroen into the long line of cars boarding the Blue Star Delios. She had purchased tickets to this ferry online in Perth. The Internet had made this whole caper so much easier. No face-to-face interaction. It was easier to lie using words typed on a computer screen; their false names requiring no authentication.

She rolled her window down and handed the tickets to a handsome young sailor. He tore the printed dockets in two and returned them, directing Jess into the hull of the ship.

The ramp ahead was swaying upon the ocean swell and she revved her engine and calmly negotiated the challenge it presented. The gradient of the flattened steel door rose and fell and Jess ignored the fear she felt and drove on, up and into the rear of the hull. Hundreds of vehicles were already squeezed in like tin cans. Jess took her place beside a small truck.

She switched the car off and opened her door. The children followed her, stepping free from the constraints of the hire car, eager to stretch their legs after twenty-five hours of driving. The swaying motion of the ocean vessel made standing difficult, Lisa and Jacob laughing as they came to grips with its effects. Lisa felt like she'd just stepped off a rollercoaster. Jacob held his little sister's hand. She was smiling and that made him happy.

Jess pulled a small suitcase from the boot. She locked the car and knelt beside the kids. 'You okay?' she asked.

A nod from the children was enough.

'Now we're going to find a seat on the top deck. Let's hold hands all the way.' They linked arms and worked their way between the maze of cars. The other passengers were disappearing out through a narrow steel doorway in the far corner and that is where they headed.

3:00PM AWST

The Blue Star ferry chugged away from the harbour, the concrete platforms below still bustling with activity. Lisa and Jacob pressed their bodies against the steel rails of the upper deck and watched as the people on the docks got smaller and smaller. The city of Athens stretched itself out into a sprawl of white buildings and marbled monuments, a mass of man-made structures, broken only by the blue sky above.

Lisa and Jacob were becoming accustomed to saying goodbye to new towns and cities and the shrinking ancient metropolis of Athens quickly became just another stop on the road to somewhere new. The people of Perth were also receding from their minds, the excitement of the here and now dominating their thoughts, saturating their minds with a mixture of aromas and emotions.

'Can we go exploring around the boat,' asked Jacob, the mainland having long disappeared over the horizon, a swathe of blue ocean surrounding them on all sides.

'Great idea,' said Jess. 'Let's go.'

The Blue Star Delios had four levels with a total length of one hundred and thirty metres. It was busy, yet still relatively spacious, the hectic heights of the summer season still a few months away. Plush carpets and polished marble adorned every surface. People reclined in padded leather chairs, all eyes trained on the big television screens fixed to the walls of each section.

Glass-walled gift shops sold irreverent mementos and knick-knacks, from miniature statues of the Acropolis to shiny collections of historically inspired snow domes. Lisa smiled as a Jacob upended a Mount Olympus themed dome sending white powder floating down over the miniature Gods spread around the mountain's base.

Jacob bit into a sugar-frosted donut, the warm Mediterranean air combining nicely with the aroma of freshly baked dough. Lisa and Jess sat opposite him, huddled together around an outside table on the rear deck, a chocolate croissant also vying for their attention. They were finally realising the promise their teacher had made to them three days ago, the amazing blue ocean massaging their minds, persuading them to bathe in its beauty.

6:00PM AWST

It was another three hours before the box-like white buildings of Paros came into view. The ferry continued to cruise upon a calm sea of glass, navigating its way around the southern tip of the island harbour, four massive wind turbines standing on the cape like white-coated guardians.

Lisa and Jacob watched as the terrain of the island rose from the ocean like a mountain range. Perth was very flat and very different from the steep inclines of this island. Paros appeared to surge from the water, its white sandy beaches a soft edge to the slate and marble-strewn topography that reached skyward. The children leant forward on the railing and stared out at this strange new world.

The harbour town of Parikia came into view as the late morning sun reflected powerfully off its lime-washed buildings. Small white houses dotted the rolling hills above, these modest structures already hinting at a simpler life. Closer to the centre of town, the buildings crowded on top of each other. This was the beating heart of Paros, where the port sprang to life, its streets crowned from behind by the towering slopes of Mount Profitis Ilias, its rocky peak smattered with shadows.

Jess stared at the familiar sight of the port windmill and beamed with joy, the satisfaction of a triumphant return filling her heart with happiness. She spied a large white church named Agios Konstantinos, its religious iconography unmistakable, high above the promenade of shops and restaurants that ran along the coast. It was a dominant site from which the parish priest could overlook his people, asserting moral order with a prevailing eye. Jess had already decided that she and the children would be attending services there every Sunday. Lisa and Jacob had attended the Marvale Uniting Church when they were younger and she felt it was important to reignite a lost family tradition.

The Community and Services Act 2004 – Principle (i) decisions about a child should be consistent with cultural, ethnic and religious values and traditions relevant to the child.

Further back from the coast and to the left was the red-tiled roof of the Church of a Thousand Doors. It was more of a tourist attraction than a working place of worship but directly behind it was the local school where Jess had already enrolled Jacob and Lisa. It lay tucked away deep in the soul of this historic civilisation and Jess looked forward to making a fresh connection with a new teaching institution, one far removed from the system she had rebelled against.

The Community and Services Act 2004 – Principle (h) decisions about a child should be made promptly having regard to the age, characteristics, circumstances and needs of the child.

It had been easy for Jess to imagine a new life here and now, and as the water below them changed from the deep blue of the ocean to the lighter shade of shallower waters, the same sunlight that illuminated the sea, made its way into Jess's heart, transforming this new future into a reality. The damaged parts of her life were being cast off as a fresh sense of life and opportunity flooded through her.

Lisa too felt the urge to smile. 'This is a very mysterious place,' she thought to herself, her mind lost in the wonder of it all.

Jacob watched a school of fish swimming alongside the boat. He had never been fishing yet loved to hear the stories his class mates often shared, expeditions with their fathers to beaches he had never heard of.

'Miss Bell, can we go fishing some time?' he asked, hope skipping from wave to wave, his confidence growing.

'Sure,' replied Jess. 'I didn't know you were interested in that sort of thing?'

'Sounds like fun,' he explained.

'I can't say I'll know what I'm doing, but we'll get some rods, find a good spot and give it a go.' This was a bright spark on a fresh horizon thought Jess, and it brought a smile from her young friend. 'We might even catch dinner,' she said and they laughed.

The ferry powered on through the natural inlet, its curves perfectly shaped for a harbour, the hills above providing protection from both the strong winds that blew here and the high seas of winter.

Jacob wondered what lay beyond the white buildings and how they were all connected to each other. Lisa thought about all the people who lived higher up on the side of the mountain and imagined meeting the princess who lived at the top.

Jess thought about the work that had gone into planning this journey, allowing tears of happiness to well up and over, sliding down her parched cheeks. She placed both her hands on top of the small fingers of her young charges as they gripped the railing together. They looked up at her and smiled and her senses made a permanent record of this moment, forever ensuring she could always relive it in a way that only senses can.

Her eyes saw a beautiful island that welcomed her with open arms.

Her ears heard the ocean breeze and the sound of foreign accents.

She could smell the exotic aromas where east meets west.

She could taste the salt of her tears. This she decided was the taste of happiness.

Lastly, she felt the two small hands that lay beneath hers. They were the reason for everything. They *were* everything.

This island was their new home.

'Welcome to Paros,' she told them and she meant it.

33

FRIDAY 19TH MAY
MARVALE PRIMARY SCHOOL

The fallout at school was massive and unavoidable. Seven days had passed and Charles De Gaulle Airport was still a dead end. Jess and the children had literally disappeared into thin air. So had the careers of a few of her colleagues.

Sujitha Tran and Amy Tanner had been fired, their licences to teach revoked indefinitely. They were hauled across the coals for not having alerted the office to the absence of Lisa Johnstone, in particular, as well as for keeping poor records of student attendance in general. This was seen as an early warning system that could have stopped Miss Bell from fleeing the country. There were no excuses provided and it was decided the women would have to carry some of the blame. Sujitha and Amy had grown tired of the unwanted attention and just wanted their names out of the headlines as quickly as possible.

Amy fled Perth to her family's holiday home in Dunsborough. She wanted to applaud Miss Bell's actions but knew her resume had been blighted by her associate's actions and so chose to disappear herself. Thoughts of a seachange crossed her mind.

Sujitha returned to her native Singapore to be with her disappointed parents. News had filtered back to concerned relatives who felt embarrassed by her poor work standards. Her proud parents saw this as a slight on the family name and summoned their daughter home to explain herself. Sujitha felt like a child again.

Miss Bell's contract was also terminated at both a school level and with the Education Department. A full investigation was ordered and pending her discovery, a criminal conviction would be sought on her return. This involved a mountain of paperwork but it had to be done so that another teacher could be brought in to replace her. All of her students were offered counselling, as were the teachers and education assistants of Marvale Primary School.

Yasmin Neates had weathered the initial storm and was offered the opportunity to rebuild and rebrand her damaged school. A name change would be the first item on the agenda, the Marvale brand stained beyond repair. Yasmin knew that a successful rejuvenation of her school would be another feather in her cap and thoughts of retirement were placed on the back burner.

Deputy Small wasn't so lucky. Three teachers were gone, now they needed an administrator to complete the set.

It happened two weeks later, one Friday afternoon, just as the school was winding down after another long week. Exhausted staff were escaping into the anonymity of the weekend. Rupert Small on the other hand didn't know what to do. He sat dejectedly at his desk, gazing off into space, consumed by the phone call he'd just received. The Minister for Education had personally informed him he would be suspended on full pay until his role in 'The Johnstone Affair' could be fully investigated. Why so much information about the students in question was accessed using his password and identification code was of particular concern. He had professed his innocence, which fell upon deaf ears. Neither Silver City nor the police were impressed with the value he had placed upon his own cyber security.

It would have seemed a harsh penalty if not for the fact that Rupert's record already had a few blemishes resulting from a short stint as a principal in a small country town. He'd mistakenly passed on the name of a female teacher responsible for reporting a case of child sexual abuse to the local family the claim was against. The woman in question had to flee for her life after she was hounded by the child's family, her windows smashed and a series of mailed death threats forcing her to leave town. Rupert had displayed a clear disregard for the security of such professional declarations and as a result had been demoted and hauled back to the city, his tail between his legs and his head in his hands. A brief battle with a mild case of depression had ensued which was also unfortunately recorded against his name. He had become a liability and the department wanted him gone.

Rupert's relationship with Yasmin had deteriorated rapidly as a result of the school-wide investigation and he knew that, whatever the outcome, he would not be returning under her stewardship. He needed a break but struggled with the fact that he might never clear his name. His family had been supportive but the isolation of his situation sucked him in and the black dog of his past reappeared. Darkness blurred his thinking and an immediate solution to all his problems came quickly to mind. He cleared his desk and left the building for the last time.

Two days later he was discovered in his car by his own children. The engine was on, a hose running from the exhaust and in through the car window. It was a traumatic incident that finally brought the school to its knees.

34

SATURDAY 27TH MAY
9:00AM AWST
DALTON CRESCENT

Gary's own snoring woke him up as usual. Two weeks and a day had passed since he'd last seen his children and life had been far from routine. Yet he was still unable to escape the tedious biological schedules that ruled his humdrum life. He hauled his weary body up off the makeshift bed he'd constructed using the kids' mattresses and shuffled out into the cluttered hallway. Tracey had kicked him out of their room, still angry he'd chosen not to celebrate the Centrelink news with her. Gary didn't feel very happy. He felt closer to the kids in their room, with their smells and their clothes.

He tip-toed quietly up the hall, passed Tracey who was still snoozing off another night at the casino. He eased into the kitchen, his right arm reaching out for the pack of cancer sticks lying dormant on the laminate covered island bench. There was one cigarette left.

The light of the day could already be measured through the opaque windows of the front door. This was a Perth morning without daylight saving. Gary had voted for it in the referendum of 2002. Hated having to squint so early in the morning. Openly 'loathed the fuckers' who voted against it. He'd been on the losing side once again.

He thrust the retro silver handle down and pulled the front door inward. He had to shield his eyes, a burning sensation affecting the pocked skin of his face. This sudden burst of fresh air induced a yawn from between his nicotine stained teeth and his body began to awaken to the realities of his situation. The eerie silence of these early mornings encouraged a familiar weight to take up residence on his sagging shoulders.

He lowered his aching body onto the top step and sat down. The front yard and road beyond it were static. Jacob and Lisa would normally be up as well and he missed the sound of the whining that always greeted him. Not that he took much notice of them before. Now they were gone, though, it all felt different and their absence pained him. 'Bitch,' he thought to himself.

He was hankering for a fag and upended the pack, jolting the lonely brown stick of nicotine free from the crumpled foil that encased it. He slid it between his fingers and flicked a flame from his lighter. He sucked hard, his first drag of the morning, a fresh coating of tar lining the fragile inner tubes of a broken man.

The high-pitched whine of a 50cc engine broke the unwanted serenity of Dalton Crescent, a red and white scooter skipping into view, a brightly dressed postman driving along the footpath. He didn't notice Gary, who had been rendered almost invisible by the coffee coloured robe he wore amid the backdrop of mission brown bricks. The entrance to the house was a recessed nook and Gary kept as still as a skink. He was getting good at going undetectable. Liked it much better than the attention he'd been subjected to of late. The response hadn't been kind. He was better off unseen.

The postie pulled to a halt beside the letterbox. He looked at the registered mail in his hand then looked up at the house. A light trail of smoke gave Gary's position away.

'Excuse me,' shouted the postie, 'Is your name Gary Johnstone?'

A nod.

'Mate, I need your signature for this one.'

'Well I ain't moving.'

The postie hated the attitude he got from some of the people around here but knew better than to piss off a customer. He twisted the accelerator and sped up the long, straight pathway toward the front door. Gary snickered at his poor excuse for a motorbike. Practicalities weren't part of Gary's world-view. 'If it didn't have any grunt, then it was for girls.'

The postie skidded to a stop at the base of the steps and passed Gary a clipboard and a pen. 'Just beside your name thanks,' he directed, a finger clearly outlining the empty box.

Gary scribbled across the rectangle and handed it back.

'Thanks pal.' The postie slotted it all in the basket across his handlebars and quickly completed a U-turn on the grass. He raced back across the lawn and pulled up beside the letterbox.

'Just in here then?' he asked, the mail still in his hand. He slid the solitary item in through the slot. Gary's eyebrows furrowed. The postie knew what he was doing. Wasn't going to make it that easy for the lazy bastard at number ten.

'Fuck you!' said Gary.

The postie grinned as he sped off. Got his way in a roundabout fashion. 'A win's a win in these parts.'

Gary allowed his anger to simmer in the hot sun. After the last few weeks he had appreciated the concept that no news was good news. It had become a favourite slogan of his. This new piece of mail did not fit that rule, but his interest had been piqued and as soon as the postie had accelerated out of sight, Gary got to his feet and crept gingerly down the steps to the pathway.

He hobbled toward the gate like a man approaching seventy. Took him all of a minute to travel the thirty metres required. He lifted the small metal door at the rear of the letterbox and reached in. It was a post card. He flipped it over and gazed at the picture on the front. A photo of a tropical beach covered one whole side with the words 'Dazzling Dubai' emblazoned across the top left corner. Gary didn't know anyone who lived there. Didn't really know anyone who'd ever left the country. Except for his kids of course. Where was Dubai anyway? World geography wasn't his strong point.

The Community and Services Act 2004 – Principle (k) a child's parents and any other people who are significant in the child's life should be given adequate information, in a manner and language that they can understand.

He spun the card over and scanned the neat hand writing. Someone had a lot to say and so he started reading it.

Dear Gary and Tracey,

By now you must have realised that I have taken your children. I know it will come as a shock and you may never get over it but I will not be bringing them back in the foreseeable future. I am sorry that it has come to this but I tried everything and everyone else without success.

I don't doubt that you once loved your children but as parents you are failures. You neglected and abused Lisa and Jacob daily and I could not stand by and watch it continue anymore. I had nightmares that I would wake up one day to news of their death at your hands.

The teacher's code states that you should always act with the best interests of the child and that is exactly what I have done. It took me two long years to get to this stage and I have covered every angle and catered for every possibility. Please do not try to find us. I will keep you updated on Lisa and Jacob's progress once a year via a postcard just like this. Please contain your anger in the knowledge that your children are safe and happy.

Yours sincerely,
Miss Jessica Bell

Gary sucked the last bit of life from the end of his fag, then blew smoke out of his mouth until a veil of white haze surrounded him. His world was clouded and uncertain. He felt anger rising from within and he clenched his jaw, his lips starting to wobble like jelly.

'You little bitch. I'll get you if it's the last thing I do!'

He drove the butt of his cigarette hard into the rusted surface of the letter box lid until it crumbled to the ground in a pile of nicotine tinged ashes.

PART TWO

TEN YEARS LATER

35

WEDNESDAY 17th SEPTEMBER 2015
3:00PM CET (CENTRAL EUROPEAN TIME)
PAROS ISLAND

The copper bell atop the Church of Aghios Fokas swung from side to side. The clamour of metal on metal rang out across the rocky cape, a flock of Yellow Legged Seagulls scattering into the air, seeking refuge in the sky above the still waters of the crescent shaped harbour. The birds regrouped and headed east, up along the coast and away from the chiming bellows of prayer.

They followed the gentle curves of the bay, white sandy beaches emerging from pristine blue water. A sealed road hugged the coast like a border, separating the ocean from the rolling fields above. The land was parched and dry after a long hot summer, each plot separated by long meandering walls of stacked slate, the hillside resembling a patchwork quilt of sunburnt browns.

Clusters of boxlike buildings dotted the land, their white walls reflecting the sun's rays with intensity and glare. The cool blue tiles of a swimming pool graced many of the boutique hotels and homes popular on this side of the island, tanned bodies bathing in loungers, soaking up the afternoon sun whilst also taking in the breathtaking views across the harbour toward Parikia.

A light breeze drifted down the hillside, blowing away the

cobwebs of the afternoon, carrying with it the fresh aroma of the wheat farms to the north. The gulls lowered their altitude as the land below them flattened out, the popular beaches of Marcelo and Krios packed with the post siesta crowd, electronic music drifting from the boho beach bars and out across the sand.

Krotiri Road snaked like an artery between the town and the beaches, twisting and turning with the curves of the coastline, buzzing with the sound of vehicles. Scooters raced around blind corners, whilst hire cars navigated their way carefully up and down the narrow confines of this very old road.

The land hooked right, running toward a jagged point, before the coastline spiked back like a bite mark in the hill, a set of Sandstone cliffs thrusting themselves from the water. The birds flew out across this rocky outcrop, high above the Cabana Beach Bar and on towards the beaches of Blue Bay and Livadia. The water was shallower here, a protected haven for the smaller yachts anchored just off shore.

The beach volleyball courts of the western end of Tango Mar were busy too, the seagulls drifting above the thump, thump of balls, before they headed down toward the gathered buildings of the busy port town. Here the coastal promenade of Christoi Knostavtopoiloi kept the Aegean Sea at bay, a low sea wall protecting the white washed buildings from any tidal excess. An eclectic mix of restaurants and gift shops welcomed the afternoon trade, having earlier fallen quiet with the expectations of *mesimeri*.

Holidaymakers filled the slate paved streets, flitting from shop to shop, snapping up last-minute bargains, ensuring another season finished with a flourish. Contented shop owners chatted warmly, the riches of another good summer filling both their hearts and pockets.

The gulls continued to skirt the breeze, avoiding the larger masts of the yachts and launches moored within the marina, each boat tethered to the wooden jetty by a single rope. The birds drifted left, across the medical centre, above a small garden of trees; a welcome reprieve from the vast swathes of concrete that dominated.

The imposing architecture of The Church of a Thousand Doors loomed up ahead, the deep orange hue of its old clay tiles visible for miles around. Its ancient arched tiles created a gorgeous contrast against the smooth rendered surface of the white bell tower soaring high above. The gulls took refuge within the shadows of the overhanging lemon trees, planted to softened the Byzantine chapel's central square.

Surrounding the church were the wide-open spaces of the piazza, its large marble tiles cascading across the floor.

Behind the chapel, a narrow pathway leading to a set of stone stairs. A source of interest for curious sightseers, it lures them up toward the centuries-old entrance of the local high school. Two wrought iron gates framed the gorgeous gardens which surrounded the school. A light trail of young voices reverberated across the basketball court beyond, this two-story building busy with afternoon classes.

Several large windows flooded the classrooms with light, the students well dressed and fashionable. Packed classes discussed subjects and debated opinions, the flow of their native tongue broken only by the chorus of laughter. A young woman at the front of a class, her small desk a cluttered mass of books, her eyes focused on her teacher, his hands as expressive as his words.

'Romaios skotothike apo enan filo,' he explained. *Romeo was killed by a friend.* He waited for his words to sink in. 'I Loulieta pire ti diki tis zoi, alla giati? Giati to ekane?' *Juliet took her own life, but why? Why did she do it?*

The woman thrust her right hand into the air. She was beautiful, her blonde hair a mass of sundrenched wild curls, a short tartan skirt and plain white t-shirt strikingly youthful. The old disguises of the past had long been forgotten. Little Lisa Johnstone had grown up.

'Nai Zetta,' said her teacher. *Yes Zetta?* He referred to her by a different name. A straight translation from English to Greek.

'Giati ton agapise,' she said. *That's because she loved him.* 'Den eiche alli epilog.' *She had no choice.* That gentle, raspy voice the only vestige of an old life, her Greek perfectly delivered.

'Yparchei panta epilog,' said the teacher. *There is always choice.*

'Romeo was dead,' said Zetta. 'What else could she do?'

'Go on a date with someone else instead?' interrupted the boy to her right.

'He was her life. She didn't want a replacement.'

'Neither do I,' continued the boy. 'Will you go out with me Zetta, please.'

'In your dreams, Gino.'

'You're already in those.' His classmates laughed, a smile from Zetta affording him some comfort.

'And that's where I'll stay, thank you,' she replied.

Gino slid from his chair and knelt on the floor. 'Where for art thou kind heart?'

The scream of the school siren left his question unanswered. Zetta lifted her backpack off the floor and pushed the pile of books inside.

'Kali apogevmatini taxi,' said the teacher above the noise. *Good afternoon class*. 'Kalo savvatokyriako.' *Have a nice weekend.*

'Kalo Kyrios Anagnos,' yelled the students above the din.

The corridor outside the classroom was suddenly flooded with students, their chatter and clatter bouncing off the dark grey lockers that lined both sides. Zetta jostled her way between their juvenile bodies and opened her locker. She shoved a thick pile of books upon its narrow shelves and looked up the corridor. Her gorgeous green eyes sparkled with life, evidence of the spirit that was alive and free.

A young woman stepped in beside her and smiled. 'Geia sou Zetta.' *Hello Zetta.*

'Geia sou Carissa,' said Zetta. 'Skopevete stin plateia apopse?' *What are you doing this weekend?*

'Fysika kai eimai,' replied Carissa. *I'm working most of Saturday.* She, too, wore a simple plain t-shirt and a short, patterned skirt, her long dark ponytail bouncing from side to side with her words.

'Do you want to come to the beach?' asked Zetta. 'We're spending the afternoon at Paros Poros.'

'Okay,' said Carissa. 'I've already got my bathers underneath.'

She hoisted her skirt up one leg, revealing a pair of black bikini bottoms underneath. An admirer whistled as he walked past. Carissa dropped her skirt, embarrassed but smiling.

'You always wear your bikinis to school?' asked Zetta.

'Only on Fridays. It's always beach time one way or another.'

Zetta closed her locker and strode up the hallway with her friend. They stepped through a set of double doors out into the sunshine and descended the stone stairs that lead to the main gate.

A small blue Mini Cooper sparkled amidst the dust covered cars parked across the road. Zetta waved and smiled.

A young man, seated behind the driving wheel, waved back. His long dark hair and tan could not cover those honest eyes of ten years ago. Jacob Johnstone was no longer a child, dark stubble on his chin, a simple black t-shirt showing off a pair of strong arms, the word CHAOS emblazoned across his chest. Beside him another boy, his best friend Anton, playing with the volume, music oozing from the car speakers. Jacob watched as the girls navigated the steps.

'Is Carissa coming as well?' asked Anton.

'Etsi fainetai,' said Jacob. *Looks like it.* His voice was strong and deep, his Greek very smooth.

'Here's your chance. You really should tell her...'

Jacob turned and scolded his friend. 'Not now, alright.'

Zetta leaned in through the passenger window. 'Hi bro, Hi Anton. You guys ready to go?'

'Neh,' said her brother. 'Jump in.'

The girls opened the rear doors and climbed onto the back seat.

'Hi Iakovos, hi Anton,' said Carissa. Jacob's name was also different. It suited him. Pronounced Ya-ko-vos, it was strong like him.

Carissa pulled the door closed and the mini accelerated away.

Anton turned and faced the girls. 'How's your mum and dad's bar going Carissa?'

'Great. It's been a very good season.'

'I've hardly seen you around all summer.'

'I worked almost every day. Made a tonne of money, so I don't mind.'

'I wish mum would let me get a job,' said Zetta.

'Not now school's back,' said Iakovos. 'You're only a few weeks into your last year and you can't afford to mess it up.'

'She's just comparing me to you. It's so unfair.'

'I only finished top of my class because mum made me study so much.'

'And still you work nights in a bar.'

'Because I choose to, not because I have to.'

Carissa and Anton watched the banter between brother and sister like they were watching a game of ping pong.

'Carissa's getting great marks and she's got a job,' said Zetta.

'She works for her parents,' replied Iakovos. 'It's different.'

'You sound like mum.'

'I can set you up with some after-hours lessons teaching English.'

'And be a part-time tutor like you, no way.'

'You could tutor me,' said Carissa. 'English is one area where I could do better.'

'You're my friend,' said Zetta. 'That would be too weird.'

'Iakovos can tutor you Carissa,' said Anton with a smile.

Iakovos gave him a wicked stare.

'Sure. That would be great,' said Carissa.

'Not sure you'd get much work done,' giggled Zetta.

Carissa and Iakovos both turned red.

'Human Biology is one of Iakovos's favourite subjects,' laughed Anton, before he was thumped in the arm by a wayward fist. 'Ouch!'

'You want to get dropped off here?' said Iakovos.

'No thanks,' said Anton. 'Just having a joke.'

'Not funny.'

The Mini left the school car park and pulled out into Perifereiaki Road. This stretch of tarseal was the backbone of the old town, always busy with cars, trucks and scooters, zig zagging their way off in every direction, keeping the port town alive and happy.

Iakovos steered the car past the old church and up toward the clifftop road with its views toward Butterfly Valley. The traffic thinned out, the buildings either side slowly shrinking in both size and number, gradually giving way to the hay-filled fields of a small farming community.

The mini crossed a low-slung bridge before indicating right and pulling off the main road, down into a dry river bed which led to the coast. It was a particular feature of Paros, these natural land forms often used as access routes during the summer season. A quicker route than the road that looped its way around the coast, these short cuts become very popular once the rainy season has ended.

The teenagers jolted their way toward the beach, the Mini's suspension unable to suppress the bounce of the uneven surface.

'I'm so hungry,' said Zetta. 'Are we staying for dinner?'

'No. I think mum's booked us into Evinos,' said Iakovos. 'It's fireworks night, remember.'

'Of course. I completely forgot about the festival.'

'Don't let Mum know.'

'The festival was only created to keep the tourists happy,' said Anton.

'Yeah, but it's a personal milestone for us,' said Iakovos. 'We arrived here just over ten years ago. Moved into the mountain house pretty much straight away. It was and always will be a very emotional day for our mother.'

'The fireworks go off and so does she,' said Zetta.

'Your Mum loves a good party,' said Carissa. 'It's why I like her so much.'

The Mini zipped in between a narrow gap in a low stone wall to the right. Ahead of them was a large sand covered car park. Iakovos guided the car up beside a large stone taverna.

The four friends strolled across the grass-covered bank situated just in front of the open-air restaurant and past a large wine barrel. The familiar sounds of Radio Active spilled out from the bar to their right, large blooms of pink bougainvillea wrapped around the white wooden beams of a pergola. Small groups of people lounged across a mix of chairs and tables, food and drink being enjoyed under the shade of this bushy green arbor.

A raised hand, then a wave from beneath the trees just in front of the taverna. A woman surrounded by towels, all draped neatly across the sand like a carpet of colour.

Zetta waved back and smiled. 'Usual spot, of course.'

The woman on the beach stepped forward as the children approached.

'You came,' she said, her arms spread, that slender frame unchanged if not better than a decade earlier. Jessica Bell looked great, the plunging neckline of her black one piece adding glamour to a stripped back physique most women would die for.

'Of course we did,' said Zetta. 'It's our special day.'

'How could we forget,' grinned Iakovos. They all hugged in a triangle of warmth.

'Hi Carissa, hi Anton' said Jess, peeking across her children's shoulders.

'Hi Yiskah,' they replied. Another new name, a beautiful sound for a beautiful woman. A straight translation of Jessica into Hebrew *(Yiska)*.

Zetta and Carissa undressed, their bikinis showing off tanned and toned bodies, so similar in shape they could be twins. Iakovos shed his t-shirt to reveal a muscled torso, his skin a golden brown. Anton too, his body a skinnier version of his good mate.

The five of them ran toward the water together, a race that screamed of a ritual, bodies bounding past the thatched umbrellas and diving into the clear blue water of the bay. White water crashed over them, the larger waves a particular feature of this horse-shoe shaped bay.

Ten minutes later and they were exhausted, milling around in shallower water.

'Do you remember our first day at this beach?' asked Yiskah.

'Yes, we'd only been here a few weeks,' said Iakovos. 'I think a friend from school wanted to meet here.'

'That's right,' said Yiskah. 'You were still quite small and I had to come and make sure you were safe.'

'Which meant I had to come as well,' said Zetta.

'We did everything together back then,' said Yiskah.

'We still do,' said Zetta.

'You're both getting older. You don't need me as much.'

'We'll always need you,' said Iakovos.

'I hope so. I know I'll always want you around.'

'Did you book Evinos?' asked Zetta, trying to change topics.

'Yes, for eight-thirty. I'll try to close the gallery early if I can.'

'Ta pota einai etoima,' called a voice. *Drinks are ready*. The family looked back to see Anton beneath the trees, a full tray of beers and cocktails in his hands.

'I'll race ya,' said Iakovos.

Zetta was off before she'd even answered, a head-start on her brother a definite advantage. Yiskah watched them go, strong feelings of pride churning through her. Her family as perfect as it had ever been. A decade of happiness. New names, new lives, a wonderful existence in a new world.

The sun was poised behind her, ready to begin its final descent. Yiskah's time had also come. She was a very happy woman right here, right now but she knew her own natural cycle was coming to a close. There was still work to be done and nothing could be guaranteed. Not even love.

36

7:55PM CET
PAROS ISLAND

The white crested waves of Paros Poros rippled across the canvas, a lavish layering of oils creating a multi-coloured patchwork of light and dark. The thick brush strokes of the sun blazed down upon the beach, its orange hues tinting a sky that was as empty of clouds as the sand was of people. A light olive wood frame encased the artwork, its position fixed high against a white rendered wall.

An older woman gazed at it from just a metre away. 'It's beautiful.'

'Yes, it is,' said Yiskah, stepping in beside her. 'The artist was in her element when she painted it. One of her favourite places in the world.'

'She has a soft touch, a playfulness that says anything is possible.'

'That certainly was her approach to life.'

The woman turned. 'You sound like you know her.'

'She is my daughter.'

'How wonderful. You must be so proud.'

'Yes, I am. She painted this a few years ago. Yet nothing else since.'

'What a shame. Does she live here on Paros?'

'Yes. She is a few years older now of course. More constrained. She knows how the world works. The innocence of this painting is long gone.'

'Innocence is so fleeting. Which makes this a very rare painting indeed.'

'It's definitely one of her best.'

'Is it for sale?'

'Everything is for sale,' smiled Yiskah.

'I'll buy it.'

'Don't you want to know the price?'

'No. It is worth any price. I buy paintings for the stories behind them. The work itself is important but the person behind it is the heart.'

'I agree. It's where the soul of the piece comes from. The truth.'

A white card beside the painting explained its detail. 'That's its title. The Truth. How beautiful.'

Yiskah smiled. 'Shall I wrap it up for you?'

'Efharisto. *Thank you.*'

Yiskah lifted the painting off its hook. She turned and carried it toward a large wooden desk in the far corner of the gallery. The walls surrounding her were filled with paintings, soft white light cascading down from the chrome fixtures in the ceiling.

'Here's my details should you need anything else,' said Yiskah, her customer accepting a blue business card, the words White Island Blue Art Gallery emblazoned like snow across the front and below it the name Yiskah Apostilides.

A man stepped in through the front door of the shop. He saw Yiskah and waved. She smiled back, her hands continuing to wrap the painting. The man wandered over to the nearest corner and looked at some of the work, his blue linen shirt untucked, atop faded blue jeans and brown sandals. His attire hinted at the warmth of the night. His smile hinted at love.

'Thank you so much,' said the woman as she accepted the painting.

'Efharisto,' said Yiskah.

She watched as her last customer of the night stepped out

through the main doors of the gallery, a pair of arms surprising her from behind, wrapping themselves around her stomach.

The man with the smile kissed her neck. 'Yassas, my darling.'

'Yassas,' she said, spinning round and meeting his lips with hers.

'You made a sale?'

'Yes. One of Zetta's. I think that lady was from Australia.'

'What a coincidence.'

'She was very nice.'

'All you Aussies are.' Another kiss. 'Are you ready to go?'

'Of course. I'll cash up the till.' She turned and glided across the bare wooden floors. The gallery was a classic take on Greek style, the white washed walls and bare oak floors, allowing the art to take centre stage.

He followed her across the room. 'The children said the sunset was glorious.'

'Yes, it was pretty special,' replied Yiskah.

'You should have called me. I would have finished early.'

'I'm sorry, but you know how I feel about today.' She turned to face him. 'It was the beginning of a journey. A new start for me and the children. A moment for us.'

'And tonight?' he asked.

'Tonight is a celebration for all of Paros.'

'When we thank God for your arrival and prey that you will never leave.'

'Why would I ever want to do that?' Yiskah kissed him again. 'Thank you Kosta, for putting up with my little rituals.'

He stepped forward and grabbed her around the waist. 'It is I who have needed you most. Thank you for always inspiring me. Making me the best I can be.'

They pulled the large wooden doors of the gallery shut. The sounds of night followed the two lovers down the slate-hewn path toward the ocean. They walked hand in hand down Market Street and up the steps that led to the old castle ruins.

'I never get bored of walking up here at night,' said Yiskah. 'It's so tranquil, so old.'

'Like we will be one day. Still here, walking hand in hand.'

'Oh, I hope so.'

'What do you see, when you look into our future?' asked Kosta.

'I never look too far ahead. It's bad luck.'

'Wouldn't you like to travel though. See another part of the world.'

'Of course I would.'

'But you never leave the island?'

'The right place, the right man, he could take me anywhere.'

Kosta smiled. 'I could see you in Scandinavia. Huge mountains and the softest snow everywhere.'

'Sounds tempting. Will you be there with me?'

'Of course I will.'

She laughed. 'Maybe next year then.'

Kosta stopped walking and Yiskah turned to face him. 'And what about us?' he said. 'Do you think we could ever live together?'

Yiskah stepped toward him, wrapping her arms around his waist and resting her head on his shoulder. 'You're full of questions tonight?'

'I'm excited. For you, for us. There are so many possibilities.'

Yiskah sighed. 'Zetta turns eighteen next weekend. My children will both be adults. I really haven't looked past that day yet.'

'They're practically adults already.'

'I know, but they're still my babies and probably always will be. I want to be there for them. To help them navigate the next chapter of their lives.'

'I wouldn't expect anything less. You are a wonderful mother. It's why I love you so much.' They kissed passionately against the white rendered walls of the old church.

They walked beneath an old wooden sign that read Evinos, then under a low archway and up a narrow set of white washed steps. The restaurant greeted them with open arms, its tables busy and the sound of music and voices melding as one. They shimmied past the first few tables and toward the far edge of the rooftop terrace. The night sky was already alive with stars, the ocean below, ablaze in the glow of the moon.

Zetta and Iakovos greeted them with a wave. The children sat side by side, their school friends around them and many adult guests as well, the table deep in conversation. There were two spare seats beside her children so Yiskah and Kosta slipped around to the other side of the table.

Yiskah kissed the top of her daughter's head. 'Yassas.'

'Yassas.'

The other guests looked up.

Yiskah kissed Iakovos on the cheek. Kosta greeted the others with a big hug.

'Great spot, Yiskah,' said a bearded man up the far end.

'We should do this every year,' said the woman beside him. 'It's crazy that we never thought of coming here before.'

'The children were smaller,' said Yiskah. 'They needed to run around.'

'Not any more,' the man said. 'Look how big they are now.'

A waitress placed a round of champagnes on the table.

Kosta stood. 'I propose a toast.'

Everyone took a glass and raised them into the air.

'To Yiskah, Iakovos and Zetta. You have made all our lives better. You are an inspirational family. Thank you for being part of our lives. We love you.'

The clink of glasses resounded across the table just as the first of the fireworks exploded across the sky. Cries of delight and surprise could be heard across the terrace, the night suddenly filled with light, sparks shooting into space, employing all the colours of the rainbow.

Kosta returned to his seat beside Yiskah and laid his arms gently around her shoulders. He stared up at the action above. Yiskah, though, was staring at her two children, the fireworks sending light dancing across their faces, memories of when they were little clouding her mind. Yiskah didn't know what she would ever do without them; feared that living would not be possible if they were no longer a part of her life.

Two hours later and the streets were still packed with hundreds of festival goers, all of them enjoying the warmth of night. A parade of bongo drummers strolled up the coastal promenade. Zetta and Carissa danced to their crazy beat, Iakovos and his mates clapping as the drums drew closer.

Yiskah and Kosta strolled several metres behind the youngsters, their arms entwined.

'Can you believe how much they've grown?' said Kosta. 'I've only known them for four years and they've changed my life.'

'These same streets welcomed us with open arms a decade ago. They were only this high.' She held a hand just above her hips. 'Now they tower over the both of us.'

'They look really happy.'

'The world is their oyster,' said Yiskah. 'It should be a happy time for everyone their age. On this island, I think it is even better.'

'They keep you young, you know that?'

'Yes, I do. I feed of their enthusiasm, their joie de vivre. They're so much fun to be around.'

Kosta and Yiskah watched them with a smile.

'Do you remember being eighteen?' asked Kosta.

'Not really,' said Yiskah. 'It went by in a blur.'

'I remember it well. I spent the summer here too. The freedom, the excitement. The world was opening up right in front of me.'

'I hope the children feel the same.'

'I'm sure they do.' Kosta kissed her head.

'It's getting late,' said Yiskah.

'It is. Are we still climbing the mountain tomorrow?'

'Of course we are. It's a family tradition.'

'We'll need some sleep.'

'A quick visit to the ice cream shop and then home.'

'Okay. Deal.'

They walked hand in hand, turning right and following the children into the smaller streets, the maze of white walls swallowing them whole.

37

THURSDAY 18th SEPTEMBER 2015
5:55AM CET
PAROS ISLAND

An electronic bleat pulled Kosta from his dreams. He tapped the top of the digital clock with his fingers. Yiskah stirred beside him.

'Time to get up,' he whispered, before kissing her bare shoulders.

Iakovos and Zetta stepped through the front door and grabbed one of the small backpacks Yiskah had prepared last night.

Kosta stepped down the front steps and into the orchard, Yiskah just a few steps behind him. The moon was strong, throwing light upon the olive trees, their long branches bending in the light breeze.

They emerged as a family, out onto the rocky mountain road that swept around the house. The view from here was inspiring, the land falling into a valley of shadows before soaring once again, up towards the peak of Mount Profitis Ilias.

They followed the road until it forked, taking a left turn up toward the nunnery, its two-metre-high walls strangely unwelcoming, a message to unwanted visitors or possible escapees. An old wrought-iron gate provided the only glimpse beyond the fortifications, a single lamp attached to a wall, light spilling across the front courtyard, the gardens impeccable, the silence complete. The building itself was in the style of old Greece, its ornate decoration a throwback to the past.

The road became increasingly overgrown, requiring their concentration; only a few houses left before the land became too steep to build on. Vehicles rarely came this far and the weeds were tall and strong.

Another kilometre and the road had disappeared altogether, lost beneath the forces of nature, a small goat track the only surviving pathway to the top. The ground underfoot was loose and every step had to be carefully placed, the earth likely to shift at any time.

'How's everyone going?' asked Kosta from the rear. They had to walk in line, one behind the other, no room for any passing manoeuvres.

'Fine,' said Iakovos. 'It's a gorgeous morning.' He was ahead of Kosta but behind Zetta.

'Is it morning? Or still the middle of the night?' said Zetta. 'The time is going past so quickly.'

Yiskah lead them. Her pace was good. 'It's nice to be up here again. The air is so clean.' She stopped and turned around. 'Look at that view.'

They all paused and turned. The scenery was breathtaking, the land falling away in all directions. The easy light of the moon providing a softness to the open canvas of fields and buildings, blurring the edges, allowing the features to glow in their own space.

To the right was the Marathi valley, its fields cascading down toward Piso Livadia and the open waters between the islands of Paros and Naxos. Straight ahead was their perfectly formed house, the land rising momentarily behind it before plummeting down towards the coastal towns of Naousa and Kolumbithres. To their left was the port town, the earth having manufactured a groove between the mountain peak and the smaller hills in the east, the ravine running all the way down to back streets of Parikia.

'Our house always looks so beautiful from here,' said Zetta.

Yiskah smiled. 'Do you remember coming up here the day after we moved in and we were like wow! Is that really our place?'

'We'd never seen Paros from this high up,' said Iakovos. 'The whole island looked incredible. Still does.'

'I think you are very lucky,' said Kosta. 'Many people have lived here and never known this view.'

Yiskah stepped from the goat track and onto the road which had ascended from the southern town of Aliki. Several satellite towers loomed high above the mountain. Their silence as ominous as the secret signals they carried. Just a few hundred meters more, past the old wind turbine and then up to the church.

The protective shield of the valley was long gone and the wind blew hard against their chests. The metal pylons started to creak as if they might bend and tumble to the ground at any time. Yiskah led everyone up around the security fence and toward the church. They went past the copper bell and around to the front entrance. A low wall bordered a small slate-paved courtyard, the views toward Mykonos incredible, the lines of visibility changing quickly with the growing light of a new day. The whole island could be seen from here, all three hundred and sixty degrees of glorious coastline.

This well-preserved church was a nod to the gods, for it was deemed to be the closest place to heaven. It was a tradition played out on most of the islands in Greece, the highest point of which was always referred to as Mount Profitis Ilias, a translation that literally meant 'Closest to God'.

'Who's got the paper?' asked Iakovos.

'I have.' Yiskah unzipped her backpack and slid out a thin wad of A4. The edge of the sheets flapped wildly in the wind. Yiskah turned her back to the breeze and handed them a sheet each. 'Don't forget to write down your hopes and dreams before you fold the paper. It's so much harder afterwards.' The methodical approach of a teacher alive and well inside of her.

Zetta pulled out a pen and looked to the horizon for inspiration.

'This is such a great idea, Iakovos,' said Kosta.

'Thanks. I've always loved origami and one year I brought up some paper. Thought it would be a great place to launch a paper plane.'

'You were right,' said Kosta.

'Yiskah thought about adding the words.'

'It's now a tradition,' said Zetta.

'And it works,' said Yiskah. 'Whatever you want removed from your life you write on the paper, fold it up into an airplane and throw if off the cliff. Voila, give it a few weeks and it will be gone.'

'Can I write smoking on it,' asked Kosta.

'Good idea,' said Zetta. 'I hate that smell.' They all laughed.

Yiskah sat a few metres away from the others. She scrawled the word 'secrets' on one side of the paper and 'lies' on the other. She never went for specifics. She liked the anonymity of general terms instead. Had always worried about what would happen if someone found her plane and traced it back.

Zetta carefully wrote out a whole sentence before realising the others had finished. She stood and folded her plane quickly. They all stood on the low wall, poised and ready to go.

'Okay,' said Iakovos. 'We throw on three.'

'One, two, three,' they all chanted in unison before launching their darts into the air. The planes flew, taking slightly different trajectories, the strong breeze driving them away from the walls of the church and down into the valley. The moonlight glinted upon their white wings, each plane floating for several seconds before eventually crashing unceremoniously to the ground. Flight time had been brief, but the symbolism was huge. They all felt a weight lifted off their shoulders.

Except for Yiskah. It had only reminded her of the work to come.

The sun peeked above the horizon, a slither of deep orange oozing from the ocean limits.

'Here comes the sun, doo doo doo doo' sang Zetta.

'Here comes the sun,' joined in the others, 'and I say, it's all right.'

Zetta turned and skipped toward the blue door of the church. There was a rope hanging loosely down the wall to the right.

She grabbed it and pulled down hard. The bell atop the church swung right then left, throwing the iron ball inside hard against the copper dome. *Ding, dong, ding, dong.* The sound clattered across the courtyard and out across the valley. Yiskah and Iakovos started clapping and dancing. Kosta joined in the celebrations. Zetta rang the bell ten times before she too joined them. If the townspeople were to look up at this moment and see the church from so far away, they would have thought these people were crazy. And maybe they were, but they were also very happy too and sometimes the two go hand in hand.

An hour later and the sun was up, the family seeking protection from the wind, huddled together, their backs against the blue doors of the entrance, their bodies close, keeping the warmth even closer. Iakovos and Zetta were asleep, their heads resting on the shoulders of the adults.

'It doesn't get any better than this,' said Kosta, the fullness of the sun on his face. 'I can already see why you love this day so much.'

'It's where it all started. It was the promise that lay within. This view just changed everything inside of us. Made everything and anything possible.'

He looked at Yiskah. 'I love you with everything I have. You know that?'

'Of course I do. I love you too.' They shared a quiet kiss, careful not to wake the children. The sunlight grew stronger by the second, emerging fully from its resting place, baring all to a kinder world. Yiskah and Kosta closed their eyes and they too drifted off to sleep.

The trudge down the goat track was hard, the wind gusting in from the north and the warmth of the day creeping down their backs. No one spoke. Concentration was everything, the descent more prone to mishap, their minds already wandering toward the comforts of home.

'Eeeekk!' A shriek from Zetta, her body crashing to the earth.

'Are you okay?' asked Yiskah.

'Do I look it?' Zetta kept her head down, her bum on the floor.

'What is it?'

'My ankle. It's twisted.'

'Let me have a look.'

Yiskah took a few steps back up the mountain and squatted beside her daughter. Iakovos and Kosta moved a step closer.

'Can you take off your shoe?' asked Yiskah.

'I'll try.'

Zetta undid her laces and loosened its grip. Zetta supported her ankle with one hand while nudging her heel out of the shoe with the other. Her sock covered foot slipped from the hiking boot.

'Oooohhh. It's sore.' She was already in tears.

'Let's take the sock off and check if its swollen,' said Yiskah. She rolled the top of the sock gently down the shin and then around the heel. 'Keep it supported honey.'

Zetta nodded, words too painful to express. The ankle starting to throb.

The foot was already looking bigger.

'Looks pretty bad. We should get you back to the house as quickly as possible.'

'Is that up or down?' asked Iakovos. 'The road down to Aliki is probably closer but it is back up that way. Then we could arrange a car to pick us up and take us to the hospital. I have my phone.'

'Or we go straight down to the house?' said Yiskah. 'There's plenty of ice there and a first aid kit. I don't think it's broken. More just a bad strain.'

'Down we go then,' said Iakovos. 'I'll carry her.'

'You sure?' asked Kosta. 'It's a long way and steep.'

'It's okay old man,' smiled Iakovos. 'I'll let you know when I need a rest.'

'Can you stand?' asked Yiskah.

Zetta looked up. 'I think so.'

Iakovos leant in and helped her up into a standing position. He turned his back to her and bent his knees. 'Can you climb on my back?'

'I'll try.'

'I'll stay right behind you in case you slip,' said Kosta.

'And I'll clear the way from the front,' said Yiskah.

They helped Zetta onto her brother's back and off they went, stumbling carefully down the mountain, across the rocky terrain.

'I haven't had a piggyback from you in years,' smiled Zetta.

'So, you did this on purpose then,' said Iakovos.

'Maybe.'

They all laughed.

'If we sing a song the time might go faster,' said Yiskah.

'One thing we are not good at is singing,' said Zetta. 'We don't want to put Kosta through that kind of pain.' More laughter.

'Agreed,' said Kosta.

The sun was high in the sky by the time Iakovos trudged up the stone steps of the mountain house. Zetta slid down his back, placing her good foot on the floor first. She lowered herself into a chair.

'You must be exhausted,' she said.

Iakovos dropped into the seat opposite. 'Yup.'

'Thanks.' She leant across and placed her hand on his.

'Anytime sis.'

Yiskah and Kosta emerged from the house with a first aid kit and some ice.

Kosta grabbed a chair and placed it in front of Zetta. He lifted her bad foot and rested it on some cushions before laying a bag of ice across her ankle. 'It's swelling fast,' said Kosta. 'We'll keep it iced up and raised. See how it goes today then if need be we'll get you to a doctor.'

'I'm not going to Naxos, am I?' she asked.

'Let's wait and see,' said Yiskah.

'I can stay with Zetta,' said Iakovos. 'You two can have a romantic getaway.'

'I really wanted all of us to go,' said Yiskah.

'It's tomorrow Mum. Even if she could walk, spending a few days on her feet isn't going to help her recovery.'

'And I want to be okay for my party,' said Zetta. 'I've got to be able to dance with everyone. That's my thing.'

'Good point,' said Kosta. 'Your birthday has to be our main concern.'

'But I can't leave you both here alone,' said Yiskah.

'We won't be alone, Mum,' said Zetta. 'We've got each other. Anyway, we can see Naxos from here. We'll wave to you.'

'I'll be worried about you the whole time. It won't be any fun.'

'You have always worried about us Mum,' said Iakovos. 'Even when we're safe in our beds asleep.' He put an arm around her. 'This is for you. And Kosta. It'll be a great break from us, from everything and we'll be fine. One night away. That's all it is.'

Yiskah lifted a hand to her mouth, scared her emotions were going to pour out. She knew this time would come and she'd recently been trying to step back more and more, aware of the timetable she'd set over a decade ago.

'Okay,' she said. 'I'll give it a go.' She looked up at Kosta and smiled. 'You finally got me all to yourself. You okay with that?'

'I can't wait.' He smiled, his mind already making plans.

38

FRIDAY 19th SEPTEMBER 2015
8:00AM CET
PAROS ISLAND

Yiskah stumbled around the kitchen like an inebriated seagull. 'Where are my lucky earrings. I can't leave without them.'

She flapped around the room, lifting plates and envelopes, peering beneath anything she could lay her hands on. Smashing plates was a well-known Greek tradition, and Yiskah was considering her options.

Zetta watched her mother from the relative safety of the couch, her ankle still bandaged and raised. She knew that Yiskah was prone to sudden bouts of panic, her assumed Greekness only adding to the confusion of an already chaotic scene. She tried to pacify her mother. 'You look beautiful. You don't need them.'

Her daughter was right. Yiskah looked great in a tight-fitting pair of blue jeans and an opaque white blouse, hints of a red bikini top visible underneath. The Greek life agreed with her on all levels and she had grown to epitomise the freedom which it embodied. Her present, however, was clouded, her mind not so free and she failed to see the beauty that existed everywhere she looked.

'Everything good that has ever happened to me has occurred while I've been wearing those earrings,' she said.

'That's because you're always wearing them,' said Zetta.

Yiskah raised her hands above her head in frustration and screamed. 'Why is my house so messy!'

Iakovos came charging up the corridor, bursting out into the lounge room a huge smile on his face. 'I've found them, I've found them.'

Yiskah spun on her heels. 'Thank god. Where were they?'

'In the bathroom, wedged under the soap dish.'

She rushed forward and took them from his outstretched palm. 'You never fail me.' She attached the silver encrusted pearls to her ears before squeezing her young son and planting a loving kiss on his right cheek. 'I love you.'

The wheels of a small blue case trundled across the paving. The morning sun trickled between the leaves of the orchard's olive trees. A multitude of shadows danced across Iakovos's face as he lifted the suitcase down the stone steps. Kosta had returned home yesterday, needing to pack and prepare for this trip as well. Iakovos was trying to be the man of the house.

Yiskah was a few steps behind her son, her daughter using her as a lean to, hopping beneath the pergola on her good foot. They paused at the top of the stone stairs. Yiskah knew that these rocky steps were leading her away from her beloved mountain house and she still wasn't sure if she wanted to go.

She draped an arm around Zetta's shoulders, the other hand clutching a pair of red high heels, their impracticality currently rendering them useless.

'No further for you,' said Yiskah. 'We'll have to say goodbye here.' Yiskah looked into her daughter's eyes. 'And no school today, okay?'

Zetta smiled. 'You think I'm going to run down there when I don't have to. I'm quite happy to take a day off. Might even catch up on some study.'

'Good. Just look after yourself. And don't forget to remind your brother to feed the chooks.' Zetta nodded, her face revealing a hint of sadness.

Yiskah saw her daughter's doubts. 'What is it?'

'I'm a bit scared. You've never left us alone before.' The words stumbled out before she burst into tears.

Yiskah buried her daughter's head in her chest and wrapped her arms around her. 'This is a surprise. I never thought you were going to miss me this much.'

'Neither did I.'

'I'm really sad too but you said it would be good for us. That's why I'm going.'

'It doesn't feel good.'

'They say that absence makes the heart grow fonder. Sadness is an important part of that process.'

'You almost look happy to be leaving.'

Yiskah showed her pain. 'I'm kind of excited to see another island. This was your idea remember.'

'Yeah, well it was bad one.'

'You want me to stay?'

Iakovos interrupted the drawn-out pain of Zetta's mysterious mood. 'We'll be fine, Mum. I'll keep her busy.'

'Not too busy. That ankle needs to heal.'

'I'll get Carissa to come up and keep her company,' said Iakovos.

'You'd love that,' smiled Zetta.

'Ha ha,' said Iakovos, happy to take the ribbing as long as he got a smile from his sister.

Yiskah squeezed Zetta in a final hug. 'It's nice to know you care. It's only one night. I'll be home before you know it.'

Zetta nodded.

Yiskah kissed her on the cheek. 'You never fail to surprise me.'

'Yeah, well I surprise myself sometimes too.'

Iakovos stepped around a clucky brood of Longobardian chickens, their long legs and golden feathers scattering across the yard. Yiskah was just a few steps behind him.

They stopped beside her battered old car, a light film of red dust coating every inch of it including the windscreen. Iakovos opened one of the rear doors and lifted the suitcase onto the back seat. He closed it and stepped forward to embrace his mother.

'Have a great time, Mum. Don't worry about us.'

'I'll try not to. I'm just so nervous.'

'Nerves are good. You're always telling us that.'

'I know.'

'And don't you dare come back early.'

She smiled. He knew her well. 'I promise. I'll be strong.'

The hatchback rumbled down the mountain road, clouds of dust and dirt trailing behind every twist and turn.

Yiskah's hands gripped the steering wheel like she was on a rollercoaster ride, a steady stream of tears trickling down her face. Leaving the children was proving much harder than she had envisaged and she willed herself to avoid looking in the rear vision mirror lest she entertain thoughts of turning back.

The mountain slopes were quickly replaced by the white buildings of Parakia, row upon row bursting upon her from either side of the road. A scooter tore across in front of her. She slammed on the breaks, the car coming to a screeching halt.

'Signomi,' yelled the young driver, as he slipped passed her open window and down an alley way.

Yiskah caught her breath. The drive into town had gone by in a flash, the peace of the mountain already superseded by the heavy noise of traffic, vehicles whizzing around her from all sides. She felt the chaos and colour of the port swelling in her veins, its triumphant demands filling her with the excitement of travel. The sadness of her departure still lingered, but any feelings of negativity were no longer a priority.

Chaos corner was living up to its name, vehicles banked up as the well-organised madness of multiple ferries wrought havoc on the narrow access roads leading into and out of the harbour. Yiskah used her local knowledge, turning right at the bakery, down a small lane and off the main drag. The streets here were even narrower, only just wide enough for a small car. She squeezed past a line of parked scooters, washing lines hanging above the streets, the sound of her horn sending a group of soccer-loving children into the porches of their homes.

A few turns later and ahead of her lay a glimpse of the ocean. The morning sun had only just peaked above the northern slopes of Mount Profitis Ilias, a glint of light reflecting off the slow-moving water of the bay of love.

The car emerged from the shadows of the back streets, ruins on one side, a kebab shop on the other. Yiskah looked both ways before swinging the car left and accelerating quickly up the coast road. The tip of the port windmill could be seen above the procession of cars still in front of her, but with three ferries disembarking, seeing it and getting there were two completely different things. Yiskah spotted a small gap between two parked cars. She pulled off the road and into the spot, switched off the engine and checked her reflection in the mirror. Tears had smudged her eyeliner and she thought about redoing her make up. Her darkened eyes looked full of intent and she felt like a fearless young woman again.

Beep, beep! Yiskah pressed the lock button on her keys and stepped up onto the footpath. She was still barefoot, her red shoes in her left hand, her handbag over her left shoulder and her suitcase trailing behind her. She had no reason to hurry but nerves were bouncing through her and she just wanted the holiday to start.

She wove her way through the throng of passengers and taxi drivers that clogged the roundabout. She spotted her man, perched on the low wall encircling the windmill. She stopped and took him in; his smile, the stubbled chin, his long, dark ruffled hair. She allowed time to drift, ignoring the harassed tourists crowding around her. She was a barrier to their movement but she wanted this moment to last and allowed them to jostle her like a pinball.

She could still remember the first time she met Kosta. A crowded restaurant, a wedding reception for close friends in full swing. She'd taken the option of some fresh air, out across the road, seated on the low sea wall overlooking the harbour. Her legs dangled over the edge, sandy beach just below her toes, a hint of moonlight tickling the tide. She saw his silhouette off to one side, down at the water's edge, suit pants rolled up, barefoot. He was skimming stones, his movements athletic and smooth, reminiscent of a dancer. She watched the stones skip across the ocean surface.

She guessed he, too, was escaping the clamour of the party but couldn't place who he was or how he might be connected with the happy couple. Identification was rendered difficult given the low light of the harbour but time passed and her imagination ran wild, his whole backstory slowly built from scratch. An imagined man with a fictional past, her leanings toward romanticism were clear.

'Yassas.' His voice caught her off guard. He'd approached her whilst she was still lost in her dreams, no longer a piece of fiction.

'Hello.' She was breathless, his closeness too sudden. She'd had a bit to drink. Still he caught her before she collapsed, a fainting spell tossing her forward. He cared for her then, and had never stopped, their lives intertwined and unbroken from that day forward.

Kosta hoped that today would bring that moment full circle. He watched the people spinning around him. They all looked as excited as he was. He caught a glimpse of Yiskah, her eyes meeting his. She was stationary so he got to his feet. His arms were already open by the time she rushed into his embrace.

He noticed the smudged eye liner. 'You've been crying?'

'Saying goodbye to the kids,' she said. 'They're so beautiful. It was really hard leaving them.'

'We can stay here if you want?'

'That's what I told them.'

'And?'

'Iakovos wasn't having any of that sort of talk.' She wiped her eyes. 'I'll be fine.'

'We're not going far. Your son is a good man. He and Zetta will have a ball up there without us.'

Yiskah's faced dropped and fresh tears pooled in her eyes.

'Sorry I didn't mean that the way it sounded.'

'I know, I know. It's just they are so acutely connected to my heart. Like the strings we say tie us all together. Except the ones between us are as thick as rope and they are anchored deep inside of me. Ten years together has made us quite dependent on each other. I'm really torn.'

'It's hard letting go,' said Kosta.

Yiskah nodded before burying her head in his chest.

The ferry pulled anchor, the roaring engines hauling it into the open harbor.

Yiskah watched her favourite town drift away. Kosta stood beside her, his arm wrapped around her waist as Parikia shrank until the finer details were just a blur. Each building resembling nothing more than the geometric lines of a white box, the people on the streets little more than dots.

Yiskah gazed up above the towns buildings, across the valley, to the left of Mount Profitis Ilias. Her house could not be seen from here, but the ridges to the north could. The high walls of the nunnery were just visible above the mountain pass between the ranges to the north and south. God was a close friend of hers and she knew he would keep watch over her secluded piece of paradise, protecting her children, for that is who they really were.

The reality of their past rarely entered her mind anymore, her life too consumed by the day-to-day details of a present she had lovingly created. But seeing her island like this, rekindled memories of their arrival. She had achieved more than she could ever have wished for and she knew deep down that the children would be okay without her. They were very capable individuals and even stronger together. It's how they'd always been and she prayed this bond would stay unbroken through the turbulent waters ahead.

39

8:55AM CET
NAXOS ISLAND

Yiskah gazed wistfully at the island of Naxos. Kosta stepped in beside her, their suitcases in his hands.

'It looks so beautiful,' she said.

The buildings of the main town rose up around the port, its restaurants and shops surrounding a centuries-old castle. The turrets and walls of the fortress had been proudly restored, the castle still capable of guarding the port with honour and aggression.

To the north of the town stood the mythical Portara, a massive ancient marble doorway surrounded by ruins. Built to honour the god Apollo it had been designed as the entrance to a temple that was never finished.

'This is where the story of Dionysus and Ariadne unfolded,' said Kosta.

'Who were they?' asked Yiskah.

'She was the daughter of King Minos of Crete and he was the wine god. She helped Theseus slay the Minotaur and was then abandoned here on Naxos. Dionysus found her sleeping and made her his wife.'

'They got married here?'

'Sure did.' Kosta leant over and kissed her, lingering long

enough for the horn of the ferry to interrupt them.

Yiskah's arms were wrapped tightly around Kosta's waist, her long hair blowing in the wind. Two helmets were secured upon the rear rack of the quad bike as they raced away from the port, the castle ramparts and turrets receding in the distance.

The coastal plain behind them was wide and flat, the road ahead a slow climb into the mountains. This scenic route took them higher and higher, the views across the island spectacular, quite different from Paros both in size and colour. Fertile farmland stretched as far as the eye could see, its heavy population of olive trees bringing varying shades of green to this striking agricultural canvas.

The slopes of the mountain were exposed and raw, a smattering of marble quarries slicing their way into its heart. Massive cubes of marble stood like creations from outer space, a geometric certainty amid the wild terrain of nature.

Kosta steered the quad bike off the highway and into a small town called Apiranthos. They parked the bike and strolled down a small path into the heart of town. Most of the homes here had been cut into the hillside, a host of beautiful archways supporting them around every corner.

Kosta asked an old lady if she would take a photo for him. He wrapped his arms around Yiskah in front of an intricate set of stairs and kissed her on the cheek just as the lady clicked the camera. The old woman smiled and said they looked lovely together.

They ambled past a small café which overlooked the valley.

'I could live here,' said Yiskah.

'It's an incredible town. We could lose ourselves here.'

'I like the sound of that.'

They stopped for a drink. Coffee was brought out to them by a young man. He looked like any other teenager which reminded her of her children. The Western side of this mountain felt so removed from the tourism of the harbour. Growing up here must be quite different, its isolation reminiscent of her mountain house. She felt lucky to be so alive.

They returned to the quadbike, soaking up the freedom of the open road, the lack of responsibility it offered. Yiskah was in her element, her mind uncluttered and unwound.

Kosta steered the quadbike over a small one-way bridge, past a sign welcoming them into the hillside town of Halki. The assistant at the car rental place suggested they break for a late lunch here, the moussaka, he explained, was very well regarded. Only half an hour from the harbour, Yiskah and Kosta were keen for some traditional Naxos fare before they returned to the hustle of the port.

Parking was easy, traffic non-existent, just a few old cars parked haphazardly to one side of the road. Even the streets were empty, hardly a soul to be seen, the unexpected emptiness almost eerie.

Kosta pulled in beside the curb, switched off the bike and waited as Yiskah swung her legs off and onto the footpath.

'Mípos boreíte na apoláfsete ti vólta?' asked Kosta. *Did you enjoy the ride?*

'Itan panemorfo,' smiled Yiskah. *It was beautiful.*

'Now for lunch.'

They walked hand in hand down a narrow street. A small dog watched them pass, Jess having added a woven sun hat to her attire. The puppy was curled up on the front door mat, his eyes only half open, his demeanour indicative of this sleepy little town.

They passed a collection of small shops. A young woman stepped out to greet them. 'Yassas,' she said.

'Yassas,' said Kosta.

Yiskah smiled. 'Kalimera.

An much older woman sat on a chair opposite, her lined face full of smiles, a cluster of small tables around her displaying a mixture of copper and silver sculptures. Yiskah stepped forward to admire them. Each piece of art appeared to follow a theme of foliage, with leaves, branches and full-blown trees moulded, scratched and brushed upon different types of materials. They reminded Yiskah of the small orchard of olive trees she had inherited with her mountain property. She tended to them religiously, watching them grow with the children.

'Afta einai dika sas?' she inquired of the old lady. *Are these yours?*

She smiled. 'Einai oi kores mou.' *They are my daughters.* She gestured toward the younger woman.

'They're amazing,' said Yiskah.

The artisan smiled. 'Thank you.'

'You have an affinity with the trees?'

'Of course. This is Naxos,' gestured the artist. 'We have over ten thousand olive trees. They dominate our landscape. They provide us with a very good economy.'

'The land here is so fertile,' said Yiskah.

'Yes, we are lucky. The mountains bring down the rains and the land is healthy. We are very proud.'

'Boroúme na páme sto esoterikó?' asked Yiskah. *May we go inside.*

'Of course.'

Yiskah stepped up into the shop, clusters of art displayed beautifully around the small but perfectly formed room. Kosta followed closely behind, his quiet steps matching the peace of the space. Yiskah picked up a small piece of marble. She turned it, encouraging the light of the day to bring out its translucent qualities. A painting of an olive branch had been delicately applied to the green stained streaks of this natural resource. The cut of the marble worked well with the bronze of the artwork, making the piece both strong and inspirational. She felt the same way about Kosta. He had been her rock over the years and she closed her eyes and prayed he would be around forever.

'Efharisto.' They departed the shop and continued up the narrow streets toward the main square. Each house had its own personality, with grapevines and bougainvillea wrapped around every available surface, bringing colour and drama to the peaceful streets of Halki.

The main piazza opened onto a central restaurant, with leafy pergolas on both sides. An open hearth had been built into one side of the whitewashed walls of the eatery, its fuel of wood burning brightly, orange tipped flames lapping upon the well-basted crust of a slow turning lamb roast. It was as inviting a picture as the travel brochures that had brought Yiskah to this part of the world in the first place. She smiled, unusually conscious of the choices that she'd made in the past. Kosta smiled too. He was not a choice. He was a necessity. She'd been alone too long. When they first met she was more than ready to become someone's woman.

A young tattooed waiter led them toward a table off to one side of the restaurant, a long curtain of grape leaves draping down the wall. The unmistakable tunes of traditional Greek music played softly in the background, the mouth-watering aromas of well-honed dishes drifting across the table tops. Kosta pulled a chair out for her and Yiskah slipped into place. She felt like she'd been here before. Wine was ordered, as well as two of the much-feted moussakas.

The food proved scrumptious and didn't last long on their plates. Neither did the red wine, the calmest of atmospheres proving heady and liberating.

The coming together of these two lost souls had been a reason for celebration back on Paros. The Nazars and talismans of the evil eye had worked hard to keep them together, warding off the misfortunes and mistakes of the past.

'Eísai charoúmenos?' said Kosta. *Are you happy?*

'Neh,' smiled Yiskah, 'Para poly.' *Yes, very much.*

'I look at you and I see a very beautiful woman. Of course you are gorgeous, that is obvious, but it is what is inside that I find so mesmerising.'

Yiskah was moved to tears, all the years of struggle pinnacling here. The children would be so proud. They liked Kosta too and had accepted her need for a companion. A friend she could kiss was how they explained it.

'You are seeing what you have created,' whispered Yiskah, not because she wanted to be quiet, there was no one else near them. She spoke quietly because it was all she could manage. 'You have been my rock for so long.'

'It's funny you should say that. I bought you something. To symbolise us.' Kosta reached down into his leather satchel and pulled out a small paper bag. He reached tenderly across the red and white checkered table cloth and placed it in Yiskah's hands.

'You shouldn't have,' she said.

'I wanted to.'

Yiskah opened the top of the little white bag and looked inside. She reached in and lifted out a small tissue wrapped rectangle and placed it on the table. She unfolded the opaque wrapping paper to reveal the painted slice of marble she had handled in the artist's gift shop earlier.

'I thought of you when I saw it.' She leant forward, rising out of her chair and kissing Kosta on the lips. He lifted a hand, brushing her right cheek in a lingering touch of love. 'Thank you.' She kissed him passionately, then whispered in his ear. 'I think we need to get a room.'

The quadbike pulled in past the castle of the port and parked outside the rental shop. Kosta leapt off the seat and threw the keys to the man who'd hired them the vehicle. He gave them the thumbs up.

They ran up the cobbled streets laughing, Yiskah's shoes once again dangling from her hands. An old man watched as they raced past his small café. He raised his cup of expresso, saluting their happiness.

They burst in through the door of their modest pension. Yiskah pulled Kosta toward the bed. This would not be the first time they had made love, but the urge was greater than she had ever known. The desire to be together was overpowering.

Yiskah lay on the bed with Kosta above her. She smiled as he unbuttoned his shirt, his long hair hanging down past his tanned shoulders. He was fit, hours of tennis and yoga keeping him toned and tanned. He threw off his shirt and lay atop her.

'Se agapó,' he said. *I love you.*

'S 'agapó pára polý,' she whispered back his lips meeting hers with passion. His hands unbuttoned her shirt, revealing the red bikini. Yiskah arched her back allowing Kosta to reach around and unclip it. He slid both the shirt and bikini off her like a sailor unfurling the mainsail, his hands brushing across her breasts. She held his chin in her hands and pulled his face in hard against her lips. He slid down and nuzzled into her neck then down her chest, using his tongue to caress her swollen nipples. His hands worked on the top button of her jeans, wiggling them free, down toward her ankles, her red bikini bottoms, showing off her long, tanned legs. He worked his way back up, kissing her thighs, her navel and returning to her lips.

'I fucking love you,' she said before they were once again consumed by kisses.

40

7:42PM CET
NAXOS ISLAND

The evening sun glowed above the silhouetted island of Paros, its hues of yellow and orange spread like wild brushstrokes across the sky. Hundreds of people had surrounded the Portara, a ritualistic meeting place from which to watch the sunset.

Kosta rested on a large limestone rock, taking in the view through this ancient structure and out across the water. It framed the sunset like one of Zetta's paintings and he felt as close to the children as ever. Streams of tourists continued to swell up the rocky path toward the temple. Kosta scanned their faces for the one he loved more than anything else in this world.

He had woken from siesta to an empty bed. A note resting on the pillow beside him had asked that he meet Yiskah here at sunset. Shopping had been her excuse for slipping out but Kosta was nervous. He wondered if Dionysus had ever worried like this about Ariadne. He wished for the rest of the evening to go as he had planned.

People started filling the space around him, cutting off his views down toward the entrance. He gritted his teeth and stood. Her strong and sexy walk caught his eye straight away. Nerves jangled through him and he tried to control his breathing, arresting the growing disquiet in his chest. Her smile was clear. She was happy, the glint in her eyes the same one he'd first fallen in love with. That hint of excitement, of the fire in her soul.

He held out his hands as she approached. She stopped just in front of him, took his hands and smiled. 'You like?' She gave him a twirl. The long flowing dress she wore was light blue in colour, its sleeveless style showing off her tanned arms, a graceful v neck line showing off her well-cut shoulders.

'It is beautiful.' he said.

'Being here made me feel like the beginning of something new. What better than a new dress to celebrate with.'

'I love it. You look gorgeous.'

Yiskah snuggled against his chest, his bare arms wrapping around her. The warm night air was light and fresh, the soft breeze coming off the sea a welcome respite from the intense heat of the day.

'How were the shops?'

'Amazing. The art here is incredible.'

'It is busier than Paros, yes?'

'It feels that way. I don't like the crowds so much, but I feel so safe with you.'

'They are all here for the same thing,' said Kosta. 'The romance of history. The Portara draws us all in. It frames our lives. Helps us to realise what is important.'

'You have been here before, yes?'

'Many times. I find it very captivating.'

'I feel so young here. Maybe it is the incredible history. The drama of romance.'

'You do look incredibly happy.'

'I am,' said Yiskah. 'This scene is like a Hollywood movie.'

Kosta lowered himself down onto one knee. 'I too feel like I am in a movie.' He smiled, pulling a small container from his pocket.

Yiskah gasped, a hand to her mouth.

He looked up at her. 'I love you Yiskah. Always have, always will.'

She was trembling.

Kosta was sure. 'I want to spend the rest of my life with you, Yiskah. I want to wake up with you every day and fall asleep beside you every night.' He eased the lid off the box. 'You have made me a better man and your kindness and care are inspirational.'

Yiskah spoke nervously. 'But there's so much you still don't know about me.'

'I know what's in here.' Kosta clasped a hand above his heart. 'That is all that matters.' Light glinted off the ring as he lifted it toward her. 'Yiskah, will you please marry me?'

Yiskah's lips were trembling uncontrollably. 'Oh Kosta, not here. Not now.' Her face was contorted and torn. 'There is so much I have to tell you. I don't even know where to start.'

Crowds of people had turned to watch, their interest piqued by Kosta's position on one knee. Yiskah looked over at them, concerned with the attention they were receiving.

Kosta saw only the wild colours of the setting sky behind her. 'I know what I know. That is enough. We will have our whole lives together to uncover the rest.'

'Oh god, can't we just stay as we are. I never expected…'

Kosta's face struggled to retain its smile. 'Please Yiskah, I thought you wanted this. Please, just say yes.'

'I can't.' Tears tumbled down her cheeks. 'Not yet. I'm so sorry.' She turned and ran down the same track she had only just walked up. Kosta watched her go, his face a distraught mass of lines and pain. He thrust the ring into his pocket and chased after her.

The crowds had blocked off her exit, forcing Yiskah to veer off the track, running toward the eastern edge of the rocky island. Several tourists pointed, watching her with concern, worried about her intentions. She came to an abrupt halt at the edge of the cliff. A set of large waves crashed hard against the rocks below her. She felt trapped. 'Not again,' she thought.

Kosta stopped a few metres behind her. 'It's okay,' he shouted. 'It's okay. I can wait. I'm so sorry for putting you through this. I thought you were ready.'

'I am ready to love you. I'm just not ready to get married. It's complicated.' She turned to face him. 'I've kept you in the dark for so long. Too long. I've told you layer after layer of lies. It's not right that you love me so much when you don't even know the real me.'

'We all have secrets, Yiskah. I'm no different.'

'Not like these. You won't forgive me when you find out.'

He took another step towards her. 'I love you. I will forgive you anything…'

Her anger simmered on the surface. 'You say that without knowing what it is I have done.'

'Then tell me. Tell me what it is and let me decide.' He too was struggling to cope with their predicament.

'I wish I could.' Yiskah rushed toward him. He opened his arms but she brushed them aside and kept on running.

This time there would be no chase. The assembled audience watching as Yiskah pushed her way past the hordes that filled the tracks, running down, desperately toward the bridge that linked the Portara to the port. Kosta did not see her go. He refused to turn and watch her leave. He could only stand and cry, the world beneath his feet breaking apart once again.

Yiskah was fueled with an outpouring of emotion, sprinting up the cobbled path toward the old castle, her shadow keeping stride for stride with her every move, navigating this labyrinth of twists and turns.

Kosta stepped up to the counter of the port ticket booth. 'What time is the next ferry to Paros?'

'Nine thirty,' replied the young lady behind the counter.

'Is there nothing earlier?'

'Sorry.'

'I'll take one ticket.'

Yiskah had slowed to a stroll, wandering aimlessly around the backstreets of the port, her vision blurred, the lighting of the old castle an ominous warning to the darkness inside her head. Tears streamed down her face as she struggled to control her swaying emotions. The streets felt like they were closing in on her and she tripped and fell. Her balance was off. She was no longer sure of anything.

She lay on the ground and tried to catch her breath. An overwhelming sense of loss was all that she could be sure of.

Kosta stood at the railings of the departing ferry and looked up toward the castle. The day could not have gone any worse. His heart was broken.

41

SATURDAY 20th SEPTEMBER
8:00AM CET
MARKET STREET

The lime-washed houses of Parikia awoke to the soft sounds of morning. Barefeet tiptoed down hallways as children woke to the early morning sun. Parents stirred from their beds as the sweet smell of coffee, poured into small white cups, encouraged them from slumber. This light menagerie of noise slipped out through the open doors of the pensions and drifted down through the paved back streets of town.

The low-lying rays of the morning sun forced their way through the gaps and down these intricately spaced mazes. Some pathways held onto their darkened corners, sleepy areas yet to shrug off the shadows of the previous night.

Market Street though was already busy, greeting its locals with the smiles and smells of a new day. People sauntered in and out of the shops, others walking the short distances to work.

The Port Café met the hushed tones of its customers with a light smattering of jazz, both parties showing respect to those still lost among their dreams. It was early but the temperature was already a comfortable thirty-two degrees, mirroring the warmth the locals had for one another.

This calming island was a refuge, far from the pressurised cities of the world.

Yiskah stepped into the grocers, her suitcase trailing behind her. She wore a blue linen shirt and white shorts. Her attire projected order, but her dark sunglasses hinted at something else.

She had only just stepped off the early morning ferry, keen to see her children. She selected a large zucchini from a wooden box, rolling it in her hands like an expert.

She had not long been awake and this time of day had always been one of her favourites. The slow pace of the morning intersecting with the excitement of the new day. It was where fresh expectations met the promise of a new sun, all falling into the opportunities of a singular wonderful moment. Yiskah's own mind though was cloudier than usual. She was searching hard for any signs of optimism.

Yiskah reached over and grabbed a small basket from the stack at the end of her aisle. She placed the zucchini gently inside and continued to shop, selecting a wide variety of vegetables to fill her basket. She strolled over toward the register, a dark-haired man awaiting her. He was older than she and dressed simply in long black pants and a white singlet.

'Kalimera, Yiskah,' he said, his smile wide.

'Kalimera, Mikhalis,' smiled Yiskah. 'Pos Alexia pigainei stin Athina?' *How is Alexia going in Athens?*

'Poly kala.' *Very good.* 'Though she misses her family and especially you.'

'I miss her too. Tell her we will have plenty of time to paint together on her return.'

'I will. You are good teacher my friend. You help her very much.'

'She is a wonderful young lady. Her brushwork has come on quickly.'

'How is your own daughter?'

'Nervous.'

'It is her big day, yes?'

Yiskah nodded, flashes of last night still sapping her energy.

'Then nerves are natural,' said Mikhalis.

'For her yes, but I am worse than she is. I haven't eaten today yet. My stomach is going crazy.'

Mikhalis slid a cucumber from her basket. 'Starving yourself will not solve the problem. A good meal and then a few ouzos tonight and you'll be right.'

Yiskah nodded. 'Not too many though. I want to remember these special moments.'

Mikhalis placed the collection of vegetables inside a paper bag. Yiskah pushed ten Euro's across the counter.

Mikhalis waved a hand. 'No pay. Free to you on this special day.'

Yiskah smiled. 'Efharisto.'

'See you tonight.'

She stepped out of the shop and back up the narrow path to her right. These distinctive stone paths carried Yiskah through a maze of left and right turns, their painted white edges framing each stone like it was a jigsaw piece. The white-washed walls of the houses and painted doors repeated around every corner. Yiskah knew these streets well. She had always enjoyed the anonymity offered by its labyrinth of corridors. She prided herself on being able to navigate her way out of here, remembering the early days when getting lost was a daily occurrence.

How far she had come?

Her journey had been a long one and today was a watershed of sorts. The grey clouds that had been gathering in Yiskah's head since last month were expected but the events of last night had only darkened them, her mood continuing to overshadow these last-minute preparations. She had always viewed Zetta's eighteenth birthday as a new beginning. The end of an era and the final release of both a dangerous past and her hopes for an even brighter future.

Yiskah took a left turn and saw him instantly.

Iakovos was seated at a small table outside Selena's ice cream shop. The beauty of youth was so strong in him. She envied his approach to life. The young boy who arrived here with little confidence had all but disappeared.

He watched his mother's approach. He had missed her, his love for her stronger than ever, this Saturday morning ritual something he had come to think of as important as his heartbeat.

They shared a smile as he stood, converging upon each other, hugging warmly.

'Yassas, Mama.'

'Yassas, my son. Thanks for coming to pick me up.'

'Is everything okay?'

'Let's sit. Kafes?' asked Yiskah.

'Already ordered.'

The two companions sat down across from each other.

'How is Zetta's ankle?'

'Good. The swelling's gone down and she can walk on it. She'll be fine for tonight.'

'You are a good brother. Zetta is lucky to have you.'

'How are you feeling?' asked Iakovos.

'Excited. Nervous.'

'My eighteenth was a crazy affair, so it's nice to have the chance to watch it all happen without being at the centre.'

'It's been almost a year.'

'It feels longer.'

'You're a man now.'

'Thanks to you.'

A young girl stepped forward and lowered two coffees onto the table. 'Thanks Elektra,' said Iakovos.

'No problem, Iakovos.' A flash of her smile, a beautiful young woman.

'She's nice,' said Yiskah.

'Mum!'

'I just...'

'Just don't. I can find my own girls.'

'But they always leave on the next ferry.'

'I like it that way.'

'You never bring them home.'

'It never gets to the 'meet the family stage.' He accentuated his words with quotation marks in both hands. 'They're just here to party. It's cool.'

'No attachments?'

'Something like that.'

'You'll find the one.'

'I'm not in any hurry.' He sipped his coffee. 'How was Naxos?'

'Not so good.'

'What happened?'

'Kosta and I, we had an argument.'

'And?'

Yiskah took a breath. 'We're taking a break. We both need some time to think.'

'About what?' Iakovos was pained to say the least.

'The future. In a few years, you and Zetta will be living your own lives. I need to make sure I know what I want.'

'What does Kosta want?'

'Me. He proposed and then we fought. Which is crazy I know.'

'He proposed? Asked you to marry him?'

'Yes.'

'Isn't that what you wanted?'

'Yes and no. It's difficult.'

'That's exactly why I like my relationships short and sweet. Kosta must think you're crazy.'

'Maybe. I still love him.'

'Does he know that?'

'I hope so.'

'Is he still coming tonight?'

'Of course. He and Zetta are very close.'

'I like him a lot too you know.'

'Of course you do. He's been a great friend to you.' Yiskah sipped her coffee.

'And Zetta?'

'She always wanted a father. He stepped forward. Filled the gap as best he could.'

'Thank god he convinced her to come back from Athens. I was worried we'd lost her.'

'We all were. She appears to have left those wild days behind her.'

Iakovos could sense his mother's sadness. He reached across and held her hand. 'Thase agapo tia panda.' *I will love you forever.* 'You know that don't you.'

'Yes, of course. And I love you too, Iakovos. More than you can ever know.'

And it was true.

42

8:00PM CET
MAGAYA BEACH BAR

The golden glow of the beach heralded the final descent of the sun, the sights and sounds of dusk settling on the light breeze blowing in from the north.

Cars drove in through the iron-gated entrance, the sand-covered parking lot a chaotic maze of cars and people. Passengers climbed from vehicles, mingling as they navigated their way through this orchard of overgrown olive trees, long strings of white bulbs draped from branch to branch, leading partygoers toward the bamboo lined entrance.

The rumble of samba welcomed friends and family, this cultural phenomenon a prelude to the assault of colour and texture beyond the doors. The bar was already alive, the conversation and laughter flowing as freely as the drinks.

Balloons and streamers traversed the bamboo roof, the curved bar already home to several thirsty customers. A tall bearded waiter passed by chatting with diners all vying for his attention.

Yiskah held residence in the L-shaped booth opposite the bar, Iakovos on one side and Zetta on the other. Far more beautiful together, than they were as individuals, they were enthralled with the moment and the possibilities of the night.

Zetta's black and white patterned kaftan showed off her tan to great effect and she was both relaxed and dressy, her posture strong and confident. Iakovos looked almost romantic in a loosely buttoned white linen shirt and blue jeans, but it was Yiskah who almost stole the show in a leopard print maxi dress, a glimpse of cleavage, her long hair flicked in waves off her face.

'Chronia polla Zetta,' said a young lady as she leant in and planted a kiss on the birthday girl's cheek. *Happy birthday.*

Love was everywhere, this island family surrounded by animated friends and well-wishers, all ready to reminisce with stories of Zetta's triumphs and disasters.

The tall bearded waiter leant in beside Yiskah and placed a hand upon her shoulder.

'Irthe I ora gia tis omiles,' he smiled. *It is time for the speeches.*

'Thank you, Nico.' She surveyed the crowded bar and took a breath.

She looked at her daughter. 'I'm going to speak now,' she whispered. 'I just wanted to tell you how much I love you and how proud I am of the woman you have become.'

'I love you too, Mum,' smiled Zetta and they kissed each other on both cheeks.

Yiskah got to her feet and tapped a knife on the rim of a large wine glass. Nico waved to the band who stopped playing. The guests soaked up the change of atmosphere, murmuring to one another as their attention turned to the Apostilides' table.

'Welcome everyone and thank you so much for coming. I would like to propose a toast to my gorgeous daughter, Zetta.' Yiskah encouraged her daughter to her feet. 'You are the apple of my eye and in you I see everything that is possible in life. Your love is contagious, your heart is strong and you are beautiful beyond words. I have watched you grow from a timid little girl into a confident young woman and it has been a journey I would not have missed for the world.' She paused for breath as Zetta took a moment to wipe a tear from her cheek.

'I remember at ten years old when you caught your first octopus and I saw then the fires of wonder burning inside your wide-open eyes. And then, when you were twelve, you won your first long-distance running race. You were such a tough and determined competitor. I sometimes felt that, even at the starting line, the others were already beaten.' Gentle laughter drifted through the bar.

'At fourteen you had your first crush on a boy from the city and by the end of that summer your heart was broken for the first time. My heart too was broken just two years later, when at sixteen, the same tough determination that carried you around this island in record pace, carried you away from me and into the arms of Athens.'

'But you came back and I am sure you know just how much I missed you. I love you and I always will.' Yiskah raised her glass. 'To my amazing daughter, Zetta!'

The guests lifted their drinks. 'To Zetta,' they chimed in salutation.

Yiskah returned to her seat, allowing the nerves of the last few minutes to settle. Zetta leant over and rested her head on her mother's shoulder. 'Thanks, Mum.'

'Speech, speech, speech,' chanted the crowd. Zetta lifted her head and smiled.

'My turn,' she whispered before standing, the chanting of voices slowing to a hush.

'It is true about summer romance,' she began. 'My friends, Carissa, Helena and Phebe, we all went through the same sort of heartbreak and we leant on each other, as I am sure we always will. That is island life. People come and people go. It is what we love and what we hate about living here. We love getting our island back during the winter months, but then we miss the excitement that the tourists bring.'

'I arrived here as a young girl many years ago and you all welcomed me with open arms. Paros is now my home and you are all part of my family. You taught me the importance of friendship and honesty and you all know that truth is a concept I hold very dear. Truth is what I have tethered all of my hopes and dreams to. These years on Paros have been the best of my life and I wouldn't change any of it for the world.'

Zetta's words were powerful and everyone was quiet.

'To my dear brother, thank you for always leading me down the right path. You have such a strong moral compass and I know I have angered you sometimes by going south when you suggested north.'

Iakovos smiled.

'You were always right though and I should have listened.' She blew her brother a kiss.

'To my mother,' smiled Zetta, turning to face her. 'I will always be grateful for your unconditional love and support.' Zetta leant down and hugged Yiskah who had tears rolling down both cheeks. 'This woman is amazing. She has always been there for me when I have needed her, which has been often.'

The guests laughed.

'There are not words for how much I love you all so I will not try to explain.' Tears began streaming down her face. 'I love you.' She blew the audience a kiss then returned to her seat and into the arms of her mother.

The bar filled with applause. A group of young men and women began chanting 'Iakovos' and soon the whole place was a sea of noise. 'Iakovos, Iakovos, Iakovos!'

Zetta managed a smile in her brother's direction as he stood to great cheer.

'Thank you to my disciples.' Laughter simmered across the crowd and he waited for the noise to settle. 'This is not my night but I would like to share a few thoughts on my sister.' The crowd was almost silent. 'Zetta has always been a great sister to me. At times she has protected me, too, and it has been her passionate defense that I have counted on. She is a close friend as well as an awesome sister who most of the time laughs at my jokes…' Yiskah looked across at Zetta who was laughing. '... like now. We will always share a special bond. We have shared good times and bad and as long as we remain together we will always be strong and happy. I love you sis. I always have and I always will.'

Iakovos blew his sister a kiss. The guests followed suit showering the birthday girl in kisses. Yiskah and Zetta got to their feet, embracing a man they both loved, kissing him on each cheek. With their arms around each other and Zetta in the middle, Yiskah looked to the crowd once more.

'Everyone have a great night. We love you all. May the band play all night long and the laughter flow freely. The drinks are on us.'

The Brazilian drummers hit the skins and their wild rhythms filled the room.

Yiskah held on to her grown-up children. 'I love you guys so much. Without you I would be nothing.'

'We know Mum. We love you too,' said Iakovos.

'Thanks for the party Mum.' Zetta pecked Yiskah on the cheek. 'I think I've got some dancing to do! Put my ankle to the test.' She wiggled free of Yiskah's clutches and did the cha-cha all the way to the dance floor.

Yiskah looked to Iakovos for confirmation. 'She okay?'

'She's doing great,' said Iakovos. 'We both are, Mum.'

'Have you seen Kosta yet?'

'No. Has he called you?'

'No. It's Zetta he's here to see.'

'Are you sure he's coming?'

'He wouldn't miss it for the world.'

Iakovos draped his arm around his mother. 'So, stop worrying. He'll be here.'

Iakovos guided Yiskah toward the busy bar, its wooden top surrounded by extended family and friends. They stepped around the back and helped the staff serve drinks. They received hugs and high fives as cocktails were shaken and fresh pints poured, the whole place a sea of colour, noise and laughter.

People stepped out between two large wood framed glass doors and onto a wooden slatted deck. They milled around tables filled with food and drink. A set of wooden steps led down onto the beach, the moon full and large, throwing a beautiful white light across the water. The contrast between light and dark created human silhouettes everywhere.

Down at the water's edge sat two people, side by side, like they were sitting for a portrait. The moonlight caressed one side of Zetta's face, beside her was Kosta, his long dark hair still wet and his olive skin glistening. Zetta looked out over the ocean.

'Oriana voutia,' she asked. *Nice swim?*

'Omorfos. Mou iremei panta,' replied Kosta. *Beautiful. It always calms me.*

'Have you seen Mum yet?'

'No. I haven't even been inside yet. I listened to the speeches from here.'

'You must speak to her Kosta. At least say hello.'

'If I can, I will,' he offered. 'That is all I can promise.'

'I wish you'd tell me what happened.'

'The time will come and then I will tell you everything.'

Kosta looked at Zetta before gently wrapping an arm around her. She leant into his embrace.

'You spoke beautifully,' he said. 'Did you mean what you said?'

'Of course, I did. I know something's missing. I've told you often enough but it doesn't affect how I feel about her.'

'It is not always going to be perfect.'

'I know that. I never expected perfection but it's what lies unsaid between us that bothers me.'

'Yiskah's got a lot on her plate. This party...'

'It's more than that. I'm an adult now. Yiskah has been a wonderful mother and I wouldn't change a thing, but as I get older, I really wish my parents were here to see how far I have come. To see what I made of myself...in spite of all the mistakes they made.'

'They would be very proud,' said Kosta.

'You know I never went to their funeral.'

'I know.'

'I was so young when it happened.'

'Funerals are a miserable business. You were lucky you missed it. I hated burying my parents. Watching them get lowered into the ground.'

'Did you say goodbye?'

'Of course I did. I cried my eyes out.'

'You see I never got to do that. I mean I cried my eyes out but I never saw them again. They were just gone from my life. I think that's why I've never felt their presence. Never felt their guiding hands. Maybe they were angry or maybe they just never loved me.'

'Losing your parents isn't easy. We both know that.'

'But you feel yours. You often say they are watching over you.'

'It is true. I feel them right here, right now.'

'I have never felt that way. Not even the slightest bit. It's like there's a huge empty void where they were. It's strange but it's like they never existed.' Tears fell down her cheeks. Kosta sighed and pulled her closer, the shimmer of moonlight illuminating the small waves that crashed lightly upon the beach.

'Tonight should be a celebration. Don't make yourself sad by chasing the past. The future is yours to make in whatever image you see it.'

'I know. I just can't shake the doubts. Maybe another drink will put me into party mode.'

'It's not the perfect solution but it is your birthday, so maybe you are right.'

Kosta got to his feet and helped Zetta up. She leant in and kissed him on the cheek. 'Thanks for the chat.'

He smiled. 'Go and enjoy yourself.'

'Will you promise me you'll find her.'

'I promise.'

Zetta walked across the sand back toward the bar. Kosta watched her go, his mind filled with thoughts of tomorrow.

Yiskah stepped out onto the wooden deck that led to the beach. She stopped at the edge and took a drink from her wine glass.

'Enjoying yourself.' The question came out of the dark yet she instantly recognised the voice.

'Kosta?' She peered to her left, a corridor between two buildings, beach access for the smaller boats. She could make out a wisp of smoke wafting from a lit cigarette, her eyes slowly adjusting to the features of the person attached to it. 'I thought you were giving up?'

'I tried. Maybe once the dust has settled.'

'Well I'm really glad you came.'

'Den tha eicha chasei gia ton kosmo,' said Kosta. *I wouldn't have missed it for the world.* 'How are you doing?'

'Okay,' said Yiskah. 'The night has been a success. That's all I wanted.'

'You've done well.'

'I hope so.'

Kosta blew out some smoke. 'Zetta is changing.'

'She's eighteen. She's a woman now."

'She knows something.'

'About what?'

'You told me that there were secrets between you.'

'Yes.'

'She feels that things have changed between you and her. If there are secrets, then she needs to know the truth. And quickly.'

'I know. I have felt the tension too.'

'We are all scared of change. It's how we face it and what we do with that fear that defines us.'

'I thought I'd be okay? I thought ten years was enough time.'

'Just have faith in your plan. See it through.'

'What happened the other night in Naxos?' asked Yiskah.

'Our love got lost. This is bigger than I realised. There isn't room for me at the moment.'

'So, there's still hope?'

'There's always hope. And where there is truth, there is love.'

She took a deep breath. 'Please come in. Say hello to everyone.'

'Sorry. I'll pass. I've booked a ticket on the early ferry.'

'You're leaving the island?'

'For a while. I'll run the business from Athens.'

'Do you have to?'

'I can't always worry about bumping into you. I need to clear my mind. Allow you to do what it is you must without the complication of us.'

'I'm so sorry.'

'It is what it is. Say goodbye to the kids for me.'

'You haven't see them?'

'Zetta yes, Iakovos, no.'

'She was always your favourite.'

'He always protected you. Took him a long time to accept me.'

'He was always my rock.'

'Zetta was all open arms. He was a pair of clenched fists.'

'It was never that bad.'

Kosta smiled. 'No, it wasn't. Just tell them I love them.'

'I will.'

'Kali tychi,' smiled Kosta. *Good luck.* He stubbed his cigarette out upon the stone wall and retreated into shadow. The tread of his sandals was all that was left until that too faded away.

Yiskah leant against the pergola and dropped her head. A weight settled down upon her shoulders, her thoughts filled with the burden she must now carry alone.

43

SUNDAY 21st SEPTEMBER
7:00AM CET
MARATHI VALLEY

The church bells of Agios Konstantinos spilled out across the western slopes of Mount Profitis Ilias. Crowing roosters competed with the ringing of copper on brass, both eager to be first to announce the dawning of a new day. The solitary peace of the highlands had been shattered, a ritualised breaking of the morning that occurred every day when the sun peeked above the horizon, wilfully showing its face once more.

It was warm inside the mountain house of the Apostiledes family, the thick stonewalls keeping the coolness of the mountain air at bay. The embers of the pot belly still aglow, heat wafting through the white-washed rooms and slate floors of this traditional Greek abode.

The morning duet of the bell and the roosters had failed to wake everyone. Iakovos was still curled up under his bedcovers completely oblivious to the world. In another room Zetta tossed and turned with dreams of family and friends; some lost long ago. The third person in this triangle was already up and awake, although to say she was functioning would be a lie.

Yiskah sat hunched over the thick timber top of the breakfast table as two sources of pain racked at her brain. A stab of discomfort jabbed hard at her forehead and she knew full well that this particular agony had been self-induced. Ouzo is a clean alcohol and a friend to the body but when mixed with red wine and tequila it always causes hurt. This soreness would be temporary and she would recover.

It was another source of grief, which pained her even more; something that ran deep and would take a long time to heal.

She was currently lost in thoughts of denial. 'While the children still slept, things could remain the same,' she told herself. It was a battle with her conscience that she knew was unwinnable. This same argument had been played out over a hundred times. It was a quarrel of contradictions and doubts, each time her own reply coming back at her with the same answer and each time it was as simple as the last.

'Just tell them,' insisted her inner voice. 'You must do what you had planned all those years ago.'

This was not a rash decision, more the realisation of a promise she had made to herself and the children a decade earlier. It was a vow she must keep if she was ever going to be able to live with the decisions she'd taken. Decisions that brought them half way around the world, changing their lives irrevocably and forever.

When they first bought this building and the land that surrounded it, they had skipped hand in hand up the path toward the front door. Yiskah felt like they were leaping toward the gates of heaven. This old farmhouse had been in her sights from across the other side of the world and she had purchased it on arrival.

From that day on they had restored and revived this near ruin into a romantic hideaway. It was a home in the strongest sense of the word. Love lived in every stone and every corner of this building and living here was as easy as breathing the oxygen-laden air that surrounded it.

Today, though, Yiskah's inner voice needed to be as strong as the limestone walls that protected her. The sound of footsteps made every bone in Yiskah's body bristle. Zetta emerged from the hallway and trundled into the kitchen. She lowered herself to the seat beside her mum and kissed her shoulder.

'Godd proi,' she said huskily. *Good morning*.

'Proi,' replied Yiskah.

'Thanks for last night. I can't remember if I said that already.'

'You did. Many times over.'

'I wasn't embarrassing, was I?'

'Never.' Yiskah turned and met her daughter's eyes. 'You were your beautiful self as always.'

'Mum. The truth please.'

'I drank just as much as you. Why would my truth be any clearer than yours?'

'Because your older and wiser.'

'Sometimes I wish I wasn't.'

'Everything okay?' Zetta sensed a sadness.

'Yes and no.'

'How Greek of you. What's up?'

'I have something to tell you and I really don't want to have to go there.'

'Then don't,' replied Zetta simply. 'Not today.'

'It's not like I have a choice. It's a promise I made to myself. A promise I must keep.'

'Break it. I always do.'

'Thanks for reminding me.'

Zetta grinned. 'I think we need coffee.'

Yiskah fidgeted nervously as Zetta stepped away from the table. She couldn't wait any longer.

Yiskah looked up. 'It's about your parents.'

Zetta stopped in her tracks. Her mind was cloudy. An old image of them briefly flashed past her eyes. She turned to face Yiskah. 'Look Mum, you brought us here a long time ago. You made our lives better. It's been incredible and I don't stop to thank you enough for what you have done. I probably wouldn't have even got to celebrate an eighteenth birthday if you hadn't brought me here. I know my folks died and all but…'

Yiskah raised her right hand. 'Stop there!' Yiskah swallowed hard. 'That's just it,' she said slowly. 'They didn't die.'

'What? What do you mean?' Zetta was all attention, her face screwed up in confusion. 'You said they were killed in a car accident. You told us that when we came here.'

Yiskah covered her face with her hands, the tremor of her fingers dancing upon a pale forehead. She knew she must continue. Get it done before cowardice took hold.

'They never died,' she blurted. 'Your parents never died. I lied to you.'

Zetta took a deep breath, the intake of air staggered as she averted her eyes.

'It was all I could do to keep you from going back and returning to those deadbeats,' cried Yiskah. 'They didn't deserve you so I took you and brought you here.'

Zetta rebelled against the darkness filling her mind. There was a deep, dark void growing with every breath, a vacuum of emotions that threatened to tear the empty spaces apart. She just froze, hoping the whole world would stay paused like this forever. She needed to breathe but her heart was breaking.

Iakovos stumbled in past them both and flicked the stove on. He filled a small pot with water and lowered it onto the hot plate.

'Kafes?' he asked through bleary eyes. *Coffee.*

No one moved. He looked across at Yiskah and then Zetta.

'What in the hell are you saying?' stuttered Zetta as she fought back feelings of revulsion.

'I'm saying do you want coffee,' said Iakovos, clearly disturbed by his sister's outburst. 'It's a simple question.'

'She's talking to me,' said Yiskah. 'Just sit down, Jacob. We have a lot to talk about.'

Iakovos was stunned. 'You haven't called me that for years.'

'I know.' Yiskah gestured to the chair across the table from her. 'Please, I have something important to tell you.'

'Hah,' laughed Zetta, 'Now you think it's important!'

'Please sit down, both of you.'

'You liar,' yelled Zetta her feet unmoved. 'I can't believe what you've done.'

'Lisa, I need you to calm down.'

'What's with all the shouting and the old names?' asked Iakovos.

'What I have to say involves your old lives. The Greek translation of our names was just part of my plan to stay hidden. Those days are at an end.'

'Our parents aren't dead Jacob,' screamed Zetta. 'Never have been. She lied to us,' her right forefinger driving a direct line through Yiskah's heart.

'What?' said Iakovos. He turned to stare at his mother. 'What the hell is she talking about?'

'It's true,' Yiskah's face showed all the years of secrets. Secrets she'd held so close to her chest. 'Your parents did not die as I told you when you were younger. They…'

'Stop.' Iakovos held up a hand as he tried to get his head around what had already been discussed. 'This is crazy.'

'She's fuckin' crazy,' hissed Zetta. 'The world's been turned upside down and I'm hanging off the edge.'

'Zetta. Please don't swear like that.'

'Don't even think about telling me what I can and can't do.'

'So, when we left Australia,' clarified Iakovos, 'It wasn't because our parents died?'

'No, it was because the system that protected you was not working,' said Yiskah, looking for some balance, trying to find her feet. 'I took you away because I was tired of watching you wither away. I was fed up with seeing you stagger into school each day.'

'So, you lied to us,' said Iakovos. 'Told us our parents were dead!'

'Did you miss them?'

'We cried our eyes out,' hissed Zetta. 'Don't you remember? You were there!'

'I remember. It tore my heart out.'

'Poor you,' mocked Zetta.

'It wasn't easy.'

'Fuck easy,' said Zetta. 'Easy is forgetting this shit ever happened. Easy is going back to bed and waking up tomorrow oblivious to it all. Easy is taking someone else's children.'

'I've never cried so much in my whole life,' said Iakovos. 'It haunts me still. Did you know that?'

'No, I didn't,' said Yiskah. 'I cried too.'

'Yes, but we were crying for our parents, not for ourselves,' said Zetta, only just keeping a lid on a desire for physical violence.

'They may not have been good at it but they were still our parents. You had no right to kill them off,' said Iakovos.

'I know. It was a last resort. The one thing I have always regretted. A secret I have endured and protected. Until today.'

'Why now?' pleaded Zetta, fists clenched hard upon the table. 'Why my birthday? I should still be celebrating. Instead I'm mourning the death of my parents for a second time. Your timing really sucks.'

'Your eighteen now and I am no longer your legal guardian. Your parents no longer have any control over you either. Your life is yours. Your choices are yours. You are free and that is why I chose today.'

'Are you sure this isn't just another piece of your selfish propaganda,' asked Zetta.

'I gave you a future,' said Yiskah. 'I brought you this far. You are free to make your own choices now.'

'We will never be free of our past,' shouted Zetta. 'It will always be a stain we carry. You have made sure of that.'

'I did what I had to,' said Yiskah, her own indignation simmering just below the surface. 'I am sorry if I caused you pain but I am not sorry I did it. I will never be sorry that I took you.'

'How did you do it?' asked Iakovos, his concern with the finer details as genuine as Zetta's red-faced aggression. 'How did you get away with bringing us here? Didn't our parents, the police try and stop you?'

'They did. I planned it well. We'd been gone two whole days before they even started looking. New names and new lives on the other side of the world; we just disappeared,' clarified Yiskah.

'So, you stole us?' said Iakovos.

'Yes. I stole you. I had exhausted every other avenue to improve your lives and nothing worked. It was all I could think of. To take you away and become invisible.'

'You tricked us,' yelled Zetta, as she leant across the table, her anger rebounding off the walls.

'It wasn't a trick. You were so young. You couldn't handle the truth.'

'Fuck the truth,' screamed Zetta as she angled her face closer to Yiskah.

Iakovos tried to get in between them. 'She has made our lives better Lisa. That is a fact.'

'Now you're using our old names too,' said Zetta. 'What is this? You're on her side, all of a sudden?'

'She's the closest thing to a mother we will ever have. It's pretty messed up what she did but she's still the one who gave us a second chance at life. No one else cared for us.'

'She is not our mother!' thundered Zetta. 'Our mother is living on the other side of the world! So is our father and we have been denied access to them for ten long years.' She glared back at Yiskah. 'You say I'm eighteen and I can make my own choices but you're wrong. I can't change what you did. I can't change the fact that you took my life from me. You made a choice when I was eight and now I have to live with that.'

'You have your whole life in front of you,' pleaded Yiskah. 'I made this situation possible. Eighteen was a dream you were never going to make. I have given you that!'

'A life without the love of my birth parents and now a life without you.' Zetta turned away. 'I can't even look at you. I need to get away from here.'

'Stop being so dramatic,' said Yiskah. 'You're not thinking rationally.'

'You're killing me!' laughed Zetta, moving from anger to exasperation, thumping two fists upon the wall.

'No that's exactly what your parents were doing to you,' reasoned Yiskah, 'And I ripped you away and we all escaped to paradise.'

'How dare you accuse them of killing me,' said Zetta. 'I'm here. I am alive. And I wish you'd shut the fuck up,' she added before lifting both hands to her ears.

'Ignorance won't make this problem go away,' said Iakovos.

'I wish I'd never woken up. It was all so perfect yesterday and now look how fucked up it is.'

'Exactly,' said Iakovos. 'She gave us a perfect life. One we could only have dreamed of back in Marvale.'

'Dreams disappear when you open your eyes. This is now a living fucking nightmare.'

'You're overreacting,' said Iakovos.

'And cut it out with the swearing!' said Yiskah.

Zetta picked up a mug and threw it down hard against the tiled floor. Both the morning and the blue cup shattered into a thousand tiny pieces.

'Is that better?' she hissed.

Yiskah's hands were clasped prayer like in front of her mouth. Her fingers were trembling. She didn't know what to say. Iakovos retrieved the broom from the corner of the kitchen and started sweeping up the fragments strewn across the floor.

Zetta looked down at her brother. 'I should've known you'd side with her. Your precious little mummy. Well I missed not having a father,' tears queued up and slid down Zetta's cheeks. 'I missed not having him around to tell me how things were going to be. To help me get through it all. It was bloody hard. I thought about him a lot. Wondered why I never felt his guiding hands.' Zetta's voice was filled with pain. 'I often wished he was still here with me. It's one of the reasons I ran away to Athens. Kosta became like a father to me too and now you've pissed him off as well.'

'That's a separate issue,' said Yiskah.

'Stop being so fucking clinical. It's all part of the same bloody mess,' said Zetta. 'I've carried a weeping hole right here in my heart and I've struggled with it every fucking day. And now I find out that my real father was still alive. Just languishing away on the other side of the world, wondering where his daughter had disappeared to.'

'I'm sorry for taking you away, but your father never cared where you were. Not when you were there nor once you were gone.'

'How dare you talk about him like that,' said Zetta, storming back toward Yiskah. 'How would you know how he felt? You obviously don't feel anything!'

'I sent letters. I kept in contact with your grandparents.'

'Nan and Pop?' said Iakovos.

'Yes. Would you like to read the letters they sent back?'

'They wrote back and you never showed us?' Zetta was incredulous. 'How could you keep such a thing from us.

'I couldn't show you. It would have complicated things too much. You would have wanted to see them too. It was dangerous.'

'You calculating bitch,' said Zetta.

'Zetta! Don't speak to Mum like that.'

'Are they still alive?' asked Zetta, ignoring her brothers order.

'Your pop is. Your nan passed away about six years ago.'

'Shit, this is so tough to hear,' said Iakovos. 'I can't lie. It hurts like hell.'

'It is what it is,' milled Yiskah. 'As Zetta said, it's too late to change the past.'

'It's too late for everything,' screamed Zetta, before running back to her bedroom.

Yiskah watched her disappear up the hallway. She stood to chase.

'Let her go,' said Iakovos.

'I knew she'd be angry.'

'It's been a crazy morning. It's the last thing she expected on her birthday and she's quite right to be emotional. Throw a hangover into the mix and kaboom!. She'll come around when she cools down.'

'I hope so. Why are you taking this so well?'

'I was older when we left. I resented mum and dad. Saw what they were doing. I dreamt of getting out. You made my wish come true.'

'Thank god you think I did the right thing. I couldn't live with myself if you both hated me.'

'She doesn't hate you.'

'Yes, she does!' yelled Zetta, standing in the hallway staring back at them, a black duffle bag in one hand, her face a stream of tears. 'I always knew something was missing. Now I know what it is; your heart. You never cared about us. This was always about you.'

'Zetta,' yelled Iakovos. 'That's enough!'

'We can't hide from the truth any longer?' said Zetta. 'I've been living a lie for too long. It's time to set the record straight.'

'I agree with you,' said Yiskah, pushing her chair back and stepping away from the table. 'I too want the truth to come out. That is why I always planned to tell you the truth. I have everything ready for us to return to Australia and for me to face the courts for what I did. I never expected to get away scot-free. I just wanted to make sure you lived to see this day.'

'Well I'm here now and I'm not sure I am alive anymore. Maybe I'd be better off dead than to have lived the lie you built for me.'

'You don't mean that,' said Iakovos.

'Don't you start telling me what I should think as well. One control freak in the family is enough.'

'I know it's big news.'

'Big news?' said Zetta. 'You underestimate what she has done to me, to us. I have wracked my brain all my life, trying to make sense of what happened.'

Zetta stepped upon a forgotten shard from the mug she smashed. She allowed all her weight to fall upon it and smiled as it split in two.

'Where are they now?' she asked still staring at the floor.

'In Marvale. Still in the same house,' said Yiskah. 'Well your dad is anyway. They separated a few years ago.'

'You keep in contact with them as well?' asked Iakovos.

'I send them a postcard every year. Anonymously of course.'

'How fuckin' friendly of you,' said Zetta.

'They deserve to know what's happening in your life,' said Yiskah, trying hard to ignore the expletives.

'They don't know we're here though, do they?' asked Iakovos, trying to join the dots.

'No. They know you are alive and well. That is all.'

'Can we see them if we want too?' he said.

'Of course you can. You can call them today if you want. Take all the time you need to process this information. Ask all the questions you want. I'll be here if you need to talk and when you're ready we'll go back to Australia and I'll gladly face the music for what I've done.'

'You planned it this way ten years ago?' asked Zetta.

'Yes. This is the last piece of a very complicated jigsaw that I started when you first came into my life.'

'And now it's finished,' said Iakovos.

'The first stage is. Now we have to prove that what I did was right.'

'Good luck with that,' said Zetta.

'It won't be easy. I can see that already.'

'So why tell us at all,' asked Zetta. 'Why not just lose this part of the jigsaw. Leave it hidden in a drawer somewhere?'

'Because I lied to you and I hated myself for it. The truth is and always will be very important to me and I made a promise to own up to everything when the time was right.'

'You're not a hero,' said Zetta.

'I'm not trying to be. Please don't hate me.'

Zetta stared straight through her. 'I feel nothing for you. My old life has once again been ripped away and I hate the feeling of loneliness that is suffocating the void you have so lovingly created.'

'I'm still here for you.'

'No, you're not. You're only in it for your own needs. I wish I were dead. And I wish you were too.'

Zetta burst across the slate tiles, out the front door and down the old stone steps.

'Go after her Iakovos. Make sure she's okay.'

Iakovos sprinted out the door but she was already on her scooter by the time he burst upon the driveway. He ducked as her back tyre spat out several small stones.

'Zetta!' he yelled but the whine of the fifty CC engine drowned him out and his pleas were lost in the vast expanse of the mountains. Seconds later, she was gone.

Yiskah knelt down on the floor, picking up the broken pieces of her mug. Iakovos burst inside the house.

'She's gone. I couldn't stop her.'

Yiskah looked up at him. 'She won't hurt herself, will she?'

'I don't think so.'

'She's tried to before.'

'I know.'

Yiskah lowered her head into her hands and started sobbing.

44

8:00AM CET
MARCELO BEACH

Zetta's scooter tore through the hills above Marcelo Beach, the rough dirt road spewing a red dust into the parched brown fields on either side. Ahead loomed a large white house, its blue shuttered windows and boxlike structure typical of the Cycladic Islands. The beautiful blue ocean of the Mediterranean framed the building and added a refreshing coolness to an otherwise hot day. Zetta wasn't enjoying the scenery.

She brought her scooter to a skidding halt in front of a large set of double doors and switched off the engine. She thrust her helmet off her head and hung it loosely from the handlebars, before climbing off and running up the grey slate steps to the architrave.

She grabbed hold of the copper handles in the middle of both doors and shoved her weight forward, forcing the oversized hinges on either side to ease both panels inward. Zetta slid in through the gap she'd created, her lithe body stretching between the wood like a gymnast.

'Kosta!' she yelled, her loud voice rebounding off the white tiled floor and white washed walls which lined the double heighted entrance. 'Kosta!' she screamed louder, this second call chasing the echo of the first, down through the corridors and doorways that meandered off in all directions.

'Kalimera, Zetta,' came his light, raspy voice. Zetta traced it to a hallway to her left. It was long and wide with several closed doors on either side. Further down the end an open door, a shaft of light spilling across the hallway floor. Zetta hurried toward it.

She stopped inside the doorframe. In front of her was a large white room, bare of any furnishings or wall hangings. The polished concrete floor was also white, making her feel like she was floating through clouds. The opposite wall was floor to ceiling glass, framing a view of the Mediterranean Sea, its light and beauty flooding the room.

'Erthei kai na kathisei,' said Kosta. *Come in and sit down.*

Zetta looked around the door and to her right. Kosta sat cross-legged upon the floor, his back against the wall, his body dressed simply in a pair of white cotton pants and t-shirt. Kosta kept his gaze focused on the blue water of the horizon, his posture unchanged.

'Thank god your still here,' said Zetta, as she slumped in a heap beside him.

'I missed my ferry,' lied Kosta, knowing full well that as love and worry stirred deep within him early this morning, he had listened to his body and made a decision to stay. He had watched his ferry round the Cape in the first rays of the day and wondered if he wasn't just overreacting. Zetta's presence here now justified his indecision. 'One thing I haven't missed is your anger. I can feel it from here,' he said. 'You always were a fiery one.'

'Well now I have reason to be. Mum just told me the real story about my parents. Did you know the truth?' Zetta's tone was confrontational. Her hard voice bouncing off the walls with venom.

Kosta took a deep breath, his face no longer the picture of serenity and calm that she'd first stumbled upon. 'Did I know what?'

'Don't play games with me. This is not one of your courtrooms.'

'I don't play games.'

'Did you know the truth about my past?'

Kosta let out a deep sigh. 'I knew some, but not all.'

'Tell me what you knew.'

'Why now?'

'Because I deserve to know the truth. And as Yiskah has so kindly informed me, I am eighteen now and able to make my own decisions.' The last sentence echoed against the walls. Kosta waited for it to fade.

'She meant good decisions. When you are this angry you can only make bad mistakes.'

'Angry. That word doesn't do me justice right now. Tell me,' she thundered, her fury absolutely destroying the tranquility of the room.

'Okay. But please try to stay calm. Your mother told me what she thought I needed to know. That was all.'

'And what was it you needed to know?' Zetta's patience was growing thinner with every word.

'That you came from Australia. You have parents that did not look after you, so she brought you here.'

'And what did you think of that?'

'She is a very good woman. I trusted her. She did what she thought was right.'

'Was she right?'

'Of course. We are all right in our own minds. We all make decisions that we must live with.'

'And what does the law say?'

'Law is unbiased. It is too black or white for cases like this.'

'But you're a lawyer don't you see how wrong this was?'

'I am a lawyer, yes. But I am not a judge. There is a difference.'

'She told me that my parents had died. She lied straight to my face.'

Kosta looked to the ocean for a moment. 'That I did not know. She must have wrestled with it for many years.'

'Why didn't she tell me the truth?'

'She obviously thought it was better this way.'

'Better for who?' Zetta's fists were clenched.

'Calm down. I am as surprised as you. Your battle is not with me or the world for that matter.'

'So, you agree with me.'

'I am shocked. I can't believe your mother would create this kind of a lie.'

'She is not my mother!'

'Anger makes you rash. She looked after you. She loved you.'

'You still believe that?'

'This journey she has taken you on, it is bigger than the all of us,' said Kosta. 'Our lives have become very complicated.'

'She lied to you too. If she really loved you, she would have explained herself.'

'We all have secrets. It's our actions that make us who we are, not the words we keep hidden. If our intentions are true, then that is what really matters.'

Zetta picked nervously at her fingernails. Kosta watched on, deep furrows of concern etched across his own face.

'What are your intentions?' said Kosta.

'I want the truth. I want her to pay for what she has taken from me.'

'You know she always planned to return to Australia and hand herself in?'

'She said that. How nice of her,' the sarcasm and hate, dripped from Zetta's lips.

'I imagine she knew that what she was doing was against the law but she had to do something.'

'And now it's my turn to play the devil's advocate.'

'You want her to say sorry?' asked Kosta.

'No. That would be too easy. I want revenge.'

Kosta raised his eyebrows. 'Really? They are strong words! Your instincts surprise me.'

'My whole life has just been turned upside down. It's all one big fucking surprise to me.'

'You are not helping yourself with thoughts of retaliation.'

'It'll do the job for now. She has controlled my life. Now I will control hers.'

'You should take a while to think before you do something you might regret.'

Zetta turned away from Kosta and looked out over the horizon. 'It is too late for that. As you said before, actions count more than words. It is my intentions that will define me.'

45

10:00AM CET
MONASTERY OF AGHIOS MINAS

The morning sun hung lazily above the horizon, its autumn trajectory forcing long dark shadows across the faded white face of the old monastery. All was quiet in this remote section of Marathi, high above the ancient marble quarries. Yiskah treaded dirt as she circled the four walls of the religious fortress, searching for signs of the monk who resided here.

She stepped in through the old wooden gate that clung loosely to the crumbling stonewalls of the vegetable garden. Inside here the land was fertile, its raised beds teaming with produce, the recent summer rains providing the extra nutrition required for a late push into the cooler months. Yiskah reached up and picked a mulberry from the tree in the centre, dark red juice oozing from the fruit and dripping down her fingers. She popped the berry quickly into her mouth and licked her fingers. She already had blood on her hands. She didn't need any more.

She stepped over a section of the outer stonewall that had crumbled to the ground, the discarded rocks sharing the land with an eclectic assortment of headstones and epitaphs. The cemetery numbered some fifty dead, but it had not been a working concern for some time and the most recent burial was twenty years ago.

The monk still tended it, keeping the weeds under control. And with good reason. There was one spot left in the graveyard for the man who worked this corner of God's heavenly creation. The monk had reserved it a long time ago, having realised he would finish his time here doing both God's work and continuing the much-maligned business of living. They would end together, his life and his work, as inseparable as they had always been.

Yiskah shared a deep connection with Monk Andreadis. He'd played an important role in helping Yiskah carry her burden of mistruths. They had met irregularly over the years, the monk always available when called upon to listen to her lies. He was not a priest and had never delivered a sermon nor led a congregation, but he was wise beyond his station and she considered him a man of great honour.

She stepped around the northern corner of the building and placed a hand on the iron gate that defended the main entrance. Her hands were trembling, a physical reminder that today had not gone to plan. Zetta's eruption into anger had disturbed her greatly.

Yiskah needed the Monk Andreadis' advice. She didn't know if she would have time to return later. A thick rope hung freely off to the left of the gate. She pulled down on it, the ringing sound of bronze on bronze announcing her arrival. Yiskah waited, knowing that time was once again working against her.

10:15AM CET
CAFÉ LATTE

Iakovos fidgeted with a napkin. He sat at a table underneath the pergola of Selina's ice cream shop. He had called Zetta earlier and after a brief but terse exchange they had agreed to meet here. Being in such a public place might calm them both down.

Iakovos thought about the extraordinary life they had lived here. People came from all over the world looking for a taste of the beautiful life. The clear blue water, the ancient white buildings, the purple bougainvillea and the allure of love. Others came in search of history, chasing the oldest remnants of Greek civilisation.

The news he had heard this morning had turned his own slice of history on its head. He needed to save what he could, before it too was in ruins. Zetta entered the café with the energy of someone about to burn a few bridges.

'Afto tha parei kairo?' she asked. *Will this take long?*

'Ithela aplos na miliso,' said Iakovos, trying to wrestle control of the high ground. *I just wanted to talk.*

'Haven't we done that already!'

'Please!' Iakovos directed his sister to take the seat opposite him. Zetta stood her ground.

'Do it for me,' he pleaded. She took her seat.

'Coffee?' Iakovos needed to keep her here to have any chance of success. A nod. He raised his hand and a dark-haired young woman approached them from the shade of the doorway.

'Two short blacks, please.' Iakovos waited for the waitress to leave. 'How are you feeling?'

'Is it not written all over my face?'

'Yes, it is, but I did not want to presume.'

'Why stop now?'

'I understand how you feel.'

'No! That's where you're wrong. You don't have a clue how I feel.'

'I went through this too, you know.'

'You were always a mummy's boy. I needed something else; a father to help me understand how men think. My relationship history is proof of that failure.'

'And Yiskah is trying to take responsibility for the choices she made. She knows she wasn't perfect.'

'She's ten years too late by my count. She can't just say sorry now and hope everything will be okay.'

'She's not expecting that. She knows what she did was wrong. It was a bad situation.'

'And she made it worse.'

'That's where you're wrong. She saved us. We were living a life of abuse and loneliness. Don't you remember?'

'Not really. I was so young. Too young to lose my parents.'

'Well you'd do well to remember how bad it was before you attack our mother again.'

'Attack? She's the one who broke the bloody law. She attacked my right to choose. Now I will attack her right to freedom!'

'She had no choice. I see a lot of Mum in you and you don't always play the game as per the instructions either.'

'There's no genetic match up here. She's not my blood.'

'No, but you act like her sometimes. Impulsive, fiery, rash.'

'You think I haven't thought about that?'

'Well you've known the truth for five minutes and already you're burning the house down.'

'I've had my suspicions for a long time.'

Iakovos was visibly shocked. 'What? You already knew about this?'

'Not exactly. Just a couple of things that sparked my concern. That's why I'm so bloody angry. I should've worked it out sooner.'

'Like what?'

'Like the fact we never spoke about our wider family. You know, cousins, aunties, and uncles? Where were they? All our friends have them.'

'We have always been different,' reasoned Iakovos. 'We kept to ourselves in the beginning. We were all we had. The Johnstone clan hated us.'

'So mum told us.'

Iakovos ignored her accusation. 'We're part of this island now like everybody else. Kosta, Gianni, Stella and Nico. They have all treated us like family.'

'They have been very good friends to us but they are not our family.'

'They are enough for me.' He looked around the café and back to Zetta. 'What else made you suspicious?'

'Do you remember when I was in trouble with the police for stealing that necklace?'

'Yes. Hardly forgettable.'

'Well it should have been recorded on my criminal record,

right, but they couldn't find my name on the register. I was in the police cell and I watched Yiskah have a very terse argument with the officer who arrested me; Anton I think his name was. I'm sure I saw money exchanged and the problem magically disappeared. They released me that afternoon.'

'You think Mum paid off the police?'

'She had too. We know now that Zetta Apostilides does not officially exist.'

'Wow, Of course. And me?'

'The same. You're still Jacob Johnstone. Always was and always will be. Iakovos Apostilides is a creature of fiction, like a character in a book.'

'So, she had to bribe the police to stop them tracing us back to Perth. I never knew she had it in her.'

'She kidnapped us, didn't she?'

'Sure. We know that now.'

'Yes, but what I'm trying to say is that you never looked deep enough. You've always been happier than me. Your favourite saying is why rock the boat?'

'I had no reason to question our lives. Why destroy what I love?'

'I didn't go looking for problems either. They found me.'

'It was a team effort. You never knew when to stop pushing. Still don't.'

'Agreed…' Zetta paused. 'There's more.'

The waitress arrived with their coffees and the conversation stalled.

'Thank you.' Iakovos provided the glimpse of a smile before the waitress departed.

Zetta leant across the table. 'If I tell you, it must always remain a secret between the two of us.'

'Yposchomai,' said Iakovos. *I promise.*

10:30AM CET
MONASTERY OF AGHIOS MINAS

The interior of the rundown church was a monastic mix of stone and wood. There was very little in the way of decoration. Light flooded in through the high arched windows, playing elaborate shadow games upon the lumpy rendered walls.

On one side was a large hand-painted mural, depicting the moment the Three Wise Men came across Mary and Jesus. The colours had faded and the plaster had peeled off in places to reveal the stonework construction behind the art, but the work was still a sight to behold and a reminder of the importance of faith.

Beside the mural stood a small wooden table, a collection of unlit wax candles atop it in a long brass container. On the far side was another table, atop which a container of sand held a single burning candle.

A neat row of seven wooden pews filled the other side of the small chapel. Yiskah and the monk sat beside one another on the pew nearest the front, his full length black robe a reminder of the somber mood Yiskah found herself in.

'It is not forgiveness that I am searching for,' said Yiskah, emotional yet eloquent. 'I know that what I did was wrong.'

'Do not be too harsh on yourself. Try to remember who you were ten years ago and why you took the actions that guided you here.'

'I just wish I had told them earlier. Eighteen is a very troublesome age without this added problem to deal with. I know it was the same with me.'

'You lost your own parents at fourteen did you not?' remembered the monk.

'Yes, that's right. A drunk driver ploughed into them. They were both killed instantly. They'd been to a friend's house for dinner. I was supposed to go too but I'd refused. Our last exchange was not a happy one.'

'Do you blame them?'

'For dying?'

The monk nodded.

'No. Not anymore. I did, though, for a long time.'

'Was that reasonable?'

'No. I was angry.'

'Your reaction was probably not unlike what Zetta is going through right now.'

'Her anger is so raw.'

'As was yours. Deep down you are so alike.'

'But so distant.'

'You must allow her the space to grieve. She has been denied what was rightfully hers. The past can never be changed but the future is in your hands.'

'So, I'll just have to wait and see?'

'It is one way forward.'

Yiskah wiped a tear from her cheek.

The monk rolled his worry beads over in his hands. 'There is another question I have for you. The drunk driver who crashed into your parents? Whatever happened to him?'

Yiskah lifted her head and looked up at Christ on the cross. 'He was convicted and sentenced to ten years in jail. It wasn't nearly enough. I wanted to kill him.'

'Is he still alive?'

'I don't know.'

'You should be proud of yourself. You created a new future with your own hands. Made it better for everyone including him. His life was never yours to play with.'

'Did I go too far?'

'I think you did the right thing coming to Paros. You are a good woman, Yiskah. That is foremost in my mind.'

'I am not so sure. None of this would have happened if I'd killed him. I would have gone to prison and never been allowed to train as a teacher. I would never have met Zetta or Iakovos. Life would simply have been different. Not this mess.'

'This is your life. It's what you were born to do. Fate is still playing with you.'

'Well I wish she'd bloody well stop.' Yiskah collected her thoughts. 'My apologies for swearing.'

'That same anger is what your daughter is feeding off. You must be calm. Finish what you started. Then and only then will you be judged.'

Yiskah closed her eyes and knelt on the floor. She clasped her hands together. 'Love will be my shepherd,' she prayed.

'Yes, love will be your guiding light,' agreed the monk as he knelt beside his good friend and they prayed together.

46

1:00PM CET
CAPE MAISTROS

Zetta sat huddled and alone against the base of one of three massive wind turbines that stood proudly at the summit of Cape Maistros. This lookout appealed to Zetta during times of stress, its remoteness ensuring the privacy she so keenly sought. The last few years had seen many visits here and, as loneliness, fear and anger battled for her attention, she had attempted to clear the debris away and reflect as often as she could.

Today she stared off into the distance, the island of Mykonos only just visible through the heat haze floating high above the deep blue of the Mediterranean Sea. Her own vision was just as cloudy and as the huge white blades of the turbines spun swiftly above her head, she tore at her memories, shredding them to pieces, a desperate search for some semblance of truth.

The breeze up here was strong and consistent enabling these modern-day windmills to generate a dependable source of electricity for the island. Zetta, too, had a mission and her seething intensity was as formidable as the towers behind her. Her zeal was unwavering and it showed no respite. She was heartbroken, a situation which allowed determination and desperation to drive her every decision. Kosta's advice was not being headed and Zetta had become an irrational and unstoppable mess.

The terrain surrounding her was harsh and dry. Stacked slate walls bordered the fields, slicing them up into small parcels of land. Only one plant could survive the arid soil and fierce breeze that blew up here and the parched brown flower buds of this thriving weed swayed from side to side. It was survival at all costs.

A lone white yacht sailed across the deep blue water of the horizon. Zetta knew there would be a ferry not too far behind it. The same scheduled ferry they arrived on ten years ago. Zetta planned to be there when it docked. But this time she would be saying goodbye.

Tears streamed down her cheeks as she uncovered the mobile phone that had been cradled in the palm of her left hand. She dialed quickly then lifted it to her ear. The phone rang. She waited. Click, click.

'Australian Federal Police. How can I help you?'

Zetta wiped fresh tears away from her cheeks. 'Hi, my name is Zetta,' she stumbled, '… sorry Lisa Johnstone is my real name and I am calling from the Greek Island of Paros.'

'Hello Lisa, what can I do for you?'

'I am on your missing persons list. Have been for ten years.'

'Are you safe?'

'Yes.'

'And you're healthy?'

'Yes. Everything's fine. No one's trying to kill me. I just think it's time I came home.'

2:00PM CET
MARATHI VALLEY

Yiskah was harvesting cucumbers from the vegetable garden in front of her house when she heard the Mini pull up into the driveway. Her emotions leapt with the possibilities of a tearful reunion with her estranged daughter but she looked up and watched as Iakovos climbed quickly from his car and ran toward her.

'Grigori mama, I astynomia erchontai,' he yelled. *Quick Mum, the police are coming*. 'You must hide.'

Deep frown lines covered Yiskah's face but she did not move. Despondency and sadness had her glued to the spot.

Iakovos came to a halt in front of his mother and tried to shake the doldrums from her. 'Are you listening to me? You must run away from here.'

Yiskah could feel the increasing weight of the world upon her shoulders and it felt a lot heavier than she had expected.

'If now is the time for me to face my demons, then let it be so,' she said.

'But they'll put you in jail. Maybe take you back to Australia.'

'These are the events I have planned for. It is happening much quicker than I expected and without the reflection I craved, but I cannot avoid them now. Running would only delay these actions. I am ready to face the law. I started this whole process. Now I must finish it.'

Iakovos stepped forward and embraced his mother. 'Why are you doing this to us?'

'Because I love you and I wanted to save you. That is why.' Yiskah cradled her son's face with both hands. 'Look at me. We have had ten years of bliss and happiness. Now I must face up to the truth. Fate has brought us here. Love will bring us back.'

'This is not fate's doing. It's Zetta's. She has done this to you. To us.'

'I chose to face up to the law.'

'Not like this though? I tried to change her mind but she wouldn't listen. Zetta called the police. Both here and back in Australia.'

Yiskah's shoulders drooped, each word adding more weight to her burden.

'She must be more hurt than I ever imagined. I thought I could be everything, both a mother and a father. I was wrong.'

'So now we run.' Iakovos pulled his mother toward the house. 'I don't want them to take you.'

She dug in her heels. 'If Zetta really feels this way, then half of what is dear to me has already been taken.'

'What about me?' wailed Iakovos, brimming with tears. 'I still love you, isn't that enough?'

'Of course it is, but we have been broken. Stay here where you will be safe. I will call for you. Zetta is eighteen now and our lives may take different courses under her control.'

'But she is out of control. That is the problem.'

'She can live her life as she wants to now. Make her own decisions. That is the freedom she has craved. It is everything that she deserves.'

'But her decisions are destroying us! She should know this.'

'She knows.'

The sound of a car engine tore the heart out of the valley. Iakovos remained in panic mode.

'Please mum, don't let them take you.'

'I am ready to go.' Yiskah opened her arms. 'Let us say goodbye.' Iakovos stumbled forward into his mother's embrace. Yiskah kissed the top of his head and breathed in the familiar aroma of her son's hair.

A police car raced around the corner and came to a skidding halt behind the Mini. Two officers climbed out and approached the house.

The bearded one stepped toward Yiskah. 'You need to come with us.'

'I know.'

'This is big problem that you have caused and I cannot protect you this time. It is happening fast my friend. It appears you have kept many secrets from us.'

'I'm sorry George. I felt I had no choice.'

'The Australians are extraditing you now. Your ferry leaves at midnight. You're on your way home.'

'Paros is my home.'

'Not anymore.' The younger officer secured a pair of handcuffs around Yiskah's wrists and guided her toward the police car. She looked over her shoulder.

Iakovos held her gaze before he collapsed against the white

washed walls of their house, his sobs floating off across the hills, sadness filling what was once a valley of hope.

47

12:00 MIDNIGHT CET
BLUE STAR FERRY

The hull of the ferry struck wave after wave as all four engines drove its heaving bulk around Cape Aghios Fokas and into the rough seas of the open ocean. A thick grey blanket of clouds covered the sky as the large searchlight mounted at the bow of the ship threw its massive beam across the vast darkness of the Mediterranean Sea.

The muffled sounds of this battle between ocean and steel seeped in past the picture windows of the main deck. Tired passengers found comfort where they could, from the soft seats of first class, to the cheap seats and carpeted floors of the corridors that ran the ships length.

Two floors down and into the bowels of the hull, the ocean noise had totally evaporated. A long grey corridor of steel contained this eerie silence, at the far end a seated naval officer, his eyes closed, body drifting from side to side in sync with the listing of the boat. Behind him a door labelled 'Cell 2'.

On the other side of the door was Yiskah, cross-legged on the floor, her thin frame wedged into one corner. There were no picture windows for this passenger, just a centrally hung roof light, illuminating the cube-like space. The bulb swung without pattern, throwing shadows around the room like a swarm of enemies. Yiskah tried to concentrate on the folder open on her lap.

She flicked through the lever arch file, its pages filled with old photos, postcards and letters covering her last ten years. Beautifully bound with ribbon, each new page was lovingly decorated, each section filled with the finer details of their story. Each section organised chronologically, a mixture of birthdays and celebrations, copies of school reports and letters from the local church.

Yiskah derived great strength from the turning of every page. The world outside might be crashing down around her, but inside her own head lived the peace and quiet of the last decade, and as she relived the highlights of her life on Paros, the glimpse of a smile spread quietly across her face. The clock ticked past midnight and she sensed that this might be her last chance at happiness for a while.

48

TUESDAY 23rd SEPTEMBER
8:00AM AWST
PERTH INTERNATIONAL AIRPORT

Yiskah was escorted from the plane under lock and key, her wrists bound by a pair of steel cuff links. Two officers, one female and one male, had waited until all the other passengers had left the plane, saving their prisoner the embarrassment of an audience. The disapproving eyes of the Qantas plane crew were enough, keeping Yiskah pigeonholed as the worst kind of mother, their dislike and distrust obvious and overbearing.

'This way, Miss Bell,' directed the male officer. He had been seated immediately behind Yiskah throughout the journey and they were yet to share a real conversation.

'My name is Yiskah Apostolides. Can you please stop using my old name?'

'Sorry, but my job doesn't involve niceties. The extradition papers refer to you as Miss Bell so that's what I'll call you.'

'Thanks,' sighed Yiskah. 'It's been nice getting to know you too.'

'The pleasure ain't over yet.'

'We needn't worry about Passport Control,' briefed the female officer. 'That's already been dealt with.' She looked at Yiskah.

'And you only have hand luggage so we're just going to walk you straight out of here, okay?'

Yiskah just nodded. Thirty hours of non-stop travel had sapped her reserves faster than expected, weakening her defences and dampening her resolve. Returning to Perth had conjured up some uncomfortable memories, unease wedging itself hard within the forefront of Yiskah's mind, forcing her to remember the woman she thought she had left behind. A person she was painfully realising was still buried deep within. Jessica Bell was alive, but to say she was well would have been a grand overstatement.

'Through here please,' ordered the man, his left arm guiding her through a simple side door. A narrow corridor on the other side ran for about thirty metres and Yiskah enjoyed the anonymity of its secure walls. She badly needed a rest away from prying eyes. She yearned for some time alone.

They emerged out the other end, hundreds of weary travellers swirling around them. Their stares were heavy and penetrating, the cuffs apparently carrying some grave and contagious disease. She wondered whether they knew who she was and had already convicted her. It was her first real taste of the criticism and scorn she was walking head-first into.

Six soldiers in green uniforms burst forward from the mayhem and surrounded her. The sheer size of each man was both alarming and intimidating. A young woman appeared soon after, her charcoal pencil skirt forcing her to take small steps.

'Sorry I'm late,' she gasped.

Yiskah scanned the badge pinned to her chest: 'Airport Media Liaison' and underneath that the name 'Amanda Bennett'.

'That's okay,' said the male officer. 'We just got here.'

'Good. These boys certainly don't mess around and I'm just not built for speed.'

'The man mountains are a bit over the top,' observed the female officer. 'Just one of these guys would be more than enough for her.'

'I agree, but the media like a big story. So, we need a big photo. My bosses are keen on selling her as a real danger to society.'

'What does that mean?' asked Yiskah.

'That's none of your business. I haven't got the time nor the inclination to answer any of your questions.' She looked at the officers. 'Keys? File.'

'Sure.' The male officer handed a ring of keys and a clip folder to Ms Bennett.

'Thanks. I'll take her from here.'

'She's all yours.' The officers turned and left like they'd just dropped off a parcel at the post office.

Amanda stepped toward Yiskah, her arm extended in greeting.

'Hello Miss Bell. My name is Amanda.'

Yiskah showed her the cuffs. 'Hi Amanda. Sorry can't shake hands. I'm a bit tied up at the moment.'

'Oh, that's right of course you are.' Amanda smiled.

'What's happening? Where are we going?' asked Yiskah.

'No questions remember. You're the one in custody. I'll do all the talking. You just keep nice and quiet.' She turned to face the soldiers. 'I'm very keen on getting her to the courts and into remand. The media need to know what charge she's up for. They want their six o'clock headline and it's my job to give it to them.'

'Where is my daughter?'

'Your daughter?' said Amanda, a sly grin giving her bias away. 'You don't have a daughter Miss Bell.'

'Yes, I do. Zetta Apostilides. I know she's here.'

'That may be, but she is not your daughter. Her name is actually Lisa Johnstone and she was your prisoner and now she is free.'

Yiskah's composure weakened. 'You have no idea what you're talking about,' she stammered. 'How dare you make such accusations?'

Amanda stared her down. 'Look, she's not part of my brief. So, let's stay on task shall we and get where we need to be.' She turned away but Yiskah reached out with both hands and grabbed her arm.

'Find out where she is, or we stay put?'

Amanda shrugged off Yiskah's advances, removing her hands forcefully. 'You're not in any position to give orders. I am being paid to do a job. I will do no more than asked and certainly no less.'

Amanda stepped to the left and spoke quietly with one of the soldiers.

'Attention,' the man said to his men. 'Wilson and Miers; please escort the prisoner and follow my lead.' Two of the men stepped in beside Yiskah and grabbed her securely by the arms. They escorted her quickly and without interruption, following the lead soldier toward the far end of the custom's hall. A flash of Ms Bennett's card was enough to see the whole entourage jump the queues and pass through the checkpoints without any hassle.

A set of large metal doors below the Arrivals sign slid open and a flash of bulbs flooded Yiskah's unguarded face. A massive media throng had gathered in the Arrivals lounge, jostling for prime position behind a line of shiny metal barriers. This ambush of cameras and microphones assaulted Yiskah's personal space, forcing her to shield her eyes from the intense scrutiny.

'Miss Bell, what made you snap?' barked a journalist.

'Jess, why did you steal and abuse those two children?' shouted another, the sound of her old name separating her from reality like a leap back in time.

'Miss Bell, how did you stay undercover for so long?' shot another man, each one more impatient than the other, no time or energy for real answers.

'Jess, how do you feel about being captured?' pushed a young woman from the front.

Each poorly researched phrase nailed Yiskah's own reply hard against her tongue, the barrage of misinformation proof of just how misunderstood she was. The old names and their old lives the only information these people had to go on. They knew nothing of the last ten years. Nothing of the beauty or the love her new family had experienced. Only the fermented hate of her original act remained.

Yiskah's entourage forced their way unforgivingly through the storm of accusations.

'Miss Bell will not be answering any questions,' said Miss

Bennett. 'A press conference will be held later today at the district court house. Thank you.'

Amanda kept her charges moving. 'Don't stop until she's in the car.'

'How do you feel about Lisa Johnstone's decision to testify against you?' probed a younger male voice. The question was swiftly delivered and it hung above Yiskah like a noose, her head spinning, her attention captured by a young man staring straight into her own eyes. Yiskah sensed his hunger for a story. The fact that lives were being affected was no concern of his. Yiskah wanted to respond but she was whisked away from trouble and into a shiny black Ford Territory.

But there was one person here who knew everything about those last ten years. She was watching the mayhem from the relative safety of the mezzanine floor. Zetta had arrived just a few hours earlier, unannounced and under the radar. It appeared she wasn't expected and she had decided to stay clear of the theatrics. She watched Yiskah's car leave then waited as the media ran off to their own vehicles. Zetta had not anticipated such attention and thanked the heavens for the anonymity she knew would end soon.

She glided down the escalator and out through the doors to the outside world. A warm breath of Perth's air brought back many stolen memories of her youth. She smiled and hailed a taxi. The return journey hadn't numbed her senses. Quite the opposite. She felt very much alive. Lisa Johnstone was happy to be home.

49

10:00AM AWST
PERTH DISTRICT COURT

A black Ford Territory pulled up to the District Court steps, its tiered entrance already awash with reporters. All four doors opened simultaneously as Yiskah was ushered off the back seat by Wilson and Miers. They escorted her up the steps with military precision, the soldiers running the gauntlet of the gathered media.

They paused at the top of the steps and waited for Ms Bennett to catch up, her attire causing havoc with the climb. Yiskah took the time to scan the building ahead, a revolving glass door spinning like a merry-go-round. She felt like she was centre-stage at a circus and wished she could escape.

'I'd like to make a comment,' she told Amanda as soon as she reached the top step.

'Like hell you do. Our job is to get you in here, get you charged and get you behind bars.'

'That's pretty obvious. But I'm the one on trial here. They need to know the truth.'

'That's a negative Miss Bell. You will not be making any comments today.' Amanda looked at the lead soldier. 'Bring her this way.' The Media Liason stepped in through the revolving door before the order to move had been given and as the glass panel glided in between the two groups, she sensed a danger, anger crossing her face like dark clouds across the sky. She thrust a finger at Yiskah and shook her head.

But Yiskah seized the moment, wrestling control away from the grip of her minders, surprising them with a rush back toward the cameras.

'Ladies and gentlemen,' announced Yiskah as she descended the steps, the crowd of journalists and camera men mobbing and jostling her into seclusion. 'My name is Yiskah Apostolides and I have been living on the Greek island of Paros for ten years. Lisa and Jacob have grown into two healthy, educated adults. I have never abused them and they have led normal lives under their new names, Zetta and Iakovos Apostilides.'

Two of the soldiers tried to jostle their way through the protective wall of media, their actions cleverly thwarted by the press.

'My decision to leave this country with the children, was taken after much consideration and with their best interests at heart,' continued Yiskah.

The lead soldier wasn't taking any prisoners and forced his way through from the rear.

He stepped in beside Yiskah, suddenly aware of the camera lenses just metres away from his face. Unsure what media coverage his planned aggression would receive, he decided to stay put. Dragging her away kicking and screaming wasn't the kind of notoriety he was after.

'I am a teacher,' continued Yiskah, 'And our professional code of ethics states that I must always put the interests of my students first. I have followed that code to the last decree.'

Amanda Bennett appeared on Yiskah's other flank, all too aware that the cameras were still rolling.

'I followed that same promise when I took Lisa and Jacob from their parents,' said Yiskah, 'And since that day I have cared for them like they were my own. I am not a bad person. I am and always will be a good teacher.'

Amanda leant into Yiskah's ear. 'That's your sound bite over and done with,' she whispered. 'Now come with me. And no more surprises.'

Yiskah smiled for the cameras. 'My media liaison, Amanda Bennett and I, are committed to the truth and together we will ensure that the world knows why I had to take Jacob and Lisa. Why I had no other choice than to flee the cesspit their lives had become.'

Amanda glared incredulously across at Yiskah.

'Thank you for listening,' said Yiskah, just before she was guided willingly back in through the revolving door.

'What the hell do you think you're doing?' yelled Amanda.

'Making myself heard. I have a voice you know!'

'Not here you don't. And I certainly don't work for scum like you!'

'You have no idea what I have been through!'

'I like it that way. So, let's just get this damn job finished.'

The soldiers hustled Yiskah across the foyer of the courthouse and into a small, white courtroom. Several people milled around the rear, a judge and two suits up the front.

'Does my trial start today?' asked Yiskah as she was guided toward the pews in the middle.

'No. You're only here to be charged,' said Amanda.

'Do I get a lawyer?'

'That's up to you. I'm not sure you deserve one.'

Yiskah held the liaison's gaze. 'Do you even know anything about me?'

'I know you took someone else's kids and as a mother myself I can't imagine anything worse.'

'Do you find it easy?'

'Do I find what easy?'

'Being a parent. Are you good at it?'

Amanda glared at her with daggers. 'Don't even go there.'

Amanda Bennett tiptoed around a mountain of guilt each and every day. A full-time working mother, with no father on the scene wasn't information she was keen on advertising. Every day she forced herself out of bed and into a life she hadn't planned and she knew that in some people's minds this made her a bad parent. People like Jessica Bell made her look good, and she was determined to keep it that way.

'It was a question not an accusation,' said Yiskah.

'You're wasting your breath on me. Save it for someone who cares.'

Yiskah added this feisty attitude to the growing list of hate being thrust in her direction. Crimes against children always stir up a lot of emotion. Throw ten years of misinformation into that mix and you get a population ready to explode.

'The judge calls Miss Bell to the stand,' said a young man up the front of the courtroom. The soldiers hustled Yiskah to her feet and escorted her toward the judge. She stepped into the dock and took a deep breath. The distance she had painstakingly built between what she had done and the future she had created was gone. Both realities were staring each other in the face and her opportunities to prove otherwise would be minimal. She had to make the most of every engagement starting now.

'You are charged with kidnapping, forgery and assuming a false identity,' said the Judge. 'How do you plead?'

The list of charges was not a surprise to Yiskah. She understood the nature of each crime. What she didn't know was the sort of sentence they carried. She looked at the faces surrounding her for some advice but all she saw was a mixture of boredom and hatred. For some she was just another criminal in a line of unfortunate cases waiting to be entered into an overflowing justice system. For others, she represented the worst of life, a person who only deserved their abhorrence and loathing. A child abuser and a thief. There was no one to help her here.

'I need to speak with my lawyer.'

'Very well then. You have permission to make one phone call,' said the judge, before he struck the thick wooden desk with his gavel. 'Next.'

50

11:30AM
MARVALE TAVERN

A white Holden Commodore cruised up the rough bitumen of an empty carpark and pulled up outside the faded exterior of the Marvale Tavern. Nothing had changed, not even the cracked glass sign above the double doors. A bulb flickered behind the peeled font, the letters announcing the place was open for business, the faltering light show too early to be of any effect, the sun too high and bright in the sky.

Lisa Johnstone stared out through the clear glass of the rear passenger window. The long drive back to her old suburb had seen her slowly shed the olive skin of the last ten years. Zetta Apostilides had been discarded upon the taxi floor, peeled and cracked like the opaque membrane of a superfluous snakeskin. Zetta was moulting and the old Lisa was rising from the ashes.

The car park was huge. Several trees dotted its expanse, designed to provide shade to the sticky black surface. They all wept with dehydration, their crusty brown leaves an outward sign of inner turmoil. The oval beyond was a green oasis compared to this unforgiving desert and the cluster of familiar buildings beyond it caught Lisa's attention. It was her old school. The scene of her abduction.

'That'll be sixty-five dollars Miss Johnstone,' said the taxi driver, a pale blue turban wrapped firmly around his head.

'Thank you.' Lisa rummaged through her handbag. She pulled out a leather purse. It was an eighteenth birthday present from Carissa. She would have to decide which memories she kept.

She paid, then stepped from the car and closed the door behind her. The driver lifted the boot and hauled out a large blue suitcase.

'You sure you're okay? This isn't the safest place for a woman to wait alone.'

'It's okay. I used to live here.'

'Oh, I'm sorry. Why have you come back?'

'Family. I've been away a long time.'

'Be careful my friend. Sometimes blood is thicker than two short planks.'

'You mean thicker than water.'

'No. That would make them good people,' he smiled. 'I run from my family as fast as I could. They very, very, stupid people. I make new proverb especially for them.'

Lisa laughed. 'I could probably do the same.'

'Good luck Miss Johnstone.'

'Thank you.'

The taxi departed leaving Lisa alone, her suitcase beside her feet. She lifted one end and wheeled it toward the entrance.

Lisa pushed the door inward, stepping inside a place she had never been privy to before. Gary never allowed his children to come in here. Even Tracey wasn't encouraged to show her face at the tavern. Gary liked it that way. This was his kingdom; a secret hideaway from the injustices of the outside world.

A bald man looked up from behind the bar and grinned. 'Ya lookin' for a place to stay honey?' asked George.

'No,' smiled Lisa. 'I'm actually looking for my dad?'

'Bit old to be lost, aren't you?'

'I'm not lost.' Lisa lowered her case to the floor. 'My dad used to spend a lot of time in here.'

'Most men do. What's his name?'

'Gary. Gary Johnstone.'

'Woah. Did you say that he's your dad?'

'Yes, I did.'

'Shit, are you who I think you are?'

'Maybe. I'm his daughter.'

'Little Lisa Johnstone.'

'Just not so little anymore.'

'You got that fuckin' right. Apology for the language but I can't fuckin' believe it. Never thought I'd see you again. You're all over the bloody news.'

'Really. I just came straight from the airport.'

'I feel privileged then. Look at you.' George made his way out from behind the bar. 'Your fuckin gorgeous to boot.'

'Thank you...' His approach was too close, making Lisa feel uncomfortable.

'The name's George,' he held out his hand, which she took. 'I own this pub. You need a job?'

'No thanks. Does my dad still come in here?'

'Oh yeah. He practically lives here.'

'What time will he be coming in?'

'He's here now. That's his seat over there.' George pointed toward a vacant stool, an empty glass on the bar, a rainbow inspired umbrella balanced precariously on the rim. 'Starts on the piss pretty early nowadays. That's his favourite tipple. White Russian. He's getting a bit fancy in his old age.'

'Where's he gone?'

'To the dunny. All that piss has got to come out somewhere.'

'How's he been?'

'Same old, same old. Not sure you guys comin' back is going to do him any good though.'

'What makes you say that?'

'He'd put it all behind him. Now you're back in the news all that old hatred is gonna surface again.'

Lisa allowed the negativity to wash over her.

George grabbed her suitcase and veered it toward the bar. 'Anyway. You can ask him yourself. Let's get you a drink.'

Lisa walked over and sat on the stool beside her fathers.

'Gary will get a hell of a shock seeing you. That's a gimme.'

George leant across her lap and grabbed the empty glass and umbrella, his body brushing against hers in the process. "I'll make him something stronger,' he winked. 'What's your fuel?'

'A Mojito please.'

'What the fuck is that?'

'It's vodka, Bacardi, lime and mint leaves.'

'You're just as fancy as your no-good father.' George made his way around to the other side of the bar.

'It's very popular in Greece.'

'Ah that's right. You've been trapped on that bloody island haven't ya?'

'Not exactly trapped.'

'The newspapers said that teacher had you hostage and…'

The squeal of old hinges sent shivers up Lisa's spine. She spun around.

George was all smiles. 'Hey Gazza. You got yourself a visitor.'

Gary was still tying up the string waist of his tracksuit pants. He looked up and checked out the girl on the stool. 'You booked a whore to cheer me up, have ya?'

'Jesus what a greeting,' said Lisa. 'Never expected that one.'

'Is he just how you remembered?' grinned George.

Lisa ignored him. 'Hey dad.'

Gary shuffled closer. 'Hi beautiful.'

'What's up?'

'My dick is that's for sure.' Gary placed his hand on Lisa's leg.

'Dad, it's me,' she protested, guiding his hand away.

'I'll play any game you want darlin'.'

'She's not a whore you idiot,' said George. 'She's your fuckin' daughter.'

Gary gave George a dose of his gnarled teeth. 'I told you not to talk about her. You know it gets me angry.'

'I bloody know it all right.'

'It's true,' said Lisa, grabbing her father's right hand. 'I just got back into Perth this morning and came straight here.'

Gary reached into his pocket and pulled out a pair of spectacles.

He spread the metal arms and slid them onto his nose. He looked her up and down. 'Why the fuck would you come back here?'

'To see you!'

Gary's eyes were bloodshot and weepy. 'Is this mine?' he mumbled to George, grabbing the refilled glass in front of him.

George nodded. 'Straight whiskey; thought you'd need it.'

'You thought right.' Gary chucked it down in one.

Lisa placed a hand on his back. 'I missed you.'

Gary choked on his drink, dribble sliding down his chin. He returned the glass to the bar top and glared over at her, unsure as to what he should do next.

'Where's the boy?' he asked.

'He's coming on a later flight. Wasn't as keen to get back as I was.'

'Always had more brains than you.'

'Cheers. And I thought you'd be happy to see me.'

'This is happy,' pointed Gary, a finger directed at his dour face.

'It's hardly the welcome home I was expecting.'

"I'm not good with surprises.' Gary grabbed his drink and crushed the ice between his teeth. 'Get me another would ya, George?'

'My shout,' said Lisa, before sucking back her own concoction.

'Thanks.'

Lisa slid her glass toward George. 'And go easy on the vodka this time. I want to be able to walk out of here.'

'Where's the bitch that took you?' asked Gary.

'In the city jail. They took her there as soon as she landed.'

'Too fuckin' right. It's her turn to feel some pain.'

'I'm sorry dad. I wish it never happened.'

'Too late for that. I've got this place though. Kept me sane.'

'What about Mum?'

He laughed. 'Her whining drove me crazy. Pissed her off years ago.'

'You're divorced?'

'Not officially, couldn't be fucked with all the paperwork. Haven't see her for three good years and if I did I wouldn't even go near her with his dick.'

'Dad, can we at least talk nicely about Mum please.'

'Nah, this is me honey. I'm too old to change. Take it or leave it.'

'What an intriguing offer.'

Gary brought his face closer to hers. 'It ain't an offer. It's the fuckin' truth.'

Lisa pulled away, repulsed by the stink of his breath and unnerved by the depth of his anger. His skin was lined and covered in black heads, as ugly up close as the hate burning through the sun-starved pores on his nose. Tears welled up in her eyes, the fear and confusion of that last exchange, combining poorly with the alcohol of the last few minutes. His anger was unsettling her, doubt tugging at her heartstrings.

'You two have a lot of catching up to do,' said George. 'I'll chuck some nice music on and leave you both alone.'

Lisa stirred her drink. She thought about her friend Carissa. They'd shared many fun nights with a Mojito in their hands. She wished she was by her side now.

51

9:00AM CET
PORT OF PARIKIA

'Iakovos, Iakovos,' called out Carissa as she struggled through the hordes of tourists rushing past her. The port was once again awash with people, a swarming mass of excited individuals, most of them disembarking the early morning ferry like a wave upon a beach. A convoy of trucks and cars forced their way out through the port gates, horns blaring in an attempt to part this tide of humans.

'Iakovos, where are you?' yelled Carissa, her desperation mounting. She'd grown used to this chaotic transition having been born on this island, but she'd never wanted to see someone so badly and the bedlam surrounding her felt like a slap in the face. Her island was working against her.

She squeezed her way through, swimming against the flow, searching for a better view up on the walled surrounds of the iconic windmill. She climbed the white rendered barricades that encircled it and balanced on tiptoes. The sounds of the port clamoured around her, fresh tears of anxiety brimming on the surface. Her world was crashing and there was no one here to save her.

Yesterday had played like a nightmare. Wave after wave of the most insane news, each update churning through her gut like a twisting knife. Her closest friends and a family she thought of as an extension of her own, were being ripped apart. She was struggling to even comprehend the insinuations and accusations being levelled at them.

Carissa had lived the small life of a small child on a small island. This was bigger than anything she'd ever felt or seen before and she felt powerless to intervene.

But when she awoke this morning, her position appeared clearer and she knew what she must do. It wouldn't stop the mayhem but it might just ease some of the suffering. Fate though was wrestling with her happiness and now she found herself lost within the pandemonium of the port. Her beautiful island had turned ugly and she felt lost and alone.

'Carissa, ti kaneis edo?' *Carissa, what are you doing here?* A hand on her shoulder brought the world back into focus. She looked down and saw the face she had discovered such strong feelings for. A face she'd known so well over the years. Too well. Such familiarity had disguised the love she now knew was real.

Carissa stepped into his arms, wrapping herself around his chest, hugging him hard. Tears wracked her body, sobs of pain rising from deep within her gut.

'What's the matter?' said Iakovos.

She leant back and looked him in the eyes. 'I can't believe what's happening,' said Carissa. 'It's just crazy. The whole thing, it makes no sense.'

'What are you talking about?'

'Your life. Yiskah and Zetta. The truth about who you really are.'

Iakovos lifted her by the waist and returned her to the wall. 'Who told you?'

'It's all over the television. Haven't you been watching?'

'I've been busy, tying up loose ends. Paying bills. Mum left me a long list.'

'Is what they say true?'

Iakovos nodded. 'Some of it. Yes.'

'Why would Yiskah keep such a secret from you?'

'I'm still grappling with it myself. The sooner we all deal with it, the sooner we can get our old lives back.'

'So, you will come back to Paros?'

'Of course. Our home is here. Our friends, our jobs. Everything we love.'

'I was scared you'd never come back. Mum told me you were leaving this morning and I started to panic.'

'It's going to be okay.'

'I love you Iakovos.' Carissa burst forward and buried her head in his chest.

'I love you too,' replied Iakovos. 'I always have.'

'Why did this have to happen for us to realise it.'

'It just seems to be God's way. Sometimes the truth stays hidden. It makes no sense but at least we know now and when I get back we can enjoy it. Live it.'

Carissa stepped away, a clarity returning to her actions. 'Is there anything I can do for you while you're away?'

'Actually, there is. Could you look after the house, feed the animals and harvest the vegetables.'

'Of course. I'd love to.'

'Here are the keys to our car. It's out back in car park two. Drive up when you can and stay overnight if you'd like.'

'Okay.'

'And just keep the word positive on what's happening. The news will probably be filled with all kinds of horrible things about us. You know us. You know the truth.'

'I won't believe any of the lies.'

'I know you won't but keep our friends informed as well. We'd like to still be welcome when we return.'

'Everyone thinks so highly of Yiskah.'

'Things can and will change pretty quickly. Zetta is incredibly angry. She's running blind and I'm not sure what she's capable of.'

'I can't believe she didn't call me?'

'You know how she reacted when she left the island a couple of years back.'

'Yes. How can I forget.'

'She was a firestorm then and she's worse now. I understand her pain but she's gone crazy and I'm not sure she can be stopped.'

Carissa wrapped her arms around his waist. 'Be careful.'

'I will.' He held her tight and as the world continued to swarm around them, they both allowed themselves time to become lost inside their newly discovered love. A silver lining in the darkening clouds.

52

5:00PM AWST
SHERATON HOTEL, PERTH

The revolving doors of the hotel entrance spun as an older woman stepped between the glass panels and into the foyer of the Sheraton Hotel. Her sense of style was at odds with the marble and gold luxury she had walked into. She was all sparkles and perfume, a short skirt and long boots that were as appropriate as a cream tart in a health food shop. Her makeup was heavy, a splash of bright red lipstick and purple eye shadow creating a sense of Vaudevillian theatre. She strode purposefully toward the restaurant wing before a hotel porter stepped into view and interrupted her flow.

'Can I help you, mam?'

'Don't mam me. I'm not your bloody mother.'

'I'm sorry. Are you here to see someone?'

'Yes. My daughter is staying here.'

'And her name?'

'Lisa Johnstone.'

A flash of recognition from the porter. News of her arrival in Perth was everywhere. 'Of course. Please follow me.'

He led her into the main restaurant which was filled with early dinner guests, a violinist in one corner adding background music to the light chatter of voices.

'Over here, Mum,' called Lisa from a table beside the large dressed windows overlooking the street.

The sound of her daughter's voice made Tracey smile. She'd heard her say 'Mum' a million times before but this event was far more rewarding.

Lisa stepped away from the table and made her way toward the woman who gave birth to her. The porter stepped to the side as the two women embraced, tears streaming down Lisa's cheeks as she revelled in the warmth and affection she'd been craving.

'I missed you so much,' said Lisa.

'Me too.'

'I'm never ever going to leave you again.'

'Good.' They released each other and stepped back.

'You look good, Mum.'

'Not as good as you. You look like I did thirty years ago.'

Lisa smiled, the knee-length red slip dress she wore was pulled in tight at her waist, a slim black belt, black beaded necklace and heels adding the finishing touches.

'Can we eat?' asked Tracey. 'I'm starving.'

'Of course.' Lisa guided Tracey back toward the table.

'Are you enjoying being back in Perth?'

'Yes. I had forgotten how beautiful it was. Especially in spring.'

The porter slid their chairs out and they sat.

'But you were living in bloody Greece. How can this place even compare?'

'Paros is a beautiful island, there's no denying it but it was all a lie. A very masterful copy of a beautiful life. It wasn't real. This is my home. I can feel the difference already.'

'Life really sucked when you left.'

Lisa reached across the table and held her mother's hands.

'I'm so sorry. I never wanted to leave.'

'It wasn't your fault. You were taken.'

'I never would have stayed away so long had I known the truth. I thought you were dead.'

'I can't believe that bitch did that to you!'

Lisa looked into the eyes of the woman opposite her. The lines were deeper than expected and the down lights of the restaurant exposed her hair which was thin and wiry.

'You must tell me everything I missed out on,' said Lisa. 'All the details of the last decade. The birthdays, the holidays. Everything.'

'Weren't too many of those. Money was really tight. Always has been. Your bloody father is a useless tosser.'

'I can help you out financially. I've got some savings. It's the least I can do.'

'Thanks honey. It was very painful not knowing where youse was all this time. Without you, my life was just worthless.' She picked up a serviette and wiped a tear away from her cheek. 'Your disappearance ripped a hole in me so large I thought I'd never climb out. I still feel like I'm stuck down in that hole.'

'I feel like that too sometimes. It's all so unreal. So much baggage weighing us down.'

'You thought I was in heaven but I never even knew if you was dead or alive,' said Tracey. 'My mind filled itself up with some horrible images.'

'And Dad?'

Tracey's shoulders bristled and she leaned back in her chair. 'What about the bastard. Haven't seen that old prick for years. Wish she'd taken him as well.'

Two elderly women at a table near them glanced their way. Tracey and Lisa only had eyes for each other.

'When did you split up?' asked Lisa.

'As soon as I found out about all the abuse he'd been putting you through. I couldn't believe it. My little babies having to suffer through all his hate. Broke my heart.'

'He abused us?'

'He used to hit you and keep you in your room for hours on end.'

'I don't remember it.'

'Lucky for you.'

'Jacob might remember. He sees our lives here so differently to me.'

'He would. Loved pushing my buttons that boy. I mean, I loved youse both so much. Still do. But you was always me favourite.'

Lisa looked away, across the room and beyond, trying hard to remember the past.

'You believe me don't ya?' said Tracey.

'Of course I do.' Lisa wanted her past to be so different. Wanted the facts she had been told to be a pack of lies. They were Yiskah's facts she told herself. This woman here was the new truth!

'Where are you staying?' asked Tracey.

'Room 216.'

'What here? In the bloody Sheraton?'

'Yes.'

'You must have bought a fair bit of dough with ya, then.'

'It's all being paid for by the Department of Education.'

'Fuckin' awesome. Too bloody right. They employed the bitch who did this to us. I hope they put the tramp in jail and throw away the key.' Two elderly women at the table across from them glanced their way and this time Tracey noticed.

'What?' she asked them, her outward aggression bluffing the expensively dressed ladies into submission, turning away without comment.

Lisa pulled a hand away and sipped her coffee.

'Maybe we could get some compensation from them. You know, some money for all our pain.'

'I hadn't even considered that.'

'Well we should. Get some of that government money for ourselves.'

Lisa was quiet.

Tracey squeezed her daughter's left hand. 'Anyways, I was going to ask you if you'd like to move in with me?'

'Wow, really?'

'Yeah, really. You've been away a bleedin' decade darlin' and I need you to help get me out of that deep black hole you dropped me in.'

Lisa took a breath.

'I know you didn't mean it, but it's still partly your fault, you know,' said Tracey. 'You need to take some responsibility.'

'I understand how you feel and I'll fix it, I will. I just don't know if we're allowed to live together. We've got a court case to get through.'

'You can't expect me to climb out by meself. I need to go back in time. Have you with me again. Pretend this shit never happened.'

'Can we go backwards?'

'Course we fuckin' can.' Tracey slapped the table, raising the continued ire of the other guests. She stared them down. 'What you staring at? Look away or get outta here you old nags.' The elderly women got to their feet quickly and left the restaurant. Tracey watched them go. 'Silly bitches.'

'We'll have to be a bit quieter, Mum. Otherwise we might get kicked out.'

'Yeah, yeah. Won't be the first time. We'll piss 'em off first and then we'll leave. I've got a room at home ready for you anyway.'

'My old room?'

'Nah. Moved out of the dump in Dalton Crescent a long time ago. Got new digs now in Belmont. Much closer to the casino. You'll love it!'

Lisa was uneasy. 'Sounds all right.'

'Awesome. Let's celebrate with some champagne?'

'Not sure the Education Department will cover that?'

'Course they fuckin' will. Not often a lady gets treated like a queen.'

Tracey raised her arm and hailed a waiter. 'Oi, we'd like some drinks,' she hollered above the strings of the violin. The remaining guests looked over at Tracey. She gave them the finger. Lisa had to look away.

53

5:30PM
PERTH CITY REMAND CENTRE

'This way please, Miss Bell,' said Ms Bennett. 'I'd like to get home to my daughter before she goes to bed.'

'You have a daughter too?' said Yiskah, as they descended a set of concrete stairs, one arm held securely by an officer. 'How old is she?'

Amanda Bennett wasn't really interested in conversation, but she answered all the same. 'Seven.'

'That was Zetta's age when we left,' explained Yiskah. 'So cute.'

'Look lady, you've been gone a hell of a long time, but no one has ever forgotten what you did. I was in high school at the time and my parents were shit scared of you and your kind. It had never happened before and you broke a level of trust that had existed for centuries.'

They stepped through a double set of doors into the basement of the city remand centre. There were several cold grey cells on either side of a narrow corridor of steel doors.

'I knew that my school and the teachers there would cop a lot of flak,' said Yiskah.

'Flack. You have no idea.'

'I wasn't doing it for them. I was doing it for the children,' said Yiskah, as she was guided through a doorway into one of the holding cells.

'So you keep on saying. But you've got one hell of a fight on your hands. You are enemy number one in this city and no one even cares whether you looked after the kids or not? They just want you behind bars.'

'I can see the hate people have for me and I must admit it's a big surprise. I just need the chance to explain.'

'Mr and Mr Johnstone were feted when you left. They became overnight celebrities. Everyone felt sad for them. You, on the other hand, became infamous. Your past was dug up; how you lost your parents, went off the rails, lived alone, spent time in jail for assault. You were universally hated and now you're back and people are rubbing their hands together, saying finally, we can see justice prevail.'

'That's why I came back. To tell the truth.'

'You didn't come back. We found you and hauled you home.' Amanda stepped away from the cell. 'Lock her up officer. She's a danger to us all.'

The clunk of heavy metal reverberated off the hard concrete walls as the reinforced steel door was closed and locked. The officer peered in through the small viewing window.

Yiskah stood in the centre of her new accommodation and looked around the cold grey cell. She felt very alone. The last few days had been some of the longest of her life. Returning to Perth was proving harder than leaving.

The officer closed the cover on the viewing panel. 'She'll be easy,' he said. 'Harmless compared to some of the cattle we get in here.'

'She's more dangerous that you think,' said Amanda, before she strolled away up the corridor and out through the double doors. The officer took up a seat behind his desk in the corner of the hall, took out some paperwork from a tray and started filling it out.

Yiskah sat down on the bed which was secured to one side

of the concrete cell. She lowered her head into her hands and started to cry. This pain she felt conjured up memories of the day two policemen visited her house to inform her that her parents were dead. Something else had shattered today. Those two officers were there to comfort her on that miserable day over thirty years ago, but no one was around to witness this moment of darkness. No one even slightly interested in soothing her pain. Yiskah was scared and heartbroken. She'd only been back a few hours and already she'd begun to lose touch with the strong independent woman she had become.

One hour later and those heart-wrenching tears had broken her. Yiskah Apostilides was now just a memory. Jessica Bell had once again taken over and she curled up on the unforgiving mattress and willed herself to sleep. She felt like she was fourteen all over again.

54

6:30PM
SHERATON HOTEL, ROOM 216

Lisa Johnstone fumbled with her key card before sliding it in through the slot, turning the handle to room 216 and pushing the door wide open.

'After you,' she offered, her speech and demeanour visibly affected by alcohol.

Tracey Johnstone swanned in through the door, memories of the perks she used to enjoy as a working girl in the late nineties providing a lift to her spirits. Those days were long gone but sentimentality had taken over as she headed straight for the mini bar. She yanked the fridge door open and scanned the offerings.

'Do you mind?' slurred Tracey. 'Seeing you're not paying and all. Those education bastards owe me a few bob.'

'Go ahead. Enjoy it while you can.'

Tracey lifted out several miniature bottles of spirits and pocketed them. 'For later.' She hauled a full-size bottle of Moet from the fridge. 'Us being together again deserves a bigger celebration than a few spirits can offer.' She plonked the bottle on the table. 'I got a real taste for it now, and this looks like a bloody good drop.'

Lisa grabbed two glasses from the cabinet while Tracey ripped the foil from the neck of the bottle.

'Follow me,' said Tracey as she walked over toward the balcony doors. She twisted the latch and slid the glass panel to the right. A light breeze billowed the double set of blue curtains that covered the wall of glass. Tracey disappeared between the drapery and Lisa followed quickly after her.

The balcony was empty but for two chairs and a small round table, the steel-framed glass balustrade keeping both mother and daughter safe. Lisa stared out across the Swan River to the south. The sun wasn't far from setting and it was a spectacular view, evoking memories of the vista she'd painted from the Monastery half way up the slopes of Mount Profitis Ilias. This brief recall pained her and she pushed it quickly to the back of her mind, watching as Tracey dangled the bottle of sparkling wine dangerously over the edge of the handrail.

'Let's try to hit a car, hey?' She aimed the bottle in the direction of the busy highway opposite the hotel.

'That bottle could kill someone.'

'I'm just popping the cork you idiot. Ya really think I'm gonna smash all this piss on the pavement?'

'No, but I do think you're a little bit drunk. You already got us kicked out of the restaurant for abuse.'

'Big deal. We'll be long gone tomorrow.'

Tracey gave the bottle a good hard shake before slowly easing the cork out of the neck with her thumbs. 'Pop!' It flew through the air and down to the road below. The dink of metal told them they'd hit a target.

'Yes!' hissed Tracey. 'Got ya.'

She lifted the bottle to her mouth and took a swig. Lisa watched her mother gulp down a barrage of bubbles.

Tracey passed the bottle to Lisa. 'Your turn.'

Lisa lifted the bottle to her lips and swallowed, liquid spilling down her chin. Tracey snatched the bottle back. 'Don't waste it, ya fuckin' loser.' She stormed back through the curtains and into the room. She plonked her ass on the king-size bed and took another swig. The television remote was beside her and she grabbed it and hit the power button.

The newsreader filled the screen, the slogan 'Lost Decade' behind him. 'Child kidnapper Jessica Bell returned to Perth today after ten years on the run,' he said.

'Oi Lisa, get in here. The bitch is on telly.'

A shot of Yiskah came up behind the newsreader. 'She's been gone a decade with someone else's children and now after her capture in Greece, Miss Bell has been extradited back to Perth to face justice.'

Lisa put her head in through the curtains.

'Perth Airport saw quite the stir as the fugitive was taken from the arrivals lounge and into a waiting car.' Recorded images from today's scenes at the airport and the court steps played rolled over the screen.

'She tried vainly to obscure her identity from our cameras and it was only outside the courts that our reporters were finally able to get a comment from this much-hated figure.'

Lisa stepped into the room and took a seat on the edge of the bed, her face a blank, her emotions swirling.

A shaky shot of Yiskah from side on filled the screen, the high court in the background.

She watched as Yiskah defended herself, Tracey behind her, silent and staring.

'Must have schizophrenia,' said Tracey. 'She's got it all wrong.'

'She did look after us. Never hit us or anything like that.'

'Shut up, would ya,' sniped Tracey. 'I don't wanna hear you tell me anything good or nice about her. She's evil and that's fuckin' all there is to it!'

The newsreader's voiced returned. 'Child psychologist Doctor Stan Arthurs is here to shed fresh light on this story.' The screen switched to a shot of a man in a tie and glasses, blond curly hair framing an old weathered face.

'Thank you for having me,' said the Doctor.

'So, what makes this case so uniquely traumatic?'

'Miss Bell kidnapped two children against their free will. She imprisoned them in a life which was not theirs. Forced them to live a lie, brainwashed them into believing they were hers.'

'That's better,' said Tracey. 'At least he knows what he's talking about.'

'We haven't heard or seen anything from this woman for ten years,' said the newsreader. 'How has she evaded capture for so long?'

'She's obviously very manipulative and cold-hearted to have carried out and maintained such a calculated plan against the Johnstone family. She may be trying to hide behind this image of an ethically strong teacher but really, what professional in their right mind steals someone else's children. I think this case will show us that Miss Bell is not of sound mind.'

'Are you suggesting she's crazy?' asked the newsreader.

'The medical term would be insane and yes, I am. It is my professional opinion that she is mentally unbalanced on some level, be it schizophrenia, bipolar or a similar kind of condition.'

'I fuckin' told ya,' said Tracey. 'She's fuckin' loopy.'

'This isn't your average human being,' said Dr Arthurs. 'She's practically erased the last ten years of Mr and Mrs Johnstone's lives. Not to mention the children. I expect to see her behind bars for a long time.'

'I'm sure the public would be pleased with that result. Thank you for your time Dr Arthurs.'

'My pleasure.'

Lisa got to her feet and hit the off button.

'What's the matter?' said Tracey.

'He's just looking for his fifteen seconds of fame.'

'He's fuckin' right though. She's bonkers.'

'What she did was wrong, but she's not crazy.'

Tracey cut short another skull of champagne. 'I told you to cut it with the nice crap. Let's write the bitch a letter.'

'And say what?'

'Tell her how we really feel.'

'It's not that simple.'

'Don't go getting all sympathetic on that cow. Just copy down what I say. I've been waiting for this day and it's been a bloody long time coming. Just let me enjoy it, would ya?'

Tracey leaned over and pulled a pad of hotel paper from the drawer beside the bed. There was a pen on top and she threw them across the bed toward Lisa.

'What do you want to say?' asked Lisa.

'Tell her the truth! Make her stew like a rabbit.'

'You sure this is a good idea? They might use it in court.'

'We can do anything we want to. She's the bloody criminal. We're the victims.'

Lisa wasn't so sure.

Tracey leant back against the large pillows behind her, cradling the champagne bottle to her chest. Words rolled off her tongue like water off a duck's back.

Dear Miss Bell,

We have so much to say but so little time for cockroaches like you.

My beautiful daughter has found a new life here in Perth and she is slowly rebuilding all that you ripped from us. She and I have so much in common and we will try to claw back the years that have been lost. She still loves me and wishes you were dead.

You have taken so much from us that can never be replaced and now you will have the pleasure of finding out how that feels for yourself. Our lawyer told us that you will rot in jail and for that we are glad. You had no right to interfere in our lives. I sure as hell never asked you to.

Our family was destroyed when you took the children. Jacob is still lost to me because of what you did. Now the world will know the truth and you will be the most hated woman on the planet.

Good riddance,
Tracey and Lisa Johnstone

Lisa placed the pen flat upon the table. She felt deflated as she looked over at her mother who was grinning with delight.

'What's that look for?' asked Tracey. 'It's all true.'

'But it's hard putting it in writing.'

'Better bloody well get used to it. The wankers in court will want you to spill all the fuckin' beans you got.'

'I know and it scares me.'

'Shit, you're a wet blanket. That teacher's made you go all soft. Toughen up and grab us another drink, will ya.'

'I thought we were checking out?' said Lisa.

'Tomorrow, you softcock. I ain't throwing all this free stuff away.' Tracey had her arms and legs spread open on the sumptuous bed. 'We'll party our asses off tonight and then piss off in the morning.'

'But there's only one bed.'

'Yeah but it's a King, you silly tart. Made for two.' Tracey giggled like a little girl. 'Got a lot more than that under the covers at some of the parties we used to have up here.'

'You been here before?'

'I've been everywhere girlie. Now if you'd get us a fuckin' drink, I'll tell you a few stories about the good old days.'

Lisa did as she was told and Tracey didn't stop talking for near on four hours. Lisa had fallen asleep a whole hour earlier.

55

WEDNESDAY 24th SEPTEMBER
6:00AM CET
ATHENS

The eastern pillars of the Acropolis bathed in the golden light of a new day. Huge shadows were cast across the three-storey houses to the west, the massive marble base of the Parthenon keeping the inhabitants of these local streets in darkness well past the early light of morning. It was a pattern that had been repeated every day for over two thousand years.

The apartment of Kosta Kouros shared this morning shade with his neighbours. Its owner preferred it that way, allowing him to stay hidden within the darkness of the unknown, rather than having to face the early honesty of the morning sun.

An open second-storey window framed the image of a torn man, his body curled up on scrunched sheets, his double bed a canvas of pain. Tears tumbled down his cheeks, his muted sobs evidence of exhaustion, his emotions still raw after a late-night phone call from a frantic young man, a boy he still looked upon as a son.

Kosta's emotions had ebbed and flowed over the past few days. He'd seen it coming but the sheer size of the damage was overwhelming.

Iakovos's call had been a fraught one as he tried to shed light on the painful realities simultaneously occurring on the other side of the world. They had both wallowed in desperation, damning themselves toward the depths of the defeated.

Iakovos's unexpected news, that Zetta had been reunited with both her birth mother and father, left him pained by the opposing forces that pulled at his heartstrings. A feeling of happiness for Zetta was strong, but a nagging doubt was just as robust and it poisoned how he felt about such a reunion. Kosta had been a father figure to Zetta and considered their bond to be unbreakable. That previously unassailable position suddenly looked weaker than the proposal that had been smashed against the rocks of the Portara.

A restless night had followed and the little sleep Kosta had managed was filled with unkind dreams. He was now awake and being tortured by the slow passing of time, the whitewashed walls of his bedroom a blank canvas upon which to watch the shadows flicker and fade.

Kosta's mind sought the ingredients for a fightback, conjuring up some of the happier images of his time on Paros. His name day had been particularly memorable, a cruise around the island on the wooden boat, *Regaki*, diving and swimming with his closest friends and family. The failed proposal beside the Portara was a lowlight, a slice of what was to come. In hindsight, the bike ride around Naxos was probably the last good thing to happen to either of them, small cracks beginning to appear in the veneer of their relationship. Cracks forced on them by the dark secrets of a decade ago, fault lines that would eventually open up and swallow their love whole. He could never have predicted this course of events. His organised mind wrestled with the chaos as another wave of emotion rose and fell like a tsunami, pushing him deeper into an ocean of tears.

Kosta had fled the breakdown of his relationship with Yiskah and had tried to bury himself in the bustle of modern, populous twenty-first century Athens. He had concealed his own pity beneath the post-Olympic hangover that continued to drain this once great city and like the unloved cats and dogs that roamed these streets, he had been unable to navigate his way out of those ruins.

Iakovos's call for help had blown that hollow casing wide open and as wave after wave of excruciating grief pierced through him, he still wasn't sure whether he wanted to be alive or dead.

The ringing of his phone forced Kosta up from his bed and back into the beating heart of the city. Last night's call had made the night even more difficult and grabbing the phone in his left hand, he prayed for some good news.

'Yasu,' he croaked.

'Kalimera,' came a much-loved voice.

'Yiskah? Oh lord. How are you?'

'Struggling. I need you. It's not going well. No one understands me. No one wants to listen.'

'I know. Iakovos called me. Said you needed a lawyer.'

'Where is my boy now?'

'At the airport, waiting for a flight. They're all booked up. He's on standby.'

'Can you look after him for me. I need you both over here. I can't do it by myself.'

'Of course. I will come as soon as I can.'

'I'm sorry. I have treated you so badly.'

'Ella, Yiskah. There is no need to be sorry. I will come and together we will make them see the truth.'

'I love you.'

'I love you too.'

The phone call ended and Kosta allowed a much-missed peace to revisit him. He was encouraged by the positivity he felt and as the sun peeked past the mighty columns of the Acropolis, so too a great swathe of light began to fill his bedroom and love started its long journey to mend a broken heart.

56

TUESDAY 30th SEPTEMBER
6:00PM AWST
BELMONT, PERTH

'Good fucking job,' said Tracey. 'It's everything she deserves.'

The plastered pink walls of a cramped lounge room in the suburb of Belmont reverberated to the strains of Tracey's frank observations. Lisa watched the evening news from the discomfort of a well-used couch.

'Fucking karma. That's what it is. Fucking karma!' Tracey took a long drag on her cigarette.

Lisa processed the news that Jessica Bell would be tried in a full court, jury and all. The mug shot showed a tired and unhappy woman, far from the matriarch she had spent so much of her life with. Lisa tried to clear her mind of all the clutter. She'd been in this apartment for a week and couldn't believe how much her birth mother could talk.

'You've gone all silent on me,' said Tracey. 'You hate her too, you know.'

'She's still a human being. I did love her, once.'

'That bitch tricked you. Lied to you.'

'And now she's going to jail for it. I can't just forget the past. None of us can. Look where it's gotten her.'

'I wish we had the death penalty.'

'I don't have your hate. I don't wish that for her.'

'So, what do you want?'

'I don't know. I thought I did.'

Tracey ignored her daughter's confusion. 'Let's celebrate and go out somewhere.'

'Not again,' said Lisa. 'We went out last night and every other night before that. Can't we just stay in for a change.'

'Don't be such a loser. I'm still getting used to having you back with me. It's fun'

'Yeah well, we got in at four this morning so I might just pass and go to bed early instead?'

'No fuckin' way! Sleep is for old people. C'mon, let's go to the casino. We'll win back that money we lost the other night.'

'It's a casino. Nobody ever wins.'

'Bloody hell, what's got into you? Sound like your fuckin' father.'

'Maybe I should go and live with him then?'

Tracey felt a twinge in her hip pocket. 'Ah shit, I'm sorry Lisa. That was mean, wasn't it?'

'I'm sort of getting used to it.'

'I'm not like this all the time. I just hate stayin' in. It's so fucking boring. Eat, shit, sleep. Eat, shit, sleep.'

'I'm running out of money. I need to get a job.'

'Not my fault I can't fucking work.'

'No, of course it's not. I wasn't suggesting that.'

'I never chose this stinkin' life. It chose me. Should been livin' it up, lots of money and non-stop fun.'

Lisa climbed wearily up off the couch.

'You could take me to Greece one day,' said Tracey.

'Why would I want to go back there?'

'I heard its non-stop action. Party islands and all.'

'Is that all you care about?'

'I care about my fucking kids. And, where were they? In Paros having a ball.'

'It wasn't like that.'

'It doesn't matter what it was really like. It's what happened. Shit happens and my life got fucked because of it.'

'You've got me back. Can't we just spend some quiet time together?'

'Quiet time? Sounds like a fuckin' retirement home. Life's too short to sit around.'

'How about a movie then?'

'You're joking, right?'

Lisa shook her head. 'No, I'm not.'

'For fuck's sake girl! Get your fancy clothes on. I'm callin' us a bloody taxi. I cannot listen to any more of your sorry shit.'

Tracey grabbed the phone on the table beside her and dialed. Lisa leant forward, her head in her hands and her heart in a spin.

57

7:00PM
PERTH REMAND CENTRE

Jess sat motionless on the other side of a glass panel, an old grey handset against her ear.

'Yiskah. Can you hear me?' crackled a young voice through the receiver.

Jess nodded silently. She looked pale and gaunt. 'But don't call me that anymore. My name is Jessica Bell.'

A female guard dressed in a navy blue uniform stood at attention behind her. This same scene was repeated all the way along this front counter of the visitors block, its lack of windows perpetuating a trapped feeling.

'That's not who you are,' said Iakovos, lines of confusion etched into his face. He and Kosta sat opposite her, on the other side of the glass, huddled around the single grey phone cradled by the younger man. 'You left her behind years ago.'

'It's my real name. It's what everyone's calling me. I can't have two names.' A tear slid down her left cheek. 'It'll drive me crazy.'

'Okay, okay, if that's what you wish,' said Kosta.

A flicker from her pupils and a weak smile was all that she could offer in return. 'Did you read the letter she sent me?'

'Yes,' they both replied.

'They showed me, up at the office,' said Kosta.

'I cannot believe she wrote with such hate.'

'It's Tracey Johnstone's doing,' said Kosta.

'Her anger is growing.'

'So, we just fight harder,' said Iakovos. 'We can't let them win.'

She stared through the glass. 'I don't care about winning. What's the point? Either way I lose. I just want my daughter back. That's all.'

'She'll come around. You are the truth. We must make sure that Lisa and the whole world knows this,' said Kosta.

Jess bowed her head.

'Have a look at these,' said Kosta, as he slid a few photos through a narrow slot in the base of the glass screen.

Jess spread them out on the counter in front of her. One was of Zetta, aged ten, splashing in the water of her favourite beach, Paros Poros. Beside that was a picture of Iakovos, playing table tennis at the tennis club in Agia Irina and finally a photo of their mountain home on the slopes of Mount Profitis Ilias. Jess touched the photos gently, caressing them with her fingers.

She stared up at Kosta. 'Will you help us?' I…we cannot do it alone.'

'I'm here, aren't I.'

'Yes.' She managed a smile. 'But will you represent me in court?'

He sighed. 'Yiskah, I don't know that I can.'

'My name's Jess and you'll be perfect. You know me inside out. Everything we went through. Everything we stand for.'

'That is precisely the problem. I think I might be too close.'

'There is no one else I can trust. Only you.'

'Your laws are so different here.'

'Truth is the same all over the world.'

'Truth doesn't win court cases.'

'It is all we have,' gestured Jess, her right hand over her heart. 'Please.'

'We'll need strong witnesses. Good people to speak on your behalf.'

'They will be difficult to find,' said Jess. 'I have been back a few days and I have yet to meet someone who likes me. I feel like I'm back in high school. Everyone hated me there too.'

A siren rang out across the building. 'Visiting hours are over,' announced a voiceover. 'Please say goodbye to your guests and return to your cells.'

Jess's head dropped and her thin smile faded.

Kosta's mood though had lifted, a hint of a smile crossing his face. 'I know just what we need. Be ready to go for a drive sometime after lunch, tomorrow.'

'Where to?'

'You'll see.' Kosta was excited.

58

9:00PM
CROWN CASINO, PERTH

Tracey thumped the cash button on the one arm bandit, a golden trail of coins spewing out into the large plastic tray below. 'Woohoooo! I'm a winner.

'Sssssshhhhhhh. Not so loud,' said Lisa.

'I'm celebrating!' Tracey flicked two fingers in the direction of a few annoyed onlookers. A man and women who took particular offence to this display advanced toward a security officer.

'Let's go play the tables, hey Mum?' said Lisa.

'Woohoooo!' Tracey's fist pumped the air as Lisa guided her away.

'This is our lucky night.' Tracey's speech was already slurred, her plastic bucket of winnings clutched to her chest. 'We're gonna win ten times this amount.'

'We're down over two hundred dollars since the start of this week.'

'Yeah, but we're on the way up now.' Tracey lifted the container in front of Lisa's face. 'No stopping us now.' But stop she did. 'Shit, where's me drink?'

'You finished it back at the machine.'

'Get me another one will ya, sweetie.'

'We're out of money unless we cash in some of the tokens.'

'Fuck off. These are my winnings.'

'From my money.'

'It's the governments actually, so it's everybody's. Comes from our taxes.'

'You don't pay any tax.'

Tracey leant close to Lisa's face. 'It's all the money I missed out on when you left. I know you got plenty where that came from so let's just go to the fuckin' bar, all right.'

Tracey started walking off through the hordes of gamblers. 'Tight-arse.'

Lisa watched her mother go, a deep ache in her ribs. A sordid little memory resurfacing from long ago. The ugly face of truth being slowly uncovered. Lisa knew where it was headed but a stubborn determination to finish this journey she had started two weeks ago shrouded these fresh pieces of evidence. Lisa had forced herself into a corner and didn't know how she could get out. She was miserable and helpless, feelings not dissimilar to those she'd experienced at the mountain house a fortnight earlier.

'Oi, get over here,' bellowed her birth mother from the bar. Lisa did as she was commanded, obeying her mum like she was a member of staff.

Two whiskies thanks,' said Tracey. 'And make them doubles.'

59

WEDNESDAY 1st OCTOBER
2:45PM
HASKER PARK PRIMARY SCHOOL

A silver Corolla pulled up beside the 'Kiss and Ride' sign. The streets were quiet, a handful of parents starting to emerge from the alleyways and houses across the street.

The car doors opened, front ones first, Iakovos and Kosta climbing out and surveying the area. The rear doors followed, Jess emerging from the back seat, flanked by two prison guards, one male and one female. She was still apparently a danger to society.

Jess's hair was tied up inside a dark blue baseball cap. A simple attempt at being incognito and unrecognizable from the woman in the news. The application for her day release from prison had been approved due to 'exceptional circumstances'. Kosta's well-designed tour had proved a winner, its theme of 'memory lane' ticking all the psychological boxes required.

Today's itinerary had included a quiet visit to Jess's favourite beach, a drive past her old house and a coffee and cake in Kings Park. Kosta sold it on the likelihood it would improve his client's mental health. Her return was selling papers and the last thing the authorities wanted was a suicide. It was quickly approved, with two prison guards deemed enough security for a woman quickly closing in on her forty eighth birthday.

'Excuse me Mr Kouros,' said the male guard, 'But this place is not on my list.'

'It's a surprise,' said Kosta.

'You're not wrong.'

'Look Karl, the day's gone really well. I just want to help my client reconnect with her old home. That's what we're here for.'

Jess was oblivious to their conversation, her pupils fixed on the black garrison fence that surrounded the plain brick buildings. A rush of emotions surged through her, the flicker of recognition visible in her eyes.

'Please sir, it won't take long' said Iakovos. 'My mum needs this.'

'Yeah, but we don't. Coming back here is a mistake. Maybe even illegal. She's my prisoner and I'll make the decisions, not you.'

'I think it's a good idea,' said the female guard, her uniform crisp and clean. 'I've spent a fair bit of time with Miss Bell over the last few weeks. It'll do her the world of good.'

'Are you overriding me?' said Karl.

'If I have to, then yes,' said Pia.

'You'll take full responsibility?'

'Yes. As her prison psychologist, I'll take it from here.'

'I'll wait in the car. This mistake is all yours.'

Karl threw a set of keys to Pia. 'The cuff's stay on the whole time. That's non-negotiable.' He turned on his heels and made his way back to the car.

Kosta approached Pia. 'Could we secure those cuffs around her back. I think it will be best for everyone if we keep them covered up.'

Pia stepped forward and unlocked the restraints. Jess relaxed her shoulders, taking time to rub each of her wrists. These snippets of freedom were few and Jess was becoming used to life as a caged animal.

'All right, let's do it,' said Pia. 'In and out, as quick as we can.'

Jess swung her arms behind her back. Pia shackled her wrists.

'Thanks.' Jess was trying to be a model prisoner.

Iakovos draped a long brown cardigan across his mother's shoulders, the hem hanging low enough to cover the restraints. Jess smiled at him. 'Thank god you're here.'

'It's okay, Mum.' Iakovos could sense his mother's growing apprehension. 'We brought you here to remember why you saved us. It's my first time back as well.' He draped an arm across her shoulders. 'Let's see what we can remember.'

The school sign to the left of the gate was the first evidence of forced change.

'Hasker Park Primary,' said Iakovos. 'Kinda rolls off the tongue.'

'Marvale was a damaged brand,' said Pia. 'They needed a new name. A new future.'

'Was the park next door always called that,' said Iakovos.

'Yes. It was a sensible move forward.'

They stepped in through an open gate. A vegetable garden flanked both sides of the pathway into the school.

'School's almost out,' said Pia. 'We don't want to be too exposed. Who knows what sorts of views the staff here have.'

'Not to mention the parents,' said Kosta.

The entourage of four adults continued along the path toward the first building. Blue Block had six classrooms in all, a wall of windows all the way down one side. The glare of the sun poured in through the glass, backlighting a classroom filled with students. Rows of light blue polo shirts turned their heads, their concentration broken by the group of strangers outside.

Jess wondered whether they knew who she was. A decade ago and everyone in that class would have known her name, even waved. She was a popular teacher and making sense of her return under fire was an uncomfortable experience. The passing of time, too, was proving difficult to assess, the cream brickwork and gardens as clean and manicured as a decade ago.

'It's all the same,' she said. 'Like we never left.'

'We changed. They didn't,' said Iakovos.

The next classroom held a few good memories. It felt like a lifetime ago, her first year at Marvale Primary, fresh out of university and straight into her own class. The learning curve had been steep.

A door opened and out stepped a young boy. His similarities to a young Jacob startling her. He didn't look up, just walked toward the tidy line of backpacks, slotted like dominoes along the slatted bench. He unzipped one of the bags and slid the blue folder he was carrying inside it. Jess followed his every move like it was the first time she'd seen a human being do this. More students filed out the same door, the peace and quiet of the afternoon quickly replaced by the hustle and bustle of young bodies.

'Let's keep moving,' said Pia. 'We need to stay invisible.'

Iakovos guided Jess around the corner. A narrow concrete path ran diagonally across a grassy slope, the area split in two, a clutch of trees off to one side. Iakovos remembered the conversations and games he'd played here, the canopy of leaves there to provide some welcome respite from the midday sun. Some of his Australian memories had been worth keeping.

A woman stepped around the corner of the building above the grassy slope and followed the footpath toward them. Jess caught a glimpse of her movement and stopped.

Kosta stepped in beside Jess. 'Do you recognise her?'

Jess nodded.

'Is that Mrs Dawson,' said Iakovos from the other flank.

'I think so. It's a long time since I last saw her.'

'Will she be on our side?' asked Pia.

Jess nodded. She remembered a kind and gentle lady. She hoped the same was still the case. Mrs. Dawson was only meters away when she opened her arms up. It was the welcome Jess had hoped for as she was wrapped in a hug. Jess would have loved to return the compliment but the prison issue jewelry wouldn't allow it.

Mrs Dawson lifted her head and whispered into Jess's ear. 'You did good, Jess. I believe that what you did was right.'

'Thank you, Emily. That means a lot to me.'

Emily loosened her grip and stepped back. 'You've meant a lot to us. We've tried to keep the torch burning, but it's been hard.'

Kosta extended his hand. 'Hello, my name is Kosta Kouros.'

Emily took the offer. 'Emily Dawson. Nice to meet you.'

'And this is Jacob.'

Emily's hands flew up instinctively, her mouth covered, her eyes wide. 'Oh my god. I didn't recognise you.'

'Hi Mrs Dawson.'

'Is it really you?'

'One hundred percent.'

'But you're a man now,' said Emily. 'Do I get a hug?'

Iakovos stepped forward and embraced the woman who had cared so much for him.

'You really are a sight for sore eyes,' said Emily.

'Wasn't sure I'd make it, hey?'

They released each other.

'I used to worry so much about you. And your sister.'

'This beautiful lady saved us,' said Iakovos.

Emily wiped the tears from her cheeks. 'She sure did. Shame on the rest of us for just watching and waiting for the worst. We were so apathetic.'

'You were good to me too, Mrs Dawson,' said Iakovos. 'You helped me with my reading and my spelling.'

'Yes, but I didn't step in and protect you. Jess took matters into her own hands and she changed the big things. She should be applauded not imprisoned.'

Kosta saw an opportunity. 'Emily, would you mind testifying in court? You sound very passionate and you're a powerful speaker.'

'If you think it would help?'

'Definitely. We are in for a fight and your educated opinion would be very welcome.'

'Then count me in,' said Emily. 'If I can help you beat this crazy system it might help erase the guilt I carry.'

'Thank you,' said Kosta.

'Who else is still working here?' asked Jess.

'Only a handful since you left. Lots of retirements. Jeff's still going strong though. Have you caught up with him yet?'

Jess shook her head.

'Really. Come on then, follow me. He'll die when he sees you.'

'I was scared I'd killed him already.'

'Nah, not him. It was like water off a duck's back. He knew why you did it. We all did.'

'Who's Jeff,' asked Pia.

'I used to teach with him.' Jess was already walking.

'And?'

'They were the best of friends,' said Emily. 'Very close.'

Emily led them up the slope and around the corner of Red Block. The smoke-stained bricks and mortar of the outer walls stoked the fire inside Jess. She too was beginning to rise from the ashes.

The scream of the school bell took them all by surprise. Its piercing wail a reminder they were on borrowed time. Children suddenly poured out of every door, a heady mix of high-octane energy and pure joy.

'In here.' Emily urged them, past the heaving crowd of children toward an open set of double doors. Inside the building it was quieter, this large room running centrally down the whole building like a spine.

'The wet area,' said Jess. 'It's exactly as I left it.' She took a few steps toward a plaque on the wall. She brushed her fingertips across the engraved letters of the bronze plate. 'It's one of the last things I touched before we drove to the airport.'

'You were charged with an important task,' said Emily. 'To save two children.'

'Yes. I remember,' smiled Jess. 'Nothing could have stopped me.'

A male teacher stepped into the wet area from up the far end. He was tall and well dressed. He gazed down at a large fish tank situated in the corner. 'Hi fishy monsters,' he said. 'Thank fuck that day's over hey?'

Jess smiled at his curt language. 'Mind your language, young man,' she called out. There are children present.'

He spun around. 'I'm so sorry. I didn't realise anyone else was here.'

'Well we are and it's just not good enough!'

His jaw dropped. 'I don't fuckin' believe it!' He took a deep breath. 'Wee bit late for drinks, aren't you?'

'I'm sorry. I got distracted.'

'Well that's just not good enough.' He smiled.

'I swear it'll never happen again.'

'You bet it won't.' He ran a straight line and embraced her. 'God it's good to see you.'

They stayed entangled for a good ten seconds, Jess's head resting in the crook of his neck, his arms trapping her own in a bear hug.

A tear slid down Jess's left cheek and onto his shoulder, her hands still cuffed behind her back. 'I'm sorry for leaving without telling you.'

'I knew what was going on. Not where you went, but what you were doing. I saw your pain.'

Jess leant back and looked him in the eye. 'You knew what I was planning?'

'Every teacher has a child they want to save at some point in their career. I could see that Lisa's sadness was tearing you apart. It takes a very strong person to follow through on your convictions.'

'But the fallout must have been awful.'

'It was hell for a while but I fought a good fight. I was rooting for you the whole time. Each day that went by without them finding you, was another day to celebrate.'

'I knew you were helping me. I could feel it.'

'Who are these guys?'

'This is Kosta, my lawyer.'

They shook hands. 'I think I've seen you on the telly.'

'It comes with the job unfortunately,' said Kosta.

Jeff looked left, his eyes lighting up. 'And this must be Jacob. My god! You were just this high when you left, and so skinny. Look at you now. You're a big hairy dude.'

Everyone laughed.

Iakovos stepped forward and they shook hands. 'Nice to see you again, Mr Simpson.'

'You're a man now. Call me Jeff.'

'He's still my baby though,' said Jess.

'Too right he is. You've done a bloody amazing job. Look at him. It's incredible what a difference love and attention can make.'

'I hope we can explain that to the judge,' said Kosta.

'Don't worry, I will. Let me know when you need me and I'll shout it from the rooftops.'

Two little girls dressed in blue polo shirts burst in through the double doors. They looked up at everyone, found what they were looking for and ran at Jeff. He squatted down and greeted them at eye level.

'Hey girls. You had a good day?' They grabbed an arm each, both nodding, their long blond ponytails dancing across his strong shoulders.

'I've got someone for you to meet,' said Jeff. 'Do you remember the name of that lady I'm always talking about. The one who taught me so much.'

'Miss Bell,' they said together.

'Well she's come back here to see us all.'

The girls turned, their eyes wide with excitement.

'Hi girls,' said Jess. 'It's a pleasure to meet you, is this amazing guy your daddy?'

'Yes. I'm Charlie and this is Angela.'

'Can you take us to Greece?' said Angela.

Jeff smiled. 'I told them all about your big adventure. The fairytale version.'

Jess knelt down on the floor. 'I'd like very much to show you my island. It's a beautiful place.'

The twins high five'd each other. 'Yessss!'

'Come, I'll show you our old class.' Jeff rested a hand on Jess's shoulders and guided her up the corridor.

'So, who'd you marry?' asked Jess.

'One of the mothers. Her name's Marissa.'

'No way! That is so out of bounds.'

'I know. It was good you were gone because I knew you wouldn't approve.'

They laughed.

'I met her at the kindy sundowner. I was working the hot dog stand and she just walked up and I was a goner.'

'You always did have your eye out for a prize,' said Jess.

'I thought we were going make a go of it at one stage.'

'What a disaster that would have been.'

'When you left, I thought maybe you were running away from me?'

'That's what I'll tell the judge. The kids just happened to be hiding in my luggage.' Everybody laughed.

'You might not realise it, but I got my strength from you. You always made me feel so good. Made me strong. I ran away for both of us.'

'I know.' They rested in each other's arms, tears flowing.

'Sorry to interrupt the outpouring but we should probably be going,' said Pia. 'We've got what we wanted.'

'Okay,' nodded Jess.

The playground beside Red Block was still busy, parents lingering, chatting while their children played on the swings and slides. Emily and Iakovos led Pia and Kosta down the slope past these families. Jess and Jeff followed a few steps behind.

'You little bitch,' screamed a woman. 'What the hell have you come back here for? More innocent little children?'

Jess stopped and looked down into the playground.

'Get the hell out of here would you.' The woman whose strong opinions she could hear was short with long dark hair, a blue t-shirt and jeans stretched to capacity. The rest of the parents looked just as unimpressed.

Jeff stepped forward. 'Now calm down Mrs Bright. There are still children around and you're swearing…'

'I don't give a fuck about my swearing.' She thrust a finger in Jess's direction. 'She shouldn't fuckin' be here. She's done more damage than my bad mouth ever will.'

Kosta sensed danger. 'We'll leave right away,' he said.

'Too fuckin' right you will.'

'Don't say another word,' said Pia. 'Let's just walk out like nothing has happened.'

Pia took Jess by the arm and they all walked briskly and silently toward the exit.

'See you in hell,' barked Mrs Bright.

If hell was a packed courtroom, then she was right.

60

MONDAY 6TH OCTOBER
9:45AM
COURT 3-1, PERTH DISTRICT COURT

Kosta exited the lift alone. Court 3-1 was his intended destination but finding it was proving harder than he'd expected.

He had hoped to arrive a lot earlier, a chance to become more familiar with his new surroundings. Soaking up the atmosphere before everyone else arrived had always been of great benefit. No such luck today though. He'd been pipped for a parking spot and finding another free space in the underground car park proved to be a nightmare.

And now, as he approached court 3-1, he recognised the familiar stance of his enemy. Even the posture of this legal juggernaut was at odds with the rest of the world. They had never met in person but the image his adversary projected on the television looked very much like the one he assumed in real life, only bigger.

He had been warned to tread carefully by everyone connected to this case. 'Edward Rosenthal has no friends and isn't interested in being nice,' commented the lady behind the information desk downstairs. 'He is as abrasive as a thousand barnacles,' noted the old security guard at the main desk.

Prosecutor Rosenthal's record spoke for itself.

Kosta approached the legal giant and offered his hand. 'My name's Kosta.'

'The Greek marvel,' replied Rosenthal, squeezing Kosta's hand harder and longer than necessary. 'This shouldn't take long.' Rosenthal released him, his words seeped with arrogance, every letter sliding out past a set of perfectly aligned and pristine white teeth.

'Long enough for the truth to come out,' said Kosta.

'Such a romantic notion.'

'Some of us still believe in honesty.'

'Just stick to the script and veracity will take care of herself.'

'What script? This isn't the theatre.'

'That's where you're wrong. That's exactly what it is! And I'm the lead, so just stick to your role as the fall guy and everything will be all right. Otherwise you might just lose both your dignity and any reputation you still have.'

'I can cut my losses, as long as my client wins. You, though, will crumble. You probably haven't even entertained the idea of losing have you.'

'Of course not. I never do.'

'Entertaining fools is not something I like to do either,' grinned Kosta, 'So excuse me, I have a client to see.'

Kosta stepped away from the conflict zone and toward the recessed entrance to court 3-1. He pressed down on the large white button beside the door. The electronic buzz of the locking mechanism resembled the energy churning inside of him and he waited the prescribed five seconds for the deadbolt to disengage. The high stakes game of bluff he'd just played had enlivened his morning but Kosta knew he couldn't keep that up all day. Bzzzzzt. He pulled the door toward him and greeted the guard on the other side with a smile.

'Morning.'

'Good morning Mr Kouros. Welcome to Court three dash one.'

Kosta studied the vastness of the room and swallowed. The sheer size of these rooms always made him feel insignificant. They were the same in Athens and possibly the world over. Designed to peel back a person's weaknesses. Created to eat the meek for breakfast.

Kosta spotted Jess on the other side of the room. She looked like she was meditating, her eyes closed, her body still. A mind filled with images of Paros and of happier times. He knew she returned there as often as possible, the slopes of the mountain house and the golden beaches. This mental journey calmed her nerves and brought her some peace.

He prayed they would someday return.

Kosta decided to let her be, making his way over toward the desk at the front of the court. He gently placed his briefcase on the polished wooden veneer and started unpacking his notes.

Jess caught a whiff of his familiar scent. The cologne had been a birthday present. The associated connotations were a pleasant reminder that she wasn't alone. The man who wore it was her true believer. He made her strong. She played his voice over and over. *Let's do what we came here for. Let's clear your name and live forever without fear.*

She took a deep breath and opened her eyes. 'Yassas Kosta.'

Kosta enjoyed the sound of her voice. There was more optimism than he had expected, even some Greek. He projected his own image of calm, turning around and giving her his full attention.

'Yasu Miss Bell. How are you?' Kosta felt it was important to keep the formalities of court. Just in case anyone was listening.

'Much better now you're here.'

'You look good.'

'Thanks. I took on board all your suggestions. Thanks for the top.'

'My pleasure. It's from your favourite shop in Naoussa.'

'Esmerelda's?'

'Neh.'

Jess allowed her hand to glide across the smooth white fabric, the shirt alluding to a warmth and softness that Kosta had been keen to display. Her hair was loose and free, her face made up with natural tones. She looked radiant and beautiful. This was the woman he had fallen in love with many years before. He hoped the jury would too.

The whirr of the lock broke the spell. The door opened and in strode Rosenthal. He walked like a soldier, upright and toward a target. There were no greetings, not even a glance their way. He assumed a position on the table, front right and methodically unpacked his materials.

Fifteen minutes later and the courtroom was officially open for business. Streams of people poured in, filling up both the gallery and the area reserved for media. The case had caught the imagination of the public and they came like footy fans to a game, ready for a spectacle.

One person knew more than most and as he wandered in alone, Jess looked up and waved his way. Iakovos smiled back as he took his seat in the front row. Kosta approached the railing that separated the gallery from the court floor.

'Yasu Iakovos.'

'Yasu Kosta.'

'Thanks for coming.'

'I wouldn't be anywhere else. No sign of Zetta yet?'

'I'm not expecting to see her,' said Kosta.

'I'll let you know if she arrives.'

The simple black and white clock above the defendant's box struck ten o'clock. Jess wanted to stretch, could feel the tension returning to her legs. This dock would be her moral prison for the next five days and the repetitive tick tock of the timepiece above her head was already making her fret.

The stares from the gallery weighed her down, her role as the accused meaning she would be a magnet for scrutiny. A low railing was all that separated her from the main court room. A burly security guard sat just behind her and to the right. She felt like an animal in a zoo.

She had been saved the indignity of a goldfish bowl, noting the existence of several clear glass panels, recessed into the wall to her right. She'd spent ninety percent of her time trapped inside the walls of her cell since she arrived back in Perth. Being sealed behind a wall of glass would have been the last straw. Tick, tock, tick, tock, tick, tock. The clock was growing louder and remaining positive was going to be her first battle.

The jury filed in from a small door at the rear of the court. They were unannounced and quietly took their seats. They were of mixed age, race and sex. A good cross section of multicultural Perth. Jess could hardly bear to look at them lest they catch her staring. Kosta had asked her to appear both trustworthy and inspirational. It was her past actions that were on trial but she needed to appear beyond reproach during the court sessions as well.

At 10:05am the orderly announced the arrival of Judge Iverson and asked all present to stand. Another door at the rear of the chamber opened and in strode a woman with the assurance of someone who knew she was on the right side of the law. Her black gown with its purple trimmings denoted her standing and the fancy white collar and red sash only further dramatised the aura surrounding her. The chamber waited for the judge to take her seat before returning to their own chairs. The pageantry had begun. Rosenthal bristled with excitement.

Kosta waited patiently for the judge to address the court. The last few days had been a manic mix of last-minute meetings and misinformation. The media had been all over Jess's story and he had run the gamut of quiet requests and discourteous demands. Discrediting the untruths and protecting the children had been of paramount importance and he'd worked tirelessly to prepare a strong case. Now the moment had arrived and everything depended on his own performance. He must be strong, decisive and credible. He had a history with the defendant that went far deeper than this case and he would be representing her in more ways than one.

He had also been asked to defend his own credibility, so-called experts insisting that he was in over his head. That whilst this case was already stacked heavily in the DCP's favour, hiring a Greek divorce lawyer had only deepened the hole that would eventually bury Jessica Bell. Kosta had chosen silence as his weapon. He knew the truth could wait. Court cases were not won in the papers nor on the six o'clock news. They were important for the mindset of the client but this was not a popularity contest.

Prosecutor Rosenthal had prepared his notes in chronological order. He would be the first to stand and he knew he must be prepared. In his mind, this is what won cases. Preparation and dedication. The law would do the rest. He alone was proof that what he stood for was just and right. Today was just another day in court, doing what he loved. Winning.

The Judge's Associate stood and addressed the court. 'Would the defendant please stand.'

Jess saw the sea of heads turn. She got to her feet.

'To the charges of stealing and forgery how do you plead?' asked the associate.

Jess looked at Kosta for guidance. He nodded. She returned her gaze to the associate. 'I plead guilty.'

'And to the charge of kidnapping how do you plead?'

The gallery was quiet. This was what they had come to see.

'Not guilty, your honour.'

The shimmer of voices resembled an ocean swell and Jess felt it move through her, swaying her momentum, reminding her of its power.

61

10:30AM
COURT 3-1

Judge Iverson looked up and across at the jurors.

'Welcome and thank you for giving us your time. Mr Edward Rosenthal will be representing the Department of Education and Mr Kostas Kouros will be representing the accused, Miss Jessica Bell. What they say is not evidence, but what they present is. The questions they ask are not pieces of evidence, but the answers they elicit are. You must decide this case based on the facts presented inside this courtroom only. You must not engage in any discussion forums with anyone other than your fellow jurors in relation to the evidence or issues of this case. You must not refer to this case on any form of social media.'

The juror's faces were solemn and serious.

'The fact that a security guard is sitting in the booth with the accused carries no meaning,' explained the Judge. 'This is standard court procedure and does not infer that the person on trial is in any way dangerous. Mr Rosenthal, I invite you to open this case.'

The prosecutor rose to his feet.

'Thank you, Your Honour. Ladies and gentlemen of the jury we are here today to hear the case against a teacher, Miss Jessica Bell, who ten years ago kidnapped two of her students and fled to the other side of the world. They remained hidden for a decade under forged identities, having no contact with their parents and family back here in Perth. Miss Bell knows she has done the wrong thing and has returned now to take her punishment. I will make my plea brief and to the point.'

Rosenthal stepped away from his desk and toward the jury. 'Please do not go light on her, but instead send a very firm and clear message to anyone and everyone in positions of trust and power, that this behaviour is not acceptable. That taking children from their parents is not only wrong but morally reprehensible. I know that I can trust you to make the right decision. Thank you.' He returned to his desk and sat back down in his chair.

'Mr Kouros,' invited the judge. 'Please address the jury.'

Kosta stood proudly. 'Thank you, Your Honour. Ladies and gentlemen of the jury it is true my client, Miss Jessica Bell, did flee this country some ten years ago with two of her students, but what you don't know are the horrendous and frightening truths that lay at the centre of her heartbreaking decision to flee. This decision was not hasty nor was it self-indulgent. This decision was taken only when all other avenues had been exhausted and my client could see only one way to protect these children from the dangers encircling them.' Kosta stepped around the side of his desk and walked toward the jury. 'This exit plan was forced upon her by a system that had failed these two children. She worked for an organisation too caught up in paperwork to be effective. On one hand, the Education Department told her that as a teacher she must always put the welfare of the children first. That same entity then constructed roadblock after roadblock to stop her taking the steps necessary to enact this very principle. My client took the extraordinary step to escape, only when all other attempts had failed. She enacted the code of ethics, even when it affected her own life. I will prove that she is a good teacher and that what she did was right. Jessica Bell took the only remaining choice she had left.' Kosta paused to take a breath. 'She has returned a hero in many people's eyes; a role model for fairness and choice. Please do not punish her for doing what so many have failed to do in the past, that is, to protect the children in their care. Thank you.' Kosta returned to his seat.

A chatter of conversation rose from the gallery.

The judge waited for the public to settle. 'Mr Kouros I now invite you to begin your defence.'

Kosta returned to his feet. 'Thank you, Judge Iverson. I would like to start by offering some understanding on how The Department for Child Protection in Western Australia administers the Acts and Regulations on behalf of the Minister. These details are vital if we are to understand the actions of my client because these principles form the foundation on which she made her decisions. They are also complex so a careful explanation is very important.' Kosta stepped from behind his desk and moved toward the jury. 'The Children and Community Services Act of 2004 came into operation on 1 March 2005. It is the main legislation that governs the Department's three service areas, one of which is protecting children and young people from abuse. I have copies for you all.'

Kosta handed several copies to the Judge's Associate who passed all bar one over to the jury. He then crossed the court and passed the remaining copy to Judge Iverson.

'Please let this be known as Exhibit A,' said Kosta.

The Judge and Jury took a few moments to flick through the first few pages.

Kosta spoke as they read. 'One of the objects of the Act is to provide for the protection and care of children in circumstances where their parents have not given, or are unlikely or unable to give, such protection and care. In the administration of this Act the following principles must be observed. I will use these principles over the next few days, to put forward the case that my client did everything asked of her.' He smiled up at Jess who was watching him with pride.

'The principles are; (a) that the parents, family and community of a child have the primary role in safeguarding and promoting the child's wellbeing; (b) that the preferred way of safeguarding and promoting a child's wellbeing is to support the child's parents, family and community in the care of the child; (c) that every child should be cared for and protected from harm; (d) that every child should live in an environment free from violence; (e) that every child should have stable, secure and safe relationships and living arrangements; (f) that intervention action should be taken only in circumstances where there is no other reasonable way to safeguard and promote the child's wellbeing; (g) that if a child is removed from the child's family then, so far as is consistent with the child's best interests, the child should be given encouragement and support in maintaining contact with the child's parents, siblings and other relatives and with any other people who are significant in the child's life; (h-a) that if a child is removed from the child's family then, so far as is consistent with the child's best interests, planning for the child's care should occur as soon as possible in order to ensure long-term stability for the child; (h) that decisions about a child should be made promptly having regard to the age, characteristics, circumstances and needs of the child; (i) that decisions about a child should be consistent with cultural, ethnic and religious values and traditions relevant to the child; (j) that a child's parents and any other people who are significant in the child's life should be given an opportunity and assistance to participate in decision-making processes under this Act that are likely to have a significant impact on the child's life; (k) that a child's parents and any other people who are significant in the child's life should be given adequate information, in a manner and language that they can understand.' Kosta reached for the glass of water on his desk and took a drink.

'It's a lot of information to take in and that is why, one by one, I will be analysing each and every principle, pulling it apart so that you can put yourselves in my client's shoes, helping you to understand her decision-making process in a desperate situation. I will call many witnesses. They will help explain these principles and how they affect the teaching profession. Jessica Bell made the right choices when confronted with these guidelines and I will prove the legality of these actions.'

Rosenthal stood. 'Excuse me, Your Honour, but is it really necessary that we should investigate an Act that is already ten years old and has since been updated and improved.'

Judge Iverson looked up from the paperwork in front of her. 'Is this true Mr Kouros?'

'It is true, Your Honour,' said Kosta. 'It was updated as a direct result of my client's actions. She exposed gaps in the system. Flaws, I think the Prime Minister of the time called them. Miss Bell though used the 2004 Act as her guiding light as it was designed to inform all teachers and community workers of the expectations placed upon them. She applied this law to her actions for this law was current at that time.'

'She never applied the law, Your Honour,' said Rosenthal. 'She broke it.'

'Objection.' said Kosta. 'That is yet to be proven.'

'Sustained,' said the Judge. 'Mr. Rosenthal, you must keep your opinions to yourself.'

Kosta continued. 'The jury cannot be expected to rule on this case unless they understand what inspired my client to take the actions she took.

'I would hardly say she was inspired,' said Rosenthal.

'I would prefer it if you hardly said anything at all.'

'Thank you Mr Kouros,' said the Judge, 'But we must keep the personal remarks to a minimum. This is a very serious case and I will not allow such childish behavior to negatively impact its outcome. We shall adjourn for thirty minutes. Gentlemen, please use this time to sort yourselves out before we return.'

62

12:26PM
INTERVIEW ROOM ONE, DISTRICT COURT

'How do you think we're going?' asked Jess.

She was seated across a plain white table opposite Kosta, a plate of club sandwiches in front of them. The neutral decor of the cell-like interview room threw a pallor over the conversation.

'It's your country. These are still your people. What do you think?' Kosta took a piece of food.

'Judge Iverson is great. I was expecting some old bloke with grey hair, so she was a breath of fresh air.'

'She's good. Gets straight to the point.'

'Is it good for us? Having a woman at the top?'

'She's only guiding proceedings. She doesn't make the final decision.'

'I know, but will she be sympathetic to our cause? Will she understand why a woman would take another woman's children?'

'I think that once she has studied the facts and heard from all the witnesses she will be swayed. Judge Iverson will be given the same opportunity as everyone on the jury.'

'Do we know anything about her background?' Jess took a sip from her coffee.

'Married, two children, teenagers, wealthy, successful and by all accounts happy.'

'I'm so nervous.'

'That's understandable.'

'Zetta hasn't shown up yet, has she?'

'No. She's probably too embarrassed to show her face.'

'I feel sorry for her. Is she going to testify?'

'Rosenthal said she wasn't. Although he might be playing games.'

'Iakovos looks relaxed. He's so calm.'

'He knows that what you did was right. He's expecting everyone else will see the truth as well.' He took another sandwhich.

'You hated me when I first told you that Jacob and Lisa weren't my children,' said Jess.

'I never hated you. It hurt that you hadn't seen fit to trust me earlier.'

'I had to be sure my secret was safe.'

'You knew I loved them and we both did everything for them so to find out they weren't yours, I was disappointed. Felt like they would never be ours.'

'I always felt like they were ours.'

'I know, but it worried me. That one day you might have to give them back.'

'That's sort of what I'm doing now I guess. They're old enough to make their own decisions.'

'And it's ripping you apart.'

'Love is what keeps families together, not blood or laws.'

'I agree with you. Without love, there is only obedience.'

'Does it scare you that I had the audacity to take someone else's kids?'

'Your strength of character was always a standout feature. Although at times you could be very stubborn. I knew you must have had a good reason for taking them. As a divorce lawyer, I see a lot of idiot parents who couldn't care less about the children and you definitely weren't like them.'

'You thought a lot of me?'

'Still do.'

'Do you ever wish we'd had our own children?'

'If god had wanted it that way then it would have happened.'

'I wanted children with you.'

'You never talked about it.'

'I know. I wasn't sure if we were ready. I thought that having a child of our own would have cemented our status as a family and given Iakovos and Zetta a brother or a sister to care for.'

'It's all in the past now.'

'Might have been the glue that held us together?'

'Maybe.'

Jess reached for Kosta's hands and grasped them between her fingers. 'Is there still a chance for us?'

'Not here.' Kosta pulled his hand away. 'We need to stay focused on this case. Complicating our lives by dissecting the past isn't going to help.'

'I know you're right. I just can't help wondering, that's all.'

'Well don't. If they find out about the two of us, then it might just kill your case altogether.' Kosta got to his feet. 'Let's keep our distance over the next few days. The last thing we need is another media storm.'

'Okay, I'm sorry.'

Kosta walked toward the door. 'I'll see you on the other side.'

He opened the door and left. Yiskah watched the door close.

She prayed his heart was still open.

63

1:00PM
COURT 3-1, FIRST WITNESS, HEATHER ROBINS

(Principal a) the parents, family and community of a child have the primary role in safeguarding and promoting the child's wellbeing.

The courtroom clock ticked over as Kosta rose to his feet.

'Principle A is where I shall start. The truth is where I will end.'

Several screens, situated around the court lit up with text of 'Principle A'.

'I hope that you shall refer to these facts whenever doubt is cast upon the actions of my client. 'Principle A' states that *the parents, family and community of a child have the primary role in safeguarding and promoting the child's wellbeing.* So, let us first define what it is to be a parent.'

Kosta lifted a copy of the Oxford Dictionary off his desk and flicked the bookmarked page open. 'The Oxford Dictionary states the definition of a 'parent' as either a mother or a father. The term 'parenting' means to give warmth and attention. I know that certificates can and will be provided to prove that Tracey and Gary Johnstone are the blood parents of Jacob and Lisa Johnstone. That is irrefutable. But did they show good parenting skills? Did they provide warmth and attention? Absolutely not.'

Rosenthal was quick to his feet. 'Objection.'

'On what grounds?' asked Judge Iverson.

'Parenting is not part of this principle.'

Kosta was ready. 'Parenting is simply the verb of the word parent and so cannot be separated.'

'I'll allow it,' said the Judge.

Kosta continued. 'The definition of the word 'Family' is a group of people related to one another by blood. This again refers to Tracey and Gary Johnstone. It also includes the grandparents who I can reveal had been frozen out of their grandchildren's lives.'

'Objection. Where's the proof?'

'That will come.'

'Allowed,' said Iverson.

'The Oxford Dictionary also states that the term 'family' can be used to define a group of people united in criminal activity. Tracey and Gary Johnstone have a long list of criminal infringements. To say they have a checkered history would be to underplay their dealings with the police.'

Judge Iverson smiled. 'This lawyer was good, if not unconventional,' she thought to herself.

'The definition of a 'community' is the people of a district or country considered collectively, especially in the context of social values and responsibilities. This is where Jessica Bell and the teachers of Marvale Primary play such an important role. Principle A states that they must be involved in safeguarding and promoting the child's wellbeing. To absolve themselves of this responsibility would be negligent. And negligence, in this profession, is punishable by law.' Kosta looked down at his notes then turned to the bench. 'To further explain this professional expectation the Defence calls Mrs Heather Robins to the stand.'

A dark-haired woman in her fifties rose from the last seat in the last row of the gallery. She approached the low swinging gate separating the audience from the court. The guard allowed her through and she took her place in the witness stand.

Heather Robins placed her left hand on the Bible and raised

her right hand in the air. 'I swear by the Almighty God that I will give a true account according to the evidence being tried here.'

'Thank you,' said Judge Iverson. 'You may be seated.'

'Good morning Mrs Robins,' said Kosta.

'Please call me Heather.' She spoke with a clipped English accent.

'Of course. Heather, what is your occupation?'

'I am an early childhood teacher.'

'And early childhood covers what ages?'

'I am qualified to teach children between the ages of four and seven.'

'Are you aware of Principle A of the Children and Community Services Act?'

'Yes, I am.'

'What is your understanding of this principle?'

'Principle A relates to myself as being part of the community responsible for safeguarding and promoting a child's wellbeing. Parents enrol their children in school, safe in the knowledge that I am trained and certified to teach and care for their children.'

'Who else, in your opinion, helps form this community?'

'The whole school does. The teachers, education assistants and office staff. Everyone at Marvale is involved.'

'And how do you go about safeguarding and protecting these children?'

'We make decisions every day that puts their best interest at the centre of everything we do. We communicate with other teachers on a professional level and with the children's parents and family to ensure we are providing a safe and happy environment for learning.'

'So how do you work with parents to achieve this?'

'We have a parent-teacher meeting at the beginning of each year where we outline our expectations. We also have one-on-one meetings if required and then throughout the year as issues arise.'

'And are all the parents appreciative of your efforts?'

'Most are. There's always one or two who just drop off their kids like we're a bunch of babysitters.'

'And how does that affect you?'

'Those kids are usually the ones who arrive without a good lunch or a clean uniform. The ones who haven't had enough sleep to get them through the day.'

'What happens to them?'

'We have to step in and fill the breech. We feed them if necessary, sew up and clean their torn uniforms. If they feel sleepy, we let them have a nap.'

'Why do you do this?'

'Because we want then to be healthy and happy.'

'You want to safeguard and promote their wellbeing?'

'Yes.'

'And in the absence of their parents being capable of this, you are prepared to take on that role.'

'We feel that we must. It is an extension of our roles as teachers.'

'Did you ever have to step in and help Jacob and Lisa Johnstone?'

'Yes, I did. From their very first day of school, they were obviously being neglected and malnourished. Their story was a sad one.' Heather lifted a handkerchief to her face and wiped away a tear. 'It still pains me to think about what they had to endure.'

'You say their story *was* a sad one. What do you mean by that?'

'Well thanks to the extraordinary efforts of Miss Bell, they have been rescued.'

'Did she safeguard and protect their wellbeing?'

'My oath she did! She is an amazing teacher and a sensational human being.'

'Do you know if she ever met with the children's parents to discuss the school's concerns?'

'Several times. It became quite a serious issue for the school because of the lack of success we were all having with them.'

'Lack of success. What do you mean by that?'

'Just getting the parents to turn up was hard. It was the same when I taught them but they were just little then. In Year 4 and 5 these issues were becoming more serious and, in some instances, there were legal concerns, problems that needed to be dealt with. But nothing could be done without the parent's consent. Any real change was impossible. The whole process was stagnating under their refusal to cooperate. Jess was very worried about the children. We all were.'

'Was this normal for a teacher to be so concerned?'

'All teachers worry about their students but usually it's just a reading or a math problem, something educational. Something we can fix during school hours. Lisa and Jacob's whole life was a concern. Every day was a battle for them. I haven't seen a worse case of physical and mental abuse in my entire teaching career.'

Jess glanced over at Iakovos, concerned that these ugly facts might be painful to hear. He was all concentration.

'And when the parents did turn up,' said Kosta, 'What happened then?'

'People shouting, wild accusations and a lot of swearing. Jess would have her meetings in the administration block just up the hall from the staffroom. It was a precaution we all followed, in case the parents turned violent, as they nearly always did. The teachers would be at recess or lunch and the noise coming out of that office was unsettling. But we'd all been through it before. We knew what would happen.'

'Objection. This is hearsay,' said Rosenthal, jumping to his feet.

'Mrs Robins is a qualified teacher,' replied Iverson. 'I believe she is qualified enough to ensure that her version of events is at least heard.'

'But she wasn't even in the room where these meetings took place.'

'No but she has had prior experience and knows what she heard,' said the Judge. 'That is all she has commented on so far. Overruled.' Rosenthal sat down in his leather-bound chair.

'Sorry Mrs Robins you may continue,' said the Judge.

'This noise. Who was making it?' asked Kosta.

'Mr and Mrs Johnstone were. They were going off their trolley. They never listened to what was being said. Jess and Rupert Small, the deputy, couldn't get a word in edgeways. Jess genuinely cared for those children. We all did, but Gary and Tracey Johnstone only saw how people were pointing the blame at them and they couldn't handle it without aggression. It was pandemonium sometimes. We were all prepared for a lockdown every time they were scheduled to come in.'

'In your opinion, what do you think might have happened had Jess not acted and fled the country with Lisa and Jacob?'

'The children wouldn't have made it to eighteen.' Heather looked across at Iakovos then back at Kosta. 'We'd probably be here talking about two dead kids.'

'Objection' yelled Rosenthal. 'That is totally out of order.'

'My witness is a teacher with thirty-five year's experience,' said Kosta. 'Twenty-two of those years were spent at Marvale Primary School. I think she is qualified to share her qualified opinion, Your Honour.'

Judge Iverson was not impressed. 'Well clearly she has already done that. Objection sustained! I direct the jury to please ignore the comments just aired by Mrs Robins. We are not here to predict what might have happened, only to observe the facts as they stand.'

'Thank you, Your Honour,' said Rosenthal.

Kosta returned his attention to Mrs Robins. 'Why do you think Miss Bell did what she did?'

'Because she, along with the rest of us, would have probably been prosecuted for failing to safeguard their wellbeing.'

'That happens?'

'Our guidelines are very strict. If we see abuse, we must report it or face jail. You either struggle against a system that is failing or you act. Thank god, our Jess acted when she did. She saved us all, not just the kids.'

'Is this problem of poor parenting a common issue?'

'It's a growing problem for sure. The definition of a family can be one related to criminal activity. We see our fair share of that in Marvale and it's the kids who always bear the brunt. Maybe this case will change things. Reveal a few home truths. It's about time the government included themselves in what we call a community and stopped hiding behind all the paperwork they ask us to produce.'

'Thank you Mrs. Robins. I have no more questions.'

'Mr. Rosenthal.' said the Judge. 'You may cross-examine the witness.'

The prosecutor rose. 'Good afternoon, Mrs Robins.'

'Hello.'

'My apologies for being so frank but what is it about your profession that makes you think you can run roughshod over the wishes of the parents and the family.'

'It's not just what we think. It is what the Education Department expects of us. It's mandated and so must be carried out.'

'But not everyone does what Miss Bell did?'

'No, they don't. Dealing with ineffective and irate parents is the bane of all teachers. The child is never to blame. Fault always lays with their parents and they don't like it when we tell them so.'

'I expect they wouldn't.'

'So, it's easier to avoid an awkward situation by not creating it in the first place.'

'So, you're saying Miss Bell created this situation.'

'By alerting the authorities to a system of neglect, yes.'

'Isn't it true, however, that five teachers before her had not taken such a drastic step as to kidnap the children because they knew that was not safeguarding a child's wellbeing. They knew that this would be considered a criminal act.'

'Well … yes … but …'

'Thank you. I have no more questions.'

'But they ...'

'Thank you, Mrs Robins,' said Judge Iverson. 'You may return to your seat.'

'But I …'

'Mrs Robins,' said the Judge, 'You've answered the Prosecutor's questions and you must now leave the stand.'

'But I haven't finished answering.'

'I understand that, but the Prosecutor has finished his cross examination of you.'

Heather Robins stood and shuffled out of the dock.

64

2:00PM
SECOND WITNESS, EMILY DAWSON

(Principal b) the preferred way of safeguarding and promoting a child's wellbeing is to support the child's parents, family and community in the care of the child.

Kosta strolled in front of Judge Iverson and toward the jury.

'What happens when this support system breaks down?' he asked.

Emily Dawson sat confidently in the dock, her red and white floral dress providing a striking contrast against the backdrop of dark polished wood. 'Nothing gets done,' she answered. 'The child's wellbeing is at the mercy of fate.'

'Do Jessica Bell's actions come under this umbrella of fate, Mrs Dawson?'

'Definitely. Everything else had broken down, several times in fact. Nothing appeared to work. It needed something special to break the cycle and she was it.'

'Was she still working within the boundaries of Principle B?'

'She is Principle B. She wasn't just the support, she was the whole structure that cared for these children, so yes, in my eyes she had become the parent, the family and the community.'

'Was leaving the country her call to make?'

'Sometimes life doesn't ask you what you'd prefer to do. It just thrusts these issues in your face and forces you deal with them.'

'Did Jessica make the right decisions?'

'Absolutely! She made decisions that most of us are too weak to carry out. We think about it but we are too scared to act. She supported these children at the expense of her own life. She continues to support them today even though they are the reason she is here.'

'Isn't the fact that she is being tried here today evidence enough that she was wrong?'

'No. Only one of the children is driving this case. Her son is here in full support of her. The Education Department is at fault. This whole circus is its doing. It needed a scapegoat to hide its own failings.' The clock above Jess's head clicked past 2:15pm.

Prosecutor Rosenthal prowled in front of his desk. 'In what country can we read kidnapping a child as supporting the parents?' he asked.

'Here in Australia, where some cases don't quite fit the box built to hold them.' Emily Dawson's sarcasm was clear as day. She was at her fighting best.

'You appear quite negative toward the education system, Mrs Dawson.'

'I've had my battles.'

'And were you a winner or a loser?'

'I lost them all if that's what you're asking. They weren't fair fights.'

'They never are when you're not victorious. Hoping to win this one?'

'You better believe it.'

'Teach those Education Department cronies a lesson hey?'

'For sure. We'll show them who's right.'

'That doesn't sound very supportive of the people who run the system.'

'It wasn't meant to be. They pay my mortgage, that's as far as we go.'

'Nice sentiments Mrs Dawson. I believe we all know which side you're barracking for. Thank you for your time.'

'My pleasure.'

65

6:00PM
DALTON CRESCENT

A green Corolla hatchback sat with its engine off at the intersection between Dalton Crescent and O'Neill Drive. Hertz Rent-a-Car stickers were emblazoned across both doors.

Iakovos and Lisa sat in the front seats. She took a sip of her takeaway coffee. 'You weren't in court today?' said Iakovos.

'Couldn't face it. They don't need me anyway. Yiskah's done enough to hang herself without me being there.'

'You're wrong. They'll see the truth.'

'You're always so bloody optimistic.'

'I believe in our mother. I still believe in us.'

'Believe all you like. It won't change a thing.'

'So why agree to meet me here then?'

'You're my brother. I miss you.'

'I miss you too.'

'I've tried to visit our old house three times already,' said Lisa. 'This is as far as I got.'

'Too scared?'

'Just numb actually. Not sure what to feel.'

'Just seeing the old street sign makes me want to vomit.'

'Good old Dalton Crescent,' she said. 'Did you know that

all the street names from around here are sourced from famous educators?'

'No, I didn't.'

'Anthony Dalton wrote the first Curriculum Framework. Marvale was themed around school life. It was created as a learning community.'

'That's a joke. It certainly died a quick death with us.'

'I wonder what happens between the design process and the reality? What causes ideas like this to fail?'

'I don't think you can control all of the outcomes,' said Iakovos. 'Shitty parents are a disease wherever you go. You can hope and you can put down a level of concrete that will support a particular concept but in the end the quality of the people will decide whether you're successful or not.'

'Did we ever have the chance to decide?' asked Lisa.

'Not really. The architects' dream was already over by the time we were old enough to read.'

'Then suddenly we were whisked off to a better place.' Lisa's sarcasm was painful for Iakovos to hear.

'Anything was better than here.' Iakovos took a sip of his coffee, a strained silence taking up residence inside the car. 'How do you know all that info about the street names anyway?' he asked.

'Lawyers. They're pretty good at delving into archives and pulling out all manner of interesting stuff.'

'They're just digging for dirt. For people who are charged with upholding the truth they sure know how to twist it.'

'We all do it to some degree. Look at us. I have my truth and it's so different to yours, yet we shared the exact same life.'

'I wrestle with that fact every day. What happened to you? Did I miss something?'

'I needed a father and unfortunately he was on the other side of the world.'

'You and I never had a father. He was absent from our lives even when we were living here.'

'He was taken from me and there's nothing you can do to change that fact.'

'Shit happened! I agree. It wasn't perfect, but you have to try and imagine what our future would have been like had we stayed.'

'I don't have to do anything I don't want to.'

'That has always been your mantra.'

'And will be till the day I die.'

Jacob was losing her and he knew it. 'How's it going with Tracey?'

'Mum's fine thanks. She really wants to see you, you know that don't you?'

'Not interested. I wish she had died like Yiskah told us.'

'That's a horrible thing to say.'

'Can't change how I feel.'

'No, we can't.'

'How's the old man,' asked Iakovos.

'I'm not really sure. He won't return my calls. I caught up with him at the pub when I first arrived but that's been the only contact.'

'What did he have to say?'

'Nothing too deep. His brains are pickled in alcohol. We had a few drinks but he got pretty agro toward the end, so I left.'

'You left. But he's the one you came home for?'

'Yeah he is and I'll just have to wait until he comes around. Maybe once the court case has finished he'll soften towards me.'

'You'll be lucky. He's always been a hard man.'

'Mum admitted that us being taken made him go a little bit crazy.'

'That's a joke. He's always been aggressive, irrational, pigheaded. Nothing's changed. Maybe she's just woken up from her own drug-induced slumber.'

'She's clean now. Doesn't touch the stuff.'

'And alcohol?'

'Here and there. She's no saint.'

'I never said she was.' Another wave of silence rose up between them.

'Let's try and park outside the house?'

'You think it might change how I feel?'

'You came half way around the world to find out.'

'I came for justice.'

'Well this is where it starts. Or are you too scared?'

'Is that a challenge?'

'You bet.'

Lisa switched the car on. 'Let's drive!'

The house at number twenty-three had paint peeling off the weatherboard exterior. The garden was filled with metre-high weeds. A battered old Commodore sat in the driveway, its left rear wheel missing, a car jack rusting away in its place.

A smashed window in the front room had been covered by black polythene. It billowed with the breeze, in then out, in then out.

The hire car rolled into view and parked across the road. The street was quiet, filled only with the long shadows of the afternoon sun.

The driver's window descended with a whirr. Lisa sucked on a freshly lit cigarette.

'You sure you should be doing that in here?' asked Iakovos.

'It's a hire car. Who really cares.' Another drag. 'Paros gave me this disgusting habit. If I'd grown up here, chances are I wouldn't have picked it up.'

'No, you'd already be dead from the secondary smoke of our kind and loving parents.'

Lisa took a long suck then blew a plume of smoke in her brother's face.

'Hey.' Iakovos waved his hands to clear the white cloud.

'Just making a point.'

They stared across at the house they'd grown up in.

'It hasn't changed,' said Lisa.

'I know. I think the resident is a gardening enthusiast.' They both laughed.

'Why doesn't the government just do it up?' asked Lisa. 'They own it.'

'Are you sure about that?'

Lisa turned and looked at Iakovos. 'Of course I am. No one

around here could ever afford to buy this 'decorator's delight'. The price of houses around here makes this trash heap look like a palace on paper.'

'This palace is where we grew up.'

'Yeah and I thought I was a princess.'

Something over Lisa's shoulder caught Iakovos's attention. 'Well here comes our King?'

A broken fly screen clanged against the portico wall as Gary shuffled out the front door atop the steps. A brown towelling dressing gown hung off his lopsided shoulders. He grabbed hold of the railing and descended two steps, then lowered his bum to the top of the first.

Gary looked like he should be in hospital. He grimaced, allowing the nagging pain in his back to settle. He reached inside one of his pockets and lifted a lighter and a fag to his mouth. A flick of metal, followed by a flame. Same old, same old, thought Iakovos. Probably the millionth time he'd done this set of actions. If he could count that high?

'Always has a fag in his mouth,' said Lisa.

'That's the old man in all his glory.'

'You think he can see us?'

'Nah. He's blind as a bat without his glasses.'

'He wears glasses?'

'He's meant to. Can't see past his hand without them. Likes it that way though. Means he can't see the truth even when it's right in front of him. I spoke to him the other day. Or rather tried to. Walked up to the front door to say hello. He answered the door but he didn't have the slightest idea who I was.'

'Really? Well he thought I was a prostitute when I visited him at the pub.'

'You're kidding. What did you say?'

'Nothing. We've been away a long time. It's not his fault.'

'We're his children for fuck sake.'

'And he can't fuckin' see! What do you expect from him?

'An apology. I wanted him to know that I was happy. That Yiskah had done a great job as a parent.'

'That would've just pissed him off.'

'Maybe that's what I wanted as well.'

'We both want so many things. Some of them different.'

'Our father had forgotten about us long before we left. They both had.' Iakovos looked his sister in the eye. 'Tracey is just as culpable as he is. They were partners in crime. Happy with the money they got just for having us under that roof.'

Lisa turned back and looked at her father.

Iakovos needed to confront her. 'Why are you so scared of him if you're fighting on his side?'

'My battle is not with him,' said Lisa. 'It's for me. I'm the one who got shafted. I'm the one who never got to choose.'

'Is that what this is all about. Choice.'

'Damn right it is. Yiskah decided our future for us. She was wrong to do that.'

'We were only nine and ten years old. What sort of decision-making skills did we have?'

'She was our teacher. She should have guided us toward a better reality instead of forcing us to accept hers.'

'See how the truth can be so different. She did guide us, away from this hellhole. Away from that fat bastard and his god damn useless wife.'

'Away from our families, our grandparents,' said Lisa. 'The life we knew.'

'Our grandparents were happy we escaped. Sure, they missed us but they'd already been removed from our lives. They weren't allowed to see us, or even talk to us.'

'And Yiskah only made that gap between us greater.'

'Look around yourself. Can't you see the despair and the loneliness that surrounded us? Don't you remember the dark shadows that followed us everywhere we went. Yiskah gave us hope. She gave us a second chance at life.'

'She gave us some good things. I'll give you that. It's what she took away from us that I can never forgive her for.'

'And you want her to go to jail for trying to do the right thing.'

'I want her to know I'm pissed off.'

'Oh, she already knows that, don't worry. You showed that hand back in Paros.'

'Fuck off!' yelled Gary. Lisa and Iakovos stared as he advanced along the pathway toward their car, too caught up in their own fight to realise he'd moved.

'He's seen us,' said Lisa. 'Thought you said he was blind?'

'He is. Probably thinks we're the coppers.'

Gary's fastest was still just a slow walk. 'Fuck off, you parasites.'

'And maybe not?' said Lisa.

'Quick let's get out of here.'

'Look who's scared now?'

'I'll give you a bloody nose, not a story,' screamed Gary. 'Now fuck off before I get my hands on you.'

'He thinks we're from the newspaper,' smiled Lisa.

'I'll piss on your car before I'll talk to you little fuckers.' He fumbled with his dressing gown, loosening the rope around his waist.

Iakovos was laughing too now. 'It brings back memories. I remember him calling us little fuckers.'

'He sure has a way with words.' Lisa turned the keys and the car burst to life.

Gary tripped upon the raised grass of the verge and tumbled across the soft ground. His face was all screwed up. Lisa thought he looked like a troll who'd just woken up from under his bridge. She put the pedal to the floor and screeched off, wheels spinning with black smoke. Gary raised his fist in the rear vision mirror.

'He sure is an ugly man,' she observed. 'Inside and out.'

'And you want to defend him.'

'I already told you. I'm not on his side.'

'The rest of the world thinks you are.'

'The rest of the world can go fuck themselves. All I care about is me.'

'You sound like Tracey.'

'Piss off.'

'That's how she used to talk.'

'Still does.'

'Living with her is rubbing off on you.'

'So, what if it is?'

Iakovos raised his hands. 'Just an observation.'

Lisa took a long drag on her cigarette before indicating and turning left onto the main road.

'Nice car,' said Iakovos. 'Must be costing you a bomb?'

'Not me. The Education Department. It's their way of keeping me mobile. Lots of meetings and media.'

'They're paying for it? That's a bit dodgy.'

'It's all a public relations exercise to them. My pain is their reward.'

'That sit okay with you?'

'I started this action. Now it's their campaign to finish it. Can't be seen to let the teachers of this world think they can up and run away with someone else's child. It's not very good for business.'

'Who cares about the Education Department. This is about Yiskah and us. It's our story not anyone else's.'

'It's bigger than that now. It's got a life of its own.'

'You've created a monster.'

'I think you're right. Our future is in his hands.'

'What future. The us we used to know is long gone.'

Lisa slowed down for a red traffic light.

Iakovos checked his watch. 'I'll get out here thanks.'

'It's okay, I've not got anywhere else to be. I can take you all the way to your hotel.'

'I'd rather catch the train. Be alone for a while.'

'Did I offend you?'

Iakovos opened the door and looked at his sister. 'You're trying to erase the past. I don't want that to happen. I don't agree with what you're doing.'

'You don't have to agree. It's not you I'm taking to court.'

'I know that.' Jacob climbed out and closed the door. He looked back at her through the wound down window. 'I still love you. I always will, but I can't stand by and watch you ruin our family.' The light changed to green. 'It's time to choose; a life with them, or a life with Yiskah and me. You can't have it both ways.'

The car horn from the vehicle directly behind them hurried them along.

Jacob stepped away from the car. Lisa watched him turn and go, tears welling up in both her eyes, sliding down her cheeks and off her chin. The car behind put in another complaint. Lisa gave him the finger before accelerating slowly away.

Iakovos watched her go. He'd wanted to make a stand for Yiskah, for Paros. He hoped he hadn't lost her.

66

TUESDAY 7TH OCTOBER
10:00AM
COURT 3-1, DAY TWO, THIRD WITNESS - CHILD X

Principle c) every child should be cared for and protected from harm.

A young woman sat composed and ready, the wooden railings of the dock set squarely around her. Her long hair was shiny and black, a collection of silver ear and nose piercings shimmering across her stark white face. She was emotionless and still, her posture projecting the qualities of an oil painting.

Kosta leant on the rim of the witness stand. 'Can you tell us how you felt when you heard the news that Lisa and Jacob Johnstone were returning to Australia.'

'It's tough to hear that someone got saved. It made me feel like I wasn't important enough to rescue. But it's given me a chance to speak out. I'm looking forward to telling the world my story.'

Kosta turned and addressed the court. 'Please let it be known that Child X's identity has been protected for legal reasons. She has volunteered to come here today to share her opinion on a delicate matter.'

Rosenthal looked restless.

Kosta turned his attention back to the witness. 'You were a pupil at Marvale Primary School about twenty four years ago. Is that correct?'

'Yes, I was.'

'Did your teachers ensure that Principle C was effected?'

'No, they did not.'

'What makes you so sure?'

'Because I had to suffer through a life with a shit family. No one at the school offered to help me at all.'

'What was happening in your life at that time?'

'I was being physically abused by both my parents.'

'The jury should know that this has been proven in a court of law and that Child X's parents are currently in prison for those crimes against her.'

The jury showed the pain that came with such heavy news.

'Were there any obvious signs which may have alluded to the problems in your life?' asked Kosta.

'There were always marks on my wrists. Bruises on my legs. I cried a lot. Was always in trouble.'

'Did any of the teachers ever ask you about it?'

'They did but I was a nightmare to talk to. And I was violent. They couldn't get through the wall I'd erected. It got to the stage where they just punished me as well.'

'How long did this go on for?'

'Ten years. No one at high school came to my aid either. I was fifteen when I finally ran away. I managed to live on the streets until my eighteenth birthday. I could decide my own future then without anyone's help. Without anyone's abuse.'

'Looking back do you feel like your right to be cared for and protected from harm was enforced?'

'No way.'

'Do you think Jessica Bell has enforced that principle in relation to Lisa and Jacob Johnstone?'

'Absolutely.' Child X smiled, her facing lighting up, her eyes locking with Jess's. 'I was cheering her on when I heard the news. I was in Year Seven when she arrived at my old school, so I remembered the name. She was too late to help me though. I was already pigeonholed as a troublemaker.'

'You are now thirty-two years old. How did it make you feel when you followed her story in the papers?'

'Elated. A bit jealous. Mostly happy that the two little kids she took weren't going to have to go through what I went through. I didn't know all the ins and outs but I was sure she was saving them from a world of pain. I was just like Lisa Johnstone. We could have been sisters.'

Iakovos looked away, his old life haunting his thoughts.

Child X continued with her story. 'I know there were a lot of questions hanging over the teacher's head, but as the days went on and the picture became clearer, it was obvious she was a good lady. She did what no one else was prepared to do. I wish I'd had her as a teacher. I really do.'

'And what is life like for you now?'

'It's okay. I'm in counselling. Done a couple of stints in jail for minor offences. It's not easy but I think I'm on the right path now. I've got some good people in my corner who are caring for me and protecting me from harm. Principle C is pretty bloody important. It may just be the secret to a happy life.'

'I think you're right,' said Kosta. 'I hope your life continues to get better.'

'Thank you.'

Rosenthal stepped from his desk and approached the witness.

'I'm sorry for your pain too. We are all very sorry. The community is sorry. The police are sorry. Your teachers are sorry. But there really was nothing more that could be done for you.'

'I was a lost cause? Is that what you're saying?'

'Yes, the law could not protect you but the people responsible are now behind bars so ultimately the system worked.'

'Better late than never, hey?'

'Couldn't have put it better myself.' Rosenthal leant forward on the railings. 'The powers that be got it right. The law is protecting you. The legal process we have for these types of situations works. Job done. Thank you.'

'You're just as messed up as them.'

'You may return to your seat,' said Rosenthal.

Child X stood and thrust her badly scarred forearms forward, in full view of the Prosecutor. 'Do I look like the result of something that works.'

The courtroom gasped. Rosenthal turned and walked quickly toward the safety of his chair.

Child X didn't move other than to pull up her t-shirt, revealing a litany of scars across her stomach. 'Are these the signs of success?'

Rosenthal slid uncomfortably into his chair.

'I am a product of the system that you defend,' said Child X.

Judge Iverson pounded her gavel upon the desk. 'Would the witness please step down.'

'Too much for you to handle, is it?'

'The Prosecution has finished with you as a witness.'

'The world finished with me a long time ago lady. You all need to wake up. Your bloody system sucks!'

Judge Iverson waved to one of the guards. He quickly approached the stand.

'Please, don't make the same mistake again,' said Child X, before she exited the box and accepted the escort from security. She walked past Rosenthal with her finger raised. He didn't know where to look.

67

11:00AM
FOURTH WITNESS - POLICE OFFICER HARRIS

Principal d) every child should live in an environment free from violence.

Police Officer Harris sat straight-backed and attentive. The dock was a place he knew well. It was part of his job.

Kosta stood behind his desk with a sheet of paper in his hand. 'How many times were you called to attend a disturbance at number twenty-three Dalton Crescent?'

'Twenty-eight times over the course of three years,' said Officer Harris.

'Is that a lot in your opinion?'

'Yes, it is. If you took a snapshot of the city and the number of calls we get, that would definitely be one of the highest averages.'

'I have that snapshot in my hand and would like to enter it as exhibit J.' The attendant approached Kosta and took the document from him. Kosta turned his attention back to the officer. 'And what action did you take each time?'

'Well the first call is usually just a knock at the door and a quick question and answer session to ascertain the scope of the problem. It's an information gathering exercise. Hopefully, given the weight that comes with our involvement, they can see the importance of solving the problem themselves.'

'And after that?'

'Well each new report or complaint increases the level of seriousness and other services might be alerted as to the situation if we think it necessary.'

'What kind of services?'

'Department of Child Protection, Social Services.'

'Was violence ever a factor in any of the incidents concerning the Johnstone family?'

'Yes.'

'How many times?'

'All of them.'

'All twenty-eight.'

'Yes. The report you have in front of you details the dates and times of each call.'

'Thank you. Please enter this as Exhibit K.' Again, the attendant accepted the document and passed it to the judge.

'And to what degree was violence a factor?' asked Kosta.

'From threatening behaviour to pushing and hitting. Most occasions included verbal abuse as well.'

'Who perpetrated these acts?'

'The father mostly, Gary Johnstone, but the mother sometimes.'

'Who was it directed at?'

'The children. They were unfortunately at the epicentre of every single display of anger.'

Iakovos shuffled uncomfortably in his chair, arms folded tightly across his chest.

'Sometimes it would spill over into the neighbours' yards if they tried to stop it. Then they would call us. But it always began with the children. They always bore the brunt and they were the ones I was there to protect.'

'Did you succeed?'

'No. Not in the long term. The short term was covered because we spoke to them, and issued a warning or a fine if necessary.'

'And long term?'

'The parents never paid the fines and always repeated the behaviour without fail. It was a very poisonous cycle of abuse and our powers weren't sufficient enough to stop it.'

'Do you think that every child should live in an environment free from violence?'

'Of course I do. It's one of the reasons I became a police officer.'

'But you couldn't stop it?'

'No. Not in this case. It used to keep me up at night.'

'What would you have recommended in trying to bring a satisfactory solution to this situation?'

'I can't recommend anything because there are no other legal steps for the police to take. We tried everything we had at our disposal but nothing would stick.'

'So, isn't it somewhat contradictory for the law to, on one hand insist that we free children from violence, yet neglect to provide you with the powers required to do so?'

'It's complicated.'

'I disagree. I think it is a very clear cut but no one wants to make the call.'

'Make what call?'

'The call to remove the parents from the equation,' said Kosta.

Officer Harris held Kosta's gaze, then looked away.

Kosta walked up to his witness. 'Do you believe these parents should have been removed?'

'As I said before I don't have those kinds of powers.'

'No, I know that, but do you believe it should have been done?'

Officer Harris shifted uncomfortably in his seat.

Judge Iverson leant toward the witness. 'Answer the question please.'

'Yes, I do,' said Officer Harris. 'But no one would listen to our pleas.'

'Did my client's actions remove the parents from the equation?'

'Yes, they did.'

'Did my client make sure that these children had the chance to live in an environment free from violence?'

'Yes.'

'So, you agree with my clients' actions?'

Officer Harris grabbed the rails in front of him. 'I know that what Jessica Bell did was illegal, but she solved a huge problem for me and my partner. I'm happy she did what she did. I wasn't at the time but now I know who she is, I look at her and I wish there were more people with her strength.'

Jess allowed a smile to spread across her face.

'I see case after case where simple intervention is the key,' said Officer Harris, 'And it's not taken because of the red tape that binds us. Sometimes you have got to step outside of what is written, because actions speak louder than words.' Officer Harris leant back in his chair, a lone tear falling down his right cheek.

An older woman in the gallery stood to applaud him. Others followed her lead, until the show of praise included almost the whole gallery.

'Thank you,' said Kosta. 'You are a good man.'

Officer Harris took a breath. 'Thanks.'

'I have finished with the witness Your Honour,' said Kosta.

Rosenthal stood slowly, keen to allow the standing ovation to fade. 'Feels good to receive some applause?'

'Yes, it does. We're usually greeted with a barrage of insults.'

'You ever assault your wife Officer Harris?'

'Sorry?'

'Is that why she left you?'

Officer Harris shuffled uncomfortably in his chair. 'What does my marriage have to do with this case?'

'Just answer the question please. Have you ever assaulted your wife?'

Officer Harris looked down at his feet. 'We argued.'

'And you hit her. Isn't that right?'

'Yes, but I didn't mean to.'

'So, you are simultaneously both law enforcer and law breaker?'

'I had a drinking problem. The pressures of my job got to me and I haven't coped well in the past.'

'And was violence an issue in your home as well?'

Officer Harris sighed audibly. 'It was.'

'So, aren't you a little bit like the kid in the greenhouse who shouldn't throw stones?'

'I'm trying to deal with it. It's not easy.'

'That's what they all say,' said Rosenthal. 'Do you have children?'

'Yes.'

'Should they be removed from your custody?'

'No, of course not.'

'Thank you, Officer Harris. I have finished with the witness, Your Honour.'

68

12:00PM
BLUE SKY CAFE

Prosecutor Rosenthal stepped powerfully through the entrance to the Blue Sky Café. Its location on the ground floor of the law District Court meant it was filled with lawyers and their clients. Rosenthal's suit was crisp and dark. He approached the food counter.

'Hello Mr. Rosenthal,' said the Asian woman behind the till. 'Your usual, sir?'

'Yes thanks.' Rosenthal spun on his heels and scanned the room. He spotted his target and hit his stride. This was Rosenthal's turf and everyone here knew him, for better or worse.

He stepped in beside Tracey and Lisa's table.

'You order for us?' asked Tracey.

'Rosenthal looked down at her. 'No. Are you hungry?'

'My cup's empty. Needs a refill.' Tracey pushed her coffee cup across the table. 'And I want one of them cream donut thingies.'

'I'll get it, Mum,' said Lisa.

'Ahh, you are a darlin.'

Lisa collected the empty cup. 'You two can get reacquainted.' She left the table.

'What are you doing here?' asked Rosenthal as soon as Lisa

was out of earshot. 'You're not called for at least a couple of days.'

'Just spending some quality time with my daughter.'

'Yeah, yeah.' He took a seat and looked over his shoulder at Lisa who was queuing at the counter. 'I only asked Lisa to come so we could talk tactics.'

'Lucky I came then.'

'You haven't told her, have you?' he asked turning his attention back to Tracey.

'No, of course not.'

'Good. She mustn't know. Not yet anyway.'

'Your secret is safe with me.'

'It's not me I'm trying to protect.'

Lisa returned with a donut and took up a seat beside her mum. 'So, how's the trial going?' she asked.

'Early days yet,' said Rosenthal. 'It's a walk in the park at the moment.'

'Glad you feel so confident,' said Lisa.

'You not so?'

'I don't really understand it all.'

'That's the beauty of it. You don't have to. Just leave it up to me. I'm not the government's number one prosecutor for nothing.'

'Show off,' said Tracey.

'Just consider yourself lucky you've got me.'

'I've got you babe,' sang Tracey, mimicking the Sonny and Cher track.

Rosenthal looked at Lisa. 'Why'd you bring her here?'

'Oi, I can still hear, ya know.'

'Oh, I'm sorry.' Rosenthal's sarcasm was something he couldn't hide.

'I thought Mum could help us.'

'Umm, yeah, well, check with me in future, all right?'

'Okay.' Lisa was on the back foot. 'Will you still need me to be a witness?' she asked.

'Maybe. Like I said it's pretty much an open and shut case. Your testimony would just be the icing on the cake.'

'Not so sure I want to anymore.'

'Why the fuck not?' said Tracey. The customers on the tables closest turned their heads to identify the source of such aggression.

'Mum! Quiet. I said you could come but just listen all right. He's my lawyer. Not yours.'

'Don't you get all bolshie with me.'

'Mum! We've been through this before.'

'Stupid bitch.' Tracey spoke loud enough for the tables around them to hear.

Lisa put a hand to her head and closed her eyes.

'Is this the kind of quality time you were referring to?' asked Rosenthal.

'Ha fuckin' ha,' said Tracey.

Lisa composed herself. 'It's just that I'd rather not have to point the finger at Miss Bell. Not if everybody else can do the job for me.'

'What a cop out.'

'Mum, you don't understand.'

'Course I fucking understand.'

'Sssshhhh !' said Rosenthal.

'Don't you sssshhhh me, you great big leech.'

'This is a public place. Let's not argue here,' said the Prosecutor.

'I'll do what I fuckin' well want. I'll tell her our secret.'

'No, you won't.' Rosenthal tried to stare her down.

'Yes, I will.'

'Tell me what?' asked Lisa.

'This is not the time nor the place,' said Rosenthal.

'Your father killed Jess's parents,' said Tracey.

'You're an absolute idiot,' said Rosenthal, the intensity of the moment forcing him to his feet. He always thought better on his feet.

'What the hell are you talking about?' said Lisa, her face screwed up in confusion.

'Tracey, stop right now,' said Rosenthal. 'Just walk away.'

But Tracey had a head full of steam. She loved the drama. 'Your father, he was the drunk driver who killed your old teacher's mum and dad. Thirty-two fuckin' years ago today as it so happens.

That's why the little bitch took you.'

'We don't know that for sure,' said Rosenthal.

'Just put two and two together. It's pretty bloody obvious.'

'Is this for real?' asked Lisa.

'It happened,' said Rosenthal, returning to his seat and leaning in close. 'But we have no proof that Jessica Bell knew about your dad's past. If anything, the evidence points the other way.'

'She never said anything to me about it,' said Lisa. 'Are you sure it's true?'

'Yes, I checked his criminal history. Miss Bell never used it against your parents before she took you and it's never been mentioned before as far as we can tell. Your dad covered his tracks pretty well. Taking your mother's name when they married was central to leaving it all behind him.'

'Of course,' said Lisa. 'And the lack of photos of him as a child.'

'He burned everything,' laughed Tracey. 'Tried to delete the past.'

'And it looks like Gary never made the link to Miss Bell either,' said Rosenthal.

'He's too bloody dumb to link anything together. Still has trouble tying shoelaces,' said Tracey.

'So how did you find out?' asked Lisa.

'Wasn't me,' said Tracey. 'Kept these secrets to himself didn't he.'

'I hired a private detective to delve into Miss Bell's background,' said Rosenthal. 'To uncover some dirt from her life. Thought it might have been useful. Funny how things go the other way sometimes.'

'I can't believe it,' said Lisa, tears in her eyes.

'You can't let anyone know,' said Rosenthal. 'Especially not Miss Bell.'

'Someone's got to tell her.'

'It's too sensitive. I'm not sure how it would affect your case. Could go either way.'

'Forget the courtroom,' said Lisa. 'This is about her mum and dad. She needs to know.'

'She already fuckin' knows,' said Tracey. 'Weren't you listening to me before.'

'I haven't stopped listening to your crap for weeks,' said Lisa.

'Look, after the case you can do what you want with it,' said Rosenthal, 'but for now it has to stay in a sealed box. Not a word gets out.'

Lisa leant forward on the table and broke down in tears. Tracey placed an arm around her daughter.

'You have to promise me,' said Rosenthal above the sobs.

'Would you just shut up,' said Tracey. 'She fuckin' promises all right?'

Rosenthal nodded and sighed, his own body language more a symbol of defeat than triumph.

Tracey cradled Lisa's head in her left arm and stroked her back. 'It's okay baby,' soothed Tracey. 'Mumma's here.'

69

4:00PM
KARRAKATTA CEMETERY

The afternoon rain landed heavily upon the large stones at the entrance to the Karrakatta Cemetery. Jess walked briskly, a prison guard on either side, her wrists cuffed in front of her.

The distance of time had changed many things in her life. The graveyard she'd visited many times, however, had stayed the same. The large Moreton Bay fig trees still loomed over the main intersections, paved avenues radiating out from this maze of circles. Fallen leaves were scattered throughout the beautifully manicured gardens like discarded tears. These miniature streets provided easy access for the silent and forlorn visitors who came to see cherished loved ones.

Jess's arrival hadn't been announced, but her instincts were on high alert. She hadn't been here for a decade and knew to expect both water works and fireworks. Jess used to come here often and the cathartic nature of those visits had been sorely missed.

She'd last showed her face here just days before leaving the country with Lisa and Jacob. It had been the twenty-second anniversary of their death and she knew then that she would be unable to return and needed to say one last goodbye. She hoped to close this chapter of her life once and for all. Had hoped to be returning under better terms than those of today, the shackles she wore around her wrists on this wet Tuesday afternoon a reminder that she wasn't yet free of anything. She'd been in command of her future when she last walked through these gates of remembrance. That control no longer existed.

They'd parked the prison issue van outside the cemetery after Jess's heartfelt pleas. She wanted to make as few waves as possible. Being transported here by a grey Ford Transit van with large white letters proclaiming 'Greenhough Women's Prison' across both sides was hardly an exercise in positive self-promotion. The dark blue prison uniform she wore was statement enough and reasoning that at least one tenth of the corpses in here had died at the hands of criminal activity, it was an easy bet to suggest that the people who came here did not want to see prisoners treading these well-worn paths as well. A licence plate would make it too easy for those pesky journalists to track. Jess wanted to get in, say a few words and get out. No media please. Not here.

Getting a pass-out had been a lot easier than she thought. Kosta was, of course, instrumental in pulling a few strings. He could see that Jess needed to come here and he made it happen.

The cemetery was like a ghost town. Rain pooled on the surface of the paved roads, Jess's prison-issue boots throwing off large sploshes with every tread.

'You do know where you're going right?' checked one of the guards.

'Just up ahead. Then left at the roundabout.'

'Good.'

They turned left down a narrow avenue. Jess tried to remember her first visit here. She had come alone. It could only be described as a traumatic experience. She was still a young girl and already losing her way. A big night meant she was still drunk when she'd arrived. The sun had yet to rise and the darkness was an added difficulty. She'd missed a pile of dirt and had almost tripped and fallen into an empty grave that was being prepared for another funeral. Could have been her own, the way she was going.

She finally found what she was looking for that day, through the same alcoholic haze that had accompanied most events of that summer. She'd sat down and said nothing for a whole hour, eventually falling asleep against one of her parent's head stones. She woke up just as the sun had whittled its way through the trees. A good hard prod from the gardener's rake roused her from slumber. He was worried she was a ghost.

'You alright?' he'd asked.

Jess opened her eyes and stared up at him, gathering her broken thoughts. Her dreams had not been happy ones and he had startled her. She jumped to her feet and bolted out as fast as she could. Her emotions were under lock and chain, making the territory of grief very difficult to handle. She'd realised then that she'd needed to change.

A decade on and she still managed to recognise the frangipani tree that marked the spot. Seeing it drew a breath from her. Such a gorgeous tree at any time of the year, it had been chosen to signify the beauty that also lay beneath the earth. Currently in full bloom, the abundant white and pink flowers brought colour to this bleakest of venues.

Jess stopped at the base of the tree and looked right. There were two headstones. Inscribed on the first was the name *Elizabeth Bell, loving and kind, a mother to all, taken too early, may she rest in peace.* And on the second; *Jim Bell, loving father of Jessica, strong and dependable, stolen away before his time, may he rest in peace.*

The words were Jess's own. Part of the grieving process they told her. It was nice now, knowing they were hers. That she hadn't given this job over to some funeral professional. Not that she'd wanted to say anything. Back then she had no words to describe her pain. Her trauma counsellor had pushed and pushed, until she gave in. She was happier now, realising those same people who drove her to the edge, also knew what they were doing.

Jess looked back at the officers, a few respectful steps behind her. 'Would you guys mind waiting back at the roundabout? It be nice to have some time alone.' The officers nodded and left her at the graveside. Jess wasn't dangerous. They knew that..

Jess eased her body toward the leaf-strewn ground and sat

cross-legged in front of her parents.

'Hi Mum, hi Dad,' she said softly. 'Sorry it's been such a long time since my last visit but as you probably know I've been out of town. I hope you approve of what I've done. You brought me into this world and I don't know what you've seen, so I wanted to make sure you knew all the facts.'

Jess leant forward with both hands and scrawled a question mark into the dirt with her index finger. 'It's a fine line,' she said, her finger continuing to trail through the dirt, 'between wrong and right. I wish you were still here with me. Could really do with your advice.' She finished scrawling an 'f', having worked in reverse to complete the word 'family?'

'You left me way too early. Had to do so much on my own and I still feel like it's just me against the world. Maybe all this wouldn't have happened if you were still alive. Probably would have talked me down, but what then? What happens to the kids? How would their lives have been saved?'

Jess rubbed out the question mark and added an exclamation mark to the end of the word. 'As you can probably tell, I'm very confused. My forty-eighth birthday's coming up in a few weeks and I'll either be celebrating my freedom or lamenting my incarceration.'

She wiped a tear from her right eye. 'I miss you a lot. Would have loved showing you around Paros. You always preferred the warmer weather. Lisa and Jacob would have called you Nona and Baba and I know you would have loved them too, just as you loved me.'

Jess collected some leaves together and placed them in a pile. 'The man that killed you is probably still alive. He was only a few years older than me when it happened. Just a young man. Five years wasn't enough for what he did.'

The breeze lifted the leaves, breaking the pile and spreading them across the ground.

'I'm still angry with that drunken idiot but mostly I just get on with the job at hand. Some days I think I'd like to track him down and question him about the past and see how he feels about the accident but it's all so complicated now. He probably wouldn't understand. I don't think he'd be as interested in closure as I am.'

A strong gust of wind blew across the cemetery.

'How crazy is it that he's a free man and I'm now the one facing jail. Who knows what my life would have been like had he not stripped it so violently away from me.'

Leaves swarmed around each other, flying to waist height, the gust driving them between the head stones of the dead.

'I should probably track down my psychologist once this is all over. I hated him when I was younger. I think I'm ready to talk now.'

Jess lifted both hands to her lips and blew her parents a silent kiss. 'Thanks for listening to me. I love you both so much. See you again soon.'

She got to her feet and ambled up the avenue toward the guards. An old song that she hadn't sung since she was a little girl came into her head. It was her dad's favourite. She hummed the tune until the lyrics began to fall from her lips.

Que sera sera, whatever will be will be, the future's not ours to see, que sera sera.

The rain continued to fall. The world continued to cry.

70

10:00AM
COURT 3-1, DAY THREE
FIFTH WITNESS - RUPERT SMALL

Principal e) every child should have stable, secure and safe relationships and living arrangements.

Prosecutor Rosenthal sat behind his desk, arms folded across his chest.

Kosta walked in front of him. 'As the Deputy Principal of Marvale Primary, what was your role in this whole saga?'

Rupert Small had aged quicker than most and the thinning grey hair that covered his head was testament to the burdens he had shouldered.

'I was in charge of student welfare,' he said from the confines of the witness box. He was overweight and sweaty. 'I was the contact point between the parents and the social services. Sometimes the police, too, if it was necessary.'

'Sounds like school is very different to how I remember it.'

'There were and still are a lot of troubled people out there. Difficult parents make problem children. It also creates a mountain of paperwork and I was the one who was expected to push it.' His voice was strained. Bringing up the past wasn't something he enjoyed doing. He'd learnt that it was better to forget.

'You sound aggrieved with that situation,' said Kosta.

'I am or I was. I don't work in the education system anymore.'

'Because of this event?'

'Yes. Most definitely. It was the start of the end for me. I lost heart in the system.'

'It wasn't working, was it?'

'No, it was broken. This principle for starters. It puts so much pressure on us as educators, yet it's almost impossible to achieve. I mean we all know that every child should have stable, secure and safe relationships and living arrangements. It's common sense, but to put that pressure onto someone other than the parents, to make an individual outside of the family unit responsible for something so clearly out of their jurisdiction, is grossly unfair.'

'Was Miss Bell able to provide a stable, secure and safe relationship and living arrangements?'

'She's the anomaly. She's proof that sometimes you have to step outside of the law to achieve what they demand of us.' He looked over at Jess. 'And now she's the one paying the price.'

'Was leaving with the children her only option?'

'Looking back, I believe it was. God knows we tried everything else.'

'Were you a supporter of Jess's actions at the time?'

'Hell no! I was one hundred percent against her. That was when I still believed in the system. I was blinded by all the paperwork and the data. I'd lost my humanity.'

'What brought you round to seeing her as a champion rather than a criminal?'

'The children. I met Jacob again just the other day. So mature and level-headed. Believe me, that is no mean feat. He was damaged goods but he's turned out beautifully.' Rupert found the face of Iakovos and smiled. Iakovos smiled back.

'Can you tell the court the lengths you went to, to help these children?' asked Kosta.

'Sure. We wrote many letters and coordinated a lot of meetings with the parents and the DCP. We communicated with the police and the court system in a bid to try and find a program or a punishment that would work, both for the parents and the children. You have to exhaust all avenues, even when you know you're pushing shit uphill.'

'And why did your efforts fail?'

'The parents just didn't give a damn. Pardon my language, but I can't put it any better. That's it, plain and simple. It's like trying to build a mountain out of ice cream on a hot day. The environment and the conditions are all wrong. Tracey and Gary Johnstone should never have become parents. Their whole attitude to life was never supposed to involve little people. It was always going to end in disaster.'

'But it hasn't. As we have seen, Lisa and Jacob are happy adults now. Why is that?'

'Because a very brave woman did a very brave thing. When I think about the two damaged little children she took under her wing, it really is a miracle the degree to which she has changed their lives. She shouldn't be on trial. Tracey and Gary Johnstone should be the ones under the microscope. They should be the ones facing jail.'

'Thank you, Mr Small.'

Rosenthal rose opposite the retired Deputy Principal. He was paused in thought, playing for both ideas and time. 'Mr. Small, is it true that you attempted to kill yourself when your school was audited after those terrible events of May twelfth, two thousand and five?

'Yes, that is true.'

'Gassing, wasn't it?'

'Yes. I hooked the exhaust to my car and said goodbye to the world.'

'What happened?'

'My children saved me. They wanted me to play so they came out to the garage looking for me. I'm always fixing things in there. I was in the car and already unconscious when they burst in. They opened the door to the car and dragged me out. Paul and Alice didn't know what was going on. They thought the car was on fire.

My wife knew and she called the ambulance.'

'The media got hold of what happened?'

'Sure did. They weren't very forgiving. It was front page the next day.'

'Do all teachers act in such a desperate way?'

'It's a tough gig. You should try it some time.'

'Or maybe we should screen our teachers for mental deficiency?'

'We should probably screen our lawyers too!'

'Is it true that the teaching profession has the highest divorce rate in Australia?' asked Rosenthal.

'I believe so.'

'Are you married?'

'I was.'

'Hah. The pattern continues. Do you think that teachers as a cross-section are under too much pressure?'

'Yes, most definitely.'

'Can this lead them to make bad decisions in life?'

'Yes, of course it can.'

'Decisions that can have disastrous effects on others?'

'Yes, all decisions come with consequences.'

'Did Miss Bell's decisions have disastrous consequences for others?'

'Yes, but ...'

'Thank you, Mr Small. Your Honour, I have finished with the witness.'

71

11:00AM
SIXTH WITNESS, JUNE CARTER (DCP)

Principal f) intervention action should be taken only in circumstances where there is no other reasonable way to safeguard and promote the child's wellbeing.

Kosta reclined against the rail that separated the jury from the rest of the court. He flicked through the same Oxford Dictionary that he'd started the case with.

'Intervention is defined in the Oxford Dictionary as an action which affects another's affairs. Is that how you see it in your work?' he asked.

The woman in the dock was dressed smartly in a grey business suit, a light brown bob dropping just above her shoulders. 'Yes, and because it affects the lives of others it should only be taken as a last resort.'

'Was this not a last resort for Jessica Bell in her role as a teacher?'

'She may have reached a point where she felt she had exhausted her options but she is not and never should be in a position to take such action,' said Mrs. Carter. 'Her job specifics did not stretch that far and she was not charged with the responsibilities that came attached to such a decision.'

'Yet she took that decision and she has returned a successful outcome. Shouldn't that be enough?'

'She broke the law. It's as simple as that.'

'Is it? Are we sometimes too quick to use the law to rule upon what common sense and truth can resolve with greater satisfaction?'

'You're a lawyer. You know how it works better than most. It's a system we use to make sure judgements are always balanced and fair.'

'Is that what we are doing today?'

'I think it's why I was brought here. To help the jury understand what happened that day.'

'So, in your work for the Department for Child Protection, how many interventions have you been privy to?'

'I think that might be classified information.' June looked to the judge for reassurance.

'You think so?' pushed Kosta. 'Surely it's just a number. I'm not after any names or specifics.'

Rosenthal stood quickly. 'Please don't badger the witness.'

'I haven't even begun to badger her,' said Kosta. He turned to the witness. 'You really think this is classified, Mrs Carter?'

'I'm not sure.'

'Well blurt it out and we'll see.'

Judge Iverson leant in toward the witness box. 'Please answer.'

'Five,' said the witness.

'Only five? Such a small number. You've been doing this for ten years and you must have dealt with hundreds of cases.'

'That is right but as the Principle F states, intervention should be taken only in circumstances where there is no other reasonable way to safeguard and promote the child's wellbeing. We would prefer to find other ways to affect a positive outcome.'

'But do you? I have some statistics here that don't share that outlook.'

'We deal in people not numbers.'

'But if the facts and figures don't stack up then you don't act. Isn't that true?'

'We have to be thorough. Intervening in someone else's life can have massive ramifications down the track.'

'I would argue that not intervening can have an even bigger affect. Child X is proof of that.'

'She was a glitch in the system.'

'A glitch? She's not a computer program.'

'I mean, we never expected such a terrible outcome for her.'

'That's not what the figures tell me.'

'Figures can lie!'

'Surely not. Your data collection is thorough and with only five interventions across hundreds of cases there must be more of her ilk. Isn't she just the tip of the iceberg.'

'Look we are not perfect. We do a tough job just like everyone else involved in the lives of children. We do what we think is right at the time.'

'Which is exactly what Jessica Bell did, and look where it got her.'

'We have to take responsibility for our actions.'

'Is that why you don't take action? So that you're not responsible?'

'We don't hide from the tough calls.'

'No, you just dawdle long enough for someone else to move first. They do your job for you whether they be murderous, suicidal or both.'

'Now you're being unfair,' said the witness.

'Am I? I don't see you in that seat over there, charged with rescuing the lives of two children under your jurisdiction. I see a teacher there instead. A woman who is being vilified for taking exactly the action you consistently shy away from. I see a woman being put through the wringer for something we all believe was right. She acted while you still hide behind the law. Why is it this way?'

'You tell me. I'm just here to answer your questions.'

'That is a question. So please answer it.'

Mrs. Carter gritted her teeth. 'The law protects us.'

'Exactly. It protects people like you who couldn't give a damn about the people at the coalface. You hide in your clean white offices while the teachers and the police and the nurses face up to the rolling injustices they see every day. The law doesn't protect the children you ignore and it's certainly not protecting my client. It never protected Lisa and Jacob. The only people enjoying the shelter it provides are those who we unanimously agree should be feeling its wrath. Namely Lisa and Gary Johnstone.'

Rosenthal stood to attention. 'The parents are not on trial here today.'

Kosta was angry. 'They should be!'

'Mr Kouros,' said the witness. 'This case was, and still is, a very complicated one. There were so many factors to take into consideration.'

'Your intervention could have simplified it. Instead indolence was all you could offer us. Thanks for your time. Leaving your office and coming here today must have been hard decision to make.'

'I beg your pardon.'

'You heard me.'

Kosta informed the judge that he had finished with the witness then returned to his desk.

72

1:00PM
SEVENTH WITNESS, JOHN JOHNSTONE

Principal g) if a child is removed from the child's family then, so far as is consistent with the child's best interests, the child should be given encouragement and support in maintaining contact with the child's parents, siblings and other relatives and with any other people who are significant in the child's life.

Kosta approached the jury. 'I have laid out principle after principle and I have outlined how Miss Bell met her responsibilities. Now I need to let you know where she failed.'

He held up a piece of paper and pointed to a sentence half way up. 'Principle G was the one guiding light that my client was unable to accommodate. There will be other more successful principles to follow this, but for now we need to stop and accept that her efforts in relation to trying to maintain contact with the children's parents and other relatives were unsuccessful.'

Kosta took a deep breath. 'The brother and sister relationship that the children shared took care of the reference to siblings, but whilst some of the family were informed as to the progress their offspring were making, they were never granted contact with Lisa and Jacob. It just wasn't possible to do that and keep their whereabouts secret.' Kosta turned to address the judge. 'And it is for this reason that I call John Johnstone to the stand.'

There was movement in the gallery as Iakovos got to his feet. Beside him an elderly man, full head of grey hair, a walking stick in his hand. He used it to lift himself to his feet. Iakovos took his other arm and guided him along the row of seats. They hugged in the aisle.

'Good luck Grandad,' whispered Iakovos.

Mr Johnstone smiled. He'd been waiting a long time to have his say. He shuffled up the aisle, relying on his cane for support. He stepped carefully up the steps of the dock and took a welcome rest on the chair provided.

'Thank you very much for making the effort to come here today Mr Johnstone,' said Kosta.

'Please call me John.'

'Can you please explain your relationship with this case?'

'I am Tracey Johnstone's father.' The murmured reaction from the gallery suggested his presence was a surprise. 'More importantly I am also the grandfather to Lisa and Jacob Johnstone. They are and always will be my grandkids.'

'When did you see them last?' asked Kosta.

'Jacob brought me here today. He's been staying with me. Lisa came to see me at home two weeks ago.'

'Nice having them back?'

'Most certainly is. They are both in great health and I love them dearly.'

'You must have missed them?'

'It was hard. But I do not hold any grudges against Miss Bell.'

Jess gained strength just from hearing his kind words.

John placed a hand on the rail in front of him. 'Miss Bell was forced into action by my daughter and that poor excuse for a man she used to call her husband.'

'Do you understand the expectations of Principle G, John?'

'I do.'

'And how do you feel about my client not being able to commit to these expectations?'

'Fine. This principle was made redundant way before she came along. My wife and I had been cut off from our grandchildren's lives some three years earlier. Tracey and Gary never followed principle G, so why should anyone else.'

'Why did they cut you out of the picture, John?'

'Because we wanted them to raise their children right and we thought they weren't doing a good job at the time, so we told them so.'

'And what was their reaction?'

'We'd planned a holiday to Bali with the kids, so they cancelled that straight away. It was all paid for and everything. Good break for them we thought. Take the kids away and allow the parents to clean themselves up. Parenting isn't always easy. We know that. But they didn't want our help anymore.'

'And then what happened?'

'They froze us out. We called but they wouldn't answer the phone. We drove around to the house, but they wouldn't even open the door. It was very painful. We could hear the kids crying inside the house, wanting to come see us, but they never let them out.'

'Couldn't you have visited them at the school?'

'Tried that as well. They told the school we weren't allowed to see them. Said we were trying to steal them.'

'And the school acted against you?' said Kosta.

'Yes. The Deputy Principal asked us not to come onto the school grounds. It was before he really knew the depth of the problem. I don't blame him. Tracey's a difficult woman to deal with at the best of times.' John collected his emotions. 'You know we used to have the kids over our house at least twice a week. Sometimes more when Tracey was having a rough week. They stayed overnight on a regular basis. Those children meant the world to us.'

'Did you try to defend yourselves against these lies?'

'We did but no one wanted to know. The gossip machine went into overdrive. The whole neighbourhood was against us.'

'It must have taken its toll?'

'Yes, it did. Our general health deteriorated and even our doctors were telling us to find a quick solution. The stress, the tears; they were killing us. We didn't know who to turn to so we just up and left. Sold the house and moved to the country.'

'Did anyone ever arrange for you to see the children before they left the country?'

'One person did.' John looked up at Jess. 'That wonderful lady over there. She gave us a chance to see them a few weeks before they left. She never told us what her plans were. Just called us out of the blue and said she needed some adult volunteers for a whole school excursion to the zoo.'

'Why do you think she did this?'

'Miss Bell knew the accusations against us were lies. She'd recruited us years before to help with the school reading program. She knew we were good people.'

'Did anyone ever find out about this secret meeting at the zoo?'

'No. It had been so long since we'd seen the children, that Lisa and Jacob had forgotten what we looked like. We wore hats and didn't ask any personal questions. We'd both aged about ten years as well thanks to the emotional trauma of the situation. They thought we were just a couple of helpers; someone else's grandparents. It made my wife so sad.' John swallowed hard, tried to recompose himself. 'But we got to spend the day with them. That kept us going for a few more years.'

'I bet you wanted to tell them who you really were.'

'Of course we did, but those kids had already been through hell and back. None of it was their fault and I didn't want them to suffer again. Not for me, not even for my wife, god bless her.'

'How did the children look when you saw them?'

'They were very skinny and they weren't quick to smile. Even at the cute animals. A lot of the zest and energy I'd known was gone.'

'How long were you with them for that day?'

'A few hours. Jess had assigned us to their group. And as anonymous as we were, it was still the greatest joy. To be with them again. It filled our hearts with love.'

'Your wife, Eileen, passed away a few years ago, didn't she?'

'Yes. The doctors couldn't find anything wrong with her. Said it might have been heartbreak. Not because of what Jess did, mind you. She gave us hope.' John looked up at the judge. 'A few weeks after that trip to the zoo and the kids were all over the news. We knew she'd be looking after them. We spent every night imagining them all together, smiling and laughing as they flew across the world. It probably sounds strange us thinking that way, but our daughter had really lost her way by then. She wasn't fit to be a mother anymore. The kids were better off without her.'

'Did your wife, Eileen, see your daughter before she died?'

'Once. She called us out of the blue, from the local hospital. We shouldn't have gone to see her. It was the final nail in my dear wife's coffin.'

'Why did she want to see you?'

John swallowed hard. 'She'd had another abortion.' There were tears in his eyes.

'Objection,' said Rosenthal.

'Overruled,' said the Judge. She too was absorbed by John's testimony.

'We found out she was pregnant from the DCP. They called us to see if we were interested in caring for the child if they took it from her at birth.' John stopped talking. His hands shook with emotion.

'Take it slowly, John,' said Kosta. 'There's no hurry.'

'Tracey found out we'd said yes. She hated us for wanting her baby, so she killed it.' Tears fell down his cheeks. 'That's why she called us. She'd just terminated it. Wanted to tell us in person.'

'This is hearsay,' said Rosenthal.

'I have all the necessary documentation,' said Kosta, holding up the hospital records.

'Sorry Mr Johnstone, keep going,' said Judge Iverson.

'It was a home-style abortion but the hospital couldn't prove it. She said she'd fallen. That part was true but both the doctors and Social Services were concerned she'd thrown herself down the front steps on purpose. She was just skirting around the law once again. We were absolutely shattered. Eileen never recovered. She died five months later. On the due date of her grandchild.'

'It's a tragic story. Some things just don't make sense.' Kosta handed John a tissue.

'Everything about my daughter's life was and is depressingly sad and tragic. We didn't raise her to be this way, but life is strange sometimes, and takes a few twisted turns along the way. The only thing good that ever happened to Tracey was Jess taking her children away.' He looked over at Jess. 'Thank you, Miss Bell. You gave us hope when there was none. Eileen always thought the world of you. And thanks for the postcards. They were like a treat from heaven.'

Tears began to roll down Jess's cheeks too. She mouthed the words 'Thank you'. She was too choked up to speak.

Kosta blinked his own tears away. 'Thanks John, that's all.'

'Prosecutor Rosenthal do you have any questions,' asked Judge Iverson. Rosenthal looked at Mr Johnstone with a rare show of sadness. His quiet reflection surprised Kosta.

'No questions, Your Honour.'

The attendant helped John from his chair and the courtroom was silent as this good man shuffled back down the aisle. Iakovos stood and guided him back to his seat. They sat down, Iakovos's right arm across his grandfather's shoulders.

73

2:00PM
EIGHTH WITNESS, ELIZABETH MALM

> *Principal ha) if a child is removed from the child's family then, so far as is consistent with the child's best interests, planning for the child's care should occur as soon as possible in order to ensure long-term stability for the child.*

'In your professional opinion, as the resident school psychologist at Marvale Primary, did Jessica Bell plan for the children's care in order to ensure long-term stability?' asked Kosta.

'Yes, I do believe she did,' said Elizabeth Malm, her features still as refined and delicate as they had been a decade earlier.

'Can you explain why you feel that way?'

'Well the preparation and research she would have put into the escape and staying hidden, it must have been so complete that she'd left no stone unturned.'

'And how did this ensure long-term stability?'

'She knew that during those first few days of upheaval and change, that any uncertainty and discomfort experienced by the children would be magnified and so she worked to minimise this undesirable outcome.'

'You sound in awe of her efforts, yet I must make it clear that you are still on the payroll of the Education Department, isn't that so?'

'Yes, I am, but I speak from a professional point of view only. My thoughts are not personal, rather they come from the background of a psychologist who values greatly the efforts made by people to limit the damage done to another human mindset.'

'And you believe that Jessica Bell executed her plan with great care and respect for the mindset of the children.'

'Most definitely. She knew exactly what she was doing. This wasn't some half-baked idea she was creating on the run.'

'How well do you know the accused?'

'Very well. We shared a lot in common when we worked together at Marvale Primary and due to the enormous lengths Jess went to, to ensure both the physical and mental health of her students, we would often meet, sometimes twice a week, to talk about various issues in her class.'

'Would you characterise her as impulsive or vindictive?'

'Neither. She was always thoughtful and thorough; an optimist, almost to a fault. She believed there was always a way to solve every problem, if you looked hard enough.'

'Did she get it right in this case?'

'Well she found a solution, didn't she?'

'One that some people have a hard time accepting.'

'Yes, that is true but it's hard to make everyone happy. Her plan worked. For the issue that presented itself and after having exhausted every other avenue, Jess found an answer and she executed it with precision and care. I know she crossed the line of the law, but let's not be petty about this. She has succeeded in protecting Lisa and Jacob Johnstone from two very destructive parents and in doing so has safeguarded their futures. Every day I see situations where a vicious cycle perpetuates itself, with generation after generation infecting those who follow. If we regard the children's lives as paramount, then we must regard Jess's action as a win. She broke the cycle and that can be very difficult to do.'

'But the parents lost their children.'

'They were given more chances than they deserved to lift their game and rise to the challenge of being even half decent parents. We're not looking for perfection by any means. But they couldn't even manage the responsibility of being adequate human beings. Their loss was our gain, as far as I'm concerned.'

'Thank you,' said Kosta.

Prosecutor Rosenthal thumped his fist on his desk. 'You work for the department Mrs Malm. How dare you go about commending those who break the department's rules.'

'I am a psychologist, not a lawmaker. I think, and therefore I do. These are my mottos. I am not under anyone's control.'

'You are an employee, Mrs Malm. That comes with expectations.'

'Yes, and so are you. They pay us for our expertise. Not because we are robots.'

'But we must toe the line!'

'Not if the line needs crossing.'

'Laws are not made to be broken!'

'No. They are a guide rail that sometimes needs a softer grasp.'

'Is that how you live your life?'

'Have you ever had a parking fine or a speeding ticket?' asked the psychologist.

Rosenthal was hesitant to respond. 'I don't have to answer any of your questions.'

'No, you don't. And I don't have to follow any of your rules.'

'Are you refusing to answer my questions?'

'No. Are you mine?'

'Your place in this courtroom is as a witness Mrs Malm. Please remember that.'

'I will, but you seem to have a problem with me telling you what I witnessed. The law does not change what I saw and how I see it. My employer cannot alter what I have witnessed. And you most certainly will not stop me from telling what I see to be the truth.'

The power of her words forced Rosenthal onto his heels. He tried to gather his thoughts, walking back to his desk.

'Have you finished with the witness Mr. Rosenthal?' asked Judge Iverson.

Rosenthal was lost in his own thoughts. He sat in his chair like a beaten man.

'Mr Rosenthal?'

A flicker of recognition from the prosecution. 'That is all, your Honour.'

74

3:00PM
NINTH WITNESS, EFFI BAGHDATIS

Principal h) decisions about a child should be made promptly having regard to the age, characteristics, circumstances and needs of the child.

The courtroom gallery was overflowing, a host of foreign journalists packed in at the rear.

Kosta approached the witness box where a young lady with dark hair and olive skin waited patiently. 'Hello Effi, how are you feeling today?'

'I am well, thank you.' Effi spoke calmly, her demeanour reflected in her choice of a yellow blouse. She glowed in contrast to the bland environment surrounding her.

'I hope you are enjoying your time in this country.'

'Yes. I have family here, some I have not seen for many years. It is a home away from home.'

Kosta addressed the jury. 'Now, before I continue with the witness, I would like to make something clear. Miss Baghdatis is from Paros and knows my client and her children by their Greek names of Yiskah, Zetta and Iakovos. For this reason, I will address all my questions using those names and not their

Australian versions.' Kosta approached the witness. 'When did you meet Yiskah and the children for the first time?'

'The first day of Term One. It was 2005. I was a school teacher in Parikia. I meet them face-to-face that first morning.'

'Your school year is scheduled differently to that of Australia?'

'That is true. We have summer holidays in July and August, so we start the school year in September.'

'Anything unusual about that first day?'

'No. The children were happy and friendly. They spoke some basic Greek. I learn later on that they had arrived on the island a few months previously and that Yiskah had been teaching them during the summer holidays. They picked it up easily. We get lots of foreign children coming through our doors, mostly English, and sometimes they struggle with our language. Zetta and Iakovos were different. Their motivation was strong.'

'Did Yiskah make decisions promptly, regarding the age, characteristics, circumstances and needs of the children?'

'Yes, she did. She was always there when I needed her. We met often to talk about their progress. Yiskah was very hands-on. She knew what she wanted.'

'And you never had any suspicions as to her arrival on the island?'

'I sometimes wondered where the father was. Yiskah is such a beautiful woman. It did not make any sense, but my job is to make sure the children can read and write. That is all.'

'It must be nice to have such simple goals.'

'Yes. Yiskah always made sure the children were healthy and happy. She made my job easy.'

'And how is their Greek now?'

'Very good. Iakovos and Zetta have excelled.'

'Thank you Effi. I hope you enjoy your stay in Perth.'

The prosecutor prowled in front of the dock. 'Have you ever had to step in and save a child?' he asked.

'No. On Paros our community is small but proud. We stick together and help each other. If there is a problem, it gets fixed early on by everyone.'

'What about Galen Khaneski?'

Effi was visibly shocked. 'My god, I haven't heard that name for a long time.'

'That's understandable. It was six years ago when he left your island for good.'

'Do you know where is he now?' asked Effi.

'Six feet under.'

Effi looked around the courtroom as the jury and gallery gasped. 'What does that mean? I do not understand.'

'He's dead,' said Rosenthal.

Effi leant back in her chair, her hands clasped at her face. 'Oh no!'

'Oh yes. A drug overdose, in Berlin.'

Effi rocked forward, her head in her hands.

'You were close?' said Rosenthal.

'Yes.' She was on the verge of tears. 'He was troubled. I wanted to help.'

'You contacted his parents?'

'I did. They were Romanian and didn't like mixing with the local Greek community. I tried to reach out to them.'

'Your involvement was not welcome?'

'No, it wasn't. They were embarrassed. They are a very proud family and word spread quickly about Galen's problems.'

'What happened next?'

'His family spun out of control. It happened so quickly. His parents broke up and Galen ran away from home.'

'But he was just twelve years old.'

'I know. Far too young to be alone.'

'Would you agree that your intervention broke his family up?'

'That was never my plan. He needed help so I did what I thought was right.'

'But it didn't stop there, did it? You also gave him a place to stay.'

'Yes, I took him in. I didn't know what else to do.'

'Did it help?'

'No. He was mean and abusive.'

'So, your attempts at fixing his problems weren't successful either.'

'No.'

'And he ended up fleeing the island?'

'Yes. I had to call the police. He was getting very aggressive towards me. I give him a choice and he ran.'

'There were rumours of a relationship between the two of you.'

Effi's eyes were raging and she leaned forward. 'They were lies. He was like a son to me. That is all.'

'Unfortunately mud sticks once it has been thrown.'

Effi raised her hands. 'I not understand you.'

'He died two years later,' said Rosenthal. 'Not what you would call a positive outcome.'

'I did all I could. It wasn't enough.'

'And it resulted in a broken marriage and a dead child.'

Effi began to sob, slowly at first, until her body was wracked with guilt. 'It killed me to see him in such pain,' she cried.

'It killed him full stop!' said Rosenthal. 'This is what happens when teachers intervene in other people's lives. Thank you for coming. I hope your stay in Perth is happier than Galen's trip to Berlin.'

Effi grabbed the railing and pulled herself up. She walked away from the dock, her head down her smile gone. Her pain was Kosta's pain, was Yiskah's pain, was Iakovos's pain. They had all known Galen. They had all lost a friend.

75

4:00PM
TENTH WITNESS, REVEREND STUART NIELSEN

Principal i) decisions about a child should be consistent with cultural, ethnic and religious values and traditions relevant to the child.

An elderly man wearing the black and white cloak of a priest placed his right hand upon a leather-bound Bible. He looked up and across at the jury. 'I swear by the Almighty God that I will give a true answer according to the questions being asked of me.'

'Please be seated, Reverend,' said Judge Iverson.

'Thank you.' He sat.

Kosta stood from behind his desk. 'Thank you, Reverend, for appearing here today. I know you must be busy.'

'It's the least I could do. Being here is all part of God's work.'

'Of course. Now, Reverend, I have invited you here today, to help us understand the cultural, ethnic and religious values prominent in the suburb of Marvale and particularly within the Johnstone family as a unit.'

'Yes.'

'Can you tell me if the Johnstone family were churchgoers?'

'They were. I've been at St Mary's Church in Marvale for thirty years now so I've seen the family come and go. Lisa and Jacob's grandparents, John and Eileen, were devoted Catholics. They never missed a Sunday service.'

'Are they still part of your parish?'

'No, they moved out to the Hills. A bit of a sea change I think. There were a few problems in the family. I didn't pry. They made the decision to leave Marvale. People come and go.'

'Did their children attend church?'

'When they were very young, yes; Tracey and her brother, Steve, came with their mum and dad but they were never happy. Frowns the size of airplanes. It pained John and Eileen but it's a common occurrence nowadays. The church is struggling to keep pace with those electronic gadgets we have for competition. Children find it hard to concentrate.'

'Did Gary and Tracey Johnstone ever bring their children to a service?'

'Three times in total. They didn't get married in my church but a few years later both children were baptised here. It was before the families broke up. Long before John and Eileen moved away. It is my understanding their visits were more to do with routine than a deeper commitment to the church.'

'Did you know that Jessica Bell was also a Catholic?'

'Really. That's great.'

'She also continued attending a Catholic church with Lisa and Jacob as soon as they arrived on Paros. Do you think this is consistent with the children's traditional religious values?'

'Of course, it would be,' smiled the Reverend. 'Is that true? Did she really take them to church?'

'Yes, she did. Could I present to the court Exhibit L, which is a letter from the Catholic priest of the Holy Trinity Church on the island of Paros. This document clearly states that my client and her children were regular attendees at church and were highly regarded members of the congregation.'

Reverend Nielson's grin lit up his face. 'That makes me very happy.' He acknowledged Jess with a few quiet claps. 'Just proves that God indeed does follows us everywhere and anywhere, if we choose to allow him into our lives.'

'Can you make comment on any cultural or ethnic values within the Johnstone family?'

'Well they were second generation Australians, of Irish heritage, hence the Catholic leanings. Gary on the other hand was Serbian, or his family were anyway. I remember his surname. It was… Raonic. I remember this because I was surprised that he had taken Tracey's surname when they got married. I'd never seen that before, the man taking the woman's name. The children were being baptised and I wanted to make sure it was legal, so I called head office and they confirmed it was okay.' The Reverend looked up at the judge. 'I think he had a past that he wanted to leave behind.'

'A criminal past?'

'I couldn't say for sure.'

'So, in your opinion,' said Kosta, 'did Jessica Bell make decisions about the children that were consistent with their cultural, ethnic and religious values and traditions relevant to them?'

'Without a doubt. She has gone above and beyond the call of duty. God is our judge and by what I have seen and heard, Jessica Bell has followed her heart and acted when and where she saw a need. I cannot condemn her for that and I will not force judgement upon her.'

'Thank you for your time,' said Kosta.

Rosenthal ran a set of rosary beads through his hands. 'This necklace of rosary beads used to belong to Lisa Johnstone,' said the prosecutor. 'It was given to her by her priest in Paros and she wanted me to return it to you.'

'I was not the one who gave it to her, so I cannot receive it back,' said the Reverend.

'She says she no longer has a use for it. She no longer believes in the power of prayer.'

'That's a shame. I am sure it has comforted her in the past. Provided her with a lot of love.'

'She feels that hate is a better word to describe the help she has received.'

'Objection,' said Kosta. 'Mr Rosenthal is pretending to speak on behalf of a young woman we have yet to hear evidence from.'

'Agreed,' said Judge Iverson. 'Please keep your opinions to yourself, Mr. Rosenthal.'

'Sorry.' He walked toward the waste paper basket beside his desk and symbolically dropped the beads into the bin. 'That is all. You may go.'

Kosta watched as the Reverend left the witness box. Rosenthal had taken to his seat, a look of contempt throwing his face into shadow. His cross examinations were shrinking by the hour and Kosta was worried. A man of such stature would not succumb so easily. Something was not right.

76

WEDNESDAY 8TH OCTOBER
7:30AM DAY THREE
23 DALTON CRESCENT

Knock, knock, knock. The rap of knuckles on glass resembled a short burst of machine gun fire.

Gary's eyes flicked open. He knew it couldn't be family or friends. 'Don't have any of those,' he thought to himself.

Knock, knock, knock! Faster and heavier this time. Gary struggled to lift his aching body off the couch. He wiggled his way into a seated position, his torso supported by his arms.

Knock, knock, knock, knock! An extra strike. The noise was starting to annoy Gary, his rising anger driving him up off the soft cushions of the faux leather couch and propelling him toward the door. His dressing gown flapped around his legs while he tried to secure the rope string around his waist. He caught a glimpse of himself in the hallway mirror and grimaced. He knew he looked like a living corpse but 'it's them on the other side of the door that have to look at me,' he grinned. It was a form of self-defense that he had created in his mind. 'I may be an arsehole and ugly to boot but I'm not the one who has to wrestle with yours truly. It's the rest of the world that has me in their sights. They want to hassle me, then they can deal with who I am.'

He'd decided long ago to be his own man, whatever the costs.

The blurred image on the other side of the see-through door revealed a large dark human shape. It was still and quiet. Patience was a virtue but Gary strode toward it with a growing impatience. He turned the handle and pulled the door toward him.

'What!' said Gary in his usual aggressive manner. He did it for impact. Hated what he saw on the other side of the threshold.

'Is your name Gary Johnstone?' asked the man from the top of the front porch. Another guy at the bottom of the steps watched on impassively, his arms crossed and legs astride. Both men wore grey suits and ties.

'What do you think?' said Gary.

The man grinned as he thrust an envelope at Gary's chest. The sudden jab of his arm surprised Gary just enough to make grabbing at it instinctual.

'I am a representative of the court. I present you, Gary Johnstone, with a summons to appear as a witness in the case of 'The Government versus Bell.'

Gary stared at the envelope in his hand before chucking it back at the man who gave it him. 'Fuck off. I ain't going to no court case.' The envelope rebounded off the man's chest and fell flat upon the floor at Gary's feet.

'Sorry sir, but I have presented you with it and you are now bound by law to appear.'

'I ain't bound by nobody. You can stick your envelope up your arse.' Gary was serious.

'I must warn you sir, that whilst I myself have no powers to use physical force upon you, these gentlemen do.' Both men stepped aside, their arms directing Gary's attention toward the police car parked in the road directly opposite the house. The officers waved up at Gary, chilling him to the bone.

He knew them well. Hated them with all his might. They were pigs before his ungrateful children pissed off but now they were like rats, hiding around every corner, nibbling at his feet, ready to pounce if he did something, anything wrong. When your natural instincts have an illegal leaning to it, it's like wearing a straitjacket twenty-four-seven. 'I can't even fart without worrying what's gonna happen,' thought Gary, an on cue he let one rip, the bad smell drifting across the steps. He was not in a tolerant mood. Been waiting for the shit to hit the proverbial fan and now that it had, he couldn't help himself, his right arm rising belligerently in a one-fingered salute targeted at the lawmen.

Click, click. The car doors opened so quickly it surprised even Gary. The officers were on his lawn in three seconds flat. Gary's defiance wavered momentarily but he didn't move and inch. He knew the rundown. Been through it enough times to be an expert in avoidance; the warning, the back down, the repeat and finally the exit, before he could triumphantly shut the door. He knew how to play this game. How to push just enough and then retreat before it was too late. Been doing it all his life.

The policemen advanced up the garden while the two suits retreated down the steps and away from the front door. They knew what was coming too. Could see it in this idiot's eyes. Gary thought he still had the situation under control but it was a different ball game today. The stakes were higher and he'd misjudged the moment. Underestimated their intent. Math was never a strong point and he had miscalculated this problem by a few hundred degrees.

The officers ascended the steps without the expected verbal warning. It was the first action that struck Gary as unusual. They usually talked to him from the lawn so as not to provoke his naturally aggressive nature. His eyes widened at this unexpected turn of events.

They took the steps two at a time, their very deliberate actions a mental attempt at making sure the brief they were given was carried out to perfection. They'd been given the word early that morning, halfway through their shift. Go in, use the slightest provocation and arrest the target. They were thankful that Gary had played his role to perfection. Giving them the bird was typical of someone with his limited vocabulary and whilst an increasingly common reaction from the locals in these parts of the city, it was still a legitimate reason to put someone in the slammer.

Gary felt his muscles tense up with growing disquiet. The fat encircling his physique prevented them from showing themselves but he still had enough strength to trouble them and his stubbornness was legendary. 'My words, my world,' he reassured himself.

'Gary Johnstone, you are under arrest for assaulting a police officer,' said Officer Barrett. 'Please place your arms behind your back and face the wall. I will need to cuff you for the trip to Marvale Police Station.'

Gary felt the sharp edges of the morning prodding him awake and he bristled with a restless fervour. 'What you going on about? The bird's not a form of assault? Here have another one, you fuckin' arseholes.' He tried to raise his finger again, but his arm was stopped before it got to its planned destination. Both policemen had stepped forward in unison and turned Gary around like he was a shop window mannequin. They used full force. No time for the nice-guy routine. This also struck Gary as highly unusual but he wasn't capable of changing his spots.

The cuffs were on him before he really knew what was happening. He tried to flail his arms around but he was powerless. He threw his shoulders to one side, hard against the glass of the open door. Smash! One of the panels cracked and shattered, large shards of glass falling to the ground. Blood splattered upon the debris, a flash of red atop the torn arm of Gary's dressing gown. The policemen ignored the injury, one of them collecting his legs in a waist high lift, the other throwing his arm around the shoulders and neck. The grasp they had on him, restricted Gary to such a degree, that sharp pains shot across his back and up his shoulders. His own body weight was being used as an anchor against his spine and he almost lost consciousness.

The court reps watched in awe. They'd never seen this before and happily stood aside as the real enforcers carried their bloodied target down the steps and up the pathway toward the patrol car.

Gary continued to struggle for all he was worth as they forced him onto the back seat of the vehicle. A few grunts and a bashed head later and he was in. The rear door was slammed shut. The suits and the uniforms said their goodbyes before the police car disappeared around the corner. One of the suits looked back at the house and realised that the front door had been left open.

'Back in a sec, Harry.'

He jogged up the pathway, leapt up the steps to the door, leant forward and grabbed the handle. The morning sun directed his gaze up a hallway that was better off sealed in utter darkness. The floor was covered in clothes, plates, newspapers and piles of rubbish. This man was as messy as they come. This house was as unloved as the children who used to live here.

He thought for a moment about the case he had been following with interest and how today he had played his own small part in it. He had now met one of the main characters in the story and he wondered what the others were like. Surely the teacher wasn't as low life as this dude. He crossed his fingers and hoped for the right outcome. Prayed that good would prevail. He'd only been working at the courts for a year and already he'd seen more bad guys go free than was palatable.

He twisted the catch behind the lock and pulled the door toward him. The click of the deadlock was the last sound he heard before leaping down the steps in one jump and leaving the house to its own devices; alone and quiet; a moment of peace, after a history of shame and violence.

77

10:00AM
COURT 3-1

Prosecutor Rosenthal rose to his feet. "We've heard from all the extras. Now let's get to the main characters. The ones whose opinions really matter.'

Kosta watched his adversary. He'd been concerned about this part of the trial. Knew that it could all hinge on these last few days.

Rosenthal stepped from behind his desk. 'The people who were really affected by the accused actions have stayed respectfully quiet. Today is their turn to speak. Their side of the story is what we came to hear. Their truth is real. Their lives have been painful.'

The courtroom became silent with expectation.

'Ladies and gentlemen, I call Tracey Johnstone to the stand.'

The jury's eyes darted toward the gallery, wildly searching for signs of the tortured woman they'd heard so much about. Seconds ticked by and no one rose to their feet. The court attendant walked over and whispered something to the judge. The judge whispered a reply before the attendant strode down the aisle toward the secure entrance. The female guard beside the door took fresh orders, a hushed conversation between them before she opened the doors and exited.

The foyer outside courtroom 3.1 was quiet and bare. The orderly looked left, down past several other doors and cushioned chairs but no one lingered. She looked right past the doors to the emergency stairs and a corridor which led to the toilets. A trail of smoke drifted past the sign for the restrooms, below it a glimpse of an elbow around the corner of the passageway. The orderly smiled and headed in that direction.

She stepped around the corner and addressed the person attached to the arm. 'Mrs Johnstone?'

Tracey looked older and sadder than she had done at the casino. Her hair resembled a bird's nest and her clothes were wrinkled and loose. 'Yeah,' she shot back. 'What about it?'

'You're being called as a witness.'

'Yeah, yeah. I know that. Why the fuck do you think I'm here?' Tracey lifted the fag end in front of her face. 'Just finishing me fag.'

'You're not allowed to smoke in this building Mrs Johnstone.'

'I know that too. Like I said, I'm almost finished.'

'I'll let the judge know you won't be long.'

'You do that.'

The orderly turned quick smart on her heels and made haste toward courtroom 3.1.

Sunlight poured down on the people strolling down Hay Street. Small groups of lunchtime workers lurched back toward their uninspiring office spaces, the second half of the working day still ahead of them. They were full of smiles though, a skip in their steps, a quick liquid lunch making everything look a little bit rosier.

The steep steps of the District Court were also bathed in the midday light as a police car pulled up beside the curb. Two policemen exited the front doors on either side and regrouped on the footpath beside the rear door. They chatted briefly before opening the door and leaning in.

Gary was encouraged to come out by the strong arm of the law. The harsh light of day wasn't his best friend but he looked a different man from the person who'd been hauled down the garden path earlier that morning. Someone had obviously spent time on his appearance. He was clean and well presented in a pair of black pants, a black belt, white long sleeve shirt and black shoes. A cleanly shaven chin revealed more than his fair share of wrinkles but his hair was washed and still wet, slicked back off his forehead. He looked ten times better. The blotchy skin and poor posture though couldn't be hidden, evidence of the real man simmering beneath the new threads.

He was free of the cuffs, a quiet swagger returning as he meandered up the steps toward the court entrance. He was a willing participant now, the day's festivities upon him.

The briefing he had been subjected to in the local police station was very one-sided. The Education Department's representatives were clear and uncompromising. They'd harassed him, whittling away at decades of stubbornness. He was compliant on the surface, but the rumble of resentment stirred deep within, a fundamental fact they would never eliminate.

The officers guided him through the metal detector. Court security watched him with care. They saw all different types come through their space. Gary Johnstone was like a caricature of the small-time thief and the energy he exuded was a reaction to the nerves of court. He hated being harassed by the media but the thrill of having an audience bubbled and built, brick by brick, inside of him. He was going to have his moment in the sun today and just the thought of it made him crazy with excitement.

Gary waved goodbye to the staring eyes of the foyer as the doors of the elevators closed, trapping him in the mirrored box with his police escort. Gary caught sight of his reflection and wondered who that man was. His over stimulated brain failed to make a connection at first, instinct informing him he must have miscounted, that there were actually four people in here. He'd grown accustomed to avoiding his own image, age having sucked his youth away. It wasn't until he scratched an itch on his freshly shaven chin that he finally made sense of it all. The man in the mirror did whatever he did.

'Shit,' he said out loud.

'What is it?' shot the officer to his left, suddenly on alert.

'Is that me?' pointed Gary.

A laugh from the other two in the mirror. 'Yeah mate. That's your ugly mug.'

Gary turned side on and sucked his stomach in. He adopted the stance of a boxer, his fists closed, arms poised to strike. He looked back at the mirror like he was in a photo shoot, striking pose after pose.

'Calm down Rocky,' said Officer Barrett. 'This ain't Friday night boxing.'

'I've got the eye of the tiger, haven't I,' said Gary.

'Knock 'em out mate,' said Officer Thompson.

The elevator slowed, an automated voice announcing their arrival at level three. The doors sprung open just as Gary let rip with a flurry of air jabs. A light shove from one of the coppers forced him from his raging bull state, creating enough momentum for them to bundle him out into the foyer.

They knew where they were going, turning left and walking toward the signs for courtroom three-one. Gary followed like an obedient dog. He'd spent his fair share of time in courts but they were never like this. This was for the big cases. He was big time now. These were the events you read about in the papers. It reminded Gary that he was known to people he had never even met.

It had irked him when the media first came calling. The spotlight drove him mad. He had nothing to say and a hell of a lot to hide. Today was different though. His fame was a positive and he had plenty he wanted to gloat about. The coppers had made him see the light and he'd accepted his grasp on celebrity with glee. Today was a day for notoriety and fame. This was his chance to shine. To tell the truth and be revealed for the great man he really was.

Gary's swagger slipped when he spotted his ex-wife off to one side of the landing. She was huddled down the narrow corridor to the toilets. The last remnants of a fag dangling from her mouth, smoke being sucked into the ventilation shaft above.

Gary stepped in between the cover of his uniformed escorts, hoping to avoid the aggression and embarrassment she always dished out.

'You still look like shit,' hollered a voice and he felt the day close in around him. 'Fancy clothes can't hide a loser like you!

He sighed and closed his eyes momentarily, conjuring up just enough hate to be effective. He stopped walking and emerged from his hiding place. He looked straight at Tracey. 'Can't say the same for you. Never could dress yourself properly.'

'Got your mates with you?'

'Yeah. I'm in bed with the law now. Lookin' after me real well. Better than you ever did.'

'Limp-dicked little bastard,' she shouted. 'You couldn't fuck a cat. You'll just disappoint them, like you've disappointed everybody else in your life.'

Gary squirmed, his new outfit was giving him the itch. He advanced toward her. 'You get personal in there and I won't stop 'til I bring you down.'

'Oooh, I'm so scared. Why the fuck did George think you were ever tough enough to collect his drug debts. Your about as frightening as a perfumed poodle and nowhere near as cute.'

'I'll be listening to every word,' said Gary, his clenched fist poised just underneath his chin.

'Good. I hope my honesty makes you scratch like a flea-ridden rat.'

'I fucking hate you.' Gary took a step closer but the officers grabbed his arms and held him back.

'Makes two of us. I hate me as well.' It was a rare moment of insight. Gary laughed.

'Mrs Johnstone?' The court attendant had stepped out from the doors of court 3.1. 'The court can't wait forever.'

'Yeah, yeah, almost fuckin' finished.' She walked towards Gary. 'Here,' she said, handing him the roach of her cigarette. 'You sucked the life out of me. Now do the same to this fag.'

Gary took it from her and sucked it dry in one go. He blew a haze of smoke Tracey's way but her back was already turned and a few seconds later she'd all but disappeared inside the courtroom doors.

'Bitch.' Gary flicked the roach to the ground.

78

10:30AM
ELEVENTH WITNESS, TRACEY JOHNSTONE

Principal j) a child's parents and any other people who are significant in the child's life should be given an opportunity and assistance to participate in decision-making processes under this Act that are likely to have a significant impact on the child's life.

Tracey Johnstone stepped into the dock. She faced the court, a sea of heads staring at her. She thought she could feel their thoughts. Carried their gaze like a barbed wire crown. The bright lights were focused her way. Darkness used to be her friend but even he was on thin ice.

The court attendant passed her a copy of the Bible. There was a slip of paper on top of it. Tracey leant in and peered at the piece of paper. 'I swear by the Almighty God that I will give a true account according to the evidence upon the issues being tried here.'

'Thank you,' said Judge Iverson. 'You may be seated.'

Tracey lowered herself into the chair.

Prosecutor Rosenthal approached the stand. 'Thank you, Mrs Johnstone for coming here today. It must be very hard to have to relive the emotions of the past ten years?'

'Is what it is.'

'Are you well?'

'I'm okay. I suffer from a lot of emotional and physical pain but I'll get through. Always have, always will.'

'You sound like a strong woman?'

'Had to be after what happened, didn't I. Otherwise I might have killed meself.'

'We've heard testimony as to what happened the day the accused took your children. They all range from teachers, to academics, to church leaders, but surely no one else really knows how it feels to have their children snatched away. Surely it is only the mother who can really understand the pain.' Rosenthal placed a hand on the rail of the witness box. 'In your own words, can you please tell us what happened on that black day in 2005.'

'My life ended. Fell apart piece by piece, until there was nothing left. The kids were everything to me.'

'Did you know that the accused had taken them?'

'Not straight away. The police took a couple of days to name her as their number one suspect and that's when it all started to make sense. I always worried about her relationship with my kids. She was very close to them. A teacher shouldn't be so touchy feely.'

'Objection,' said Kosta, jumping to his feet. 'That is an allegation which is clearly unwarranted and baseless.'

'Mrs Johnstone is only expressing her feelings your Honour,' said Rosenthal.

'Let's just keep within the facts, shall we,' said the Judge.

'Of course,' said the prosecutor. He returned his attention to the witness. 'Having taken your children, Miss Bell went into hiding for ten years. What did you feel when news first reached you that your children were on their way back to Australia?'

'I was elated at first and then my heart broke again. I had to live through it once already and here it was, happening all over again. I'm too old for this sort of rubbish. The damage has been done. That woman over there needs to pay for what she did.' Tracey pointed angrily at Jess.

'Have you had time to catch up with your children? To rekindle what you missed?' asked Rosenthal.

'Yes, I have. Lisa's been living at my place. Has been for a few weeks. We're trying to bridge the gap left by the last decade. Trying to get back to where we left off. It's bloody hard.'

'And your son?'

Iakovos watched on from the back row of the gallery.

'No contact so far,' lamented Tracey. 'He won't see me. Jess made sure of that.'

'Would you like to meet with him?'

'Of course, I would. It kills me that I can't hold him.'

'He's here today. Is there anything you'd like to say to him?'

Tracey searched for her son. Iakovos looked away.

'I love you Jacob. Please come home.'

Rosenthal smiled. 'Thank you, Mrs Johnstone.'

Kosta waited down the far end of the juror's box. It was his turn. 'Could you please rate yourself out of ten as a mother?'

Tracey's nostrils flared, her dislike for this man was palpable. 'Is this a quiz? No one said it was gonna be fuckin' quiz night. Would've worn my Sunday best.'

'No, it is not a quiz, but I will be asking some questions and I would like you to answer, where you can.'

'Sounds like a quiz.'

'What sort of mother are you?'

'Ask the bloody kids. They seem to know everything.' The creases on Rosenthal's face deepened.

'I'm asking you Mrs Johnstone.'

'Call me Tracey for fuck's sake.'

'Please watch your language Mrs Johnstone,' said Judge Iverson.

'Sorry, your Honour.'

'Tracey, what do you think of your skills as a mother?' asked Kosta for a third time.

'Not sure. Haven't been one for ten years. She nicked my kids. Can't be a mother without children can you.'

'What about before they left?'

'That's a decade ago. I can't remember back that far. Lucky if I can remember where I live.'

'And where would that be?'

'Erm … Forty-six … Tafferty Court in Orange Grove. Real nice spot.'

'How long have you been there?'

'Best guess would be about six years. And it's a bloody rough guess.'

'I have documents here that show you moved in seven years ago.' Kosta passed the documents to the attendant.

'Ha! See, told ya I was shit with history.'

'Why did you leave the home you shared with your husband?'

'Because he's a little fucker.'

Judge Iverson leaned in toward the witness box. 'Mrs Johnstone please keep the bad language to a minimum or I will have to close this court.'

'I heard you the first time,' said Tracey.

'But your language hasn't changed.'

'Did too. It's a description ain't it. He's a little fucker. The truth is what you want right?'

'Yes, we do, but without the swear words thank you.'

'Can't talk about that little bastard without swearing. It's who he is.'

'Well please try.'

'Alright.' Tracey clenched her teeth.

'You left the marital home,' said Kosta. 'What made you do that?'

'Marital? What the fu…heck's that?'

'The marriage home,' said Kosta.

'I just got tired of the same old shit. He's always been a bit of an arsehole, but I was stuck with him I guess. Then one day I saw this advert on the telly for Orange Grove and it looked nice, so I researched it on the quiet and booked myself a spot.'

'It's for over fifty-fives, is that correct?'

'Yeah. I lied about my age. They were desperate for people. Didn't ask any questions. Not like you.'

'So now, when you look back on your life, what do you see?'

'A massive train wreck. Those kids leaving like they did forced me off the tracks and nearly killed me. I know I wasn't the best parent in the world. We can always be better, but losing your own flesh and blood is hard. I reckon I aged ten years in one day. Probably the reason I was able to sneak into the retirement home.' She looked over at Jess. 'Thanks for that, Bitch!'

'Mrs Johnstone,' said the Judge. 'One more outburst and you will be sent from my court. I cannot and will not allow such language to be thrust upon this jury. Do you understand me.'

'Yes, your Honour,' said Tracey.

Kosta waited for the court to settle. 'And what about the children?' he asked. 'How do you feel towards them?'

'May as well be dead.'

'But you said your daughter was living with you these past few weeks?'

'Yeah, that's right.'

'Well how healthy can your relationship be if you wish she was dead?'

'I never said I wished it. Just that after all that's happened, they might as well be buried in the ground. They don't know how to treat me right.'

'Is Lisa still staying with you?'

'Who you been talking to?'

'Lisa Johnstone called me,' said Kosta. 'She said there was a problem.'

'She pissed off didn't she. Just left in the middle of the night.'

'I'm sorry to hear that.'

'Sure, you are.'

'May I ask what happened?'

'Objection.' Rosenthal looked worried. 'What bearing does this have on the case?'

'I'm not sure yet. That is why I'm asking the question,' said Kosta.

'I'll allow it,' replied Iverson.

'So, what happened?' asked Kosta.

'She ran out of money.'

'That's it.'

'Yeah.'

'Surely you didn't kick her out?'

'Nah. Just woke up the next morning and she was gone. Snuck out like she did ten years ago.'

'This time she acted alone, though, didn't she?'

'That teacher woman is still controlling her.' Tracey glared at Jess.

'From a jail cell?' asked Kosta. 'With limited access to any forms of communication?'

'She's brainwashed her. Ten years of torture.'

'Lisa told me you gambled all her money away.'

'Hearsay,' yelled Rosenthal, jumping to his feet.

'Agreed,' said the Judge. 'Please Mr Kouros, stick to what you can prove. Nothing more.'

Tracey tapped her fingers on the side rail. She was agitated. Rosenthal picked up on her body language and crossed his fingers.

'Where is Lisa now?' asked Kosta.

'Who knows. Who bloody cares.'

Rosenthal gritted his teeth.

Kosta stepped toward the witness box. 'This is your long-lost daughter we're talking about. How have things gone so bad so quickly?'

'Just wasn't meant to be, was it? Too much pain to get over.'

'Was there a fight between you?'

'Objection,' said Rosenthal. 'This is a private matter between two people. Their disagreement has no bearing on the case against Miss Bell.'

'Sustained. Mr. Kouros, you must refrain from this open line of questioning.'

'Do you still love your daughter Mrs Johnstone?' asked Kosta.

Tracey smiled at Rosenthal who was staring intently at her. Tracey swung her gaze back to Kosta.

'Yes, I do!'

'Does she still love you?'

'Too bloody right she does. I'm her freakin' mum. You only get one of those.'

Rosenthal breathed a sigh of relief.
One down, one to go.

79

11:30AM
TWELTH WITNESS, GARY JOHNSTONE

The court security guard gave a nod. The police ushered Gary into the security chamber.

'Stop pushin' me would ya?' said Gary. 'I'm walkin' by myself!'

Beads of sweat were building on Gary's neck. The door into courtroom three dash one beeped. The guard pushed the silver handle.

The courtroom was hushed as Gary made his entrance. He looked straight ahead and swaggered up the aisle, making his way toward the witness stand. He ignored the stares, allowing the buzz of the chamber to wash over him. Everything was happening in slow motion, like he was in a movie. Gary felt like a star.

Jess watched him with interest. She hadn't seen Mr Johnstone for a decade or more. Thought about the angry father she'd encountered so many years ago. Time had not been kind to him. The tick tock of the clock had aged them both.

Gary sensed her curiosity as he climbed the steps into the witness stand. He took it slowly, milking the moment, heart beating out of his chest.

He stood proudly, met the enemy's gaze and glared back with interest. He wanted Miss Bell to die in jail. She'd won so many of their little battles but today the power was his. Today was the big one and he was prepared to do and say whatever was necessary to bring her down.

The court attendant slid the Bible toward Gary. He lifted his right hand and placed it on the leather-bound cover. 'I swear on the Bible that I will give a true answer according to the evidence and in relation to the questions being asked of me.'

Religion wasn't Gary's strong point but he'd been advised to take a straight run at proceedings. He'd have sworn his allegiance to Hitler if they'd wanted him to.

Gary pushed the Bible toward the attendant and took a seat.

Rosenthal stood. 'Good morning, Mr Johnstone.'

'Good morning, Mr Rosensplatz.'

'It's Rosenthal.'

'Oops. My bad.'

'It's understandable given the situation. Are you nervous.'

'Nah, I just forgot your fancy name is all.'

Rosenthal looked down at his notes. 'Mr Johnstone, you have been brought here today to tell us exactly how the accused, Miss Bell, ruined your life.'

'Yes. And about bloody time. It's only taken ten years.'

'Ten years of hell, I'd imagine. Can you take us back to the day it happened? Tell us how it felt?'

'It was horrible. I didn't have a clue what was going on from one day to the next. I'd wake up each day with tears streaming down my face. I was a wreck.'

'Who looked after you during those first few weeks?'

'Everyone. Had more help then, than I'd had my whole life.' Gary faced the jury. 'They all came running didn't they. Felt guilty. The school tried to provide us with counselling, the police checked up on us regularly and our neighbours brought around frozen dinners. It was awesome.'

'Yes, but it must have been a struggle to stay positive?'

'They fed me but they couldn't heal me. My heart was broken. Couldn't even get out of bed.'

'Was there a low point?'

'Too many to count. Thought about topping myself. Couldn't see the point in living. Not without my kids. They were everything to me.'

'Have you seen them?'

'Once or twice.' Gary wiped away a tear. 'A broken heart takes time to fix. We'll get there. I love them.' He started to whimper, held his head in his hands.

'I'm sorry you have to go through this again.'

Gary lifted his head. 'It's alright. It needs to be done.'

'You survived the injustices that were forced upon you and now justice is finally taking its proper course. It must be very satisfying?'

'Bloody oath it is! Miss Bell stole my life away from me. I was damaged goods. I hope she gets life for what she's done.'

'Is the woman that ruined your life here today?'

'Yes, she is.'

'Can you please point her out?'

Gary lifted his right arm and pointed at Jess. 'It's that bitch over there. She's the one who nicked my kids.'

'Has she ever spoken to you about what she did.'

'Nah, nothin'. She never cared about me or my children. This was always about her. She took my kids because she didn't have her own.'

'Is there anything you'd like to say to her?'

'Nah. Actions speak louder than words. I've leaked blood, sweat and tears over what she did to me. I've got nothin' left to give. Nothin' more for her to take.'

'I'm sorry for your pain. Thank you for coming today.'

Gary gave him the thumbs up as he got to his feet. He looked at the judge. 'That it?'

'No, Mr Johnstone, the Defence will now cross examine you.'

'He ain't touching me!' said Gary.

'He won't need to. He just has some questions for you.'

'Oh.' Gary sat down.

Kosta stood behind his desk and looked across at the witness. They'd never met before but the dislike was already mutual. 'Mr Johnstone, were you working when the children left your care?'

'Objection,' said Rosenthal. 'That has nothing to do with this case.'

'I am trying to get an idea of what Lisa and Jacob's home life was like,' said Kosta. 'What they left is just as important as why they left.'

'Allowed,' said the judge. 'Please answer the question Mr Johnstone.'

'Well I forgot the fuckin' question, didn't I.'

'Language please,' said the Judge.

'What is the question?' Gary was feeling bullish.

Kosta stepped around his desk. 'Mr Johnstone, were you working when the children left your care?'

'I was in between jobs.'

'So, you weren't working?'

'No.'

'What were you and your family living on then?'

'The government. You know the dole. Tracey organised all that.'

'How much were you receiving?'

Gary shrugged his shoulders. 'Enough to get by. Wasn't a lot.'

'I have documents here your Honour that show Mr and Mrs Johnstone were receiving $823 a fortnight in family payments from Centrelink.'

'And why is this important?' Rosenthal had stayed on his feet.

'Because the payments on these sheets continued for up to three years after the children went missing,' said Kosta.

'Objection,' said Rosenthal. 'My client is being asked to declare his financial records. This case is about two children. It has nothing to do with money.'

'We deserved that money,' said Gary. 'Lost our bloody kids. Someone had to pay.'

'Your Honour, I am trying to show the court that the distress Mr and Mrs Johnstone suffered, was nowhere near as bad as they have suggested. In fact, it was quite the opposite,' said Kosta. 'They lapped up this windfall and laughed all the way to the bank.

'Hah, the bank never even saw a dime. We spent it all. So, you can't have it back if that's what you're thinking. It's long gone.'

'We don't want the money,' said Kosta. 'I just want to know what you spent it on?'

Gary grinned. 'Parties, fun.'

'And all the while your children were missing,' said Kosta.

'I was drowning my sorrows wasn't I. Anyway, what would you know about having kids. I read that article in *Woman's Day*. Your kids don't even want to see you.'

'Mr. Johnstone!' said the judge. 'Mr Kouros is not the subject of this investigation.'

'You turned gay or something?' Gary was trying to stare Kosta down.

Judge Iverson slammed her gavel upon the desk. 'Mr Johnstone, you are clearly out of order. Please refrain from the personal nature of your attack or get out of my court.'

Gary didn't budge, his eyes trying to pierce through Kosta's chest.

Kosta continued his attack. 'There was also a lump sum payment, once the police called a halt to the case after three and a half years. It was equivalent to three months of family payments, around five thousand dollars.'

'Spent that too.'

'On putting your life back together, I assume?'

'No. On a horse. And she won.' Gary laughed like he was down the pub. 'The bloody kids came through for me after all. Paid all me debts and more.'

'What kind of debts?'

'That's for me to know and for you to find out.'

'I'm trying to find out. If you'd answer the question.'

'Fuck off. I ain't telling you nothin'.'

'Mr Johnstone,' said the judge. 'This is your second warning. That kind of language will not be tolerated in this courtroom.'

'Don't you go tellin' me what I can and can't do. I've been bossed about by women all my life. A female judge for Christ sake? What the fuck were they thinking?'

'Mr Johnstone, this is my courtroom. Respect the rules and

regulations of this place or be removed from it!' Judge Iverson loomed over Gary like a spider inspecting her prey.

Jess couldn't take her eyes away from proceedings. She'd seen this sort of bravado many times before. Knew how it was going to end.

'Your fancy get-up doesn't scare me,' smiled Gary. 'I'll do what I want, when I want, so take your silly little sash and stick it up your ass.' He got quickly to his feet. 'I'm done here.'

'You most certainly are,' agreed the Judge. 'Security,' she hollered, 'Get this man to a holding cell.'

'I'm not going into any cell. I'm a free man.'

'Contempt of court is a chargeable offence,' said the Judge. 'Freedom is something we have to earn Mr Johnstone.'

Two security officers stepped in and flanked Gary as he tried to exit the dock.

'Don't fuckin' touch me alright?'

'Calm down and we won't have to,' said one of the officers.

'I am fuckin' calm.' Gary took the steps carefully, anger bubbling its way to the surface. They were trying to wrestle control back from him. Not again he thought to himself. Gary bolted down the aisle, his body about as aerodynamic as a mould of jelly. The security officers were well trained and they tackled him to the ground before he could reach the gallery. The public gasped as he fell hard upon the wooden floor. The assembled media took the photos that would grace the front pages of most of tomorrow's Australian newspapers. Gary was still the star of the show. 'Fuckin' bastards', he screamed.

Rosenthal dropped into his seat. He probed the lines on his forehead with the fingers on his right hand. A few new ones had been added thanks to today's interrogations and he could feel the rumblings of a headache.

The officers cuffed Gary's wrists which were pinned behind his back. An expletive laden, stream of abuse spewed from between a pair of split lips, his face having taken the brunt of the fall. Gary's nose was also bleeding, his moment of glory over. It hadn't gone as planned.

80

2:00PM
DISTRICT COURT HOLDING CELL

Gary slept heavily upon the cold steel bench of the holding cell. The polished cement floor was cold, the walls as unforgiving as the steel bars on one side. Built beneath the ground floor of the district court, the cell saw no natural light and as Gary's garbled snores echoed against the hard surfaces of the basement, a visitor stepped forward and spoke.

'Wake up.' The voice was a blast from his past, but Gary didn't even twitch. 'I need to talk to you.'

Iakovos stared at his father through the bars. He had to pity the man. Hadn't changed a bit. Consistency was his only redeeming feature. Iakovos pulled a set of car keys from his pocket and jangled them against the black steel grill. The shrill racket of metal on metal pierced Gary's rhythm, his brain spluttering back toward consciousness. A stream of dribble slid from one corner of his swollen lips. He wiped it away with his arm as he wrestled his sweaty body in to an upright position. 'What's your problem?'

'You are,' said Iakovos. 'You and your sneaky little wife.'

'And who the hell are you?'

Iakovos muffled a laugh. 'I'm family. Your family.'

'Should I know you?' asked Gary.

'Yeah. Probably.'

'What's your name then pretty boy?'

'Iakovos Apostilides.'

'That's a wog name. Ain't no relative of mine.' Gary got to his feet. 'You here to support that bitch teacher?'

'Yeah, you could say that.'

'She's a bloody liar,' ripped Gary. 'Got secrets coming out her arse.'

'Haven't we all.'

'Nah mate. Not me. I'm an open book.'

'That no one wants to read.'

'Ha de fuckin' ha. You sound familiar. Like the shithead son I lost.'

'I am the shithead son you lost.'

'Fuck me,' brightened Gary. He walked toward his visitor, trying to improve his vision. 'You've grown.'

'Time will do that.' Iakovos clenched his fists. 'I came down here to have it out with you. To finally tell you what I think of your shit-arse parenting skills.'

'Can't be good at everything,' smiled Gary.

'I'm going to be a father too one day and I know I'll do a much better job than you ever did. One, I'll love my kids and two, I'll never hit them.'

'You never deserved my love,' said Gary. 'Always up to no good. I hit you because that was the only language you understood.'

'You hit me because that was the only language you knew.' Iakovos was shaking. 'No one deserves a father like you.' Iakovos stepped forward and grabbed hold of the steel bars which separated them. 'You should've topped yourself when you had the chance. This world would be much better off with you gone.'

'Look at that. You're just like me. The old Serbian anger rising from the dust. Some things you just can't run away from.' Gary reached for Iakovo's hands but his blood son stepped quickly away. Gary wasn't finished talking. 'Does it burn you up inside knowing I enjoyed it when you disappeared? That I was happy you were gone.'

'It doesn't matter anymore. My life took a different twist. I was given a second chance at life.'

'Thanks for the money. I'll always take the cash over you kids.'

Iakovos stared into his father's blood shot eyes. 'You are a complete waste of space. You'll never change. I realise that now.'

'Took you fuckin' long enough. You never were that bright.'

'I'm smarter than you ever will be.' Iakovos turned and walked away.

'Good riddance,' yelled Gary. 'I said goodbye to you ten years ago. Fuck knows why you ever came back.'

Iakovos climbed the stairs at the end of the corridor and disappeared around the landing.

Gary started laughing. 'Someone get me a fucking drink!' he yelled through the bars. 'And make it a double!'

81

THURSDAY 9TH OCTOBER
10:00AM, DAY FIVE
THIRTEENTH WITNESS, JESSICA BELL

Principal k) a child's parents and any other people who are significant in the child's life should be given adequate information, in a manner and language that they can understand.

The media jostled each other for prime position. The normal routine of setting up the equipment had been complicated by the meagre space they'd been given. This case had grown in stature and newspapers were flying off the shelves. News sites were paying big money for coverage. The defendant had split expectations down the middle. Her actions were a huge point of discussion all around the world.

Jessica Bell arrived early and watched the circus from her special seat off to one side. She looked relaxed and happy, resplendent in dark trousers and a white blouse. Her hair was blow waved, her make-up perfect. She knew the case had gone as well as could be expected. Now it was her turn to speak. A chance to allow her side of the story to join the conversation.

A steady stream of spectators glided in through the security doors, drifting left and right, looking for the best vantage point. Jess watched them as they arrived, some she recognised from the previous four days. Others she had never seen, possibly only coming today after having read the papers. They were dressed like they were going to the theatre. The suspense and the twist and turns of the last few days had played itself out like a piece of performance art.

Two of her closest supporters arrived together. Iakovos guided John Johnstone in through the doorway and over to their favourite seats in the front row. Seeing them together like that gave Jess strength. Made all the pain and ridicule seem worth it. They both waved up at her. Iakovos added a kiss. Today was for them.

Kosta was upfront, deep in concentration, a spread of papers on the desktop in front of him. He looked handsome and smart, a crisp white shirt and dark blue tie chosen to display strength and honesty. It was working.

Rosenthal looked up as Judge Iverson entered the court from above. He drummed his fingers impatiently upon the desk. Final day nerves weren't a feeling he was used to and he tried to ignore them. The drycleaners had burnt his new shirt. An ironing mishap. Pulling on yesterday's clothes wasn't what he was used too either. He felt unclean.

The judge took her seat. She could see the finishing line and was glad it wasn't hers to decide upon.

The jury members entered the chamber and filed in along the rows. They took up their seats, one by one, dropping into position like a Mexican wave. They'd grown into the job like most juries do. Felt important now. A necessary cog in the giant machine of justice.

Kosta stood. 'I call the defendant, Miss Jessica Bell, to the stand.'

The same guard had been beside her all week and he stood with her, opened a gate in the railing beside them and took a few steps down to the floor of the main court. He encouraged the accused to follow him and she took his outstretched hand, taking the steps one by one.

The pressure she felt was immense. This room had been her cage and with all these people watching her, she knew she had to finish what she'd started. She took a deep breath. The witness box was just a few steps away and before she knew it she was taking the Bible in her hand.

'I swear by the almighty God that I will give a true account according to the evidence and the issues being tried here.' She spoke clearly.

Kosta approached the dock. 'Welcome, Miss Bell, and thank you for taking the stand today. I know the last few months have not been easy for you.'

'It's been a journey. Had its ups and downs. Now it's drawing to a close, I wouldn't change a thing. I knew this day would come.'

Kosta smiled then turned and faced the jury. 'Ladies and gentlemen of the jury, today I will examine the final principle of the Community and Services Act. Principle K states that a child's parents and any other people who are significant in the child's life should be given adequate information, in a manner and language that they can understand. I will prove to you today that the defendant Miss Bell did just that. My client went to great lengths to ensure the children's parents knew how they were doing.'

Several of the jury shifted in their seats. Their interest was piqued. Kosta was buoyed by their attentiveness. If it all came down to his performance today, then let it be worthy of an Academy Award.

Kosta turned to his client. 'We will move chronologically through the last ten years, trying to recreate each scene as best as we can so that the jury can appreciate how hard you worked to make this principle a reality.'

'I understand,' said Jess. They had rehearsed their delivery many times. Knew exactly what each other would say.

'To the court I present Exhibit F.' Kosta held aloft a photo. 'I have also scanned it so the rest of the court can see it on the monitors.' The television screens dotted around the courtroom burst to life. 'The postcard in this photo was sent from Paris the day after Miss Bell left Australia with Lisa and Jacob Johnstone.

The date has been digitally imprinted on the photo and it read 13 May 2005.' Kosta handed the exhibit to the attendant who passed it onto the jury.

Kosta watched as the jury assessed the evidence. 'This photo forms part of a file that Miss Bell put together over the past ten years. It has been kept in meticulous order, ready to be revealed on a day just like this. She thought long and hard about what she was doing when she first made the decision to run and wanted to do the right thing by the law, where she could. She always planned to return to Australia to defend her actions.'

'The original postcard would have been received by Tracey and Gary Johnstone, sent via registered mail, four days after their children first left the country. I have attached a copy of the delivery receipt, courtesy of Australia Post, which has been signed by the recipient, Gary Johnstone.'

The exhibit was scrutinised by the judge. Kosta passed a copy of it to Jess. 'Miss Bell, you were the author of this postcard. Could you please read out what you wrote?'

Jess stood carefully and cleared her throat. 'Dear Gary and Tracey, by now you must have realised that I have taken your children. I know it will come as a shock and you may never get over it but I will not be bringing them back in the foreseeable future. I am sorry that it has come to this but I tried everything and everyone else without success.

I don't doubt that you once loved your children but as parents you are failures. You neglected and abused Lisa and Jacob daily and I could not stand by and watch it continue anymore. I had nightmares that I would wake up one day to news of their death at your hands.'

Jess looked up at the jury before continuing.

'The teachers code states that you should always act with the best interests of the child and that is exactly what I have done. It took me two long years to get to this stage and I have covered every angle and catered for every possibility. Please do not try to find us. I will keep you updated on Lisa and Jacob's progress once a year via a postcard just like this. Please contain your anger in the knowledge that your children are safe and happy. Yours sincerely, Miss Jessica Bell.'

Kosta looked at the jury. 'Thank you for sharing this with us.'

'I enjoyed that. It reminded me how absolutely clear I was with my intentions.'

'Why did you send this postcard, Miss Bell?'

'I knew it was my responsibility to keep Lisa and Jacob's parents informed. I had always planned to send some form of correspondence as often as possible. They deserved to lose their children but no one should ever have to suffer the pain of not knowing whether they are alive or not.'

'When did you send this?'

'As soon as we arrived in Paris. I had purchased a box full of postcards in Dubai, wrote the words on the plane, then posted it from Charles De Gaulle airport.'

'So, you knew this was one of your obligations?'

'Yes. It was one of the principles I needed to carry out.'

'And did you do this regularly?'

'I sent a total of thirty-three postcards during the ten years we were away.'

Kosta lifted a small packet from his desk. 'Please let the court know that I have photocopies of all thirty-three postcards, all complete with international receipts, showing the day and the country from which they were sent. Please enter this as exhibit G.'

The court clerk took the package from Kosta and entered it into a book. She crossed the room and handed the set of postcards to the lead juror. The jurors' interest in these letters was obvious.

Kosta allowed them time to open the package before continuing. 'Having sent all of these postcards, can you please explain how you avoided detection? Surely these messages could have been tracked.'

'I planned it well. I spent time a lot of thinking it through. It might sound callous but I was determined to be successful. Determined to give the children a second chance at life. If we were found and hauled back to Australia then I would have only compounded the children's pain.' Jess looked up at the judge. 'The system I decided upon, ended up being the simplest. You see I had a lot of friends in Paros and I asked them to post the cards from wherever they went on holiday. I wrote on the postcards and took a copy before they left. I gave them the cards with strict instructions that they were not read them. I asked that they be posted as soon as they arrived at their holiday destination. And never registered post. The receipt from the post office for the stamps would hopefully be enough to prove that they had been sent.'

'So, each card was sent from a different place in the world by different people?' said Kosta. 'It was traceable as a single entity but with no common geographical link between them all?'

'Exactly. It performed just as I had hoped. Keeping the Johnstone family in the loop gave me enormous pride.'

'Could I ask you to read out loud one of the other cards for me?

'Of course.'

'It's from 2010, five years after you left the country.'

Kosta passed another photo to Jess. 'This card was posted from Nepal.'

Jess stood. 'Dear Tracey and Gary, I have just enrolled Lisa and Jacob in high school. I have chosen a good local school where I know a few of the teachers. The school is small so the children will get the necessary attention they need. They are sad to say goodbye to their primary school but they are more than ready to make the leap having scored very well in end-of-year reports.' Jess wiped a tear from her eye. 'With regards to their home life, I have been in a relationship with a man for two years now and they see him as a father figure. He will never replace you officially but I just wanted you to know that they are being raised in a loving family environment. Socially they are doing very well, with lots of good friends. Jacob has a couple of mates and they will be lifelong buddies. Lisa's friendship group is less permanent, which is of some concern. She will need a lot of guidance going into her teenage years. I will be there to support her all the way. That's all for now. Thanks for listening and I hope you are well. Yours sincerely, Miss Bell.'

Kosta placed a hand on the rail of the witness box. 'How does that make you feel?'

'It takes me back. I can still remember writing that one.'

'Are the other postcards like this?'

'Yes. It was written as a conversation piece. My professional responsibility needed to be met but it also allowed some of the guilt to slip from my shoulders. I felt better every time I sent one.'

'And your friends weren't curious as to all the secrecy?'

'We all have secrets. Paros is no different. It is an island filled with people escaping old lives. Families looking for a fresh start.'

'The file you kept was also part of your professional responsibility, wasn't it?'

'I always knew that I was coming back to face the music. I knew that without proof of my efforts, all of this work would have been worthless. I knew I couldn't depend on Gary and Tracey to keep the postcards. Why would they?'

'Your concern for the children is admirable. You thought of everything.'

Kosta gestured toward the Prosecutor. Rosenthal stood like a steel rod.

'Yes, Miss Bell, you are a meticulous woman.' An awkward silence followed the prosecutor's measured words. Jess was unsure whether he wanted a reply or not. She stayed quiet.

Rosenthal stepped around his desk and approached the jury. 'Let's not beat around the bush here. Miss Bell is a very cold and calculating human being. I would not be proud of the fact that I ticked all the boxes. I would be disgusted with myself, appalled by the thought that I could reduce two young lives to a set of eleven principles, and thirty-three post cards. Miss Bell set out to destroy a family.' He turned and faced her directly. 'That's all you were successful at.'

Rosenthal waited as his words trickled down through the audience. 'You wrote the post cards to unload your own guilt. You kidnapped someone else's children to mend your own damaged childhood. This cannot be undone by a couple of letters a year. And it will not be forgotten. Not by me, not by Mr and Mrs

Johnstone and certainly not by this jury.'

'Objection,' said Kosta. 'The prosecutor's opinion is not relevant to this case. He cannot speak for this jury.'

'Agreed,' said the judge. 'I would like to instruct the jury to ignore what Prosecutor Rosenthal has just said. Prosecutor, what you think is not what we are here to listen to. Please allow the facts to speak for themselves. You have been warned before and I will not tolerate it.'

'Sorry, your Honour.' Rosenthal's apology lacked any real conviction. His cross examination did not end there. 'Miss Bell, did you realise that on receipt of each one of those postcards you continued to feed the parents hope that their children would be found.'

'That was never my intention. I only wanted to keep them informed of their children's progress. To make them aware of the fact that they were still alive.'

'Every time a postcard arrived on their door, the world was turned upside down again. The police got excited, tracked the postcard down to a location somewhere in the world. The media frenzy started up and a well-publicised search was conducted. A search that always came to nothing.'

'I thought they would have given up after a few years,' said Jess.

'Given up? On their children. Who are you? What are you?'

Jess showed the pain of the misunderstood.

'Did you ever think about how much police time and government money your little game of hide and seek wasted,' said Rosenthal.

'I did what I thought was right.'

'Nice of you to be so selfish.'

'I gave up a life to rescue those children.'

'Really. I looked into your life and found very little in the way of family and friends. You had no significant others in your life when you absconded with the children, did you, Miss Bell?'

'No, I did not.'

'So, in fact, you gave up nothing. The sacrifice was all theirs.'

Jess had nothing to add.

'That all changed when you arrived in Paros though didn't it?'

'I'm not sure what you're talking about.'

'In the postcard you just shared with us, you spoke of a relationship with a man. Can you tell us his name?'

Jess looked panicked. 'Is that relevant to the case?'

'I'll decide what is relevant Miss Bell, not you. I believe the jury would be very intrigued by his identity.'

'It's not mine to give.'

'Then I may have to.' Rosenthal was grinning.

Kosta rose to his feet. 'Objection. As my client has already stated, it has no bearing on this case. Can we please focus on the charges the accused is facing? We don't need a witch hunt.'

Rosenthal wasn't about to give up. 'I feel that this relationship might expose a conflict of interest your Honour.'

Judge Iverson couldn't work out which one of them was playing her for a fool. 'Approach the bench please.' Rosenthal and Kosta stepped out from behind their desks and leaned in before the judge. 'What is all of this about?' whispered Iverson.

Rosenthal spoke first. 'I believe the man in question is here in Perth and that he is having a bearing on this case your Honour.'

'You believe?' said Iverson.

'I have evidence that can prove it.'

'What evidence do you have, Mr Rosenthal?'

'The girl, your Honour. Lisa Johnstone.'

Kosta was angry. 'She's going to testify?'

'If she has to.'

'I don't believe it.'

Judge Iverson was concerned. 'She's not on my list of witnesses.'

'I know but she's outside, ready to go, if I call her in.'

'She's here?' said Kosta.

'Yes.'

'Sounds like you had this planned all along.'

Rosenthal's grin said it all. 'I was given the man's identity last night. I doubt you'll be as shocked as I was Mr Kouros.'

Kosta had to look away. 'We should have received prior notice your Honour.'

'It was a late decision. A change of heart shall we say. Lisa called me with the information and suggested that she take the stand.'

'May I speak with my client?' asked Kosta.

'Of course,' said Iverson.

'Kosta stepped in front of the witness box. Jess leant forward eager to know what had been discussed.

Kosta spoke first. 'Lisa wants to testify.'

'She'll tell the court about us, won't she?'

'Yes. I'm not sure what the court will do. Nor how the jury will take it.'

'It is what it is. Lisa has a right to a voice. Let her speak.'

'Are you ready for this?'

'Probably not. It'll be nice to see her though.'

'Se agapo,' whispered Kosta. *I love you.*

'Ki ego se agapo.' *I love you too.*

Kosta looked over at Judge Iverson. 'We'll allow it your Honour. She has a right to speak.'

'Thank you Mr. Kouros.' The judge turned to address the prosecutor. 'Have you finished with Miss Bell?'

'For now, Your Honour, I have.' Rosenthal was all smiles. Gone were the nerves of the morning. He felt excited.

82

10:45AM
FOURTEENTH WITNESS, LISA JOHNSTONE

Lisa Johnstone walked into the courtroom with the air of royalty. She had been untouchable during the court case. No media interviews, no bad press. This fight was over her, not about her.

Still, she entered carrying the weight of the world. And it had changed her. Jess was both captivated and distressed. From her vantage point, her daughter's face looked skinnier than ever and her eyes showed signs of little sleep. Her sense of style was still alive and well though, her body immaculately dressed in a black pencil skirt and blue sleeveless top. Jess craved a hug as much as any mother would. She also felt immense pride. Zetta Apostilides was her daughter and no one could ever change that.

Iakovos and John had remained where they were since the start of the day. Lost and confused by the events of the morning they were on the edges of their seats, following Lisa's entrance with great care and concern. They loved her equally and for different reasons, but were torn by her appearance here today. None of it made any sense to them.

Tracey too felt emotional. She had slipped in between sessions, a text message from her daughter early this morning alerting her to the fact she was most probably going to testify. She hid up the back to hear her daughter's words cut deep into the heart of Miss Bell. The pain they would inflict would go a long way to healing her own wounds. The end was tantalisingly close. She could smell the money.

Lisa stepped into the dock and stood to face the gallery. She looked over at Jess briefly before turning her gaze back to the court attendant.

'Hello Miss Johnstone. Will you be swearing on the Bible?'

'I will.' The attendant past the leather-bound book to her, which she took in her left hand, placing her right on top. 'I swear by the almighty God that I will give a true account according to the evidence and the issues being tried here.'

Jess had watched every nuance of her oath, down to the last hair on her head. She hadn't been granted a visit since arriving here, their last exchange the terse battle in the mountain house they had shared. Hearing her voice made her heart beat wildly. She had missed her daughter greatly. She had been unsure how she would feel when she set eyes on her again but knew now that she still loved her. This would not change, no matter what the outcome.

Lisa felt the claws of doubt picking at her skin. Being here was proving to be more uncomfortable than she could have imagined. Everyone she had ever loved was here except for her grandmother and her father. Nana had been a casualty of this whole affair. A broken heart, a broken woman. Her father's absence had been an issue for most of her life. This time it was his own fault. He'd let anger and stupidity cloud his judgement. She wondered if that had always been the case.

'Morning Lisa.' Rosenthal interrupted her train of thought.

'Kalimera,' smiled Lisa weakly. 'Good morning.'

'I know it is hard to be here today, and we all appreciate your efforts to speak at this time.'

She nodded, a glimmer of happiness superimposed across her face.

Rosenthal held a small package in his hand. 'Are you aware of the postcards that Miss Bell sent to your parents?'

'I wasn't until recently. I have read some of them. Some I cannot finish through my tears.'

'I have them all here. Would you like to see them?'

'No, thank you. Being up here is tough enough without adding to the pain.'

'What makes them so distressing?'

'I can see my life passing before me once again and I realise how much time I have missed with my own parents. Miss Bell knew they were alive and allowed herself the pleasure of communication. A pleasure that she denied me.' Lisa glanced across at Jess. 'I think of the letters and all I see are my parents reading the words, their eyes overflowing with tears.'

'Indeed. It must have felt like they were being tortured?'

'Objection,' said Kosta, jumping to his feet. 'He's putting words into the witness's mouth.'

Lisa leant forward and gripped the railing. 'These are my words thank you, Mr Kouros. It was torture and I don't need anyone's help to explain my pain. We all know exactly how I feel.'

'Yes, we do.' Kosta backed down. He knew how strong she could be. 'Sorry for the interruption.' He returned to his seat.

'How are your parents?' asked Rosenthal.

'Which ones?' smiled Lisa.

'Your real parents, of course. The ones who actually gave birth to you and are legally recognised as your mother and father.'

'They're not in a good place. Losing their children has had a massive effect on their lives. They are divorced now and lead desperate and disappointing lives. Coming home has been a very sad return for me, seeing them this way. It's been difficult to say the least.'

'They deserved better?'

'Not really.'

Rosenthal's flow was interrupted. 'Sorry?'

'I said not really. They got what they deserved and more.'

'What makes you say that?'

'They're just not nice people.'

Tracey bit her nails. Staying quiet was going to be very difficult.

'And this is because of what Miss Bell made them endure?' The prosecutor tried to lead her away from the edge of a cliff.

'No. I thought that was true. The anger inside of me wanted to believe they were good people. Wanted so much for them to embrace me and love me.' Lisa's emotions boiled over, tears filling her eyes. 'But they are not capable of love. Not even for themselves.'

'Did your mother not welcome you into her home?'

'Yes, she did. She thought I would fund her drinking habits and pay off all her debts. I wanted to talk but she just wanted me to take her to the casino every day. She only wanted my money. Love doesn't mean anything to her. She kicked me out when she discovered that my bank balance was finite.'

'That's not true,' yelled Tracey from the gallery. People spun around, stared at her, shocked by her outburst.

Judge Iverson looked toward the rear of the court. 'Would the gallery please refrain from commenting or they will have to leave.'

Lisa continued. 'She only ever wanted me because I brought in the cash. It was that way when I was a little kid and nothing has changed.'

Rosenthal's face was bright red. 'The family payment was important to them. They needed to feed you, buy you clothes. Your father could not work because of the depression he suffered when you were ripped away.'

'That's just not true. He used our disappearance as an excuse to stay at home and get wasted. He's depressed for sure, but so would you be if you'd made the same stupid mistakes that he's made all his life. He deserves to be where he is. He is rotten to the core.'

'But you said earlier that you had become more aware of the truth. You, of course, were referring to your mistreatment at the hands of the accused?' Rosenthal clambered for a new line of questioning.

'No, I wasn't mistreated at all. I've grown up a lot since I've been back in Perth. I have had to. I've also learnt a lot of hard truths about my early life here and some events have been really tough to accept. One thing that stands tight is the fact that truth isn't always clear or obvious. It has many layers. Some layers are there to deceive you and some are totally imaginary, invented even. I have been very fortunate in that I have had two people in my life who have always tried to protect me and love me. I see that now and that is all the truth I need.'

'And they are Tracey and Gary Johnstone.'

Lisa grabbed the railing and pulled herself to her feet. 'No, that is not who I am referring to. I'm talking about Jessica Bell and my brother Jacob. They have always been there for me.' Lisa looked over at Jess. 'Jessica Bell is an amazing woman. She seeks out truth and acts on it. Sure, she committed a crime in fleeing with us to the other side of the world but she did this to prevent an even greater crime from happening. Life needs to be balanced and that is what Miss Bell brought to my life. I am sure my brother and I would not be alive today had she left us languishing in the house we grew up in. She, too, would probably not be alive because she would never have forgiven herself for allowing our situation to continue. The Education Department may even have jailed her for not doing her job and protecting us. I see this now and I am so sorry I ever sought to hurt a woman who gave up everything to save me. I love you, Yiskah.'

Tears fell down Jess's cheeks.

'Fuckin traitor,' came another scream from the rear of the gallery. Tracey had given up staying incognito and was on her feet hurling abuse. 'Ungrateful bitch.'

Judge Iverson got to her feet as well. 'Guards. Please escort that woman out of my court.'

'Piss off back to Paros. I hope I never see your face for another ten years.'

The gallery scampered clear of Tracey, clearing a path for security to intervene. Two guards grabbed Tracey by the arms and hustled her from her seat and out the main door. 'I hate you Lisa!' They were the last words she muttered before the doors sealed closed behind her.

Judge Iverson looked toward Lisa. 'Are you okay?'

She nodded. 'I knew she wouldn't like what I had to say.'

Rosenthal glared at Lisa. She gave him nothing. He looked at the judge. 'Can I ask for a recess your Honour. I need to talk with Miss Johnstone.'

'I'm fine to continue your Honour,' said Lisa.

'But she has changed her tune your Honour,' said Rosenthal. 'She needs some space.'

'That's not true,' said Lisa. 'You asked me to testify and that's exactly what I'm doing.'

Judge Iverson glared at Rosenthal. 'Your client's position in this case is of paramount importance. Her version of the events must be heard.'

'She is not my client. I am working on behalf of the Education Department of WA. Miss Johnstone is merely a witness.'

'Who was called by you!'

'And I have now finished with her. She may return to the gallery. Or even leave altogether if she so chooses.'

Judge Iverson had never felt so frustrated. 'Approach the desk please Prosecutor.'

Rosenthal had never felt so unhinged. He stepped forward and stared up at the Judge.

'Mr Rosenthal,' whispered Iverson. 'I have allowed Miss Johnstone's surprise testimony because she was going to tell us who the mystery man in the postcard was. That has not happened yet. What the devil is going on?'

'She has turned on me. I don't know what she's going to say anymore. She has become more damaging than useful.'

'The truth is not something you can control,' said the Judge. 'Now get on with it and do your job properly! I'm this close to reporting you.'

'Yes, your Honour.' Rosenthal stormed off toward Kosta's desk, a delaying tactic while he fought his demons.

Kosta watched him contort, a strange mixture of both dread and delight coating his actions.

Rosenthal stopped in front of his adversary's desk. He looked briefly at Kosta before turning and addressing the gallery. 'Did

Miss Bell ever form any relationships while you were living with her on the island of Paros?'

'Yes, she did.'

'Did you form close fatherly bonds with any of these men?'

'Yes, although Miss Bell was very careful to shield us from unnecessary distractions.'

'Distractions. How so?'

'Well, she didn't want us to form any emotional connections with people who might not be permanent fixtures in our lives. She had already put us through so much, I think she was trying to protect us from any more confusion.'

'That was nice of her seeing she had already kidnapped you and lied about your parent's deaths.'

'Objection,' said Kosta.

Rosenthal pinned his eyes upon his enemies. 'These are the facts.'

'And they have already been presented to the court,' said Kosta. 'They do not need repeating.'

Rosenthal grinned. 'So, let's say she had a few relationships. Are any of those men here in this court today?'

'Yes.' Lisa's answer was greeted with a wash of hushed voices and rushed glances.

'Could you please point that gentleman out.'

'There is a wonderful man here today. A man who has been like a second father to me and that person is the lawyer for the Defendant, Mr Kosta Kouros.'

The whole chamber gasped. Judge Iverson clasped her hands to her face. She took a moment to allow the clamour to recede. 'All quiet in the court.' She smacked her mallet upon her desk just to make sure they heard. She couldn't believe it but a bad day had just got worse.

83

11:15AM
COURT 3-1

Judge Iverson waited as the chamber settled. 'Ladies and gentlemen of the jury, we will be taking an unscheduled break. You shall be excused from the chamber and asked to return in thirty minutes.' The jury stood and exited.

She turned her attention to the witness. 'Lisa Johnstone, you are also excused. You may return to the gallery if you like.'

'Is everything okay?'

'No, it is not.' Judge Iverson turned to address both lawyers. 'Mr Rosenthal, Mr. Kouros please approach the desk.'

Lisa shuffled off toward the gallery where she was embraced by her brother and grandfather. She blew a kiss to Jess.

Judge Iverson stared down at both men. 'Mr Kouros, is what she says true? Have you been in a close relationship with the accused?'

'Yes, your Honour.'

'Why did you not declare this to me, before the case began?'

'My client needed me. I felt removed enough from the case to be impartial.'

'You were both a father figure to the prosecution's star witness and a previous partner to the accused. How did you think you could remain impartial?'

'It's been three months since our relationship ended, Your Honour. I thought enough time had passed.'

'Well you put up a great act. I would never have guessed.'

'Our relationship ended mutually. We're now just friends.'

'Still, you have deceived the court.'

'I'm sorry, your Honour.'

'And how in god's name do you recommend we proceed? Your selfish actions have put your clients case in serious jeopardy.'

Rosenthal took his chance. 'This case should be thrown out and a retrial ordered, your Honour.'

'I wasn't asking you.'

'I'd like to take the stand your Honour,' said Kosta.

Judge Iverson leant back in her chair and exhaled every last bit of air she had left inside her body. 'You're going to give me a heart attack.'

'It can't happen,' said Rosenthal.

'Be quiet,' slammed Iverson. 'I will ask for your opinion when I require it. Not before, not after and definitely not for the benefit of hearing your own voice.'

'The case is almost over,' said Kosta. 'I shall be the last witness. My client can present the final address to the jury instead of me. She is allowed this without my representation.'

'Are you stepping down from the case?' asked Iverson.

'Yes, your Honour. I feel it's what I must do.'

'It is highly unusual Mr Kouros.'

'I have never heard of this happening in my whole career,' said Rosenthal.

'Which may be cut short if you don't shut up!' Judge Rosenthal gritted her teeth.

'There are legal precedents your Honour,' said Kosta. 'I have done some research.'

The judge looked straight into Kosta eyes. 'You planned for this to happen, didn't you?'

'No, I wanted to avoid it at all costs. It was Prosecutor Rosenthal who brought it to a head. I did accept that there was a small chance it could happen and I looked into what choices there were.'

'Well done, Mr Kouros.' Iverson clapped softly. 'It will be as you wish. I'll ask the jury to return and I will explain the unusual situation we are faced with. I will then ask you, Mr Kouros, to take the stand.'

She turned to Rosenthal whose face looked like it was frozen in time. 'Prosecutor Rosenthal you will be asked to cross examine the witness. Is that alright with you?'

'No, it is not! This is a mistrial at the very least. Lisa Johnstone has exposed a conflict of interest which must be investigated.'

'Which I have done and which I have resolved,' said the judge. 'Thank you both for your input, now please return to your seats.'

The jury filed back into the chamber and took their seats.

Judge Iverson addressed the jurors. 'Members of the jury, the situation we find ourselves in is highly unusual. But then this whole case has been highly unusual. The lawyer for the defendant, Mr Kouros, has admitted to a prior relationship with the accused, Jessica Bell. He has also accepted he was a father figure to the prosecution's star witness. I have decided that due to this conflict, Mr Kouros will have to remove himself from his position as lawyer for the accused.'

The jury looked at each other in confusion.

Judge Iverson waited for it to sink in. 'He will not be dismissed from this court entirely though. He is now a person of interest and therefore he is required to take the stand as a witness. This is legal under our constitution and necessary if we are going to find a resolution to this problem. Thank you for your patience.'

Judge Iverson turned to face the gallery.

The court attendant stood. 'I call Kosta Kouros to the witness box.'

11:30AM
FIFTEENTH WITNESS, KOSTA KOUROS

Kosta left the seat behind his desk and made his way across the front of the court and into the witness box.

'Prosecutor Rosenthal,' said the Judge, 'You may examine the witness.' Rosenthal's demeanour had not thawed and he struggled to find the necessary desire to question the man in front of him.

Kosta looked across at Lisa. She had taken a seat beside her grandfather and brother. Memories of happier times flooded in and out of his mind.

'How involved were you in raising the children Miss Bell kidnapped?'

'She did not kidnap anyone, and I was very involved. I looked upon them as If they were my own children.'

'Did Miss Bell ever tell you the truth?'

'She did.'

'And how did you take it?'

'Not well. I felt betrayed.'

'Yes. A lot of people have felt that way after dealings with the accused.'

'I'm not like the others. I loved her. I would have preferred she told me earlier, that is all.'

'And what happened once she did?'

'Our trust was broken and I broke off our relationship.'

'Just like that? How many years had you been together?'

'Four years.'

'How did this breakdown affect the children?'

'I'm not too sure. Yiskah told the children about their parents a few days later and here we are now. There hasn't really been time to process anything else.'

'But surely they would have been heartbroken. You were like a father to them.'

'Maybe. Like I said we were busy. Zetta had her eighteenth birthday and then our lives exploded.'

'Were you forced to provide legal guidance to your client?' Rosenthal was looking for friction.

'No. I was asked to defend her and I agreed.'

'Knowing that your connections would eventually come to light?'

'I thought I could separate the two.'

'Did you succeed?'

'The jury will decide that. Not me. Nor you.'

Jess's eyes were wet with tears.

'You have told the court that you felt betrayed by the accused's secrets?' said Rosenthal.

Kosta felt the pain of her disclosure like it had only happened yesterday. 'Yes, that is true.'

'Well there is another secret she did not share with you.'

'What do you mean?'

'It concerns the drunk driver who killed her parents.'

Lisa gripped the rail in front of her.

'I never knew much about that part of her life,' said Kosta. 'It wasn't something she liked to talk about.'

'Well this piece of information will make you rethink this whole case.'

'What is it?'

Rosenthal picked up a sheet of paper and walked across the floor. He laid the page gently on the wooden ledge in front of Kosta.

'This is the official accident report from the scene of that crash. It states that it was eleven o'clock at night when a Holden Commodore, travelling at fifty kilometres over the speeding limit, travelled across the median strip, onto the other side of the road and crashed into the car being driven by Jim and Elizabeth Bell. They were killed on impact and the driver of the Commodore was sentenced to eight years in jail.'

'Why are you telling me this?'

'The driver's name is in the report,' said the prosecutor.

Rosenthal ran his hand across the sheet of paper, leading Kosta to a box in the bottom left corner of the form.

'Gary Sideski,' read Kosta. 'And?'

'Mr Sideski was freed after just five years. But somethings never change and he is currently enjoying a quiet rest in the courthouse jail below us.'

Kosta was quick to connect the dots. 'Are you trying to tell me that Gary Sideski and Gary Johnstone are the same man?'

'Yes I am. Well done.'

'That's crazy.'

'No, that's Perth. The rest of the world has seven degrees of separation. We have four. From Miss Bell's parents to Miss Bell, to Lisa and Jacob and onto Gary Johnstone. He was the man that killed her parents. Talk about a vicious cycle.'

Jess was frozen.

Lisa looked worryingly toward her mother.

'Has this been proven without doubt?' asked Kosta.

'Yes, it has,' said Rosenthal. 'I offer up this document as Article Eleven.' Rosenthal took the accident report from Kosta's grasp and handed it over to the Lead Juror.'

Rosenthal turned his attention back to Mr. Kouros. 'Did Miss Bell ever mention this connection to you?'

'No and I still can't believe it's true.'

'Well believe it.' Rosenthal turned toward the jury. 'If Miss Bell knew of this coincidence, then could we not propose that revenge may have been the real motivation for Miss Bell's flight to the other side of the world.'

'Objection,' said Kosta.

'Sorry mate.' Rosenthal was all smiles. 'You're not her lawyer anymore.'

'But she wouldn't have done that.'

'It's a possibility. Just another secret in a long list of lies. There's no telling what that woman is capable of. I have finished with the witness your Honour.' Rosenthal had discovered a new source of energy.

'Miss Bell, would you like to examine the witness,' said the Judge, looking over at the accused.

Jess was trembling.

'Miss Bell? Are you okay?'

'Sorry,' said Jess. 'Yes of course.' She struggled to her feet and looked out across the courtroom. The walls were swaying and the twelve Jurors' were a watery blur of colour. She used the shoulders of the guard to ease herself down the steps into the court.

Memories of boarding a plane some ten years ago flooded her mind and much the same as they did that day, her legs crumpled beneath the strain of the last few hours and she tumbled hard to the polished floorboards below.

84

12:30PM
DISTRICT COURT FOYER

Lisa strode purposefully across the marbled surface of the courthouse foyer. Her face was as ashen as the day Yiskah told her, her parents were still alive. Her world had been turned upside down once again and she wanted it all to stop.

A security guard stood beside a wooden door, his arms crossed, the word 'Medical' engraved upon a metal plaque.

'Could I please go into that room,' said Lisa.

'Sorry, no visitors allowed,' said the guard.

'I'm not a visitor. I'm the daughter of the woman being treated.'

The guard blinked. 'Your name?'

'Zetta Apostilides.'

'Please wait.' The guard turned and opened the door. A gap appeared below his outstretched arm and Zetta ducked through it and into the room.

Jess sat upright on a bed as a nurse administered a blood pressure check. Kosta stood to her right, her hand in his. Zetta burst toward them.

'Did you know?' asked Lisa.

The guard grabbed Lisa's arms and thrust them behind her back.

'I told you to wait!' said the guard.

'Its' alright,' whispered Jess, her voice gravelly and light. 'What she asks, needs to be answered.'

'She pushed past me,' said the guard. 'The rules need to be followed.'

Jess slid her hand from Kosta's grasp and raised it in surrender. 'Please let her go. You're doing a great job but I am very tired and I need to talk with my daughter.'

The guard clenched his jaw and released Zetta. He stepped outside the room and slammed the door shut. The room settled except for Lisa who was still very agitated.

'So, what's it all about?'

'Have a seat,' said Jess.

'I'll stand,' said Lisa.

'I never knew,' said Jess. 'I still can't believe it.'

'Why should I believe you?

'Because we all have secrets. Even Gary.'

'Surely he knew who you were?'

'He probably wouldn't have even known that my parents had a child.'

'But didn't you hear his name when it was read out in court? At his original trial for manslaughter.'

'I was kept away from the case. For my own protection. I only appeared once and he wasn't allowed to be present.'

'The papers, people talk. Surely you heard or saw something.'

'Grief consumed me like a black cloud. I hated the world. I wasn't listening to anyone.' Jess started to cry. 'I blocked it all out. Drank myself silly.'

Lisa ran to her mother and embraced her. Jess closed her eyes, the time between hugs had been immense.

She whispered into her daughter's ear. 'Do you really think I am capable of revenge?'

'I'm not sure of anything anymore. My life has become a bloody circus and I'm the ring leader. It's doing my head in.'

'It's my fault. I started this circus ten years ago. But it's almost over.' Jess squeezed tighter. 'I'm so sorry.'

'I know you are.' Lisa stepped back. 'Are you going back in?'

'She has to,' said Kosta.

'I have one more speech to give, then my fate will be in the jury's hands,' said Jess.

'Our fate,' said Lisa.

'Will we ever recover from this?' asked Jess.

'I hope so,' smiled Lisa.

85

2:00PM
COURT 3-1, CLOSING SPEECHES

Jess stepped clear of the large desk that Kosta had been using during the case, allowing her fingers to trace along its polished surface. She sensed the anticipation in the room as she walked across the floor. She stopped in front of the jury.

'Thank you for being here every day and for suffering through my life's story. I hope it's been worth it.' She clasped her hands in prayer.

'I too have been here every day, doing what I thought was right for Lisa and Jacob Johnstone and no matter what the outcome of this trial, every hour and every minute that I spent with them was worth it. Life became beautiful with them in my life. Knowing what I know now, I wouldn't change a thing.' She collected her thoughts.

'Twelve years ago I came across two precious children whose lives were being destroyed and instead of watching them die, I decided to act. This case is that simple. The revelations of the last few days, while huge, have had no bearing over that original decision. I never knew Gary Johnstone killed my parents. I may have done more than just take his kids if I'd have known.'

The murmurs from those assembled, informed her she was on

thin ice. She didn't let it slow her down.

'I know that what I did was right, and well, it worked! You only have to look at the adults Lisa and Jacob Johnstone have become. I will always love them like they are my own. Nothing can or will ever change that.' She smiled at them both from their seats at the front of the gallery.

'I believe in the rights of the child. I also believe in the rights of adults too, but once they cross a line and become abusive, they relinquish those rights. Gary and Tracey crossed that line many times. I made a decision to take their rights away by removing the children from their care. And in doing so I restored what was rightfully the children's. A chance to have a future where anything was possible. I protected their rights and I will always be immensely proud of that achievement.'

'Your decision is a tough one. Do you side with the law and the red tape that complicates it, or do you see the situation for what it was? Bad. Something had to be done. Someone had to act.' Jess took a breath.

'Now it is your turn to act. You alone will be asked to decide whether my actions were fair or not. I accept that I stole the passports and used forged identity papers to start a new life. I am not contesting that. But I saved the lives of two wonderful children who deserved better than what they were being given. No one can ever take that away from me.'

'Your decision is a grave one and I thank you for giving up your time away from your own families and friends to be here.'

Jess curtsied, a graceful end to a powerful speech.

86

FRIDAY 8TH OCTOBER
10:00AM
DAY FIVE, COURT 3-1, JUDGEMENT DAY

The orderly of the court stood. 'Please stand for the Judge.'

The door behind the judge's desk swung open and in stepped Judge Iverson.

Kosta watched her entrance from the public gallery, with Iakovos to his immediate right looking very smart in a dark suit and tie. John Johnstone stood beside him, Iakovos's arm draped across his grandfather's back.

Jess smiled in their direction and John smiled back, squeezing his grandson's hand. In the row behind were the witnesses who were called to testify from Emily Dawson to Child X. They were all here and everyone was on edge.

Lisa was conspicuously absent.

Prosecutor Rosenthal looked strong and flashy in a shiny grey suit. His face revealed nothing, neither happiness nor fear. Ignorance had always been his favoured default.

Judge Iverson sat, allowing the courtroom to follow suit.

'The jury will now enter,' said the orderly.

'A side door to the left of the jury box swung open and in strolled the twelve members of the public who had heard every snippet of evidence. They assembled themselves almost without sound.

'Welcome,' said Judge Iverson. 'To the jury, prosecution, the accused, witnesses and general public, this case will end to day and I thank you all for your input.'

Judge Iverson turned and faced the jury. 'Would the jury foreman please stand and read out the verdict?'

The lead juror got to his feet.

The judge spoke first. 'In the case of The Education Department of WA versus Miss Bell, how did you find?'

'In reply to the charge of stealing and forgery we find the defendant guilty your Honour,' said the juror.

The gallery filled with a low murmur, as people double-checked that this was the lesser of the charges.

The juror continued. 'In reply to the charge of kidnapping we find the defendant not guilty, your Honour.'

The court erupted with cheers. Jess looked over at her supporters, her smile tempered by the tears already streaming down her face. Rosenthal sat stony faced at his desk, a clenched fist slowly destroying the pen in his grasp.

Kosta, Iakovos and John hugged each other.

Judge Iverson whacked her gavel upon the desk. It was almost celebratory and the court went quiet.

'For the conviction of forgery, I give Miss Bell a suspended sentence of six-months jail,' directed the judge. 'Should she reoffend she will be jailed for three years.'

Yiskah smiled at the Judge. 'Thank you,' she mouthed, the noise of the court drowning her out.

'You are free to go Miss bell,' smiled Judge Iverson.

Yiskah descended the few steps to the courtroom floor and ran toward her family. She embraced them all, collapsing in a tangle of arms, her sobs almost drowning out the cheers.

87

ONE YEAR LATER

The morning sun burst upon the upper deck of the Blue Star ferry, its massive engines churning the water below into a frenzy of foam. The white painted hull reversed carefully beside the rubber-rimmed edges of the concrete port of Parikia. The land around it already a sea of cars and people.

At the railings of the upper deck stood Iakovos and John Johnstone, both casually dressed in shorts and a polo shirt. Their hands waving, both faces filled with smiles. Time had aged the old man even more but his eyes sparkled and there was love in everything he saw. Iakovos looked well, as handsome as ever, his white top a stark contrast to his deep tan.

A sailor below threw a coiled rope toward the port. It was well caught and quickly wrapped around a large iron pole. The boat's engines settled, allowing the ropes to guide the hull into land.

Iakovos pulled a silver suitcase from between the shelves in the storage compartment of the lower deck. He hauled it out into the hallway where John was waiting for him. Scores of travelers were also disembarking.

'You ready, Granddad.'

'Yes I am.'

'Follow me.'

He grasped John's hand and they stepped slowly down a short flight of stairs. Crowds of people were gathered just inside the main doors of the hull. John and Iakovos were up the rear of this impatient press of bodies. There was no rush and so they preferred to step away from the hustle and bustle of the main group, allowing them some breathing space.

The rear ramps began to descend, a burst of afternoon light pouring in around the gaps, the warm air of the Mediterranean blowing in past the breech. John took a deep breath of the salt drenched oxygen. He had looked forward to this moment for a long time. 'Wow, that smell is pretty special.'

'It's the smell of home.'

'I'm on the other side of the world, aren't I.'

His grandson smiled. 'Yes, you are Granddad. And you're here to stay.'

They moved with the masses and stepped out onto the docks. People poured in all directions. Iakovos wheeled the suitcase behind him, his grandfather's hand firmly in the other. They walked past the concrete pillars of the open-air ferry terminal and through the gates. Hordes of people held up signs, advertising hotels and vehicle rentals. John saw something up ahead and smiled.

Yiskah stepped out of the fray and walked toward them. Their smiles said everything as they greeted each other with a long, warm embrace.

'So good to see you,' whispered Yiskah.

'The pleasure is all mine,' said John.

They stepped back.

Kosta appeared and shook hands with John. 'Great to see you, mate.'

'Likewise.' John was captivated by his surrounds. 'Sure is a beautiful day.'

'The gods are smiling,' said Kosta.

'How was your flight?' asked Jess.

'Great. No problems,' said John. 'Iakovos met me at the airport. The only real problem was putting up with all the girls who were staring at him.'

'Get used to it,' laughed Yiskah. 'It's even worse here.'

'Yeah, yeah,' smiled Iakovos.

John was looking over their shoulders. 'So, where's my darling baby girl?'

'Granddad!' came a scream as Zetta burst through the pack surrounding the old port windmill and sprinted toward her grandfather. She threw her arms wide and almost knocked him over with her love.

'Oh my god. You're really here,' she laughed, tears streaming down her cheeks, her arms wrapped tightly around his back.

'My girl, my darling girl, I'm so happy to be here,' he croaked, emotions brimming over.

'I love you, Granddad,' cried Zetta.

'I love you, too,' said John.

Yiskah, Iakovos and Kosta embraced them both, a circle of love, a modern-day family bonded by more than just blood.

A lone photographer took the photo that would make it into a few of the worlds newspapers. Jessica Bell no longer divided people. Her story of redemption was over.

The port of Paros was awash with love and happiness. Truth had found its way home.

To Telos – The End

About the Author

PJ Kelly is a primary school teacher who lives and works in Perth, Western Australia. He has a wife and two sons and having travelled widely, considers the world to be his home. PJ is very passionate about his teaching career and believes that all children have the right to feel safe and be free from harm. It was from the strength of these convictions that *The Good Teacher* was originally born.

PJ has a Bachelor of Arts Degree as well as a Diploma in Education. This is his first novel.

You can follow PJ's career at:

www.thegoodteachernovel.com

www.facebook.com/goodteachers/

and on Instagram at; the good teacher

Printed in Australia
AUHW010905250319
310222AU00004B/4

9 780646 597997